FIRST CAME ANTHONY OLCOTT'S MURDER AT THE RED OCTOBER ...

"Far superior to *Gorky Park* ... Olcott knows Russia on many levels. He writes with first-hand knowledge of the shabbiness and demoralization of everyday Russian life."

—*Chicago Tribune*

AND NOW, ANTHONY OLCOTT'S NEWEST TRIUMPH— *MAY DAY IN MAGADAN*

"Told with even more vim and spice ... This story begins with Duvakin's grabbing a cleaning woman as she is trying to steal a sackful of furs. It ends, many murders and much intrigue later, with great irony, justice, revenge and insight. Olcott creates an enormous appetite for more, more, more—and the sooner the better."

—*The New York Daily News*

"Olcott is a fine writer. His delineation of the massive corruption afflicting Soviet society is in the great tradition established by Gogol ... his comic gifts are considerable, and Duvakin is a wonderful, wonderful character."

—*The Cleveland Plain Dealer*

"A corker of a tale, as relentless a police novel as we've had in some time and an insightful, credible look at everyday Russian life ... *MAY DAY IN MAGADAN* is much more than a spellbinding mystery; it is a penetrating dissection of Soviet society."

—*American Way* magazine

"Fast moving and well told ... A most readable story and a convincing account of life in the Soviet hierarchy."

"Murder, double-dealin[g] in the Soviet Union ...

May Day in
* Magadan *

Anthony Olcott

BANTAM BOOKS
TORONTO · NEW YORK · LONDON · SYDNEY · AUCKLAND

MAY DAY IN MAGADAN
A Bantam Book / May 1985

ISBN 0-553-17167-4

Published simultaneously in the United States and Canada

Bantam Books are published by Bantam Books, Inc. Its trademark,
consisting of the words ''Bantam Books'' and the portrayal of a
rooster, is registered in U.S. Patent and Trademark Office and in
other countries. Marca Registrada. Bantam Books, Inc., 666 Fifth
Avenue, New York, New York 10103.

Printed and bound in Great Britain by Hunt Barnard Printing Ltd.

O   0 9 8 7 6 5 4 3 2 1

for Martha, Alison, and Andrew

May Day in
★ Magadan ★

⋆ ONE ⋆

The toilet woman—stout, elderly—shuffled along in carpet slippers and black housecoat, dragging behind her a brown paper cement sack two-thirds as tall as herself. Like the "honey merchants" of her grandfather's day, she found easy passage through the crowds of soldiers, Yakut women with bawling children, battered Chukchis, all the human log jam that made up the Magadan airport; her bag was filled with the used newspaper from a wire basket beside each stinking toilet, which it was her job to collect. "The sacred dignity of labor," Duvakin said under his breath, watching from his perch on the second level, where in theory he was measuring the railing for May Day banners; in fact, he was simply leaning on the rail, watching the chaos below, and trying to clear his head of the hum of having risen too early. "It's too crowded in the day, get out there before the first flights—five, five-thirty," Sutrapian, his bibulous superior in the propaganda bureau, had ordered. So Duvakin had done, though he had no idea why Party headquarters could not keep records of such dimensions.

May Day, after all, did come around regularly.

Once Magadan had been the El Dorado of a nightmare, capital of an empire fabulously wealthy in furs, diamonds, gold. And slaves. Men came to Magadan either to die in frozen mine shafts and icy stands of virgin timber or to drive these first to death, then pluck the kopeks from their dead men's eyes. The camps were closed now, Stalin's "error," and those who came to work did so voluntarily. So it was said, anyway.

Most had "volunteered" as Duvakin had. Given the choice of Magadan as free men or Mordovia as prisoners, few failed in their enthusiasm for the Far East and this tiny city huddled between harsh crags and frozen sea. Years, age, and boredom had inured him, but still, on days like today, when his head hummed like a defective fluorescent lamp, Duvakin at times wondered. He looked over the railing to the lobby—where men slept on the huge bosoms of their stoic wives; children slept on mounds of overcoats; soldiers slept on one another; and single arrivals, who sought in vain for taxis or friends, slept on their luggage. The air was thick with strong tobacco, the smells of urine and watery cocoa; the glint of the April sun on the torpidly circling flies made the airport, the city, the world seem dusty, vile, and close.

Duvakin noticed the cleaning woman go into the far toilets, near the empty ticket kiosks. He glanced at his watch. Not quite six; early for a cleaning woman. Very early, he thought.

Duvakin straightened himself up from the railing where he had been leaning, rolled up his tape, and stretched. He was getting old; he could feel it. His feet hurt and his teeth ached with boredom. He jotted down his figures in a grimy notebook.

It was a long way from hotel security in Moscow to

measuring railings at the Magadan airport, and now Duvakin felt every centimeter of his slide. Long ago he had
given off trying to make sense of that plunge and had
concentrated instead on trying to make sense of himself,
his life. In its way, agitprop work wasn't too bad, by local
standards, a plum even. Mostly you just put up posters,
arranged for wall newspapers and tablets of honor in the
microregions, and occasionally gave lectures on American foreign policy or the neofascist émigrés or the obvious
falseness of religious claims when scrutinized scientifi-
cally. The lectures were sent from Khabarovsk; the au-
diences mostly were Chukchi (who seemed to worship
reindeer or moss and who didn't speak Russian anyway),
and Magadan was so small that three hours of slow walking let you cover it in posters and slogans, giving the rest
of the time free.

Besides, you had to be a Party member, so you also got
a choice apartment (in fact, a small room with an erratic
coil to cook on and a communal bog down the hall) and a
special ration card, which bought the occasional kielbasa
to relieve the endless flow of cod with which the rest of
Magadan had to be content.

A quiet life, Duvakin thought, glancing over to the
militia man who snoozed, feet up on his desk. As quiet as
being dead, except that Sutrapian wanted you back with
the measurements by the start of work, which, depending
on how drunk he was, couldn't be for at least four hours.

Duvakin sighed, then headed downstairs. The railings, Sutrapian had said, but suppose they decide there
must be a "No to the Arms Race!" behind the ticket
counter or a "The People and Party Are One!" above the
buffet for May Day? After all, 1982 was a double-anniver-
sary year—65 years since the Revolution, 60 years since
the formation of the USSR. Duvakin wasn't going to risk a
second five o'clock rising; may as well measure everything.

[3]

He picked his way slowly through the mounds of
sleeping people, who had made no attempt to keep aisles
clear or to stay in their seats. The airport, as always, was
jammed; the schedule of flights was so anarchic it had
become chaos. People came to the airport like they used
to go to the railroads during the war, like Duvakin's father
said they used to during the civil war, to live in flittery
hope and bored despair for departure. The airport was
always a boiling fury of people rushing through stolid
walls of hopeless waiting. He thought of the militia man
asleep upstairs, remembered his own days as a security
officer. Duvakin knew from watching that here there was a
simpler kind of crowd handling than he had learned in
Moscow. Bang, a truncheon on the back of every head you
can reach, then throw whatever falls to the ground outside. In summer an unconscious man would be nibbled
by blackflies and mosquitoes until he was red with his
own blood; in winter when the cold oozed out of the
mountains like a gelid slime, a man would freeze so solid
in an hour that you had to wait for spring simply to fit him
into a coffin. The clotted crowd that shuffled in and out
knew this, and respectfully it let the corpulent officer
upstairs sleep.

Duvakin reached the window and tried to rub clear a
spot in the sweaty, grimy glass. He could just make out the
mountains, pinkish-white in the early sun. Down below
the snow was melting, almost entirely gone from wind-
swept southern exposures, but up higher the snow would
stay through June; some summery days the wind crept
across that snow to stab an icy shaft of winter even into
the whitest of midsummer's nights.

He turned, leaning against the glass. A glance at his
watch told him he had hours yet to kill. People were
beginning to stir, fitfully stretching and scratching, like
campers; Duvakin watched a tight knot of busy Chukchis
and recalled a circular, about how the locals sometimes

built cooking fires on the marble floor of the airport. He watched for a moment, hoping he would see such, but quickly grew bored. Besides, if he had seen it, he might have to do something about it. Soon after civic participation had fetched him up here, on this rock isthmus between frozen oceans of mud and seawater, on the farthest edge of the civilized world, Duvakin had vowed that his sole and proper concern was the safety and quiet of Duvakin. Let the snoring peasant upstairs worry about Chukchis.

The cleaning woman emerged again, dragging her sack from the nearby big men's room toward the far end, where there must be smaller toilets for airport and airline personnel. What a god-awful job, Duvakin thought, heaving himself up from the window to amble in her direction. Hard enough to spring out of bed for banners; imagine getting up so early to clean toilets. An old habit of militia work tugged at his curiosity, idly making him think again that it was unusually early to find a solitary cleaning woman. He shrugged, then set to work measuring the wall behind the ticket kiosks.

He was at the door to the offices when she scurried out. He must have startled her, for she jumped, hand to heart. Her eyes opened very large, red-rimmed and weepy.

"Saints in heaven! Where did you come from?" the toilet woman said after a little shriek, stepping back onto her nearly full bag.

"Usual place, mama's bed," Duvakin answered offhandedly. He glanced at her indifferently, then looked beyond her, down the corridor, a dirty line of closed, blind doors.

He looked back at her. She stood against the wall, her bag behind her; she watched him apprehensively.

"You've got nothing to do but roll your eyes?" Duvakin asked, amused at her goggle-eyed study of his worn, black suit, which she appeared to find important.

She released a long-held breath and dashed, bobbing in a half curtsy of gratitude and relief. Her bag wobbled precariously; Duvakin stepped well away, in no desire to see *that* load tipped out.

He closed the hall door softly, then crossed his arms to watch her scuttle across the lobby. He shook his head gently; she thinks I'm somebody, so I act like I'm somebody.

To his right was a short hall, with triple doors leading outside. Baggage handling and holding areas were under three jurisdictions, and so almost taboo. The militia kept away the curious, while Aeroflot guarded bags, carts, refueling equipment, and the KGB took care of the rest: valuable cargo, state necessities, and god knows what else. No place for us mere mortals, Duvakin thought.

However . . . he looked over the lobby, then down the hall again. It would be nice to duck out for a quick breath of air; inside, people were stirring, and he didn't wish to talk. He dug in his coat pocket for a cigarette, lit up, and pondered for a moment. Perhaps the cold would invigorate a bit, remove the tight lump of fatigue from its place at the base of his throat.

Magadan itself wasn't much colder than Leningrad, just as far north and thousands of kilometers to the west, but the ameliorating effect of the sea was quickly overpowered with each step inland. The airport was only twenty kilometers northwest of the city, but far enough that winter battered hard at even these triple doors, as thick and solid as airlocks. Duvakin had seen the thermometer creep down toward −50 degrees; he had seen truck tires shatter on small bumps; he had seen the air grow soupy with the exhalations of Magadan eddying in the nearly liquid air. The doors did not open easily.

Outside, his first breaths bit hard at nose and throat, forcing his eyes open wide in surprise. Even so, those sharp involuntary breaths carried a faint tang of salt, and Duvakin felt quickened. Salt meant spring; the sea ice was rotting.

Duvakin sidled along the south wall in the narrow space that had melted clear against the building; he sought a niche out of the wind, where the few rays of the distant sun might collect. The sun was already well up, even though the day was just on six, but it was powerless in the frozen wastes it gilded. Duvakin leaned back, drew on his cigarette, enjoying the surge of warmth against numbed fingers.

Spring. More springs than he cared to count had been buried again in winter, yet Duvakin still felt a bouyancy at the thought. Spring in Magadan was not lilac, bird cherry, and apple blossom, but even its spring of blackflies, glutinous mud, and freak blizzards exuded occasional wild crocuses, deep purple on fuzzy stems, vivid as new hopes.

Hopes, hell. Duvakin shrugged. What could he hope for? He could burrow in Magadan, quiet and invisible, eventually to collect a pension of eighty-one rubles a month. Or he could try to return to Moscow and right the wrong done him, reclaim the woman whom he had loved such a short time.

And get himself arrested. And worse, get her arrested, as an accomplice. Her daughter, they'd put where, in a state orphanage? Or would she be too old now? Duvakin tried to remember, but could not. He found his treasured memories of that old intimacy painful and confining. That world was gone, beyond reach.

Not so much as a postcard, Vanya; not so much as a two-second phone call, they had said. You even try, you even think of trying, and that Tanya of yours has a shaved head and her cunt swabbed purple. You think we're joking? It's easy to find out . . .

So here I am, he thought, staring vacantly at a battered green luggage cart, sitting tight, to protect a woman who has to figure I abandoned her years ago.

The cold had stolen deeper into his clothes, finally brushing icily along his ribs and up his spine. He shivered, then turned to go back inside. He heaved hard at the doors, stamping his feet to clear them of snow.

Inside, Duvakin paused for a moment to regain his breath and look about for what else might support a banner if the Party decreed it. The airport was waking up, nattering in Chukchi and Yakut and even Russian, preparing for a day of tedious, anxious waiting. Somewhere far away the Aeroflot people still slept in their tiny apartments, not yet ready to deign service this gently roiling mass.

Out of the corner of his eye Duvakin noticed the office door was open. I closed that, he thought, unsure.

He walked over, grabbed the handle. Force of habit made him look down the hall. What the devil? The toilet woman was shuffling toward him, dragging her bag behind. Her head was down and turned, watching behind her. Duvakin waited until she was almost next to him, then boomed, "Shock work today, grandma?"

The result was spectacular; the toilet woman snapped upright so fast she almost fell, then stepped back, stumbling on her load.

"The devil take you straight to hell, you spotted demon! What do you think you are, scaring an old working woman like that? You don't have a mother maybe?"

"Let's put a little honey on that tongue, grandma, it's too tart for my taste right now." Unconsciously, Duvakin squared himself to meet her attack with his dignity.

"Honey, is it? I'll give you honey, stinking sacks of it! Fine thing, scaring people half to death, and me still with work to do." Her right lower lid twitched spasmodically as her eyes blazed an angry brown. She was jabbing at his chest with a thick, horny forefinger. Duvakin shrank from contact, as well as from the strong odors of garlic, sweat, and toilet she exuded.

"All right, all right, so work . . . but keep a civil tongue in your head." He stepped aside, flattening himself against the wall.

"And you don't shit, I suppose," the woman sniffed. "Fine thing." She spat at his shoes, glared again, then refreshed her grip on her cement sack and shuffled on.

Duvakin watched, almost grinning. For all their deference to authority these Far Easterners still had some vinegar the inlanders lacked. Probably the soft ones died, he smiled to himself. A woman like that, built like a Kama truck and probably as durable.

As he chuckled, a thought suddenly stabbed him. Her bag was full. Just as it had been fifteen or twenty minutes earlier. So where did she find the used paper to fill two empty one-hundred-kilo sacks, in two one-stool toilets?

To his horror his foot moved faster than his mind, shooting out to step firmly on the sack's ear that dragged along the muddy floor. The toilet woman was scurrying fast enough to lose her grip and let the bag fall.

A cornucopia of smeared newspaper tumbled out onto the ground; then Duvakin just had time to see a rich slither of fabulous fur pelts roll onto the pile of stinking newsprint before the furious toilet woman was clawing at his throat and face.

⋆ TWO ⋆

"**S**top wriggling, fool . . . you're making it harder to get this stuff on you!"

"It hurts, damn it!" Duvakin yelled, as much to expel the pain in noise as to be heard.

"Of course it hurts. But who asked you to get your face this way?" The doctor gave a final brutal swab with the gauze pad, then stepped back to admire her art. "Can't say it improves your looks, to be honest. Want to see?" She waved at a grimy mirror on the wall.

The stink of the antiseptic nibbled at the inside of Duvakin's nose, triggering spasmodic sneezes; each sneeze dragged a stinging net across his face. No, he didn't want to see—it hurt enough without having also to remember that his face was streaked with emerald cleanser and brown scabs. And that not a soul in the clinic could look at him without laughing.

"Berry picking, at this time of year?" some nurses hooted at him, and others yelled "Pick one that *wants* kissing next time." In truth, Duvakin could count himself lucky still to have eyes. The toilet woman not only had had passion and surprise on her side, but she also knew her business. Duvakin's natural reluctance to hit a middle-aged woman had disappeared when he felt himself going over backwards, as she in her fury clawed at his face. Quicker than he could think, he had brought his fists up and down, bang on her neck, silencing her. He had stood over her a second, his face dissolving into a dripping agony that brought tears welling up. They had spilled down his flayed cheeks in burning salt rivulets.

Then he had shouted for help.

"Here's a prescription for more of that disinfectant. No telling what was under your lady friend's fingernails." The heavy, middle-aged doctor with dyed blond hair and two gold teeth studied him speculatively, then dug a cigarette out of her soiled smock. "Smoke?"

"Thanks . . ." He took a crumpled Tu-144. "Will I find this stuff anywhere?" He held up the scrap of paper scrawled with unknown Latin letters.

"They told me you were Party," she said in surprise. "You can't use the closed apothecary?"

"Sure, but . . . Really vital stuff they'll send to Moscow for, and that takes—"

"Days . . . I know, don't I?" She shrugged with open palms, indicating a mute fatigue with the endless struggle to procure. "Try. If yours doesn't have it, maybe Number One, downtown. Use your Party card."

Duvakin nodded, conscious now less of pain than of a hardening crust on his face.

The doctor studied him again with hard gray-green eyes, then moved closer. "You in a hurry? I've got some alcohol put back . . ."

Duvakin stared at her for a moment, surprised at the invitation in her voice, then he glanced at her spare and dirty office and shook his head.

"I can't; they want me back at the station . . . papers

to sign . . ." He stared as he choked out the answer, watching the doctor's plump back and wondering whether he had dreamed that sudden note of warmth he thought he'd heard.

She half turned, smiling girlishly over a shoulder. "You sure? It's not often one gets to talk intelligently. Besides"—she patted him on the thigh—"it's good clean stuff, medicinal . . ."

Duvakin froze, his heart pumping and his mouth dry. "I can't," he finally said, his face flushed. He felt the woman's hand as a warm, damp weight. The doctor eyed him coldly for a second, then shrugged.

"If you can't, well then . . ." She turned her back, dismissing him. Duvakin stood slowly, still shocked. What had she had in mind, a quick pull of spirits, then up on the examining table?

"You said you were in a hurry," the doctor said acidly.

In truth, Duvakin did have to hurry. Captain Pivovarov of the militia seemed to prefer justice and punishment be done simultaneously, with no paperwork; he had scowled heavily when Duvakin was brought in with the toilet woman. "Get that looked at," he had snarled, "then be back here—by nine."

In something less than ten minutes.

Duvakin's breath came slightly raw as he tried to walk briskly through the chill air back up Twenty-Fourth Party Congress Street towards militia headquarters, cursing his bad luck.

The woman had had twenty pelts in the bag he had spilled plus another twenty in the first bag. Mostly blue fox, ten pelts wired together through the nose, but also sable, red fox, and marten. The pelts were from the first of what would become a flood in summer as pelts moved from the trapping and breeding stations to Leningrad and beyond. They left Magadan in locked wire hampers, the contents protected from moisture and view by a kind of waxed paper lining; in turn these cages were locked into airline cargo containers.

What the toilet woman must have noticed was that the cages often stood about waiting to be loaded until containers were available. All she had had to do was jimmy a spot-welded flange at a corner, then make a slit in the paper; the furs slid out easily, leaving no immediate evidence of a major crime against state property, while making one toilet woman a good deal wealthier. And leaving Duvakin to loathe his meddling foot.

He walked as swiftly as the crusted frozen slush on the sidewalk would allow, anxious to be done with the formalities. All morning he had recalled the scene, wishing he had never bothered with any of it. Instead of a leisurely morning of ducking Sutrapian and pretending to inventory May Day bunting, Duvakin had to sit in the militia office, the doctor's office, the militia office again. And see that damned toilet woman, for formal identification. Why had he stuck his foot into other's affairs?

He turned down Komsomolsk, a narrower side street of squat log houses, punctuated by occasional cinderblock barracks. Militia headquarters was a rambling log building painted a peeling green, with a low porch out of some provincial production of Chekhov. A high wooden fence did not contain the yapping of the guard dogs in the yard next door.

Duvakin pushed inside, conscious of the stares his face was getting. The station was in a lull between the end of the night duty and the start of the day. A few late officers were straggling in; others stood around gossiping. The walls were thick with circulars, posters, notices. Captain Pivovarov apparently was as unconcerned with tidiness as he was with most other fine points, but then why not. As the old people said, God is high and the tsar far away. Pivovarov answered to Khabarovsk hundreds of frozen kilometers to the south. As long as the gold and furs continued to emerge, Pivovarov could do as he liked.

Duvakin walked timorously on creaking boards up to the receptionist. "You have the paper I am to complete?" he asked politely.

"Wouldn't you be in trouble if I didn't?" she rasped, then handed him a coarse tan sheet. She watched as Duvakin ostentatiously slapped his pockets.

"Pen? Use the wells over there." She pointed to some scarred and splintery benches by the window.

With a sigh Duvakin sat down to scratch out his version of events with the clotted ink and tearing, blotting nib.

The pen scraped and belched, occasionally poking through to the rough bench below. Duvakin was too near the radiator; he grew more and more torpid as the heat sank into his body. He yawned, first reluctantly, then luxuriantly. He began to imagine the cool linen of his bed.

Damn, getting up at five. What did Sutrapian think he was, a milkmaid? And now *this* business . . . Duvakin shook his head, trying to revive himself. He recalled the dumpy old woman, her fiery reaction the second time, when he startled her. He half smiled, thinking of her spirit, though the grin pulled at his new scabs, reminding him what that spirit had cost him.

Well, she'd find out how far spirit would take her now, he thought, a little bitterly.

Theft of state property is no joke; Duvakin knew too well the penalties, for that was the threat they had used to club him to Magadan—minimum five years, plus five years exile. And for furs? Furs weren't like boards or wallpaper; furs foreigners bought, for dollars. The powers did not look at loss of dollars kindly; the woman had a steep path ahead.

Still, Duvakin thought half to console himself, an old woman, a widow probably . . . she'll beat her chest and wail, and maybe they'll let her off with minimum.

He gnawed absently at his lip, trying to believe that was true, not so much because he felt sorry for her, but more because he disliked having brought her trouble. Why had that blasted foot meddled, he thought again.

Oh well, soon enough done.

There was a creak on the floorboard behind him. "You finished, comrade?"

Duvakin looked around at the high voice.

"This second, comrade Captain, this second . . ."

Duvakin scrawled his concluding sentences while Captain Pivovarov drummed his stubby fingers impatiently on crossed arms.

"Done? Bring it here . . ."

Pivovarov was very short, barely a meter and a half, with stocky frame, wiry hair, and dark brown eyes. There were those in town, Duvakin knew, who whispered that Pivovarov was a Jew, but never to his face. Pivovarov's voice might be a high tenor, and his nose might reach only to the average Ivanov's shoulder, but no one holds the captaincy of the Magadan militia because of his gentle mercies. Magadan is not the papacy.

Pivovarov put Duvakin's blotchy report in a cardboard folder, then chucked it onto a pile on his desk; the impact toppled another pile, which slid into a third. Pivovarov watched impassively, then waved a hand in disgust. He sat on his chair, signaling Duvakin to sit as well.

"Fucking nuisance, that's what this is . . ." He sounded tired.

"Comrade Captain?"

"Look at all this stuff, just look at it!" He spread his hands, palms up, over the piles of folders on his desk. "Reports of stolen bottles, drunken fights, petty prostitutes, requests for clarification, requests for projections, interim plans, long-term plans, bloody fucking socialist competitions. How in the devil can they figure me to project our planned reduction of crimes against state property for the next five years?"

He paused, turning to look out the window.

"And now this . . . Duvakin, have you any idea what you're going to cost me because you tripped over that shit sack?"

"Comrade?"

"For starters . . ." Pivovarov's short thick thumb folded down a stubby finger. "It was furs, so that means duplicate reports, one for us, one for the organs . . ." A vague wave indicated the wall. "And it was already consigned cargo, so another report, for Aeroflot. And then because it's a closed area, a security report. But that one doesn't just get written up, you know . . . that one has to have an investigation first . . . *with* outside evaluators. And they'll criticize our vigilance, and then we'll have to acknowledge it and promise to do better." He sighed heavily, still half turned toward the window.

Duvakin sat uneasily, not sure of his status in relation to the captain; old habits made him shrink, but then he was a Party member too now. Even after four years it was a new and ill-fitting mantle. And what to say in reply?

"Well, at least it's a straightforward affair," he returned hesitantly. "I mean, there she was, and there I was." He shrugged.

Pivovarov took a last look outside and snorted, then nodded. "Straightforward enough, you're right—only the old bitch won't sign her confession."

"Won't sign her confession?" Duvakin was startled. "But I—"

"I know, I know . . ." Pivovarov waved him down with a stubby hand. "She still won't sign."

Duvakin's hopes fell. No confession meant a trial, witnesses, more mucking about. And who was the main witness? The *only* witness? He glanced again at his guilty foot. *Damn* him for a meddler.

A thought occurred. "The reports are logged?"

Pivovarov now looked surprised, so Duvakin hastily explained. "I served in People's Control . . ."

"Yes? How long? Where?" For a moment interest replaced the dreary fatigue in Pivovarov's eyes, but quickly ebbed.

"Oh, a time," Duvakin mumbled, thinking darkly, "all my life," then he added, "in Moscow."

"Then," Pivovarov said summarily, "I expect you know what comes next. Yes, the reports are logged, not that we had much choice, being as it was furs, so yes, we have to go through all the other steps too." He stepped forward, to indicate that they were to walk.

"Confirmation of identity," Duvakin said mechanically, angry at himself, the world, this captain, and the stupid laws. Of course it was her there in the cell, since he had watched her led off, but the laws said . . . They never do anything by halves, he thought. Now they decide we're a nation of laws, and there's a rule for each step of every day. And what difference does it make? They'll nail this onto the toilet lady regardless.

He stood. "Very well, but quickly. I've got to get back to headquarters." Pivovarov again looked quizzical, so Duvakin added importantly, "Party business."

"You're Party?" Pivovarov asked with interest. "Odd . . . I wouldn't have thought." He shrugged, and gently touched Duvakin's elbow. "Please . . ."

They went out into the hall.

"Which cell did our toilet lady get chucked into, Elizaveta Arkadievna?" Pivovarov asked the front desk clerk, who looked as coarse and vicious as her name sounded delicate.

"C, sir, the far one. You'll find her all right, carrying on like a hen in a string bag." She laughed.

Militia usually held miscreants for only short periods

before consigning them to prison and the courts, so most of the cells they passed were little more than cages. C, however, was a proper cell, with double log walls and a small Judas hole in a solid door. His catch must have awakened in a temper, thought Duvakin, with a scabby smile.

Sure enough, even at the head of the hall he could hear a muffled shouting and some kind of banging, as if of a foot on the door.

"Open C for us, would you?" Pivovarov asked the harassed-looking guard.

He looked up, partly with exasperation, partly with relief. "Be happy to be done with *her*." He rose as if exhausted, then dug out his keys.

Usual procedure in such cells, Duvakin remembered, was to flip on the light from the outside, to dazzle the occupant, then to rush inside while the occupant was still blinking.

It seemed, however, that the toilet woman was not in C for the first time; even though she could not prevent her dilated pupils from blinding her, she stood solidly in the doorway, flailing madly. Duvakin felt a searing slash across his scabs before the guard chopped the woman in her kidney. She collapsed, moaning, and Pivovarov kicked her back against the iron cot.

"Well, my greatly respected Firsovna," the guard said with heavy irony, "still with the wind up your tail, eh?"

Her response was so coarse that for a moment Duvakin could only stare, openmouthed.

"Just a minute, granny, let's remember where you are, all right?" Duvakin could not help saying.

"I remember right enough, you sniveling owl. For half a kopek, I'd . . ."

"I'd think, that's what *I'd* do," Pivovarov interrupted, a stern look on his face. "You've got a big slice on your

[19]

plate right now, you know. Theft of state property, assaulting a Party member . . . You want to spend the rest of your life inside?"

"What business of yours is it? What do you care?" The woman was heavy and squat, with disheveled gray curls and a doughy face, but a lynxlike fury burned in her small brown eyes. "Who asked you to nose around?" she barked at Duvakin.

"Enough, granny. Let's get this done with, eh? Where's your passport?" Pivovarov asked in a tired, businesslike voice.

"Brezhnev took it to wipe his ass with."

No passport, Duvakin thought. A runaway state farmer? Or an escaped criminal? Everybody else had to have a passport.

"Your name, then?"

"Nadya Krupskaya."

"Her name's Maria Firsovna Osmushkina, sir," the guard said deferentially to Pivovarov. "We're old friends, aren't we, Masha?"

"Nationality?"

"Russian, like he ought to be, the stinking crossbreed!" She tossed her head at Duvakin.

"I'm Russian, grandma, and what's more I know better than to take what's not mine," Duvakin answered stiffly, too heatedly. He wished the identification were done.

"If you're so Russian, then you ought to stick up for your own. What the devil is it to you if a few pelts go missing?" The woman's fire seemed to be subsiding, but there was still a good deal of heat.

"Address?" Pivovarov continued.

"A dormitory, down on Karl Liebknicht Street, number sixteen." Her voice grew more resigned.

Duvakin studied the shabby figure before him; those dormitories were bearpits, tiny cell-like rooms with one toilet per building, washup in the courtyard. On most holidays they caught fire.

"Well, Maria Firsovna, you know the charge. Theft of state property, assault, resisting arrest. The comrade here caught you fair and square. You'll save yourself a lot of trouble if you'd sign this confession." Pivovarov extended a prepared sheet.

"I'll sign nothing, you stinking shit!" The woman spat at the sheet, then turned away.

"I suppose you didn't know those pelts were valuable? You just happened to find them in the toilets?" Pivovarov's sarcasm was acid; he held the paper nearer her face.

The toilet woman spat again. "Of course I knew they were valuable. Why the devil would I take them, otherwise?"

"So you do confess?" Pivovarov leaped forward, waving the paper; Duvakin felt his heart rise in hope.

"I sign nothing. Make the bloodsucker there work for his furs!" She glared at Duvakin.

Pivovarov raised his hand, as though to backhand her across the mouth, but the woman cringed, threw up an arm.

"Sure, beat the old toilet woman, put her away for a stretch. Never mind the people like him, the big thieves, the ones who steal whole crates. Just send the old toilet woman out to the log teams." She looked viperous behind her upraised arm.

"You're looking at a long stretch of socially useful work as it is, grandma," Duvakin said heavily. "You wouldn't want an anti-Party slander clause on top of that, would you?" He eyed her narrowly.

"Slander, is it?" she suddenly slumped, apparently abandoning all resistance. "Slander? More like you Party bloodsuckers all look out for each other, gnawing the living flesh from our poor workers' bones." She shook her head slightly, then, at last, began to sob. "Steal twenty pelts and you go to prison; for twenty crates they make you the chief . . ." Her shoulders shook raggedly beneath the worn black housecoat.

Pivovarov looked at her a moment, then shrugged. "You see?" He turned to Duvakin. "Looks like a trial."

Duvakin's spirits fell, as he thought of strings he might pull to spare himself the tedium, the ignominy of having to appear; there were depressingly few possibilities.

"I suppose so," he agreed. "Anyway, formally . . . that's her."

Pivovarov nodded once and left the cell. Duvakin stood a second, still puzzled by the huddled woman before him. The warden pulled at his arm to get him through the door. He slammed the heavy door home, then switched off the cell light.

Duvakin nodded and turned away from the door. The woman's behavior had puzzled him since he had first spilled out her sack. Usually old women caught pilfering state goods dissolved into tears, pleading poverty, widowhood, starvation, while pledging repentance, restitution, and unflagging future service. This one had scratched, cursed, spat and fought all morning; only now had tears come, and tears not of repentance, but of desperate, impotent anger.

"She's been a guest here before, I take it," Duvakin asked the guard, who was already heading for his well-worn seat at the desk.

"Firsovna? Mostly in the dry-out pen, but every now and again there's some brawling or public scandal. Couple of times there's been aces, a year for black market. Little stuff, sweaters, mohair hats, T-shirts—" The guard shrugged, eying his desk pointedly.

Duvakin stood irresolutely, still puzzled. "Doesn't sound like the type to go prying open crates, does she?"

"The devil knows . . . You saw her bags." The guard sat down, no longer interested. "You're the one had her arrested."

Duvakin shrugged and went up the hall after Pivovarov. The hall was quiet save for the buzzing of two sleepy window flies banging sluggishly against the dusty panes. Duvakin stood, acutely aware of his aching face, his exhaustion. What a foul life this is, he thought wearily. For a moment he entertained lunatic scenes—destroying the file on Pivovarov's desk, freeing the toilet woman, flying back to Moscow in search of the life he had lost, and the woman. But even as the thoughts reached his mind, he knew he would do nothing. He was too old, too far away, too beaten. At its best, life is a spiral, and never in any event a pendulum. What has been done cannot be undone, and for Duvakin further to act would only enmire him more, like those mammoths that turn up frozen into the taiga swamps; the best course now, he knew, was to play the little role his thoughtlessness had thrust upon him. What was it to him that some filthy old toilet lady had landed herself in the soup? She had made her mistake, he had made his. Fine—now let each play out his role quietly, accuser and accused, and then let the remainder of life come.

Duvakin grew conscious of the shuffle and stomp of feet further up the corridor. Outside, a dog's chain snaked, clanking against itself, then a raven coughed on a pine branch. He glanced at his watch; it was long ago time he were at headquarters. Oh well, with the right face put on it, maybe his meddling might even come out heroism, or vigilance at least. He sighed, then went back into the front room, where Elizaveta Arkadievna was whistling convict songs between her gapped steel teeth.

"That's it?" he asked, looking about for Pivovarov, who had vanished. "I can go?"

"Looks like," the straw-headed woman said offhandedly, indifferently. "If we want you," she smiled nastily, "we know where to find you." Then she laughed. It seemed this was an old joke with her, and one she enjoyed repeating.

∗ THREE ∗

There was still a Chukchi woman with two enormous baskets hung fore and aft on a shoulder sling between Duvakin and the door, so he lunged, forcing at least his shoulders and head out. The other passengers he shoved past shouted "Swine! Beast!" and a couple managed to land blows, but still the move worked; Duvakin caught the edge of the bus door and pulled his hips free, then, at last, stepped down onto the sidewalk. The bus doors slammed angrily, catching someone's elbow in the rubber seal, and the bus waddled farther down the Boulevard of Labor. Exhausted, Duvakin sat on a broken bench against a fence.

That the bus was packed was no surprise; the buses of Magadan were always jammed, sometimes so that old men or small women were carried aloft by the press of the crowd. However, the crush was the last straw of a day that had begun three hours too early. He leaned back against the boards, which still felt faintly warm in the sun.

The sun was just descending behind the mountain,

throwing ruddy shafts against the clouds. Duvakin watched the old women splash up the street before it suddenly hit him. "Puddles!" he said out loud, his heart now lighter. Puddles! It had been above freezing . . . and could spring be far off now?

Reinvigorated slightly, Duvakin sluggishly stood, buoyed by the thought of his room, his bed. The room was tiny, some four meters by five, and furnished like maybe they were going to film a Gorky play there, but it was his; after today he wanted nothing more than that dusty, cluttered peace.

Duvakin slogged happily up his street, Treefellers Prospekt, a name dreamed up thirty years ago by some city-planning romantic in Irkutsk or Moscow, to describe what in fact was a lane, just like the country lanes in Duvakin's native Krasnaya Sosna. Little log huts stood randomly about, facing whichever direction they wished, each surrounded by a tiny plot fenced with whatever came to hand, around and through which snaked footpaths trodden in the snow; spring would transform the lane into a quagmire of ruts and puddles. At random points, comparative civilization intervened, in apartment blocks stuck higgledy-piggledy like meat scraps in head cheese. Magadan boasted no buildings above six stories, and most went no higher than three. The apartment blocks on the Prospekt were what the wits called "Khrushhuts," for they had appeared in Magadan only with the end of the cult, when the city ceased to be a simple guard house for the vast penal colony to the north. Three stories, of crumbling cinder block, most of them erected in freezing weather so that the mortar powdered and the buildings settled, tiny apartments of two and three low-ceilinged rooms . . . and just try to lay your hands on one! In Moscow no one above floor steward in the meanest rat-infested factory would live in such, but here? Strictly for the Hotel Metropole types. And, Duvakin thought ironically as he fumbled the key in his lock, for us high Party bloodsuckers.

The room exhaled a welcoming, familiar closeness of stale cigarettes, dust, and a single man enclosed by too long a winter, and Duvakin felt himself more cheerful. When Colonel Polkovnikov had first forced this on him back in Moscow, Duvakin had balked at Party membership. How could *he* become a member? Never in his life had he done a political thing—Pioneers and Komsomol, sure, like everyone else, but the lectures made him drowsy, and the girls he liked didn't continue; so Duvakin hadn't either, and the next thirty-odd years he had passed without serious thought of the Party. So why join?

"You *have* to join, for the post, and if you don't take *this* post . . ." Polkovnikov had said menacingly. And so he became a Party member. During the endless train ride to Khabarovsk, hard class, Duvakin had had time to regret much and fear more. Magadan, a name schoolboys frightened one another with, and a Party member too, with meetings, purges, vigilance, slogans . . .

In fact, Duvakin thought as he tugged off his stiff shoes, it could be worse. At least it got him this, plus the slab of bologna in his briefcase that would, with bread and some homemade birch beer he bought at the market from a Yakut woman, make his supper. He stepped into slippers and shed his coat.

At first Magadan, the agitprop job, everything had choked like a new shirt, reminding him daily of all that Polkovnikov and his treachery had snatched from him, reminding him of his own impotence, which raged and burned in mad, frenzied nightmares. Now, though, he had grown used, had found small comforts, had settled down. Had settled, period, he thought with an edge of bitterness. He waved his hand resignedly, half talking to himself, the way lone men will. He even recognized this growing eccentricity but could not seem to halt it. If settled, then

Anthony Olcott

settled, and the devil take it. He took a small milk can from the sill, where his birch beer was chilling, and began slicing the bread into chunks. His stomach rumbled happily.

The phone rang, startling him. He turned, waited. The phone rang again.

Damn it! Duvakin thought, trudging over to the heavy Bakelite instrument, an old-fashioned affair almost the size of a radio. Party business, it had to be. He hadn't wanted the thing; who would call him anyway? But Party members got phones as a perq, and so had he. Other than the furious periods just before the big holidays, the phone sat silent for whole weeks on end.

"Duvakin here," he said gruffly.

"Where in the devil have you been? I've been calling headquarters, and I tried your apartment, but there's always no answer, and they've been asking for you close on an hour now, and he wants to go home—"

"Who is this?" Duvakin asked, startled at the pent-up flood of words.

"Semyenov, you fool . . . Look, get out there on the double. He's no small cheese, and his people have been climbing all over me."

Semyenov, Duvakin recalled after a blank period, was his younger colleague at agitprop, the stupid-looking one. His chins were well doubled, and although he was not fat, there was a softness beneath his clothes, fat to be filled in, so to say. Duvakin did not know him well but suspected him as a bully and a braggart.

Duvakin bridled at the thought of leaving even his cosy chair, let alone the apartment, on the hysterical say-so of his junior. "Who's this he?" he asked dryly.

"Rzhevsky, of course . . . He's had his people after me all afternoon."

"Rzhevsky?" Duvakin could not place the name.

[28]

"The airport chief."

"What's he want me for? I've got nothing to do with him."

"You tell him that! He's phoned maybe a hundred times and sent people over here. Send Duvakin, and right now or faster—"

"It'll keep," Duvakin said gruffly, and began to hang up the phone.

"Vanya, hold it!" Semyenov shouted, as if aware he had been headed toward the receiver cradle. "He says it's *vital*, Party business, about this morning, he said . . . He's one of the big ones, Vanya."

Damn it to the devil's ancestors! Duvakin thought in disgust. It was probably true; you aren't put in charge of an airport just because you can keep the ticket lines straight. But what about this morning? The furs? Probably this Rzhevsky just wanted to be important, getting a personal report. At the cost of Duvakin's evening. He sat a moment longer, the phone heavy in his hand. Party membership seemed suddenly less benign. Well, no help for it.

"Duvakin? You still there? They'll be asking me again, you know. I'll just tell them where you are . . ." Semyenov's voice grew wheedling.

"All right . . . I'm going . . . by bus. It'll take a while."

"Bus! Take a taxi, Vanya, he said it's really crucial—"

Duvakin silenced him with a click of the receiver. A taxi, yet! Not enough that they steal my evening, but I've got to pay for it too! He rubbed his temples to ease the ache of fatigue, then slowly put his shoes back on. He took a slice of the bologna, soft and fragrant, and a bit of the bread. He rewrapped both tightly, but knew sadly that when he finally got back, both would be dryer, a little more stale. Heavily, he donned his coat and retraced his steps to the outside. Damn that old woman and his meddling foot.

Duvakin joined the small crowd huddling in the bus shelter; like each new arrival he peered down the street, anxious for a glimpse of the pigeon-toed old bus.

When it finally arrived, it was still jammed, but a lucky opening and a hearty shove got Duvakin the favored spot in the corner of the rear platform. He settled down to the smell of gasoline, exhaust, and his own sweat, as the heat of his fellow passengers steamed him slowly in his coat.

Luck seemed intent on small compensation for the Party's excessive demands; Duvakin's second bus came quickly, and then, although it meant he had to wait twenty minutes, he arrived at the airport stop just as a new bus pulled up. He got in second and sat. Slowly, the bus filled up with soldiers, Chukchis lugging huge willow baskets, slit-eyed Emy women chattering in mounds of blanket-wrapped bundles, Russian peasant women in their high felt boots. Duvakin kept his nose buried in a soggy copy of *Evening Magadan* he found on the floor.

It was almost eight-thirty before he managed to pry himself out of the bus and hurry into the airport.

Duvakin had wandered Magadan for four years now without so much as meeting the airport administrator, to say nothing of being the object of a frantic summons. Aviation administration and routine propaganda work were controlled from different centers, and so never met. Normally, if the airport administration had something to say to agitprop, they said it to their own superiors in Khabarovsk, the regional center; these said it to theirs, in Moscow. Only in Moscow did the lines converge, to touch and send the words back, to Khabarovsk, Magadan, and at last, Duvakin. Only the Party structure permitted this unusual route, to permit one comrade (senior) summoning another (decidedly, alas, junior); even so, Duvakin felt uncomfortably as if he were breaking regulations when he entered the narrow hall where he had nabbed the toilet woman. He did not know which office, but in the darkened hall only one door threw a shaft of light. Absurdly, Duvakin held his breath as he turned the door latch softly.

"Who's there?" a voice boomed from an inner office.

"Duvakin, sir," he answered automatically, then cursed himself. Astounding really how much of the ability to command consisted in the presumption of that right.

"Who?" The speaker emerged, blinking unintelligently at Duvakin. Duvakin would not have sworn he had seen him before, but he knew the type well. The man was a little taller than average but a good deal heavier, with great stocky legs, a chest the shape and size of an oil drum, arms so powerful they hung awkwardly, like a child overbundled against winter. His forehead sloped, and his cheeks were slab-cut inward, to give his eyes the slant of some Scythian idol, glittering cold blue, like a spider's eyes seen in torchlight.

"Duvakin, agitprop . . . headquarters told me you were looking for me." Duvakin straightened himself, bolstering his authority to confront Rzhevsky's.

"You the lad what pinched the old woman this morning?"

"That's right."

"Duvakin, you say? Well, well . . ." The man's eyes narrowed a flicker before he smiled, a huge toothy affair glittering with gold. "Let me shake your hand, comrade, come in, come in." He extended a hand so thick it made Duvakin goggle, so horny it rasped as they shook. Rzhevsky's grip was crushing. The hands of some horrid smothering monster out of a childhood nightmare. Duvakin let himself be pulled into the inner office, still uncertain of why he was there.

The chief smiled broadly at him, then said heartily, "Rzhevsky, Yury Dmitrovich . . . and Yura to my friends."

There was a pregnant pause that Duvakin finally filled with "Ivan Pavlovich . . . Vanya."

"Vanya it is then! Sit down, sit down." The man all

but threw him down into a blue vinyl chair across from a smart chrome and plastic desk, then sank himself into the soft fabric of his chair. Duvakin looked around stiffly, almost at attention; the Aeroflot posters (blowup of Red Square, an unfocused ballet dancer, smiling hostess in perky hat), Eastern rug on the floor, some plants, lots of telephones . . . and one wall all streaky glass, looking out on the runway and the mountains beyond. Now only the runway lights glistened blue in the night.

There was a thud. Duvakin looked back to see a cognac service had appeared on the desk, a leather-covered bottle and a set of leather cups. He raised his eyebrows.

"Just a drop, for the sake of new friendship and to reward the clever man," Rzhevsky boomed in a jovial tone somewhere between offer and order, then poured.

For this I came out here, Duvakin thought in disgust. "I'm touched, comrade, but . . . aren't you on duty?" Duvakin finally hit on the softest expression of his question he could.

"Who's to know?" Rzhevsky shrugged, then added, "I'm in charge here, remember?" Then he winked, smiled, and added, "Vanya, I am grateful to you, and surely you wouldn't refuse a man his gratitude. Besides," he winked, "it'll heal your face. Drink!"

Duvakin looked appraisingly at Rzhevsky.

"Grateful?"

"The woman, the woman! The furs, Vanya! My god, that flea-bitten bitch walking off with those pelts . . ." He slapped his forehead with a whack that would have stunned a calf. "Trouble I could have had up to here!" He showed Duvakin his chin.

"You could have had? Those were consigned already."

"Still my airport, isn't it? And they don't fool around with fine points when furs and the like come in. Take that stuff *dead* serious, they do. *Drink!*" he clicked imperiously against Duvakin's lightly held cup and tossed off the cognac. A life of habit made Duvakin follow, unthinking. Rzhevsky inhaled through open mouth, exhaled like a gale, and smiled.

"Good. Armenian, not what you usually get around here. I've got a friend, a pilot on the Evpatoria-Novy Sibirsk-Irkutsk-Khabarovsk-Magadan run; he brings it up."

Duvakin rolled his tongue inside his mouth. "Not bad . . ." He made ready to stand.

"Can't fly on one wing, Vanya; where's the hurry?" Rzhevsky laid a hand the size of a medium rye bread on the green blotter between them; Duvakin could not tear his eyes from the man's stubby thick fingers. He found himself sitting.

There was a pause. Duvakin knew that Rzhevsky wanted something, some kind of information about the arrest probably, but he would not help the man. Let him seek out his own approach.

"You like agitprop? It's clean work?" Rzhevsky cocked his head appraisingly.

"It's all right . . ." Duvakin felt the awkward pause too acutely. "Better than working for a living . . ."

Rzhevsky laughed too loudly. Duvakin felt the hairs on his neck bristle.

"What's it like, agitprop?" Rzhevsky peered with apparent interest at Duvakin. "My job, now, it's all papers, meetings, telephones . . . not like the old days."

"The old days?" Duvakin asked this cautiously, for in Magadan those old days all too often meant "when this was a slave camp"; despite all the influx since those days, chances were still pretty good the old man jammed against you in the bus was either a former guard or one of his surviving charges. Most likely the former. Even now the explanation to most of the crimes in Magadan lay, if not in the bottle, then in scores racked up in those "good old days."

Rzhevsky laughed, well aware of Duvakin's question. "No, Vanya, not the camps. Do I look so old? No, I meant my old days, when I first started out. I was a pilot, worked the taiga, the mountains in the south. I took scientists in and out, dropped doctors on Yakut sheepherders, flew sick Uighurs to hospitals . . . their cattle too, sometimes." Rzhevsky's eyes glazed a moment as he watched his own youth; Duvakin too saw a younger, more alive Duvakin flicker before him. Unexpectedly he recalled something his old girlfriend had once suddenly demanded. "If this is the land of the future, why are we all so nostalgic?"

"Not now, though. Most excitement I get now is when they try to reduce our ink quota for the year." He smiled. "That's not your life, though . . . Another?" He reached for the bottle as he talked. "Pretty interesting, I'll bet."

"Oh, I don't know. Lot of walking, for one thing, putting up posters and the like. Hard on the feet." Duvakin's answer was guarded.

"And you think it's easy to sit on this all day?" Rzhevsky half jumped up, slapping his bottom like some Cossack folk dancer, then sat, laughing. "Anyway, today, arrests, interrogations . . . That's interesting, eh?"

"Interest like that I don't need," Duvakin indicated his scabbed face, fending off the man's question as long as he might. He had no wish to tell the story once more.

"Oh, well, it's done, and you're a hero." Smiling, Rzhevsky held up the bottle, then poured them each another cup. "To spring!" he bellowed, drank.

Duvakin drank too, this time finding that his body welcomed the warm wave of liquor. "Complaint's signed anyway, and formal investigation. Bloody nuisance . . ." He waved his hand.

"But that's the whole thing, isn't it? The crime, so to say? Your complaint says this and this, and leaves out maybe that and that, and then only this and this is what they ever investigate?" Rzhevsky indicated his "this" and "that" with huge chopping motions of those meaty hands.

Duvakin sensed the direction the man was trying to drive him, but refused to cooperate. The complaint was official; he could read it if he was so interested. "I guess so." He shrugged. "Today they only asked about passport stuff, address, name, nationality . . ."

"So they wouldn't write down anything the criminals say, or ask them any questions?" Rzhevsky's interest now seemed not polite, but intense, probing.

"No, no questions," Duvakin answered offhandedly, watching Rzhevsky closely. The huge man relaxed visibly, even smiling. Rzhevsky plain as day had something he wished hidden. Duvakin could even guess what. Airport, Armenian cognac, nice suit . . . the devil's own godfather, Duvakin thought bitterly. The man's working an angle, and he's afraid the cleaning woman might have said something compromising. "Of course," he added blandly, enjoying his own nastiness, "they do write down anything that's said voluntarily."

It took no skill to notice the stiff attention Rzhevsky suddenly paid Duvakin; Siberian pilot, Duvakin thought wryly. The type was all roughhewn, with more muscle between the ears than most men had on their entire bodies, and Rzhevsky was true to form, now clearly searching for a sly way to inquire what the woman might have said and to whom it would be reported. Duvakin studied Rzhevsky, wavering between loathing and pity; the man was so large, so powerful, and yet had through greed come to a place where he must fear the evil fortunes of a strange toilet woman.

"She said something?" Rzhevsky whispered harshly. "What? What did she say?" He slowly stood as he talked.

Duvakin suddenly felt fed up. Enough. Too much today he had mucked about in other's lives, and each step

seemed to pull him on toward another. Let this Rzhevsky
do his worrying for himself, Duvakin thought, leaning
tiredly back in his chair.

"She was an odd one," he said to the water stains
above his head, "no tears, just carrying on about how she
gets caught for twenty skins and the big people get medals
for twenty crates . . ." He sat up a little, to see whether his
words would satisfy. Rzhevsky's face now was more
opaque, more impenetrable; the information seemed to
have hit some mark.

"Usual sort of thing to say, don't you think?"
Rzhevsky asked, straining at first, but quickly achieving a
lighter tone. "That the people above are thieves . . . antisocialist elements like her, I mean? Can't get it themselves, so they get jealous."

"Something like that." Duvakin was still, watching
Rzhevsky; since his betrayal back in Moscow, he had
come to fear this kind of well-fed, complacent man,
whom a threat of any sort could terrify, and who thus was
as dangerous as a bear in spring.

Duvakin looked pointedly at his watch and gathered
himself to stand. "More?" he asked, perhaps too boldly,
but Rzhevsky's attention seemed focused in the middle
distance, beyond Duvakin's head.

Outside the runway lights flicked off; the last flight
must be away. Duvakin shifted again, mindful that soon
the last bus too would run, stranding him at the airport,
while the airport would become its nocturnal self, an
informal hotel. Like most Soviet cities, Magadan had almost no available beds. Beyond the Far East, the Rising
Sun, and the Dawn, Magadan boasted no hotels, and even
to get admitted to the rotting log hut that bore the last of
these names, one had to be at least second assistant to a
factory manager, and of no small factory at that. The hotel
shortage kept no one home, though; who in the airline

terminal was to know whether you were waiting for a plane or simply for the morning?

Duvakin, though, had his own bed, and no desire to nestle up to some native for a pillow. At night the airport would become its own little island, without bus, taxi, or hope of reaching town. Anxiously he gathered his hat.

"Comrade Director, I really must . . ." Duvakin stood.

Rzhevsky slowly focused upward on Duvakin, like a man pulling his foot from deep spring mud.

"Going? Of course—of course." He smiled laboriously. "Interesting to talk, eh? Must have another drop in here sometime . . ." He came around the desk to take Duvakin's arm. Duvakin was uncomfortably aware of the other man's sheer size, his physical proximity, as if he might pull Duvakin even nearer. To make himself feel heavier, Duvakin put on his hat.

They stood still a moment—Duvakin straining, Rzhevsky thinking deeply. Finally he asked, searching Duvakin's eyes, "So what will they make of something like that, what the old lady said?"

"Depends, I suppose . . ." Duvakin said vaguely, but watching intently from the corner of his eye.

"Depends, depends . . . Of course, it *always* depends," Rzhevsky said shortly, at the same time squeezing Duvakin's arm too tightly. "But now, in this instance?"

"I really can't say." Duvakin tried to wave his arm, as the pressure increased further. "It goes in the report, I guess, when that gets sent on."

"To Khabarovsk?"

"To Khabarovsk, I imagine, but truth to tell, what do they care in Khabarovsk? They've got the thief *and* the furs . . . The old woman didn't name any names or anything like that." Duvakin said pointedly, almost mocking the nervous Rzhevsky.

"It's true, what do they care in Khabarovsk?" The idea

obviously cheered Rzhevsky, who released Duvakin, smiled broadly, then slapped Duvakin soundly on the back. "Khabarovsk, eh? Not like they don't have what to worry about already, is it?"

Duvakin smiled and made for the door, anxious only to be out of the room. He felt he had had this conversation before, and worse, that he would have it again. That Rzhevsky was abusing his position in some way could have been made clearer only by outright admission, but Duvakin's concern now was to be gone before Rzhevsky had the opportunity or poor judgment to go that final step. Duvakin wanted no part of it; a confession he would have to report, to spare himself possible compromise; but suspicions the devil could take. Duvakin's proper concern was Duvakin.

In the corridor he heard Rzhevsky bellow a perfunctory "until next time!" but he made no effort to answer. He felt unclean and wished only to be away.

The lobby was full, as usual, and the crowds seemed edgier, more restless than they ought. There seemed a buzz, a sharpness to the wordless mass speech that Duvakin could almost taste, and that pushed him to a trot toward the bus stop. The problems of these several hundred tired, hungry, and irritable strangers were more than Duvakin needed, after the translucent scheming of Rzhevsky. He pushed through the door.

Duvakin, he thought grimly, would meddle only where his arms reached, enjoy what pleasures the world might bring, and wait quietly for the dissolution of his daily existence. He trotted heavily toward the distant stop where the last passengers were jamming onto the bus. The devil can take the Rzhevskys of this world, Duvakin thought darkly, his breath short in his chest.

* FOUR *

Duvakin was still groggy with sleep, so the knocks seemed remote. They repeated.

"Ivan Palych? Are you awake?" Knock, knock.

"What is it?" he mumbled. A half-opened eye told him it was light against his window. He fumbled for his watch. Eight-thirty. He had overslept, he thought indifferently.

"Ivan Palych, Ivan Palych, I must see you for a moment," the unknown voice repeated. It was, he realized in a second, a female voice.

A woman? Duvakin sat up straight.

He tried to remember his last visitor, without success. Certainly there had never been a woman to visit; Duvakin knew no women.

"Just a second, just a second . . ." Duvakin crawled from his daybed and reached for his trousers. His fingers, inexplicably, trembled as he buttoned the fly, then continued to shake as he buttoned his shirt. A woman, eh?

Dressed, if haphazardly, Duvakin then switched on

the light and looked anxiously about the room. The daybed was easily made up; his small bureau was jumbled, but forgivably; his table was still set with last night's plates. Duvakin looked distractedly about, then finally chucked the crockery and cutlery under the bed. Smoothing his hair nervously, he was acutely aware of his bald horseshoe. A woman? So let's have a look.

"Please . . . you are welcome," he said formally, as he fumbled with the door lock.

There was a rustle outside; then the door opened, admitting a woman of middling years, by no means unattractive. She was a beauty of Magadan scale: fleshy and firm, henna hair and glittering gold teeth, and fitted out, too! Leather boots such as Duvakin hadn't seen since he left Moscow, leather overcoat. A somebody, sure as day is long! And whatever could this all be about?

The woman shut the door firmly, then drew herself erect.

"Your name is Duvakin? You are the man who found the old woman at the airport?" she asked distinctly, watching Duvakin closely.

"At your service, madame," Duvakin said in a mock-heroic way, bowing with a flourish. Out of the corner of his eye he just noticed as the woman brought her heavy bag down smartly on the back of his skull, knocking him hard to the floor.

"Murderer!" she shrieked, aiming a kick at the dazed and astounded Duvakin. Fortunately for him there was more passion than aim in the gesture, for it caught him on the shoulder, not the temple, as she seemed to wish. "Murderer! Murderer!"

Duvakin shook his head, setting comets wheeling through his eyes, and moved instinctively. All militia men had some *sambo* training, self-defense; even four years out of the service, Duvakin remembered enough to catch the woman's next kick, twist her upwards, and throw her back on the daybed.

She screamed, but twisted in midair to regain her feet before Duvakin did. He was able to muffle the next blow, a knee to his face, but the effort was startling; the woman must run near eighty kilos.

"Who are you?" Duvakin managed to croak as the woman was on him again. Once more he felt nails rake across his face. "What's this about?"

The nails tipped the cart. Mad with the agony of his face, Duvakin chopped both fists down on the woman's shoulders, then shoved her back onto the bed again.

Duvakin grabbed for a chair and stood panting behind it. The woman made to rise, then collapsed like a mud wall in a cloudburst. Duvakin could not remember sobs so deep or so bitter. He stood, wary and puzzled, watching the woman minutely. There grew on him the awareness both that the woman's passion was now drowned and that he was bleeding. Keeping his eyes on his guest, Duvakin groped along the wall for a towel with which he mopped his stinging face.

"All right," he said as calmly as he could, "what is this about? Who are you?"

"Who am I, he asks! He makes me a widow, then asks who I am!" The woman addressed the heavens, entreating with both hands, then collapsed again into sobs.

Widow?

"I don't understand you," Duvakin said more softly; as his blood slowed and the woman sobbed on, he could feel some sympathy growing. "What's your name, at least?"

"Rzhevskaya, Rzhevskaya! Bloody foul murderer!" The name set her off again, shrieks and tears.

What in the devil's seven hells?

"You mean Yura? Yura's wife?"

"Yura, he calls him! His murderer calls him Yura!" If possible, the shrieks were even louder, the sobs deeper. Duvakin began nervously to think of the neighbors. If they were to call the militia . . . How could he ever live down losing two fights with women in two days?

"Madame, I assure you . . . I'm not a murderer. There must be some mistake . . . Why has your husband sent you?"

The sobs slowly subsided. "Sent me? How could he send me? No, I had to find out by myself. Everyone there keeps quiet, but I found out who was responsible . . ." Her blubbering stopped entirely. She looked up from the couch, disheveled and red-eyed, but still radiating venomous hostility. "My husband's blood is on your hands. I hope his dead feet will walk across your chest every night of your life."

Duvakin was aware that his jaw hung open like the scoop of a back hoe, but he could not concentrate enough to close it.

"What blood? I saw your husband last evening. He wasn't dead," Duvakin assured her absurdly. "I mean, he was in perfect health, strong as a bull calf . . ."

"Well, he's dead now, and it's your fault!" The tears welled up and ran down her flushed cheeks, but the woman's control held. "And I'll make you pay for it if it takes the rest of my life."

With that the woman stood, straightened her coat, and stalked quickly out of the room, nearly bowling over a curious neighbor who had not had sufficient warning to scurry away from the door.

The woman's abrupt departure left an almost theatrical frieze, for Duvakin stared after her, still uncomprehending, and the neighbor, Pavlovna, peered dimly at him.

It was Pavlovna who finally broke the silence.

"Is there some trouble, Ivan Palych?" she asked, concerned but also scenting a good scandal.

Duvakin snorted, but sobered immediately. "Perhaps—perhaps . . . well." He slapped his empty pockets a couple of times. "Well . . . I guess I'd best go down to headquarters," he said as calmly as he could, gently closing the door on her curiosity. He looked at his watch again, alarm and confusion hammering at his throat. He searched quickly for his wallet and coin purse, got his overcoat, and left.

Outside, the air was so warm it seemed almost stuffy after the breathsucking cold of winter. Treefellers Prospekt was already the consistency of oatmeal, so Duvakin was laboring heavily by the time he reached the bus stop. The people waiting at the battered shelter seemed edgy, restless, sullen. The weather, Duvakin decided. Warm winds from the mountains, a freak spring. When there was a spell like this the powers got excited, worrying because the fights, the stabbings, public drunkenness all multiplied like blackflies in June. Duvakin looked across the road to the beer stall that stood alone in an empty field. In summer it was a huge dust bowl; spring and fall, a hog wallow; in winter, a stinging expanse of slashing snow crystals; but as long as there was beer, there were the same unruly crowds. Sure enough, there was a fist fight going on now. Duvakin knew it was a Party duty to see to public order, but he shrugged and turned away. Enough trouble he'd caused himself already. Besides, why bother? Two drunks more or less, who cared?

All the way downtown the same thoughts repeated disjointedly—murder, the scratches, the tears, as well as patches of Rzhevsky, hale, bluff, and vital. What the devil? The conviction grew that he might well be in a soup, and Duvakin gnawed at the rim of his fingernail.

He could feel the beginnings of a headache by the

time he alighted at the town's center, Lenin Square. Most of the stores were still dark, though the working day was almost three hours underway. "Closed for Technical Reasons" the placards on each door read; like everybody else, Duvakin knew the translation. We have nothing to sell. Sold out. The thought made Duvakin's stomach rumble, reminding him that he had eaten nothing. A cafeteria breakfast was a depressing thought.

Suddenly, he knew work would be pointless, unless he made some sense of Rzhevskaya's threats. He paused, jostled by the bulky housewives going grimly about their shopping; then he resolutely turned about, to recross the square and make for Komsomolsk Street and the militia station. He found himself hoping fiercely that the captain, Pivovarov, would be in.

He banged up the split-log stairs and through the triple doors.

"Citizen? What business have you here?" The receptionist was startled, even standing.

"A little question came up . . . the captain is in?"

"Of course he's in. Why?"

"I have business with him . ." Duvakin turned and made for the door. He heard the woman bellow, "Wait!" but pretended he did not. "Party matters," he muttered for his own benefit; rights exist only if you take them they had taught him, and if he let Pivovarov decide whether to see him, he would wait outside until communism itself arrived. So, in we go.

"Captain? Comrade Pivovarov? May I see you a moment?" Duvakin knocked, asked, and entered simultaneously.

Pivovarov looked up, startled, then understanding.

"You. I should have figured it."

Duvakin's throat went dry. "So there is something?"

Pivovarov looked into Duvakin's eyes as if he were doing a mind-reading trick at a worker's hall. He spoke very slowly, choosing his words like chocolates from a box.

"There is nothing. All is well. Do you understand me?"

Duvakin stared back. "Do you know what I'm talking about?"

"I think so . . . and if I do, you should not be talking about it." Pivovarov's eyes still held Duvakin's, as if trying by force of will to impart his wordless message.

"Wait a minute, something's wrong here . . . You do know what happened to me just now?" Duvakin was growing heated. "Do you know who just came out to see me? Do you know—"

"Want to come look to the dogs with me?"

"What?"

"The dogs, the guard dogs . . . I want to go see to them. Want to come?"

"What?" Duvakin repeated stupidly.

Pivovarov rose wordlessly, leading him out of the room. Duvakin followed, uncomprehending. He knew from Party gossip that Pivovarov never walked anywhere with anyone because he loathed standing near taller men. And the dogs? There must be men paid to take care of them; certainly the chief of militia wouldn't.

The dogs were kept next to the building in a series of identical runs arranged on both sides of a narrow aisle. There must have been twenty enormous East European shepherds, and each began bellowing as soon as the two men appeared. They howled, scratched at the fencing, kicked their metal water dishes, and beat their tails against their wooden houses. Duvakin felt his temples begin to throb. There was a tug on his sleeve. Pivovarov beckoned him to bend over.

Duvakin felt only the saliva and warm breath of words in his ear.

"What?" he shouted.

"You really kicked over a shit bucket this time, comrade!" Pivovarov yelled. "Rzhevskaya see you?"

"Yes."

"Know why?"

"No."

"Because last night they picked up her husband . . ."

"Rzhevsky? For what?"

"Hard to know. The guy died."

"What?" Duvakin goggled at Pivovarov.

"It's true. They came for him at home, around eleven . . ."

"For what?"

"Story was that they had some questions about the toilet lady and the furs . . , and first thing this morning, they had to tell the widow that the guy's heart popped."

Duvakin thought back to the drinks the night before. It was possible, he supposed. Rzhevsky was a big guy, and certainly he had some reason to worry. And he liked his liquor well enough.

"That's a pity . . . Leave just the widow?"

"Widow and daughter, about ten, eleven . . . At least that's what the widow told me."

"Told you?" Duvakin coughed. The shouting was hurting his throat.

"She showed up here . . . wanted to find out what the fur business was about . . ."

"It was militia picked him up?"

"Of course not . . . KGB."

"How come?"

Pivovarov simply shrugged.

Duvakin felt a familiar knot tighten in the middle of his chest, anger and guilt intertwining so tightly it hurt.

Poor stupid unlucky bastard, Rzhevsky. Killed by the bad luck of a greedy toilet lady and my meddling foot.

"And so the guy's heart gave out . . ." he said, mostly to himself.

"What?" Pivovarov yelled; the dogs subsided slightly, but each new movement set them clamoring again, a deafening din in the confines of the dog yard.

"I just said pity about the weak heart," Duvakin shouted, indicating his chest with his hand.

"That's how come Rzhevskaya was in."

"I don't follow . . ."

Pivovarov's next words were lost as one of the biggest shepherds began to climb his fence; slavering, shaking, he dragged himself part way up before finally falling back. The other dogs went berserk.

"What?"

Pivovarov signed that they should wait a second, then he bellowed as soon as there was the slightest letup.

"Rzhevskaya said his heart was perfect. And they wouldn't let her see the body."

Duvakin's mind was slightly slower than his mouth; he opened it to speak, then closed it again, then felt it sag open as the import of Pivovarov's words sank in.

He looked about him at the foaming jaws, the sharp yellow teeth. "And all this?" He waved his hand in an encompassing, interrogative circle.

"Colonel Darmoved phoned me this morning, too—"

"Himself?"

Pivovarov nodded heavily, significantly, and then looked Duvakin directly in the eye. "Himself."

Duvakin was mystified and frightened. Darmoved was first regional secretary for state security, top cone on the tree. The head of the Magadan KGB. And he had phoned? Something monstrous was afoot.

"Why?" Duvakin finally asked.

Even here, even outside, surrounded by dogs whose baying made direct lip-to-ear shouted conversation all but impossible, Pivovarov paused to look about. Then he pulled Duvakin flat against him.

"He said that there are to be no questions. We're

done. In fact, the whole thing never happened . . . You see?" Pivovarov punctuated his speech with a sharp tap on Duvakin's chest. "You see?"

Questions ran into Duvakin's mouth like hot saliva, but one by one he swallowed them in silence. Finally he nodded. Understood.

Except for one thing.

"Why are you telling me this?" he finally croaked.

Pivovarov shrugged, then smiled. "I like you, don't I? Comrade to comrade . . . you know as well as I do, the KGB starts playing games like this, it's no place for a white man. A man could get himself hurt . . ." Pivovarov took Duvakin by the arm and led him back inside.

"Remember, now, comrade," he repeated too loudly in the sudden calm of the station, "you forget all of this; keep your health, eh?" He smiled at Duvakin and, with a parting squeeze of his elbow, disappeared.

Duvakin stumbled down the rotting log steps and out into the street, his thoughts bounding about like young jackrabbits startled from their nest.

A dead man, KGB, furs, Pivovarov and the dogs . . .

A nauseating film of dread settled on his shoulders, making him long suddenly, with vivid clarity of imagination, for a drink. He stopped, looked about, then at his watch. Midmorning, too early for the spirit stores to be open. His mouth watered and his head throbbed. Then he remembered the vodka machines in the wine shop up at the square, and with a rattling heart he set out.

These machines had been a surprise when Duvakin first arrived in Magadan, for not only did they not exist back in Moscow, they were illegal in the USSR. The laws said alcohol could be sold only in bottles. More precisely, such machines did exist in Moscow, but there served only their intended function, dispensing seltzer water and fruit syrup.

In Magadan the machines took a ruble coin, not three

kopeks, and instead of a glass full of fizzy water you got a half glass of vodka still fuming with the crude oil it was made from. Down your pipe and then, for most of the men anyway, back to the end of the line. The drinkers rotated through the line until they fell down to sleep in the slime and cigarette butts of the floor. If they were broke, they sold their clothes; if they could find no glass and had brought none, they drank greedily from cupped hands. They ate dried fish and smoked shag rolled in newspaper. A bored crone presided impassively, silently exchanging metal rubles for paper, selling an occasional glass of warm sweet champagne. When there were brawls, she simply knelt below her counter.

And yet—Duvakin thought with gratitude as he finally put his coin in and then watched the answering stream of vodka—and yet the vodka is real.

He downed the vodka and returned the glass jar he had begged from the man behind; then he wished intently for a bite to eat, to soak up the foul liquid. He settled for a cigarette. By the door, he could feel the anxious knot in his chest easing. Now for some breakfast.

Inquiries among the scurrying pedestrians pointed him to the nearest cafeteria, the Kosmos. The smell of cabbage and cigarettes clutched at his face like a rancid scarf, and Duvakin felt his stomach vault once, up and over.

He would have left, but hunger and lack of other choices pushed him to join the sullen, muttering line. It was midmorning, but the cafeteria had only just opened, delayed until food was finally delivered. The patrons were hungry, most as late for work already as Duvakin was, and the mood was ugly. Normally, Duvakin too would have muttered and growled at his neighbors while he shuffled forward, but not today; the vodka and the mindlessness of waiting were slowly making some sense from the last twenty-four odd hours.

Four years ago, back in Moscow, Duvakin had in fear
and blind enthusiasm helped investigate a black market
ring upon whose ill-kempt fringes he had accidentally
stumbled. Matters then had seemed straightforward, and
it was a pleasure to do one's duty. They were smuggling
heroin, and he, a member then of the militia, was duty
bound to assist in stopping them. Dangerous, certainly,
and often Duvakin had feared, even believing once or
twice that his death was at hand, but it was good—good to
feel part of something positive, good to feel more than a
simple night-shift security man in a seedy hotel.

And then Polkovnikov, his Judas, had smilingly
kicked him down the chute through disgrace, a jail cell,
an endless train ride, and nightmares of impotent humili-
ation, to land in Party membership and the position of
agitprop cadre second-class, lecturer in scientific atheism, Magadan region.

On the way he had learned a great deal.

"Wouldn't let the widow see the body" meant
Rzhevsky's "heart failure" was the same that all dead men
suffer. A symptom, not a cause. And the body was not
viewable because the real cause would have been too
clear, and too horribly graphic. In simple terms, Rzhevsky
had been beaten to death.

Why Rzhevsky had been beaten to death Duvakin had
no idea, but the smell—Rzhevsky's cognac, his sweating
anxiety about the toilet woman's words, the well-fed cor-
pulence of his frame—was familiar too, from Duvakin's
few days in black market restaurants and secret plush
whorehouses for generals. Rot smells like rot, and Duvakin was certain that Rzhevsky had matters enough to
hide from the organs.

Even until death?

Duvakin shrugged to himself and thought, who
knows?

A KGB hush-up like this was unusual, though. Normally the organs were quick to boast of successes. The death, perhaps an "error committed in excess of zeal"? Whatever, common sense required polite aversion of the eyes and direction of attention elsewhere.

"So, talk . . ."

Duvakin's reverie was snapped; he looked up to find he had reached the server, a florid fat woman sweating in a grimy paper cap. She cleared her abacus with an impatient, intimidating click.

"Uh, four sausages . . ."

"No sausages!"

"Cutlets, then . . ."

"None, gone, I tell you!" she shouted at the world.

"Very well, what is there?"

"Baked cottage cheese . . . some meat pies . . ."

"Any meat salad?"

"You're drunk maybe, citizen? It's April! What kind of salad when it's April, I ask you!"

Behind him the people pushed closer, muttering more audibly.

"Very well, then. Some cheese, a couple of meat pies . . . a plate of those mashed potatoes—"

"That's farina."

"Well, all right . . . with butter?"

"Oil."

"Oh, well, it's all one . . ."

"How many breads?"

"Four blacks, please . . . Is there anything to drink?"

"Yogurt."

"No beer?"

"Mors."

"What the devil is mors?"

"Cranberry stuff, just two percent. It's sweet."

Duvakin was dissatisfied, but there seemed little choice. "All right."

The woman went to fetch his order. Duvakin noticed

the cognac bottle in the cooler before him. He felt in his pants pocket. "How much for the cognac?"

"Bottle or glass?"

"Glass."

"Two seventy for forty grams."

"All right."

The woman poured precisely into her measuring glass, then poured the trembling liquid into a tea glass. Duvakin watched in horror as she tipped her head back to catch the last few drops in the measuring cup, then ran a fat moist tongue around the inside of the little glass. She winked at him.

"We're drinking partners now."

Duvakin was struck dumb; he smiled weakly as the woman slammed beads about, totaling his bill. "Three eighty." He slapped down a three and a two; the woman snarled, reaching for the can where she kept bills.

The sight of that bovine red tongue jammed into the measuring glass stayed with Duvakin as he looked vaguely for a spot at which to eat. There were no tables, just stand-up counters, most of them covered in dirty dishes. Which probably explained why there was no cutlery.

With a sigh Duvakin slammed his tray into an open space, then poured his cognac into the mors. Mixing them could only improve on the components. He rummaged about the neighboring abandoned trays until he found a fork more clean than not. He wiped it sternly on the cuff of his shirt, straightened the soft aluminum tines, and set to eating.

The food, as he expected, was glutinous and foul, but the mors and cognac combination slid down gently, spreading warm wings of pleasant numbness along his back. He thought of last night's cognac and Rzhevsky.

Four years ago Duvakin would not have understood the connection between the toilet lady and the dead

Rzhevsky; wiser now, he knew enough to know he wished to know no more. Rzhevsky was clearly working on the left, for his own gain. Whether with the toilet lady or in competition, who would say and what did it matter? This was everywhere now, corruption, the cheating. Try and stop it, he thought to himself, and you might as well go shovel the Magadan mud with this fork.

He drained the last sticky drops of his drink, wiped the last splotches of farina with his bread. His stomach was full, his heart was warm. Why worry so much about this? Silence, they said; silent he would be. It wasn't his fault Rzhevsky had a greedy soul. Besides, who didn't? The papers were filled with stories of Kirghiz school inspectors who sold diplomas, drunken factory managers who only stayed sober long enough to embezzle, Georgian doctors who for a fee would prescribe invalid's automobiles to anyone with the cash. The whole bloody world was up to something. So, God love them, Duvakin would keep his eyes in his own furrow.

Dull-heartedly, he knew though that that was only half the problem. The trick was to keep the rest of the world out of his furrow. Damn stupid foot of his, interfering in something that now bristled with militia and dead men and stolen furs and KGB.

And Duvakin wanted none of it. He had tried, once, to improve the world and look what it had got him—this island of frozen muck in a sea of permafrost, for life. The devil could have it all. He burped a greasy bubble and remembered work.

"May Day banners to count!" he mumbled with sarcastic enthusiasm, then buttoned his coat and looked about for where he ought to leave his tray. The immobile conveyor belt into the kitchen was piled high with unwashed dishes. On a hunch Duvakin peered into the kitchen. Sure enough, the dishwasher—a thin old man with one drooping lower lid and no front teeth—was sound asleep, sitting on the other end of the belt. Duvakin slammed his tray onto the nearest table and stormed out.

Irresponsible pigs, the whole bloody lot of them! he thought darkly.

Outside, the crowds of workers were thinning, but the buses were still jammed as full as tins of potted meat, their steamy windows occasionally made rosy by the smear of a face pressed tight against one. The power arms of the trolleybuses jumped and scraped at junctures, sending down periodic showers of blue sparks.

His heart was still cold and tight. He fished for a cigarette, unable to shake the dread that haunted him, that he was entangled in this amorphous mess, but ashamed too that he was so intent on remaining aloof. But how could he not stay out of it? Once burned, twice learned, he muttered, lighting up the stale tobacco.

Look where I got myself to the last time! he thought, studying the street. Lenin Square was as drab and decayed as the meanest provincial back street back home in Russia. There was some attempt at color against the dun of snow and shops, a few signs flashing a desultory "Fish" or a bright green "Call 01 for Fire," but half the tubes were burnt out. There were virtually no cars, just trucks, buses, and an occasional taxi, belching by in a blue haze of smoke.

As he looked down the street, Duvakin was suddenly reminded of a Chukchi joke someone at headquarters had been telling. Two Chukchis are out walrus hunting on the ice; one says, "You want to hear a political joke?" and the other says, "Better not, they might send us away someplace." Then the joke had seemed grimly funny—what "someplace" could be worse than the moss and snow of the Chukchis' home? In the soupy light of this Magadan spring morning, the joke seemed unaccountably serious, even profound. Because it was true—even a Chukchi had something to lose, the life he had lived and known. And so with me, Duvakin thought, suddenly fierce, what I have is mine, and I'm not risking it, damn the rest.

And that meant, among other things, that he had best get himself along to work. Another look at the crowded buses convinced him that a walk would do him good. He cut across Lenin Square and headed for Party headquarters on the far end of Dzerzhinsky Boulevard.

⋆ FIVE ⋆

April was a dreadful month in agitprop, the most frantic season of the year. First, Lenin's birthday, then the All-Union Saturday of voluntary labor to organize and assign, then ten days later, May Day to cope with. And as if that weren't enough, May 9 brought Victory Day. Each holiday demanded buntings, banners, posters, flags, and telephone calls too numerous to count.

In moments of particularly sodden chumminess, the section boss, Sutrapian, would clamp a hairy arm around the nearest underling, thrust his heavy Armenian nose in the poor man's face, and confide that he had turned to drink in just that season, in 1975, when in addition to all this, Orthodox Easter fell between May Day and the thirtieth anniversary of Victory Day, for which the Party decreed special efforts to distract the believers from sullying the socialist holidays. Office gossip was that Sutrapian was in a way telling the truth; that is, drunk, he had botched the agitprop so badly that year that he was transferred from his native Odessa to here, Magadan. Which might have improved Odessa, but not Sutrapian.

No more sober than in the past, he now had wounds to bathe as well. Almost daily Duvakin, Semyenov, and the others were harangued about the inequities of life. To escape, Duvakin inventoried fanatically, seeing which flags were faded, which frayed, making sure the municipal decorations for May Day were painted and refurbished.

After a nearly coherent dressing down for tardiness, Duvakin was delegated that day to a project particularly near Sutrapian's heart, the new Lenin. They had lots of Lenins already, but the executive committee in Khabarovsk had allotted funds for Sutrapian to commission a twelve-meter striding Lenin, to be assembled against a building just to the left of the reviewing stand.

"The eyes, Vanya, make sure they're making them slit!" Sutrapian said urgently, certain successful execution of this charge might redeem him. "Uncle Volodya's got to look slanty-eyed out here!"

"You want his face yellow too?" Duvakin asked, half in jest.

"Of course, what do you think?" Sutrapian answered seriously, then reeled off.

Duvakin shrugged, indifferent. If the "most human of humans" was to look at home here among the Chukchis and Yakuts, slanty-eyed he must be. He went to his desk and began phoning. The job was even welcome, for it would keep him well occupied. The Lenin was so big that it had had to be parceled out to three separate shops, checking on which would easily demand a day's telephoning. And if that did not, he could begin telephoning west, and south, in search of a reliable supply of lilac branches, for the spontaneous people's demonstration of peace on May Day. The sparse lilacs of Magadan generally didn't blossom until mid-June.

Even in the hugger-mugger of work, the frantic phone calls about the birthday, the frenzy to assign locations for the Saturday, Duvakin could not keep his mind fully focused on his task. The time passed, but a corner of his mind still gnawed at the events of the last two days. Most vivid of all was Rzhevskaya, especially her parting words.

"I'll make you pay for this if it takes the rest of my life."

Widow's bravado, he reassured himself repeatedly through the day, but never fully successfully. Rzhevskaya was too sure, too cruel. There was no self-pity, no appeal in the woman's attack; she was all rage and revenge, and worse, apparently certain she would get satisfaction. Leather coat, airport manager's wife, gold teeth . . .

She was not some average queue jumper, and what gnawed was the knowledge that she held him responsible for her husband's death. That he was not wouldn't matter much if she was able to bring her threats to life.

But what to do? Pivovarov had clearly warned him off, and the Magadan KGB was no joking matter. And besides, Duvakin had no idea where to reach Rzhevskaya.

All day she trembled above him, like some invisible rock poised to rumble down upon him and crush him.

His only hope, he realized slowly as the day wore on, was to convince her he was not at fault. Beautiful plan, he nagged at himself, only where is she? There are no directories, no street guides. He might ask Pivovarov, only of course the captain had told him point blank to stay away from the whole thing. He might look about for a directory at headquarters, and otherwise poke around—and be almost certain to have someone notice his unusual curiosity. Might as well just phone this Darmoved personally and say, "Look, this man you beat to death? I'd like to pay a special call on his widow."

As the day drew to a close and his fellow workers began to sort themselves out to go home, an idea hit

Duvakin. Magadan was not large, some eighty or ninety thousand souls, and the better part of them Chukchi. There weren't many places your fancy people would live, some old Party enclaves left from the prison camp days, plus one or two newer complexes. In a town this size, chances were good he could stumble on the right complex and maybe just turn up Rzhevskaya on his own.

He stood at the window, ignoring the others as they chattered past, going home. It was a risk, he knew, but then so it was too to leave Rzhevskaya panting for his blood. He had at least to try if he were going to remain at peace.

"You staying?" Sutrapian called thickly from his office, making Duvakin look about sharply. He was the last and thus in danger of being drafted as Sutrapian's drinking partner.

"No, no, Razmyk Araikovich, I'm just off." He started, hastily gathering his things. To get caught in a drinking bout now was the last thing he needed. He clattered down the worn metal stairs, wondering where to begin. The older complexes weren't far, walking distance. He felt in his pocket, to see whether there was money for taxis, if necessary.

Pausing at the entrance, he buttoned his overcoat tightly, trying to enclose himself in a sense of some security. Dread chilled him far worse than the air outside, still glowing with the setting sun. He sighed heavily, knowing that it would be a miracle to find Rzhevskaya.

And another, far greater, to convince her he was guiltless in her husband's death.

The first two apartment complexes he hazarded yielded nothing save a number of surly conversations with passers-by who would give him no information. Worse, each time patrols of militia men appeared, intent on running him off.

At first he had panicked when asked identity and business, for if Pivovarov heard he was not obeying the transparent suggestion he had been given, Duvakin would be in the soup for certain.

Happily, his tongue brought out a ready and useful lie, one he repeated easily when accosted the second time.

"I'm a teacher. I'm supposed to have a conference with the Rzhevskys, about their daughter . . . only I've misplaced the address," he protested innocently each time.

"No Rzhevskys here, shithead," the taller of the first pair said, while the second punctuated the observation with a jab at Duvakin's lower ribs.

"You teachers are all drunken wormbait," the taller of the second pair said; the second time Duvakin moved on so quickly the punctuating kick at his rear fell short.

Thirteenth Olympiad microregion was luckier for him; the newest of Magadan's complexes, it was also very loosely patrolled. The first complexes were in town, housing the old-timers, Party people who had been there since the good old days. The new microregion housed the new breed, the ones who had come since the sixties. Managers, university types, former sports heroes. They liked to live well, and would rather own a car than be driven. So they all did, and the region was planned for it. There was no bus, and when Duvakin reached the region's edge, already he had nearly eight rubles on the taxi meter. The microregion looked like a miniature Moscow, new buildings, lots of Zhigulis, opulent apartments. And no militia patrols.

Duvakin decided to try a new tack.

"Driver?"

"What?" Cabdrivers came in two varieties, garrulous and surly. This one was the latter.

"I'm looking for a lady."

"Who isn't?"

"This one's married . . ."

"So?"

"So, I don't know where she lives . . ."

"Pity."

"You find out, it's another five."

"Ten."

"Seven," Duvakin said automatically, but a little panicked. Fifteen rubles was almost two days' work, and all to find a woman who had tried to kill him with her handbag.

"Ten."

"Oh, all right . . . ten." Wonderful, Duvakin thought.

"Lie down . . . on your stomach."

"What?"

"Lie down, I told you. Pretend you're drunk."

Duvakin was mystified, but he followed directions.

"What's the lady's name?"

"Rzhevskaya."

They drove slowly forward. Duvakin felt the car pull over to the curb.

"Hey, citizeness!" he heard the driver yell.

After a pause, a woman's voice said, "What are you yelling at people for?"

"Because I've got a drunk here, won't tell me where he lives. You want him?"

"God, no! I've got one of my own at home! What's the name?"

"Rzhevsky, he says."

Outside, there was silence; inside, Duvakin could hear only his own pounding heart and silent cursing. What if the woman knew Rzhevsky was dead?

But Duvakin's luck was in.

"There's a family of that name here, seems like . . ." the voice said reflectively. There was a muffled sound now, like that of a conversation just out of earshot.

"Corpus three, seems like . . . down the way and left. Ask when you get down there."

"Thanks."

"That was marvelous!" Duvakin said, sitting up— probably too quickly; the driver shot him a sharp look.

"It never fails. Probably isn't a man in this country hasn't come home in a taxi, drunk."

"The apartment number?"

"I'll do the same thing when we get down there."

In the silence that followed, Duvakin considered forbidding the repetition of the trick, but he could not; even though the risk of discovery rose as they neared Yura's own building, there was no other way he had a chance of getting the number without calling attention to himself. He lay down again, heart knocking.

His luck, though, still held. A heavyset woman primly walking a tiny dog said sharply, with a grimace of distaste for public drunks, "Second entrance, apartment sixty-one, top floor." And why not be lucky? Rzhevsky wasn't dead a day yet, and the KGB was enveloping the whole matter in silence. Still, his hands trembled as he paid the driver.

Duvakin stood for a moment while the cab disappeared. Here the freak warmth of this late April night exhaled a dense ground fog that obscured all light; only the nearest apartments glowed dimly. The building disappeared upward, so Duvakin could not even guess whether Rzhevskaya would be home; his heart clattered at his ribs when finally he propelled himself forward.

He stepped cautiously through the triple doors, trying to keep down the noise of his thumping heart. He glanced quickly about for a doorman and was relieved to find none.

Instead, unexpected and unbidden, he found almost overwhelming memories of Tanya, Moscow, and his visits to that apartment he had polished in cherishing reminiscences over these moments, until he realized its source. The building. This building could not have been more like Tanya's if they had been stamped out in a factory—the same crackling loose floor tiles, same rusting trash chute, same dark hallways leading to padded and studded doors.

He tried to put all memory aside; he had been happy back then, sitting in Tanya's kitchen, sharing tea, for a brief time sharing even her bed. But stupidity, his own blind trust in the benevolence of others, had taken that from him, and now he had to work, to insure that nothing more of what remained to him would be snatched away. He resolutely pushed the elevator button; he had to convince Rzhevskaya he was blameless in her husband's death.

Of necessity, Magadan's buildings were on a smaller scale than Moscow's newest, for virtually everywhere the soil was hummocky permafrost, a quagmire into which buildings disappeared as fast as they were built. Even where foundations stood on stone, that sluggish frozen sea of gravel and ice often lapped up around the buildings, knocking them about, capsizing them. Duvakin's ride was just six stories, and even then a rasping sound partway up made him suspect the trueness of the shaft. However, luxury scaled down was still luxury, as Duvakin recognized when the doors opened.

The left wall—south facing? Duvakin guessed—was glass, sloping down, dirty, leaking, and yet still dazzling, even in the gloom of a Magadan night. He was above the ground haze; below, the buildings stood in milky pools suffused with a soft lamp glow. Beyond, glittered the faint lights of Magadan and its harbor, no match for the huge stars above.

Rzhevsky was no everyday Ivan Ivanych, Duvakin recognized even more gloomily; his heart began knocking again.

There were only two doors on the floor, meaning these apartments were twice the usual size. Number 61 was on the left. Padded, Duvakin noticed in awe, with real leather. He stood before it, trying to muster his explanations, his reasons, his hopes. He raised his hand to knock, then let it fall back faintheartedly.

There was a clicking scrape, as of a bolt being drawn; he made haste to knock. His hand met air, narrowly missing the nose of Rzhevskaya.

Startled, she fell back in unfocused alarm. Half thinking, Duvakin stepped forward, over the jamb.

"Hooligan! What in the devil's own . . . YOU!" she ignited from anger to fury. "Murderer! What are you, come to finish me off?" The woman's face was mottled rose and white, saliva glittering on her gold teeth. Duvakin glanced nervously over his shoulder at the other door.

"Quiet, I pray you," he muttered. "Please, it's not what you think . . . May I come in?" Duvakin answered himself, shutting the door behind. As it clicked shut, he felt relieved first, then trapped.

"Listen . . . please . . . I didn't kill your husband." Duvakin was babbling on as reassuringly as he could, keeping his hands in plain view and his eyes on the woman.

She stood against a glass-fronted bookcase, the trash she had been taking out clasped now in front of her. Her face was coarse, not easy to read, but it looked to Duvakin that rage and amazement battled in equal parts.

Duvakin noticed two more faces, a withered crone and a girl, peering in terror from a doorway down the hall. He held up his hands, like a German in a war movie; at his first movement, the two heads disappeared.

What felt like a rocket exploded in Duvakin's groin; as

he collapsed, he knew he ought never to have taken his eyes from Rzhevskaya. Her boot had found its target this time.

Duvakin fell crosswise in the narrow hall, closing off the door. Rzhevskaya was trapped inside, forced to stand above Duvakin while he retched and choked, powerless to prevent further harm to himself. For some reason though the woman held off, merely watching him.

At length he sat up, leaning against the door.

"All right . . ." His voice quivered feebly. "All right . . . kick me if you must . . . but at least *listen* to me. I did not kill your husband. In fact, I didn't know anything about it until you came to my room . . ."

Duvakin began speaking with his head down, but at the end he raised it to look at Rzhevskaya. For the first time he noticed how strained the woman seemed.

Her eyes were swollen, red, and her nose flamed like a drunk's. Her hair was all tangles and spikes, her face splotches of sleepless gray and raging crimson.

She was, Duvakin realized nervously, wound tighter than a three-ruble watch and just as likely to erupt in springs and bits. And if that happened—he glanced fearfully at the leather books, the fancy glass-fronted bookcase, the apparent opulence beyond—and if *that* happened, no telling what could happen to Duvakin.

"Listen . . ." he began, "try to believe me . . . try to understand." Damn it, he couldn't get started! "Look, I didn't know your husband . . . only met him once, in fact . . . and I didn't bear him any grudge. Your visit this morning was a total surprise to me."

Rzhevskaya stared at him with the dull hatred of a trapped fox looking up from gnawing off its own paw, but at least she was listening. Perhaps it was the angle; he was on the floor, while she towered above. He forged ahead.

"Believe me," he pleaded, his voice squeaky with pain. "I didn't even want to sign the complaint. I mean, it was all one to me. It was because the militia man heard the scream, and then the furs . . . there *had* to be a report then, don't you see? It wasn't *my* choice . . . and besides I mean, I didn't even mention your husband. I didn't know him, did I . . . ?" He trailed off.

Rzhevskaya still stared, but perhaps less intently; at any rate she wasn't kicking him. Or calling Pivovarov's militia.

"Look, I can understand. I met your—your husband, and . . . a good sort, but . . . I mean, it was a shock to *me*, he seemed so alive last night. I can *imagine* what . . ."

Damn! he thought, wishing he could bite his tongue out of his head. His last words, babbled out almost thoughtlessly, squeezed a dry, choking snort from the disheveled woman, followed after a pause by an incongruously soft bubbling noise. Rzhevskaya was sobbing—not the gargantuan wild sobs of the afternoon, not the shrieks of earlier. Childlike snuffling sobs, heartbreaking from so large and coarse a woman.

"And so I came to see . . ." he stumbled on. "Well, to ask . . ." Ask what? Don't bother me? Duvakin felt heartless in the face of so much distress, to ask to be spared trouble. He ended lamely, "Would you like a cigarette?"

Rzhevskaya continued to drip softly, like icicles on an April morning, but after a moment she nodded once.

Duvakin felt a wary relief. At least she wasn't hitting him. He dug in his coat pocket, found his crumpled pack, offered it.

He took one too, lit his. She turned away, then accepted a light. She inhaled deeply.

Perhaps worried by the sudden silence, the crone stuck a cautious head into the hall; one eye black and beady as that of a wet hen peered firmly at Duvakin.

"Valera, shall I call the militia?"

For a brief moment, during which Duvakin's heart contracted in spasms, Rzhevskaya studied him closely, then, finally, she pursed her lips and said, "No, not yet, I think . . ."

Duvakin felt himself go limp with relief. To disguise it, he took a deep drag on his cigarette; only after exhaling did he look at Rzhevskaya.

She was still studying him closely, like some new kind of bug that had fallen out of the tinned fish. Duvakin squirmed a little, setting off a heavy throb in his groin. He longed to touch, to test somehow whether there was any damage, but he could not, not with Rzhevskaya staring at him.

So he smoked, trying to get his thoughts into some coherent form. The hallway in which he sat was long and dark, telling him little save that there were many rooms. The floor was parquet, not tile, nice little patterns of strips. Duvakin wondered whether the rooms were like the lobby ouside, with the sloping wall of glass.

"Why are you here?"

"Pardon?" Duvakin asked, startled after her silence.

"Why have you come? What do you want?" Rzhevskaya sounded genuinely puzzled.

"Because, well . . ." Duvakin thought, then smiled a bit. "To tell the truth, I don't really know myself." To be forgiven? But I did nothing. And you can't say to be excused, disentangled. He thought for a moment, then surprised himself with the answer. "To understand, I suppose."

Rzhevskaya snorted. "Understand! All very simple, what's to understand? They cart off a healthy, living man in the middle of the night, and he comes back dead. What's hard to understand about that?"

"But why? What was he doing?"

"He? He doing? Get out of here!" Duvakin watched in horror as a full rage blew up again. He scrambled self-protectively to his feet.

"No, no, wait! You misunderstand! Don't scream."

[68]

Instinctively, he reached for her hands, then was startled when he touched them. Her skin was dry and cold. "I didn't mean . . . I'm just trying to help . . ." Duvakin was further startled to hear himself say.

Rzhevskaya's rage subsided so quickly that he feared she was going to faint; though he hadn't planned at all to offer it, help was exactly what this woman needed.

"Have you slept?" he asked softly.

She shook her head, a motion incongruously girllike, gentle.

"Would you like to sit . . . or have some tea or something? Or maybe I should just leave?"

The effort was palpable, but Rzhevskaya pulled herself up a bit and said, "No—no . . . it's all right . . . some tea . . ." She turned and went up the hall into a room.

After a moment's hesitation Duvakin followed.

The room into which he was led looked as if there had been a train wreck there. Books were strewn about in piles; pictures were ripped from the wall; even furniture had been gutted. The room was such a mess it took some moments to realize the apartment once would have been from out of a dream. One wall indeed was glass; far away glittered the tiny lights and primordial stars of Magadan.

"Dusya, go put on the kettle," Rzhevskaya said. The girl Duvakin had noticed earlier, a quick skinny creature with one foot in adolescence and the other on the shores of womanhood, darted off through the door.

He watched absently; the girl reminded him vaguely of Lena, the stepdaughter he would have had, if Polkovnikov and company hadn't kicked him down the chute to Magadan. Lenochka would be about that age now, he figured, for a brief moment allowing himself to meditate mournfully on what he had lost. Then he shook his head.

"What happened here?" he waved an inquiring hand.

Rzhevskaya shrugged. "God knows. I was gone, trying to find out what they had done to my Yura . . . only

Mama was here. Two men came, knocked, said they were from the organs, 'on business.' Mama took fright, bolted to the kitchen and hid. She says she could hear them rummaging around; then it got quiet, so after a while she came out, and well . . ." She showed the room with a shrug.

Curious, Duvakin thought. A crude but very thorough search, meant to intimidate as much as produce information. But why?

"Was anything taken? Anything missing?"

"How would I know?" Rzhevskaya wrapped her fleshy arms as best she could about her meaty body and shrugged, expressing utter indifference.

The room was shallow, almost like a glassed-in lip, with much more vertical space than horizontal. By Moscow standards the furniture was good, but unexceptional; by Magadan standards this was princely—real cloth on the sofa, a real woven rug on the floor. Even a television set, Duvakin noticed, though Magadan television so far had only one channel, half of that in Chukchi. But there it sat, almost a thousand rubles worth of color television. Paintings on the wall, even an icon or two.

To Duvakin this was like a return to nearly forgotten worlds, a museum of his own past. Seeing how luxurious what he knew to be Moscow standard looked gave him some measure of how barren his life had grown. Magadan isn't Paris, people always said ironically. He saw vividly now how much Magadan wasn't even Moscow. Perched here on the edge of the known world, the inhabitants even had to import their icons, the tradition back to which they pretended to hark.

"So you've no idea what this was all about?" he asked, striving for neutral words.

She shook her head, silent.

Could it be? Duvakin stared at her downcast head, trying to peer through the dark roots to an answer.

Rzhevsky had obviously been up to something, and

now the embarrassed organs were trying to ferret it out posthumously, to save face. Was it possible this strapping woman, who so obviously enjoyed the fruits of his corruption, knew nothing?

The magnitude must be breathtaking if Darmoved himself was interested. Gold? Diamonds? What could Rzhevsky have been doing? And if it had come to the attention of the KGB, then how in heaven could his wife not have noticed?

"I will tell you what I'm going to do though," Rzhevskaya spoke suddenly, as though she had been thinking. "They think they can trifle; they think Yura is just anybody, some clerk, some toady!" She spat the word like a glob of rotten food. "Yura was no toady. He has . . . had friends, *important* ones . . . and they will not allow this. They will *not!*"

Ah-ha, friends . . . Duvakin's ears pricked up, reminding him of his original mission, to protect himself. "Friends?" he inquired in a tense voice.

"You think I'm lying? That just because he's out here in this pit he's a nobody? No, dear, he's not like you. Magadan was just the bottom rung on Yura's ladder, and his friends in the ministry are going to be very upset . . ."

"Ministry?"

"Of air . . . That's the department Yura worked for, but he was no timeserver, mind. No, the ministry had its eye on him, and they are *not* going to take this quietly . . . There'll be the devil to pay!"

Sure, thought Duvakin, relaxing again. Widow talk. He allowed himself a more neutral "Oh?"

"You think this is all brave widow talk, don't you? Give me another cigarette . . ." As she reached, the daughter came in with the tea, in glasses on saucers. The smell was delightful. Talk died as they fussed with sugar, cigarettes, spoons; that domestic routine, however, somehow gave a more intimate air to the talk when it did resume.

Rzhevskaya seemed less hostile, more intent on impressing Duvakin with the seriousness of her weapons.

"You ever hear of a man named Rosenbloom, Emile Germanovich Rosenbloom?" She said the syllables like they were large fat grapes.

"No . . ." Duvakin said cautiously. "A local man?"

"No, a Volga German, but his people were sent to the Altai . . . That's where my Yura comes from . . . came from. You ever been there?"

"No, I can't say that I have." Where was all this bound? Altai, Germans? Duvakin wondered how strained this woman was.

"It's quite a country there, rich and open. The villages are prosperous, and the life is free, the mountains, fishing, hunting . . . Boys who grow up there often go back after the army, not like in Russia. So Yura and Emile were like that, both got out of the army, fledglings, but hot-blooded, you know . . . got themselves fixed up as pilots on the collective farm."

"Pilots on the collective farm?" Duvakin was taken aback.

"You have no idea, the spaces are that huge. They use light planes to take supplies in to the herders in the mountains, fly spare parts to the combine crews out in the fields. And my Yura and Emile had learned in the army, weren't afraid of a thing under God's own sun . . ." She smiled inwardly, in silence. The obvious depth of her feeling for the dead man made Duvakin suddenly wistful, acutely aware that his passing would not be so mourned. He half listened, feeling a little sorry for himself.

"Anyway," she continued, "they were young, and it was the start of the whole virgin lands thing. Yura's collective had opened thousands and thousands of hectares. To hear him tell it, the place was a sea of furrows, with dust columns all the way to the stars. Moscow sent a delegation down, big cheeses all of them. The collective farm chairman decided the best way to show off the farm would be in the airplane. Emile was older, by a year or two, so he got to be the pilot. He was scared, but he took that plane up like it was a cracked egg; his passenger never so much as hiccuped. The visitor liked it so much that he took Emile back to Moscow with him as his personal pilot." She beamed.

Duvakin smiled too, though uncertainly. What in the devil had this to do with Rzhevsky? He waited patiently while Rzhevskaya sipped her tea daintily, took a puff on her cigarette. Finally she looked up.

"Know who that passenger was?" Her voice was coy, almost coquettish; clearly for her, the story's magic was undimmed.

"No . . ."

"Brezhnev." She smiled, satisfied at the expression of shock on Duvakin's face.

Oh, my God, he thought, feeling the blood drain from his face.

"So Emile became the personal pilot of the general party secretary. He's got a big house, a country place, apartments all over, even got a ZIL, because you know what else he is?"

Duvakin just shook his head, feeling breathless.

"Assistant minister of air, that's who. Mind, all it means is that he's Brezhnev's pilot, but still, a word from him can make or break an appointment . . . and he doesn't forget old comrades." The magic of her own narration abruptly snapped, and Rzhevskaya's face grew dark. "He's not going to let them get away with this!"

"Whew," Duvakin whistled softly. So that's how it is. His growing awareness of his own comparative powerlessness, the absurdity of his desire to help, was suddenly joined by relief; thank God he had chanced to pursue this! Imagine all such well-connected wrath directed at *him*!

"So what are you going to do? Phone and ask your

friend to go after the organs?" And not after me, Duvakin added to himself. And not after me.

"Better than that. I'm going to go myself, beg him to help me, to punish these hooligans, these criminals . . ."

"How? He's only in the Ministry of Air."

"Don't you see? Through *Brezhnev.*"

Duvakin of course knew nothing of Brezhnev as a man, knew nothing of how he might respond, what his temper was, what he might think. He knew only one thing; he would not wish ever to be brought to the attention of the first party secretary.

"Valera, Valerochka, do you really think that's wise?" the old woman appeared suddenly, or had she been there all along? "To *Brezhnev,* yet. Only trouble can come of it, just trouble . . ."

"Oh, Mama, do be still. It's not the old days . . . We're a nation of laws now. Brezhnev says it himself. He'll help, he'll want to know about this sort of criminal hooliganism."

The old woman spat derisively, then wrung the tattered edge of her apron. "Trouble, trouble . . . They took your husband, but you've still got your apartment, your daughter; you're young . . . There'll be trouble, you'll see . . ."

"Enough!" Rzhevskaya snapped, so savagely that the old woman subsided into a slightly trembling silence. "I'm going on that plane and that's it! They will not go unpunished!"

Duvakin admired the woman's blaze of determination a moment, then asked softly, "Plane?"

"How did you think I was going to get to Moscow? By reindeer? I'm going on the seven o'clock flight tomorrow."

"You have a ticket? That plane is impossible; it's always full."

"Don't worry. I already phoned to arrange it." Her expression was grim; Duvakin knew she was right. So, this time tomorrow, or thereabouts, she would be in Moscow. And someone who thought he had a ticket would not.

Moscow. Unexpectedly, Duvakin found himself picturing streets, remembering scenes he had scraped painfully from his memory. He had taught himself to think of Moscow as the past, a fairy tale, more remote even than Paris; it was the one place on the globe where he could never go, not if he was to be spared God knows what kind of trouble. And this chunky hennaed woman who sat nervously smoking his cigarettes was tomorrow simply going to sit in a seat and, hey presto—Moscow.

"Could I see you off?" he asked suddenly, surprising himself again.

Rzhevskaya stared, then slowly let a smile cross her face.

"Sure . . . why not?" She continued to regard him, then added, "More tea?"

"Please . . . but don't you think perhaps? . . ."

"Yes?"

"Shouldn't you get some sleep? I mean, you look horrible . . . er, that is, you've got . . ." Duvakin felt a flush climb slowly up his neck.

Rzhevskaya, thank heaven, showed no inclination to take his mumbled comment as an insult; instead, she laughed at his confusion. "And what of you?"

Duvakin thought quickly. By rights he ought to go home; his only mission, to clear himself, was done. Rzhevskaya had accepted his innocence, and so back he ought to go, to his apartment, job, and quiet, quiet life. Except, he realized, he didn't want to, not yet. Partly, it was this apartment and its familiar unfamiliar furniture reminding him of Tanya and good times in Moscow. Partly, it was the thought of this woman going tomorrow to Moscow. For a second he pondered asking her to take a note to Tanya, or phone her, maybe.

As quickly he dropped the idea; why bother Tanya? Nothing could come of it if Rzhevskaya did get a message to her; better Tanya stayed history.

And, one tiny honest bit of his mind slyly confessed, why even let Rzhevskaya know about Tanya? It was a ludicrous thought; you don't generally woo widows the day after their husbands have been beaten to death, at least not with hope of success. Not even that he was wooing, he thought, but still . . . Drinking tea with a woman was a pleasant change from his masculine and solitary ways.

"With your permission . . ." he began haltingly. "It's far to my apartment . . . and the plane is early, isn't it? You'll have bags to carry; I could help."

"You want to stay here?" Rzhevskaya smiled.

"If it isn't a bother. I'm rather tired, you see; I came straight from work."

"You haven't eaten, then?" Rzhevskaya's tone was solicitous, although a little distant.

Duvakin was horrified at what he had said. "No, no . . . I mean, please, I . . . it's enough that I came." At the same time, his stomach began insistently reminding him of just how hungry he was. Apart from a few quick meat pies at lunch, he had eaten nothing since breakfast. He glanced at his watch. Almost twelve hours ago.

Rzhevskaya nodded decisively. "Well, then, Mama will give you something, and I will leave you. Arrange yourself as is most comfortable for you." The improbable nature of their interlude apparently dawned upon the woman, for she added more grimly, "I must get prepared."

They shook hands, stiffly, formally, then she disappeared into the hall.

There followed the muffled sounds of a brief shouting match—Feed him! I will not—and Mama shuffled into the room with a plate. On it lay a tin of sardines, some bread, and, wonder of wonders, a green onion. "There's more tea if you want," the old woman muttered.

"Please . . ." Duvakin did his best to melt her with a smile. In vain. She walked out muttering, then returned, still muttering. She slammed the glass down, sloshing the tea over some papers. And Georgian tea at that!

Duvakin glanced at the open tin; sure enough, imported sardines. The foreign alphabet and their unknown words greatly increased Duvakin's pleasure. It was almost like the old days!

He wandered once around the room, selected the spot that seemed most promising—a daybed, buried beneath a large pile of what looked to be letters, in the corner by the glass wall—and sat. He took a mouthful of fish, wiped his fingers on the bread, and began gratefully to chew.

There was no moon; nothing broke the black stillness of the night. Duvakin chewed reflectively, watching the stars trundle themselves slowly across the sky. Bit by bit the apartment grew quite.

Duvakin knew he too should sleep, but he was at peace, loaths even to move to clear more space on the bed. It was like a holiday, that's what. The last two days in their way were a last straw, the frantic tension of unexpected activity showing him how tensely, bitterly he lived.

And now? Enough . . . No more looking back. Here too was life, here too it was possible to drink tea with a woman, and here too, now that Rzhevskaya was no longer intent on his blood, here too a man would live quietly.

Duvakin glanced about at the mess around him. Perhaps he ought to work a bit for his supper, he thought drowsily. After a last cigarette, the dregs of tea, and mopping the interior of the sardine can with a hunk of black bread, Duvakin lazily heaved himself to his feet and addressed the nearest pile. What the devil, he thought, you have to clean up a bit anyway, just to find the daybed. He began sorting and straightening, but soon he was examining more closely, curious about this life into which he had unexpectedly tumbled.

Duvakin was no investigator; back when he was in the militia he had received no more than a cursory rundown of what an officer might and ought not to do upon discovery of a crime. Besides, Soviet criminal procedure was not very interested in physical evidence of crime because the confession had long been the keystone of Soviet justice. However, a lifetime of living mostly alone had made Duvakin observant, and the mess in Moscow had taught him a thing or two, including suspicion. Not much in the way of skills, but they did well enough, for him.

The Rzhevskys were normal, living a commonplace enough life. Commonplace in Moscow, that is. Here, in Magadan, their apartment had an exotic, almost lunatic quality. Receipts from scrap paper turn-ins, good for books which could not be bought with cash. Manuscripts of poetry, typed on paper as thin as Duvakin's socks, hand-bound in cardboard folders. Duvakin dipped into a poem or two, wondering what his old girlfriend Tanya might have made of them; she had followed such things, but to his eye it all seemed pretty tame, even if sprinkled with religion. On the walls, lithographs of Russian churches. A fair number of books, some old, some new. Duvakin knew few of the names, but it was enough to tell him that they were all expensive. As was that lacquer box over there, this antique desk set of marble and brass. Even a copy of the British glossy propaganda magazine in Russian, obtained at who knows what cost and brought to Magadan.

The Rzhevskys were, in short, playing at intelligentsia. The sky outside had begun to tarnish faintly gray at the far edge when Duvakin leaned back to think. Only against the frozen hummocks of Magadan and the encircling half-human Chukchis did all this seem so absurd. Why the churches? Rzhevsky would have claimed atheism with the best. Why the samizdat? Because all the intelligentsia has samizdat. Never mind if the poetry stinks. Why those books, these journals? Because "all Moscow" is, or more likely, was reading them. In Moscow, this chasing after goods, this mad race to possess, used to remind Duvakin on occasion of the old peasant remedy for greedy landlords, who suddenly found themselves literally stuffed to death with the land or grain or fleece they had coveted. Here, in Magadan, this drive to possess seemed so unreasoned as almost to be funny.

Still musing, Duvakin dropped into a fitful doze, head against the wall, one arm draped over a mound of letters. He dreamed chaotically of vast piles of goods, clothes, furniture, papers. He woke in the half-light of dawn, his mouth sour and his neck stiff. Duvakin watched the lights in the room slowly pale as the day broadened behind him; fuzzily he remembered an old story that in childhood had puzzled him. His mother used to read to him of a cruel bai who would send his hapless slave Edigai to fetch him snow; little Vanya Duvakin would stare uncomprehendingly at the enormous mountains of snow piled up outside his windows. It was only years later that he realized snow had value only because of its rarity in the bai's hot and dusty land. So too, Duvakin suspected, with all the Rzhevsky's books and pictures. What was hard to get in Moscow was rarer than moon rocks in Magadan. Meaning, the Rzhevskys were rich. Very rich, even. Maybe what he had heard about, never seen: Red millionaires.

Duvakin laughed. And I offered to help this woman! Connections, money . . . so what if she had enemies? She could take care of it.

Not that any of this said why Rzhevsky had died, but still, wealth on this scale must be illicit. This ransacking was probably to seek out hidden treasure. And Rzhevsky must have died because he had finally grown too large, too noticeable. This wealth was a common enough story, Duvakin knew, and getting commoner. The ones this age, the guys moving up, they were all like this. Zhiguli cars, Bulgarian coats, stuffing it in their faces and pockets as fast as they could.

Was it unfair that *this* man, who was shouldering himself so rudely up to the trough, should have been caught? Duvakin stood and stretched; then he turned to watch the sun thread gold through a black congealed fog blanketing the horizon. It looked to be another springlike day.

There was a rustle behind him.

"So, you are still here?"

The sleep had not been kind to Rzhevskaya. Her eyes were still puffy and red; her hair was tangled, and there was beneath her too bright makeup an obvious ashen pallor. Her manner, though, was brisk, almost gay, as she bustled around the room.

"As you see," Duvakin said with a yawn.

"You slept well?" she asked, looking about the neatened room. Duvakin blushed, feeling guilty.

"Oh, quite . . . and I straightened up a bit." He waved a hand vaguely, hoping she would ask nothing more.

"Thank you," she said softly, then looked directly at him, pondering. "I suppose it must have seemed a little odd yesterday—my hitting you and so on."

Duvakin shrugged, smiled. "Under the circumstances . . ."

There was a painful pause, then Duvakin said, "How are we going? To the airport, I mean."

"You're still coming?"

"If you'd rather I didn't—"

"No, no . . . It's just odd." She paused. "Come, by all means."

Odd it certainly was; Duvakin could not have explained even to himself, not fully anyway. But certainly there was self-interest too, for it would not do to have a woman on her way almost to Brezhnev change her mind and begin to think ill of him. And then, it was Moscow she was headed for. And so he would see her off, if only to feel again, no matter how slight, some attachment to the unreal, distant city.

"What's the time?" she asked, looking at her own watch.

"Mine says twenty past five . . . but it often does . . ."

"The taxi ought to be here soon; it's near six. Take those down for me, will you?" She pointed at a collection of bags, valises and suitcases. He flinched inwardly, but recognized the price of his trip. He set his legs, grasped, and almost leaped into the air. The bags were empty.

Rzhevskaya had disappeared, doubtless bidding the crone and the daughter good-bye, so Duvakin went to ask her *which* bags, but then realized there was no cause. They would leave empty, but those bags were not meant to return empty. He looked about the apartment again, trying to picture each item as it fit into a suitcase. Most did; the Rzhevskys had had impressive dedication to their objects.

Rzhevskaya emerged, and a hectic, frantic departure was begun. Dropping bits as he ran, Duvakin both followed and led the woman out, down the elevator, and to the courtyard, where a taxi honked energetically at the neighboring building. Yells, whistles, shouts of "Do you know the time?" flew from nearby windows; the surly cabdriver grumbled sourly because his cases of black market vodka in the trunk had to be shifted so that the suitcases would fit. At last they pulled away, and Duvakin sank gratefully into repose, vodka bottles rattling at his elbow.

Rzhevskaya, though, could not relax; she sat forward on the rear seat, fat white knees agape in her anxiety to see the road, the speedometer, and the driver's watch.

"You'll make it, you'll make it," Duvakin said vaguely, trying to be reassuring. His attention was outside, though. The sun was up fully, no longer red. The sky was soft blue, with pristine wisps of white, while the few open fields and exposed hills they whizzed past were turning a grayer, almost mud color. Could this truly be spring coming now, so soon? Duvakin bit his lip and thought, wouldn't it be lovely?

Thirteenth Olympiad microregion was on the same side of Magadan as the airport, but on another road, so one had almost to return to town before turning onto the airport highway. As they reached Aviator's Chausee, Duvakin's lyrical thoughts wilted. This woman here might be flying to Moscow, but you are staying here, Duvakin mused. In an hour or so he would return past that same log house there, sinking west end first into the permafrost, past that same abandoned apartment building, which subsidence had cracked fully in half. Depressed and aching slightly with fatigue, Duvakin lit a cigarette and brooded. Face it. Magadan it was, Magadan it must be. The prospect seemed drabber than it had last night in the lap of Rzhevskaya's flat.

The airport was awakening. There were other taxis, a few Zhigulis. Huge Kama trucks, their radiator caps higher off the ground than a man could reach, snarled and growled up to the freight docks. Duvakin could imagine the crush inside, throngs waving passports stuffed with bribes as they begged tickets, hands shoving luggage forward to the scales and baggage areas, children howling as people pushed over them to get to boarding areas. And every day the same! Every day the airport personnel seemed surprised at the crush, and each night they did nothing to prepare for the same thing the next day. And who was to blame them? he thought gloomily. It's not like you've done anything to lighten the load. His head buzzed badly; he knew he ought to have slept more.

They pulled up, stopped. Rzhevskaya gripped his arm and said urgently, "Take everything to Gate Three . . . I'll be there as soon as I can, but get them to put the bags on . . ." Then she disappeared into the milling lobby.

The thought of getting all the woman's countless bags and grips to Gate 3, on the far side of the jammed lobby, was so appalling that it took Duvakin a moment to realize that he would also have to pay the driver. Shaking his head bitterly, Duvakin spat at the oily curbside ice. You don't get to be a millionaire by paying cab fares, he thought acidly.

Duvakin's luck was still in, though; as soon as he had fished out the bags and paid the driver, he spotted a porter asleep on a cart next to the wall.

"Hey, citizen," Duvakin shouted into the man's hair-trimmed ear.

Citizen porter was a stubby, bleary-eyed alcoholic, apparently so far stewed that he lacked the power to move voluntarily.

He could, however, still obey orders. He stood, blinking watery, blood-rimmed eyes without apparent comprehension. After a moment he nodded.

"Put *those* bags on *this* cart." Duvakin spoke as to an infant or a foreigner, hoping gesture would do what words could not. "And follow me."

Mechanically, the porter obeyed. Slowly, Duvakin forced their way through the gelid masses in the lobby.

At Gate 3 the crush was, if anything, worse. The porter muttered "S'impossible, can't be done . . ." and fell asleep on the handles of his cart. Damn Rzhevskaya. Let her arrange about getting through. Duvakin jabbed the porter awake, telling him to leave the cart. The man agreed, then stuck out a trembling but insistent hand.

Duvakin's last paper ruble and a pat on the shoulder sent him off, happy, to the beer stand.

The crowd at Gate 3 was all Russians, no natives. The Moscow run was for managers, supervisors, that class. They all jostled and pushed importantly, unaccustomed to being in a crowd of peers. Each was more used to being given way to than giving way. Good luck taking away one of *their* seats, Duvakin thought.

If one mentally filled in the burned-out bulbs, the airport clock showed 06:57 when Rzhevskaya finally steamed up, tense and jittery as a covered pot boiling on the stove.

"The ticket was all right?" Duvakin asked, stepping forward.

"My bags aren't on? You," she indicated someone behind her, "get this lot onto that plane *now!*" Her face was flushed, as much with anger as with excitement. The first hurdle, so to say, was successfully cleared. "Yes, I got it. Well, comrade Duvakin, I'm off. Wish me luck!" Her eyes glittered and seemed to focus, if at all, well beyond him.

Duvakin smiled, softened and cheered a bit by her excitement now that he was no longer the object of her vengeance.

"Good luck . . . and safe journey." He shook her hand.

He had no desire to wait any longer. The milling crowd straining at Gate 3 probably contained at least one person who would soon discover his place usurped, and Duvakin could easily spare himself yet one more public scandal. Besides, he thought, as he ignored the dusty, humming airport around him, all too soon he would be back here, hanging up slogans.

By no logic for which he could account, the bus stop had been set almost 200 meters from the doors of the airport. He slogged down the icy, rutted path, acutely aware of his own fatigue, cursing himself for a fool. How was he to get through another day without sleep?

There was a high whine and the rustle of wind about his feet, the Moscow jet moving from its parking place out onto the runway. The jet was a pitted dirty white, the red flag on the tail faded almost to pink. Lights flashed as it rolled bouncing to the end of the runway, wheeled, paused, and then heaved ponderously forward. The whine increased to a roar.

"Well, then . . . good luck, Valeria Rzhevskaya!" Duvakin said, using her full name and saluting with his hand. He watched the plane clear the ground and begin to climb, riding upwards on wads of black smoke. The noise abated. Duvakin turned and trudged on, to join the knot of passengers waiting with their bundles at the decrepit bus shelter.

There was a pop, faint but loud enough to make Duvakin look back. He was just in time to see the last trace of a black and orange fireball expanding into nothingness, replaced by the merry twinkle of sun sparkling on a rain of shredded steel, torn clothing, and specks of human flesh.

⋆ SIX ⋆

The freakish warm weather continued; a drizzly rain was falling, melting the snow into filthy lumps of muck. A thick fog bellied up, making haloes around the infrequent street lamps, highlighting the glittering beads on the trees. In the park across the street a bottle smashed against the asphalt, followed by raucous laughs, a shriek or two, and silence.

Startled at the noise, Duvakin's heart leaped like a partridge from a berry bush, then settled back to its rattling, rapid knock. Duvakin shifted on the sopping wet park bench and tried again to talk himself into going home.

The day had been impossible; the slightest noise had sent him rocketing up, wild and anxious.

"Good heavens, Ivan Palych, you'd think somebody was tramping on your grave!" the inoffensive old typist had remarked when she startled him after lunch. He smiled faintly, feeling the trace of perspiration along his brow.

He wondered how close to the mark she might be.

The day was busy, with the voluntary Saturday hard upon them and Sutrapian passed out in his office, but Duvakin could not erase or submerge that vision of airplane shards tumbling in a cloud to the ground.

Part of the clammy dread that embraced his spine was memories of Rzhevskaya—firm round upper arms, glittering gold teeth, leather coat glistening taunt across her plump shoulders, all now incomprehensibly scattered across hectare upon hectare of dwarf larch and frost heaves.

He remembered back in Moscow, when he'd first found that dead American in the hotel room. His stomach had felt like this then too—icy, almost vomiting. Because although he didn't know what was to come, in a way he nevertheless did: trouble. Unspecified, but trouble for all that. And trouble that damn dead Yankee had been, a ticket to Magadan.

Duvakin lit another cigarette, staring at the faint yellow of the distant lamp.

What business was so important that you blow up a whole airplane for?

That was what most caught at Duvakin's throat. It was like in the children's cartoons he sometimes went to at the movie palace, foolish wolf picking berries, thinks the big black one is a particular find. As he picks it, he turns to the hare to boast, unaware that his "berry" is the nose of a sleeping bear.

Duvakin had felt feverish all day, certain somehow that he might soon turn around to face the fetid gaping jaws of some unknown ursine fate, and he had no idea of how to let go.

The drunks in the park chucked another empty bottle, the alcoholics' fireworks.

With a heavy grunt, Duvakin stood up. You can't sit in this muck all night; go home, he thought deliberately.

Home, once his refuge, his hole, seemed suddenly unprotected. Vulnerable. Duvakin had no idea to what; he just knew that he didn't want to go calmly home, put on his pajamas, brush his teeth, and wait quietly while fate ran him over like a turtle on the highway. Not that it would, but who'd take that chance?

He thought of Rzhevsky, beaten to death a few hours after they shared a drink.

Rzhevskaya turned to a crow's breakfast not ten minutes after they parted.

Sure, Duvakin's rational brain said, that's them, they were Red millionaires. You're not; you haven't done anything.

Fear, though, is no great respecter of reason.

As he strolled idly toward the corner, Duvakin realized what he wanted was company, not protection. Just company.

Too little had made sense these past couple of days. Life had crawled along its slot for four years; then suddenly, from nowhere, came the toilet lady, the furs, the Rzhevskys. And death—vivid, close, real.

But who was there to talk to?

Duvakin thought of Sutrapian, who if he were ever awake, would be so drunk he'd speak Armenian. Semyenov, from the office? Duvakin had never said more than a devil's dozen of words to the man and had not enjoyed those.

Tired, frightened, Duvakin knew he was sinking into profound pity for himself. Alone on the far shore of life, at the edge of the known world, and circled by dangers unknown . . .

And soon, he thought wryly, I'll start to cry, like an old drunk. He scratched his jaw nervously; the scabby scales gave him an unexpected idea.

The doctor.

There were some disadvantages to this idea, such as

that he had no idea what her name was or where she lived, as well as that he had found her forthrightness unsettling, even a shade repugnant.

On the other hand, she was alive, friendly, and not likely to want to harm him.

He looked quickly at his watch. There was a chance she might still be at the clinic, assuming the shift went until eight. He debated another moment, glancing over his shoulder at the tunnel of wet, black street, which echoed drunken laughter and concealed heaven knows what unpleasant surprises, and then he nodded his head resolutely. Very well, then, the doctor's.

He oriented himself quickly, then began to slog briskly through the muck toward the clinic; after a few paces he found himself breaking into a ragged trot.

Magadan was not a large town, but space had been infinite, so at first, buildings came and went as they wished. Streets had been an afterthought, imposed later, with little regard for existing buildings. The result was a hodgepodge of empty lots, construction sites, buildings jammed tight against the sidewalk, and labyrinthine courtyards. Prudence made him walk normally on the streets, but when he could, he jogged across the deserted spaces. Self-control combined with speed soon had him winded. Worst was the dread, unlike anything he could remember; every passerby, every corner, every shadow could have held danger, and yet Duvakin knew that to be impossible. Or almost knew. Anticipating constantly what he expected would not happen made Duvakin trembly and breathless. He debated for a moment the wisdom of going into the polyclinic, but he knew his fear was absurd. Besides, he could not lounge around outside by the automobiles, not if he wanted to find the doctor.

He arrived, breathless and flushed, just on eight. The first staff were already trickling down the stairs; he was on the point of asking, but remembered he didn't know her name. Hoping madly she was there, Duvakin pounded up the crumbling cement stairs into the lobby, looked quickly about, and approached the desk, where a reedy, bleached-out attendant was doing a crossword.

"Your name?" she snapped before he could open his mouth.

"My name?" he stammered.

"Your name, your name! How do you think we keep records here, by lot?" she asked with bored sarcasm.

"But I'm not a patient here," Duvakin said, not sure how to say why he *was* here.

"Why are you here, then? This isn't the beach at Feodosia, citizen."

"I am a patient, though. I mean, I used to be . . . I'm looking for—I want to find the doctor who did this," he pointed at the scabs on his face. "I mean who fixed this," he added hastily, blushing. "I mean she didn't—"

"You'll have to give me your name, then, won't you? It's not as if I memorize every mug what sticks his snout in, is it?"

Panting slightly, thinking hard. And just suppose it got back to that Darmoved or whoever was behind all this trouble that Duvakin had asked for the doctor? It was nothing, certainly, absurd. And yet . . . He decided on a different course.

"She's about my height, yellow hair, my age more or less, gold teeth?"

"Glasses?" the attendant asked shrewdly.

Duvakin paused, trying to recall. "No glasses," he said decisively.

The other attendant at the desk looked up sharply from her attempts to pick dried egg from her smock.

"Must be the latest one, Larochka . . . Getting older, aren't they?"

The reedy one turned and made a hushing motion, but laughed too. "But then, so's she . . ."

Duvakin felt a blush climb up his cheeks.

"It's not . . . what you think," he mumbled.

"Let me guess," the second one said. "You're really her son, lost in the war, and this is going to be your reunion."

Duvakin's blush deepened, now making his ears throb, as the two women snorted and choked with laughter.

"Just tell me her name," he said as authoritatively as possible. "And where I can find her," he added.

Still gurgling with her own wit, the second one said, "That's Dr. Berezkina, she's on children's today. Third floor."

Duvakin trudged up the narrow stairs, still burning with embarrassment. The devil take women like that.

Children's receiving reminded Duvakin of the airport; every seat in the tiny room held a mother with one, sometimes more children on her lap, and more women sat on the floor, on the fire buckets, on the window ledges. Most were Chukchi, impassive, slit-eyed natives who stared unmovingly at one another's feet. Even the children were still, stoical. Normally, a crush like that, the futility of so much sickness, would have dispirited Duvakin; this time, however, he wedged his way to the corner near the window, stood with his back to the wall, and looked out into the darkness, feeling safe for the first time since the morning.

Just at eight a beefy nurse in a greenish sweater boomed out, "That's all . . . reception tomorrow from nine." A couple of Russian women jumped up to argue heatedly, pointing vehemently at their flushed, listless children, themselves, the nurse, and the closed doctors' doors, but the rest of the women simply stood and began shuffling quietly out. After a few minutes of the nurse's adamant "tomorrow—tomorrow—tomorrow," they too finally packed up and moved off, still hurling curses.

"You too, citizen . . . out," she said to Duvakin. "Anyway, the alcohol ward is down on the ground floor."

"I'm not waiting here."

"I can see, can't I? Unless you've lost your youngster. Come on, time to go home." She made a shooing motion with her chin.

"No, I mean I'm waiting here for a doctor, Dr. Berezkina . . ." Duvakin paused, then added, "I used to be a patient."

The nurse sniffed, then looked him up and down. "Who hasn't? I'd have thought she could find herself one with hair." She spoke half to herself.

After a pause, Duvakin realized that the nurse was waiting for something.

"She's here?" he asked anxiously.

"She's here," the woman said; then, "You want me to tell her you're here?"

A tip, damn it. Duvakin dug reluctantly into his pocket, demonstratively dredging up only three fives and a three.

"Eighteen kopeks? I asked for bus fare?" the woman said nastily.

"Just fetch her, will you? You think I'm Rockefeller come calling?" Duvakin tried to sound authoritative, jingling his pockets to show there was no more.

It was very nearly true, he thought sadly, as he watched the nurse make a slow obvious turn through the muddy waiting room before finally, grudgingly, honoring his request. He had so little money it would make a cat sob, what with the taxis and all. Maybe there'd be a May Day bonus, he hoped idly.

There was a brief silence, some rustling, and then the

doctor appeared, already dressed in her street clothes. Just in time, Duvakin thought.

"So, my crusty cavalier," she said jocularly, but her eyes were bright green, alert, inquiring.

He smiled sheepishly.

"How is it with your wounds? No relapses, no infection, eh?" She was shorter than he remembered, and heavier, perhaps, though it might just be the bulk of her green overcoat.

Duvakin smiled again, unaccountably nervous now.

"No, no relapses . . ."

"Just good fortune, then, that you happen our way this evening?" Berezkina smiled up at him, dimples on either side of a smallish mouth. Her eyes were less warm, now examining him closely.

"No, not entirely . . ." Duvakin could feel a slow blush creeping up from his collar. "I was . . . I came to see . . . to . . . would you like to take a walk?" he finally blurted.

The doctor laughed deeply, even throwing her head high, leaning back.

"Some cavalier! A walk, in such weather!"

"Oh—I've no car, you see." Curse me, he thought. Stammering like a tenth-former and flushing like I was in the bathhouse. "Oh, well . . ." He turned to go.

"You give up so soon?" The doctor reached out to touch his sleeve. "I've got a car, you know."

"You're married, then?" Duvakin pulled his arm away.

"Good heavens, no . . . not in ages, anyway."

"You mean it's your car? Personally?" Involuntarily, Duvakin looked down at his feet, suddenly struck that the only transportation he possessed were his shoes.

"Of course . . . You think it's easy to get doctors to stay out here? Even ones like me? So the Party sweetens the pot a bit." She shrugged, then examined him again with her calculating eyes. "What really brings you here? You were looking for me?"

Duvakin thought for a moment. "Yes—yes, I was." He looked over her shoulder and mumbled, "I was lonely."

"What?"

"I said I was . . . wanted some company." Duvakin spoke directly into her face, hoping there were no nurses about.

"So," she said, her face now grim. She took his arm in a firm grip and led him away, down the stairs.

Duvakin was puzzled by the strength of her grip and the purposeful look on her face, but he let himself be led to the ground floor, outside, to a maroon Zhiguli. She unlocked it, and they got in.

They did not speak, but the ride was far from silent; in the light sedan Duvakin was acutely aware of how bad the streets of Magadan were. The car rattled and lugged from hole to frost heave to hole.

The doctor's building was only a few minutes' drive, on one of the cross streets near the far side of Lenin Square, a cinder block and stucco luxury block erected for the higher-ups during the cult. By prisoners, of course. Duvakin too clearly imagined those poor wretches ever to be entirely comfortable in such apartments.

Still silent, with a purposeful look on her face, Berezkina led him through an echoing granite lobby to a cage elevator, in which they clanked up three flights. Once in the apartment, she led him past two closed doors to a third, which opened into a dark sitting room. There she switched on an overhead light shaded by an old-fashioned tasseled green shade.

"Wait here," she said flatly, then disappeared.

Sheepishly, Duvakin sat, not sure whether he ought even to remove his overcoat. He looked about, seeing but not really registering the old-fashioned furniture, the large room. This was not at all what he had imagined, although he was uncertain what he *had* imagined. He could feel the shirt beneath his coat grow damp. Not nerves, he assured himself. The radiators.

"Well, shall we begin?" the doctor said as she entered the room.

Duvakin's mouth fell open and his hat slipped from his hand. In the doorway the doctor stood, wearing only some kind of nightshirt that barely reached her knees—a white fuzzy fringe hemmed and collared the shirt, making her skin look dappled rose. Worse, the hall light shone through the fine material, clearly showing her body's shape. Her belly looked as round and springy as a fresh-baked bread.

Duvakin tried to talk; his tongue was glued to the roof of his mouth.

"Well, what's the matter? This is the first time you've seen this?" Her tone was biting.

Stupidly, Duvakin shook his head.

"Well, then . . ." She turned, bending slightly. Duvakin's heart followed the slow rise of the hem up her mottled hams.

"But—" he croaked.

"But what? This is what you came for, isn't it?" Her eyes were narrowed, almost closed.

"Yes . . . er, no . . . that is . . ." Duvakin's face flamed now; sweat popped out on his brow. "That is, I was lonely. I wanted company. Chat a bit, drink some tea . . ." He looked away.

"Tea!" The doctor laughed harshly. "Tea! It's me, I disgust you—that's it?" she said threateningly.

"Good heavens, no! Not at all. You're lovely. I mean, you're very . . ." He stumbled to a halt. "That is to say . . . well, for instance, I don't even know your name!" he blurted out.

The doctor stared at him, her hard eyes trying to bore into him. Finally she said, "This isn't a joke, then?"

"No, honestly. I don't want to hurt your feelings, but—"

"So let's drink some tea . . ." She vanished, Duvakin presumed into the kitchen, then reappeared. "You're married, then?"

"No, good Lord. What makes you say that?" Duvakin was startled.

"Because I can't make you out . . . Are you normal?"

"Normal?"

"You know, everything works?"

Duvakin blushed hard, so she added, "I'm a doctor, remember?"

Duvakin laughed, choked, looked at her, and laughed again. He tried to stifle himself as he noticed the anger boiling up in her face again, turning it almost the color of liver. "No, no . . . I'm not trying to insult you, please, pardon me. It's just, well . . . you don't look so very much like a doctor right now!"

The woman looked down at her thinly disguised naked body and then chuckled. "It's true, isn't it?" She laughed. "So, come on . . . the kettle's boiling. We can sit in the kitchen."

"All right, ummm . . ."

"Galya . . . Galina Maximovna."

"Vanya, Ivan Palych."

"Charmed . . ." She curtseyed, with a ponderous swaying of breasts that made Duvakin laugh again. To her quizzical look, he said, "I've never introduced myself to a nude doctor before."

"Come . . ."

The kitchen was like most, clean and small, with a tiny table tucked into one corner. The kettle rattled its lid on the stove. Galya bustled about, apparently indifferent to her state of undress; Duvakin found in the bright light that he too grew used to her nudity.

It was pleasant to sit in a kitchen again, he thought as

he folded his bulky coat over one chair and sat in another. His back, as he loved, was against the wall. It was *this* his life lacked, the table, the steam, the clank of cups. He took out a cigarette, lit it with a deep sense of contentment.

The doctor's fussing produced tea, lemon slices, and some kind of dry biscuit. She sat too, her prim decorousness somehow overpowering the obvious immodesty of her nightshirt. Duvakin chuckled again, then shook his head. "Thank you . . . It's very nice."

Conversation began somewhat reluctantly, for the doctor continued to be suspicious, but Duvakin's clear pleasure in sitting, sipping tea, and telling tales of his home village, of Moscow, gradually disarmed her. Duvakin's native Krasnaya Sosna had by now assumed almost legendary qualities; he spoke with real love of the river, the fresh berries, the slow pace of a rural militia man's life.

Galya too was from a village, but nearer Voronezh, in the south. For a time they talked almost independently, each charmed by his own recollections; the pines of Krasnaya Sosna, the open steppe of Verkhny Khopersk, the mushrooms of the former, the wild garlic of the latter. Duvakin spoke of his years in the village militia, chasing down occasional hooligans on motorbikes, stopping drunken brawls, and snoozing away long summer afternoons of carefree inactivity on the militia station porch. He talked and smoked and drank tea, realizing as he babbled on how great a store of words he had accumulated, drop by bitter drop. The man who lives alone has no way to rid himself of the little thoughts of daily life; too often he bursts, like a milkweed pod in autumn.

Galya too seemed pleased. She brought more tea; she smoked his cigarettes; she smiled and laughed, sometimes countering Duvakin's stories with ones of her own, but mostly letting him talk. Slowly, slowly Duvakin's breast began to empty of words, of tension, of loneliness;

* MAY DAY IN MAGADAN *

in the emptiness grew a grateful sense of happiness, and of safety.

The puddles wore clear windowpanes of new ice, beneath which gurgled white bubbles. Duvakin walked stiff-legged, to avoid slipping. The sun already glinted on the snow caps west of town. Duvakin, at Galya's request, was out early, before even the buses were running. It was cold, but the crisp cold that the sun would warm rapidly.

Could this truly be spring? Duvakin felt almost dazed with fatigue and pleasure. His feeling for the doctor was not that which he remembered with Tanya, trembling at each gesture, each word, in terror that the elaborate structure of his hopes might tumble with a single clumsy touch. Rather he felt a comfort, an ease, with Galya. They had talked until the doctor was almost asleep, her lids closing heavily and reopening slowly.

Duvakin, modestly, had meant to sit on, thinking, perhaps dozing in a chair while the doctor slept, but she would have none of it. Still embarrassed and stiff with apprehension, Duvakin took a place beside her, even in the dark self-consciousness of his black cotton underwear and undershirt.

This, and spring too, Duvakin thought, enjoying how clean the world seemed now, without people. The early sun gilded the willow shoots, where grackles gargled a morning song at one another. Physical intimacy, when it came sleepily, had been a surprise as well as a comfort. Duvakin had fallen into a deep sleep, lulled by Galya's quiet sobs.

They parted warmly, the doctor promising the same pillow if he cared to return.

Now the first old women were beginning to appear, bundled to the eyes in black coats and gray scarves,

[99]

* Anthony Olcott *

scurrying as industriously as sparrows to their mysterious destinations.

Duvakin paused to watch a woman sweep the stairs before her building. There had been no new snow, but still the woman concentrated, swinging her long bundle of twigs like a scythe. It was curious, he mused, as if the action was as important as any result. Sweep the stairs, they had told her, so sweep the stairs she did, meticulously, faithfully. Just as she finished the creeping line of sunrise caught her, bathing her erect, satisfied contemplation of her own labor in bright golden light. Duvakin laughed; the effect was too melodramatic. The Hero-Sweeper. Startled by the noise, the woman turned, made a rude gesture, and spat, then walked off grumbling.

Duvakin still stood for a moment, enjoying the stately turn of the earth moving sun slowly down his hand toward his feet, feeling the warmth lapping gently on his coat. He took a deep breath, enjoying the tang of salt and diesel from the melting harbor.

His dread of the night before seemed absurd now, the delusions of a man unwell. There were no shadows, no plots against him; why should there be? It was bad luck, he realized, just plain unlucky timing that had brought him up against the Rzhevskys at the exact moment when their sins caught up with them.

He shook his head and walked, regarding the world with new eyes, like a man just out of the hospital. Or prison. It was as if the Moscow nightmare hadn't been just the heroin and the doll and the thugs and the treachery of Colonel Polkovnikov; it was more, four years of Magadan and bad dreams and the drunken mutterings of Sutrapian, scientific atheism and no fruit from September through June. His dread had come because in a way the Moscow dread had never left; every move seemed a plot against him, every chance dead man would reach out his clammy claws to pluck at Duvakin.

[100]

This morning, in the glitter of new ice and the warmth of the sun, his worries seemed as insubstantial as the crumbs over which the sparrows battled so passionately, and the devil take them all!

Life for Ivan Palych Duvakin was, in a word, looking up. He smiled to himself and set out jauntily, almost humming.

★ SEVEN ★

Objectively, the day ought to have left Duvakin as bald as an egg, his hair snatched away in angry frustration. Nothing went right. To breakfast on, Duvakin could find only rice pies, fried bits of dough filled with what might have been wallpaper paste, except it was colder, and brittle. Then Semyenov had called in, to say he'd had a mild heart attack, but would be in in a day or so. While Duvakin was pondering that, Sutrapian reeled in, growled a few vague orders, and went into his office, where he fell asleep on his conference table. By ten o'clock the agitprop office was complete chaos, with ranks of angry section bosses calling about the voluntary Saturday assignments, worker's clubs ringing up for Lenin's birthday speakers, and messengers dropping by from the newspaper office with the articles and photos neighborhood activists were to use on their holiday bulletin boards in the housing blocks. Secretaries shrieked; junior assistants pounded desks and demanded things, and around lunchtime, the one overawed, decrepit typist burst into tears and closed herself in the women's toilet.

Because of his age and perhaps because he was calm, much of this chaos addressed itself to Duvakin, until even he could stand it no more; he found the urgent need to go examine the Party stores of rakes, on the off chance enough snow would melt by Saturday to permit voluntary raking.

The rakes were stored in a nearby cellar, vile, thick with dust and mildew; ordinarily, Duvakin would have passed any time spent in that fetid dark cursing his life for offering only *this* as escape from the bedlam of the office.

Not today, though. Contentment flowed thickly through Duvakin, bubbling gently in a half-song, half-purr at the back of his throat. Occasionally, he shook his head, amused at himself; he had not felt so *relieved* since early manhood, when a lucky evening at the Krasnaya Sosna House of Culture had finally rid him of his cursed virginity.

It wasn't even Galya, he thought as he mechanically counted the filthy rakes, throwing the broken ones to one side. It was more like a change, a turn in the road. For four years he had done nothing but chew over Tanya, Polkovnikov, Moscow, as if he weren't alive but just a dog on a chain, circling eternally about the same event. These last few days were like a slap in the face, a rough shake of the shoulders.

And they had worked, Duvakin realized, as he turned out the light and clambered back up to the street. Magadan might be foul, but life was showing him that there were worse alternatives, too. Such as the Rzhevskys now enjoyed. He forced the rusty lock shut and turned back up the street.

His watch still insisted it was 5:20; it may even have been. Whatever the hour, he had killed time successfully, for the dumpy gray citizens of Magadan were beginning to pick their doughty ways home. Or perhaps it was the weather that made the scene seem so subdued; Duvakin noted absently that the sky was gray now, a slate-colored wash, and a damp breeze was blowing from the west.

He paused, uncertain of where to go. Back to the office was senseless, for the ebb of the day could still snare him. To Galya's, only she would still be at the clinic. Later, certainly. He smiled to himself.

Besides, he muttered, I ought to do something about shaving. So, home. He turned about again, ignoring what looked like the typist waving to him from across the street, and went out to the square, to catch a bus home.

The wind had picked up, but the air was still warm, so Treefellers Prospekt was primordial ooze, just rigid enough to allow a man to clamber ahead more or less clean if he moved rapidly enough. Duvakin arrived breathless but exhilarated at the door of his building, then pushed on up the stairs. He dug for his key, reaching for the door handle. At his touch, the door swung open.

A dark shadow seemed to pass across Duvakin's shoulders. The door was unlocked? He tried to recall, but he knew he couldn't have left it open.

Holding his breath, he pushed the door fully open, recalling Rzhevskaya's flat, even his own in Moscow, torn to shreds in a search four years ago. Please, not again . . .

The room could be encompassed in a glance; even so, he stared hard before finally releasing his breath in a long, relieved sigh. The room was untouched. He must have forgotten to lock up. Of course, he muttered, of course. Last time he was in the room, it was Rzhevskaya hitting him. Naturally he could make a mistake, at a time like that.

Duvakin took off his overcoat, then massaged his chest, wondering why it was that his heart still hammered. It *was* his mistake; no one had searched his room.

So he must be only a chance bystander in all this, a witness, not a player. The Rzhevskys, they were the unlucky ones. Not him.

"Ivan Palych?" A hand clutched at his elbow, and Duvakin started. Leaping violently around, he found Pavlovna, his ancient neighbor, cowering against the wall in toothless, nearly blind amazement.

"Beg pardon, Pavlovna," he mumbled. "You startled me."

"Saints of heaven!" the crone crossed herself piously. "I had no mind to make you jump like that. I just want to ask if your friend found you." She smiled up with milky blue, almost opaque eyes. She was, Duvakin knew, forty-three years old, born in Magadan. In a prison nursery. The eyes were from vitamin deficiency then, probably what had cost her her teeth as well. He had no idea where the curved spine came from. Nevertheless, he respected her, partly because she looked old, but mostly because she was tough. To survive all that, she had to be almost steel.

"Friend?" he asked cautiously.

"This afternoon, said he wanted you for a chat," she bobbed her head, birdlike. "Couldn't see him well, of course, but big he seemed, and strong, to judge by the heat off of him . . . Said he'd look for you at the office; didn't want to leave a note or a name. Just waited a bit in your room, then left." She peered blindly, helpfully at him.

The wind caught at Duvakin's throat, as if he had been punched authoritatively in the chest. He fumbled to a chair and sat.

Questions slithered about in his suddenly throbbing head: Who had been looking? For what? Why? Had he found it? But like crabs left overnight in a bucket, soon only the biggest, ugliest, nastiest remained. What was he to do?

He hung his head, feeling now how illusory his elation had been. It wasn't just the Rzhevskys; someone was looking for him. In his room.

What to do? Run away? They hadn't put the prison camps in Magadan and Kolyma because of their handy access to bus routes. Duvakin could barely make it down the street in this season, let alone go gambol with the reindeer. Get help? From whom? Darmoved, the head of the KGB, was mixed up in this mess, and besides, one of the victims here was a devil of a lot higher up the tree than any Duvakin; a personal friend almost to Brezhnev. Fight back? Where, against whom, and with what?

He looked about his room, rubbing his neck. What mere moments ago had seemed familiar and comforting now felt vaguely sinister. You make a clear case for action, comrade Duvakin, he thought derisively. In other words, the only thing he could do was continue about his business as quietly as possible, hoping for the best. Such as that whoever had come to his room had already found whatever he wanted. Party business, maybe, he hoped artificially. His doubting mind, though, presented that ignored glimpse of the typist waving across the street.

Duvakin looked sadly at his other shirt, the one into which he had meant to change; somehow the prospect of going out seemed daunting now.

"Ivan Palych? Are you all right?" Pavlovna touched his arm gently. "You seem . . . Was it important? I'd have tried to keep him if you'd said anything."

Duvakin squared his shoulders, smiled weakly. "No, thank you. I'm fine; it was nothing . . . He'll find me again, I expect." Duvakin wondered bleakly how true his words might prove.

"Well, then . . ." Pavlovna said, uncertain of what to do. Then, decisively, she patted Duvakin once more and said, "I hope so, he seemed a nice type." And with that she left.

Again Duvakin studied the room, noticing now how objects seemed out of place. No doubt; someone had been through the room. But who, and why? The KGB? That made no sense, since they knew about Duvakin and where to reach him. The militia? Maybe they had heard about his trip out to Rzhevskaya's?

Duvakin breathed deeply, trying to rid himself of that sense of entanglement, of powerlessness, which had plagued him ever since his meddling foot had caught him up in this. A tiny act, to get him into this much soup.

Outside, the night was coming early beneath heavy clouds while Duvakin continued to sit, puzzled and tense, in the darkening room.

When the phone rang, Duvakin thought his heart would stop; his mouth went immediately dry. Another ring, metallic, as if rasping at his bones. The ring came again; only then did Duvakin fumble for a lamp. As he pushed the switch on the throat of the lamp, he noticed his hand tremble. Once more the telephone, the color and size of an old-fashioned typewriter, demanded him. Finally, resolutely, Duvakin lifted the receiver.

"Hello?" he squeaked. He cleared his throat and tried again. "Hello?"

There was silence.

"Hello?" Duvakin yelled, his nerves raw. "Hello?"

"Don't hang up . . ." a tiny voice whispered, all but inaudible.

"What?"

"Please . . . don't hang up . . . I—"

"You've got the wrong number." Duvakin's intonation was neither question nor statement. The voice was puzzling, small, like a woman's, but younger. A child?

"You came to our flat? You took Mama to the airport?"

Duvakin's jaw went slack. "Mama?"

Then he remembered, but could not think of the

name Rzhevskaya had called the slender, dark-haired girl who had brought him tea. "You're . . . ?"

"Dusya."

"That's right, Dusya," Duvakin repeated stupidly. His first questions, what she had phoned him for, what she wanted, were slowly replaced by another. How had she gotten his number?

"I don't . . . look, I don't mean to bother you, I don't know you, even."

"That's all right," Duvakin muttered mechanically, acutely aware now of the worry in the girl's voice. How old was she? Ten, eleven? He concentrated, trying to recall more about her, but could only think of how very young she was.

"Do you know where Mama is?" she blurted.

The receiver slipped slightly in Duvakin's suddenly sweaty palm. "Where she is?" he stammered. "They didn't . . ." They didn't tell you, he had begun to ask, but stopped himself. Of course no one had told her; simple air crashes are state secrets, of which nothing is said (unless, of course, there is a need, like foreigners on board or the plane belly flops on, say, Paris); even more so an explosion. And certainly no one would tell a little girl such things.

She was still talking. ". . . she was supposed to phone only she never did, and when I phoned they were surprised and thought she'd changed her mind, but I . . ."

"Is your grandmother there?" Duvakin broke in. "Is she there with you now?"

"Grandma?" Dusya was surprised. "She's gone to bed. That's the only reason I can telephone; she doesn't like me to go near it even."

"Where is she? She's staying there; she's around?"

"In the next room. Mama wouldn't leave me alone!" Indignance flared briefly, but then she sounded puzzled, almost plaintive. "Look, you told Mama you came to help,

[109]

like you knew something about Daddy . . . Do you know where Mama is?"

Duvakin stood dumb, unable to make himself tell this girl who already thought herself half an orphan that this week had made her fully alone.

"Do you?"

Duvakin wondered wildly what to do. Lie? When she'd have to find out soon enough anyway? But he couldn't just tell a little girl he didn't know that her mother was dead. Blown to bits. "Well . . ." he began feebly.

"So she is dead," the girl said flatly.

"How did you know?" Duvakin was startled, and a little ashamed of his relief that he had only to confirm, not inform.

"I guessed." The girl sounded curiously emotionless, just tired. "When the man came around this morning—"

"Man?"

"Some man, said he was a colleague of Daddy's . . ." There was not a sniffle, not even a sob.

"He told you your mother . . . about your mother?"

She made a dismissive noise. "He told Grandma he was from the ministry and kept asking about us, who our friends were, who would be looking out for us . . . 'in view of . . .'" Duvakin heard her imitation of the visitor catch in her throat, become a sob. "Anyway, then he went on about the schools he was going to get me into and . . . those sorts of things." Her voice grew softer and softer.

"You knew then?" Duvakin urged gently.

"Mama would never send me to any school," the girl said flatly. "She was going to get whoever had killed Daddy, and then we were going to . . . move . . ." Here, the last of her child's strength ran out, and she erupted in tears.

"Look, listen . . . you need . . . can I help?" Duvakin asked urgently. "Can I do something?" he asked louder, before realizing that the phone was dead. She had hung up.

Duvakin stared at the receiver in his hand, impotent. He couldn't even call her back. He didn't have her number. And he couldn't go out there; he had spent his last rubles on her mother's taxi two days ago. There wasn't even anyone to borrow from. Pavlovna, who scraped by on a pittance of disability and what kopeks she got from returning scrounged bottles? Galya?

The grandmother *was* there, he reassured himself hollowly. What harm could the girl come to? And it wasn't as if Duvakin could bring her mother back to life.

Suddenly angry, Duvakin flung the receiver at the phone, where it bounced, then lay squealing in protest. The Lord blight this whole business!

After a pause Duvakin replaced the receiver and sat heavily in his armchair, staring sourly at his feet. Logically, he made little of why all this had happened, but a strong conviction of responsibility for all this death sat heavily, irrationally, on his chest. He had put his foot into this, and like some machine too finely tuned by fate, events had exploded in his face. Part of him longed desperately to go to Galya, to return to the comforting pleasures of the night before, but Duvakin would not allow himself even to consider it.

He would not risk involving Galya. Better she should be mad at him for not showing up again, than curse him for having been born, for having touched her life.

And Dusya? Duvakin recalled his own distress when his own mother died—peacefully, after grippe—and how that emptiness had throbbed at him for years. And he had been a young man then. Not a child.

He gnawed at his thumb. Tomorrow at the office, maybe he could check somehow through Party channels to make sure somebody was looking out for the girl. That ministry man, for example.

Which recalled his earlier fright, *his* mysterious visitor. All the more reason to stay away from Galya, then, Duvakin muttered to himself. He had no friends.

Feeling alone and cursed, Duvakin gradually sank into a shallow, unpleasant sleep, jabbed by the firm lumps of his chair.

He woke stiff and hungry, his neck almost paralyzed. He stretched, still angry, but feeling a little of the satisfaction of mortified flesh.

In fact, he lectured himself sternly in the cracked mirror above his bureau, its time you started to put some things right again. The old toilet woman had a just question; what business *was* it of his that she was stealing a few state furs? Who was he to question all this, especially if the consequences were so great?

So, he told the baggy-eyed, blotchily shaven wretch in the unsilvering glass, first order of things is make sure that little girl gets proper notification and all the formalities are done right, and check that grandmother is able to take care of her. Second on the list, get away from Galya; get away from where you don't belong. Back in your allotted slot.

He had himself almost convinced that this course would put right all the catastrophes of the week—almost, because a high chill cloud still shadowed his heart. The mysterious friend. And another, maybe even more nagging. How had that little girl come to have his number?

As he trudged down the creaking stairs to the street, Duvakin recalled a stray fact he had read somewhere, about how primitive peoples have two names, a public one and a real, very private, and secret one; to know someone's secret name was to have great power over him. The anxious catch at the back of his throat was like that. Duvakin felt he had lost control of his actions, his influence on events. His life.

Out there, somewhere, someone *did* have that power.

He shivered in the raw wet wind which slapped down Treefellers Prospekt.

The bus stop was crowded with sullen workers unprepared for the tedious day ahead. They muttered and bumped one another nastily, but to Duvakin the crowd was almost soothing. Life went on; it wasn't all his troubles.

Even more distracting was his ride, demanding close attention; once he finally jammed himself onto a groaning No. 7 headed into town, the closing doors shut on his arm. He had an elbow in his ear, and his nose, alarmingly, rested almost on the bosom of an impassive Chukchi woman, who smelled of animal fat and wood smoke. There was a terrible din of voices while some fool tried to collect fares from the other passengers because he had paid with a paper ruble; the only way then to get change was patiently to collect from the next twenty-four people to get on. Duvakin felt himself dissolve almost happily in the enveloping mass of flesh lurching with the bus.

Downtown was not much better. Magadan was not large, but at five minutes to eight most of it was somewhere on Lenin Square. Huge Kamas, ancient Aurochs, an occasional Zhiguli, tractors, even here and there a rubber-tired horse cart belched past in clouds of dove-gray smoke. The sidewalks were a mass of squirrel fur hats the same color as the exhaust, here and there dotted by women's hats of damp mohair in the colors of various bodily organs and fluids.

Duvakin skirted the square, almost a hectare of empty asphalt, piled about with old snow. He came to an obedient halt with a crowd waiting to cross. The traffic was thick, whipping past scant centimeters away.

Across from him was Party headquarters, reminding him of work. After checking a bit on Dusya, he better have someone look to the moorings on top, for the banners. The banners they put down the side on the holidays were heavy, and the iron hooks on top rusted out most winters. There'd be the devil to pay if one of the banners were to fall. Duvakin shielded his eyes and studied the top of the building.

In almost a continuous motion he found himself stumbling forward, lurching into the hurtling stream of traffic. Instantaneously, he heard brakes, shouts, his own strangled yell, and felt blazing pain erupt through his body.

Weightless, flying, he knew he had been pushed, and then he blacked out.

★ EIGHT ★

For one scrambled moment, Duvakin thought he was still flying, tumbling end over end through indefinite space; convulsively, he grabbed, hoping madly to hook something firm. For a second he did; then his hand was slapped, hard.

"Here! Stop that!" a female voice barked sternly.

Duvakin opened his eyes to find someone centimeters from his face, breathing onion and boiled fish into his nostrils. He slammed his eyes shut again, hoping that these watery blue and bloodshot eyes were some sort of delirium.

There was the sound of a curtain pulled along a rod, then a familiar voice said harshly, "You! What are you doing in here?"

"Looking for the bedpan, Galina Maximovna, I meant no harm," the unknown woman said hurriedly, as if bobbing up and down and scuttling out at the same time. There was the rustle of curtain, then the scrape of metal rings along a pole.

"And don't come in again unless you're called for!" the familiar voice shouted. Galya, Duvakin thought firmly.

At the same instant there was a plump warm hand placed on his leg, rather high above the knee. Again he opened his eyes in surprise.

"So?" Galya smiled broadly, patting him, but leaving her hand where it was. "You're awake?"

"What time is it?" Duvakin croaked, trying to sit up. As soon as he tensed his muscles, he discovered they had been replaced by strands of barbed wire and shards of hot glass; he let his head sink groaning back.

"Hurt?" Galya asked with interest, placing a soothing hand on his shoulder. "It will, Vanya. You should see the bruise you got on your belly; it looks like you've turned about half Turkoman. It'll hurt like the very devil, Vanya, but thank heaven for that . . ."

Once noticed, the pain became the center of his existence, as if his heart now pumped pain, not blood. He throbbed, vibrating like some colossal bell.

"What?" he scratched out, aware that he had missed something. He stared straight up at a chipped examining light of yellow enamel.

"I said you're lucky, Vanya." Galya raised her voice, as if perhaps he had been deafened. Had he been? Duvakin wondered.

"Lucky?"

"You think stumbling in front of an auto is a rest cure? The militia man who brought you in said he'd never seen the like of it." Galya had moved, so that now her face was directly over his. He saw the lines at her eyes, the chill questioning look behind her bright encouraging smile. "It was a miracle he said, like somebody was looking out for you. You landed just so on the hood of the auto, a Zhiguli, fortunately, because you slipped up the windscreen and into the air. Didn't even break the glass, Vanya!" Galya spoke with awe.

And me, did I break me? Duvakin wondered, trying fruitlessly to *sense* bones, without the need to move them. There were no gypsums anyway, he thought.

"Then, phumph, like a bird, down you come in a snowpile, without so much as messing up your hair," Galya said teasingly, running a gentle finger over Duvakin's bald spot. "And now look at you, wide awake and grabbing at nurses." She gave him a playful slap on the head; amplified by his pain, it echoed back and forth the length of his body, making thought difficult. Cautiously, he turned his head to one side, opened his eyes. He was in a cubicle of some sort, curtained off by rough plywood and a dirty canvas, with another bed, empty, across from him.

"I'm in the hospital?" he managed to ask.

Galya started slightly, as if she had been thinking.

"Hospital? No, this is the clinic." She bit her lip, one tooth glimmering bright gold against the red of her pomade. "The hospital was out of the question," she added softly.

Duvakin was coming back into himself sufficiently to wonder at Galya's tension. Since when was the hospital "out of the question" for a traffic victim? A suspicion of the answer crossed his mind.

"A Zhiguli, you say? Who'd I hit?" He raised his head slightly, ignoring the blistering knots of his stomach muscles.

"It's all right, Vanya," Galya said briskly, patting his hand. "Don't worry, there won't be any trouble . . ."

"Who did I hit?" Duvakin's voice was louder, more urgent. He sat up further, wondering whether there would be guards. He made it to his elbows; the cubicle looked solely theirs. No militia.

"Nobody very special, manager of the worker's cafeteria down at the glass factory, nobody to worry about . . ." Galya said comfortingly. "Really, don't worry about

[117]

it, Vanya. The man that brought you in said there's no charges; the manager had a half beef in the back, so he just wanted to get out of there. Didn't want people looking in . . ." She chuckled, then added more soberly, "Of course, that's why you couldn't go to the hospital."

Duvakin stared at her, then down at his own legs and torso. Although it seemed to him that his mind was functioning fully again, he nevertheless studied his legs as if they belonged to someone else, entirely unfamiliar. Knowing that save for chance those legs belonged to a dead man made him feel disembodied. He thought tentatively of wiggling his toes and was surprised a bit to see the toes respond as ordered; the movement, though, hurt like the devil.

Duvakin sank back again, feeling vague and unconnected. He wondered what time it was, what day. It was tempting to hope for a moment that all of this was delirium.

"So anyway," Galya continued after a short silence filled with the hum of the overhead lights, "I paid your fine."

"My fine?" Duvakin looked up in surprise, staring her full in the face.

"Public drunkenness, ten rubles."

"I wasn't drunk!" Duvakin protested, angry.

"Of course you weren't." Galya patted his hand, then held it. "Of course you weren't."

"You don't believe me?" he examined her closely.

She shrugged. "It's not the usual way to spend your morning, is it?" she asked lightly, but unsmiling.

"What isn't?"

"Flying about . . ."

"You can go to hell! I was as sober as an owl, you hear me!" In some cooler part of his brain Duvakin knew that this was an absurd point on which to fasten, but honor demanded it. After the horrors of this week, he thought, I've got to be taken for a drunk as well?

"It's all right, Vanya, it's probably what saved you, kept you loose. You know they say God takes care of drunks." Galya smiled reassuringly.

Duvakin grabbed her wrist and squeezed, hard. *"I was pushed! You hear me? I was pushed!"* he shouted, the effort turning his belly into a quivering gelatin of pain. He groaned, closed his eyes.

When he opened them again, he realized his hand still gripped Galya's wrist, that she still stood, though not smiling now at all. "I'm sorry . . ." he mumbled, releasing her.

"It's nothing," she murmured, after a silence. "Listen . . . can you walk, you think? I mean, there's nothing broken."

"Walk? Why?" He thought of his still distant legs.

"This isn't my ward. I'm supposed to be up in children's yet; I just ran down when they told me you were being carried in." Galya looked confused, vulnerable. "I was frightened for you," she said quietly, then, more loudly, "besides, you can't stay in here. This is just for emergencies."

As Duvakin listened, it dawned upon him she had violated clinic rules to come to his side and that, more surprisingly, he was glad of that.

He thought again of the unexpected evening, the tea-cups, the chat, the enclosing and embracing comfort of the large fringed lampshade, the surprising pleasure of sharing her pillow. It was confusing; he had only known one woman well enough to love her, and she could not have resembled Galya less. Galya was solid, plump, loud, direct . . .

And, Duvakin realized within himself, her face had been a welcome one to regain consciousness to.

[119]

"I guess I can walk," he muttered; then with great deliberation, he swung one leg, paused, then the second over the edge of the plywood examining table. The floor shocked the soles of his feet; it felt too near. He waited a second; then, with concentration, he pulled himself erect. "Ready," he smiled brightly, trying to pretend he wasn't faint.

Galya laughed from somewhere in her belly. "Come along then, grandpa." She took his arm in a firm way that told him he could lean. After a proud step or two, he was glad to sag heavily onto the spongy warmth of her arm and breast.

They hobbled heavily into the corridor, pausing frequently to let Duvakin clear his head. He eyed a clock, vaguely registering that it was still early morning, nowhere near lunch. Distantly, he wondered about work, Sutrapian, and decided the devil could have them. He would concentrate on tottering down the hall.

At the entrance, Galya assumed a professional face and demanded his file, which she was given by a carefully blank-faced nurse. Duvakin could guess that he was being laughed at, but did not care; having given himself up to Galya's care he became more childlike, waiting patiently to be diverted. Besides, his body throbbed great bludges of pain.

"Very well citizen, all discharged," Galya announced in a voice obviously meant for the receptionists. There were faint snickers from behind the wall of folders. Galya mottled a bit along the throat and jaw, but continued bravely, "I'll just give you a hand with the stairs." There were open guffaws from somewhere.

Duvakin looked wonderingly at Galya as she, almost purple with anger or embarrassment, took his arm and led him firmly to the stairs. "Cretins," he heard her mutter. He tried to pat her hand comfortingly, but with little result.

Once outside, Galya returned to her normal color, though breathing heavily. "Come on, I'll run you home," she said lightly, though artificially. "I can't stay; they'll be wanting me upstairs, but you can get some rest anyway."

"Work?" Duvakin croaked, feeling still disoriented and feeble. At Galya's wave, he sat slowly, with great pain, in the front seat of her car.

"Your work? I phoned," she said quickly, as if he might be angry. "As a doctor, understand?" Her face looked both stern and hopeful, Duvakin thought, as he lay back into the seat, closing his eyes. They shot open again.

The thought of going home was like a cold towel on a sleeper's back. All his worry, his anger, of the night before returned, magnified by the certainty that someone had tried to kill him. Something was nightmarishly out of joint, and Duvakin was frightened, like a man lost in a cave. He wanted to run, but could not; no matter which direction he might choose, who knew what abysses· might lay in front?

Yet the thought of his own flat, of waiting alone there with a battered, all but immobile body until his "friend" might come back was devastating. But how could he get Galya caught up in this? He took a deep breath.

"You know where my flat is?"

She looked over from applying fresh color to her lips. "Not your apartment, Vanya . . . Doctor's orders, you're going to rest in my place." She giggled girlishly, a little theatrically. Then, more seriously, "If you want to, that is . . ."

Duvakin sat back in his seat, unable to think what to do. His mind spun uselessly, unable to digest the jumble of events leading from a toilet woman's sack to an attempt on his life. Almost breathless with indecision, he finally nodded faintly.

The fact of Galya's newly pomaded lips gnawed particularly at Duvakin's conscience as they drove. She was intent on the road, and they sat in silence, until Galya began, ever so faintly, to hum.

Damn it! Duvakin thought, rubbing his thumb and forefinger together. He was exhausted and entangled. The torments of his belly were unlike anything he could remember, and he took no pleasure even in having survived. It was no victory, merely a stay. Whatever, whoever was after him was still there. Waiting.

He fished out a cigarette; the first, he realized, since last night. He coughed harshly, twisting the tender muscles of his stomach into brief agony. The smoke, however, helped, giving him a faint buzzing sensation just beneath his temples. What was happening? Three or four days ago he was heedlessly going about the routine he assumed he would follow until he switched to dominoes and a pension. And now, with no warning, here he sat—hiding out from someone unknown, someone who was trying to kill him for what reason Duvakin had not the faintest idea, any more than he knew why Rzhevsky had died, or Rzhevskaya. He shook his head tenderly, with a lapping of nausea in his ears.

"You seem distracted. You're not hurting?" Galya asked, putting a gloved hand on his knee.

"Me? No—no . . . well, not much." Duvakin squared his shoulders bravely, hopefully, smiling as warmly as he could.

Face on, it came to this. Someone was trying to kill him, because of something he had done, or even something he was. It made no sense, but there it was. So he could find out what it was he had done, why he was wanted dead. Or he could oblige them, die, or disappear.

Disappearing was tempting, almost overpowering. He *had* the perfect hideout now. Galya, the doctor. Even if the woman were garrulous about her conquests, the news

[122]

would not have traveled far. The perfect bolt-hole, a random connection only just initiated. Even in a city as small as Magadan, Duvakin could stay hidden for days if he suddenly were to break his old routine.

But what if he were discovered? What consequences would this have for Galya? Not that Duvakin could be in love with her yet, he reminded himself sternly, not so soon. But he remembered too clearly the threats against Tanya, the way her apartment had been searched, her daughter's piteous retching in the toilet. They hadn't asked for any of that; it had come only because of Duvakin's touch. How could he do the same again, to another woman who had treated him decently? He shuddered with momentary self-loathing. I'm a leper, that's what, he thought.

And what's Dusya then? he thought sternly. She didn't ask to become an orphan either. She hadn't been able to hide.

"What?" he said, emerging from his reverie; he realized they had stopped in front of Galya's building.

"You said you were pushed," Galya repeated a little testily. "Is that true?"

Duvakin studied the scruffy pigeons huddling against the remaining bosom of a cracked Triumph of Agriculture on the rooftop, unable to decide what to say. Nothing? Everything? And what *was* everything? Finally he nodded, once.

"By?"

He shrugged, still studying the pigeons, acutely aware of Galya's examining eyes. He thought he heard tears, and turned. Now Duvakin's conscience grew large and raw, like a blister under new shoes. The coarse, direct mannerisms of the doctor who had taken her pleasures of men like a man had disappeared like so much scaffolding, revealing beneath a woman with large translucent tears furrowing a powdered cheek, plump fingers anxiously toying with the key chain. No scant nightshirt this time. Respectability, even domesticity, enveloped her like a bridal gown. Awkwardly, he reached across and patted her knee.

"It's all right. It's nothing illegal," he said, hoping he was correct. "Just complicated . . ."

"You're what you say you are?" she asked tensely. "Party? Of Moscow?"

"As you see," Duvakin said softly, spreading his hands wide and lowering his head. The woman's agitation distressed him, further rasping his uneasiness at being forced to threaten her life with his.

In silence she rubbed her gloved thumb along the curve of the steering wheel. Then, "You didn't come last night . . ."

"No." Duvakin looked at his knee. Then, conscious of her shallow breathing, he added, "I was . . . I didn't want to . . . I mean I thought you wouldn't want . . ." He shrugged.

"Well," the doctor said after a pause, "so, have you eaten?"

"Eaten? No," Duvakin suddenly realized. "Not since yesterday," he added half to himself, acutely aware now that he wanted desperately to eat. "But," he remembered, "I should get it . . . but I'm a bit . . ." He blushed.

"Some cavalier!" Galya laughed, her powdered cheeks growing redder, more lively. "Come along, Prince Bountiful, we'll hunt up an egg or two." She got out of the car.

"The clinic?" Duvakin shouted after her, then repeated it when he had stumbled painfully from the car. "You said you had to get back to the clinic."

"They'll wait," she said airily, taking possession of Duvakin's arm.

He let himself be led; well, you can't go to battle with a mysterious visitor if you don't eat, he told himself defensively. He was, he realized, looking forward to Galya's apartment. Things will come right, he tried to assure himself. They'll have to.

The flat was as warm, as desired as he remembered; Duvakin felt uncomfortably like a snake in Galya's nest. The confusion, the fear, the nausea of the past days flitted about in him, leaving him trembling in the hallway.

"You look exhausted, poor Vanya," Galya said, her eyes bright. "You'll want to lie down?" She emphasized her sentence with her eyebrows, indicating the neighboring room.

"If I may . . ." Duvakin said, then added hastily, "but not in that way! To sleep! I mean . . . I'm not . . ."

She laughed, charmed, it seemed, even by his failings.

"It's all right, Vanya. Today is just for sleep." She chuckled again, then began to hum deep in her throat as she cleared up the table in the tiny kitchen.

Another day, in other circumstances, Duvakin might have been touched by this domesticity. Like him, Galya seemed hungry for the small felicities which Magadan so utterly lacked. Today, though, each loving pat of her plump hand, each stir of the egg and bologna glop, each quizzical gaze at his silence, his gruffness, seemed to Duvakin another accusation of his treachery.

All right then, breakfast, a rest maybe, and then he'd go. Where he had no idea. But he'd go. Out to Dusya? But then he'd have to borrow the money from Galya.

"You want any help with your things?" Galya asked breezily as she brought the steaming mass of eggs to the table. "Here, come sit. I'll get you bread. Come! It's real coffee, Vanya, don't let it get cold!"

Duvakin stumbled toward the table, put a hand on

the chair, then asked, "My things?" He sat slowly, folding his battered stomach muscles gently, to keep the pain to a dull agony. The eggs looked delicious, distracting.

"You don't think I have things for you here, do you?" Galya asked a little coolly from the stove.

"What are you talking about?" Duvakin finally asked, his mouth moist from staring at his plate. An inarticulate suspicion kept him from putting any eggs in his mouth.

She turned around, put her hands on the sink. Duvakin realized how nearly cubical she was, a squat, powerful and quite evidently female figure. "Your shaving things, shirts—your *things*."

Duvakin's heart felt tight. He slowly pushed the plate away. "Why would I need those things?" he asked, trying still to sound stupid.

"Oh Vanya. You're not going back to your apartment, you can't." She stepped forward, seeming torn between gruff sternness and pleading despair. "Not after . . . you're sick."

"You mean move *here*?" Duvakin asked, dumbfounded to find what he suspected true.

"You liked it well enough the other night," Galya said now very coldly, defensive.

Duvakin looked at his plate and knew it was the truth. "But it's only been . . . I only just met you."

Galya laughed. "Did you hear me say anything about the civil registry? Look, you're in trouble, do I understand correctly?"

Duvakin studied her businesslike face, her brisk tone, then nodded. He could think of no reason why she was offering him help.

"So? Who knows about us? You stay here, maybe things will sort themselves out." She smiled again. "Come on, eat those eggs. You think you find them under every bush? Those eggs were a trick to come by, let me assure you of that!"

Duvakin slowly took a forkful, then another. His stomach wrapped warm arms around the food, a mother embracing the returning son. He took a few more quick bites, then felt guilty again.

"But why? It's nothing to do with you . . . and could be trouble." He spoke hesitantly, not certain whether he wanted to win or lose the argument.

Galya looked at her watch, then smiled. "I like you. I told you that . . . you were kind . . ." She trailed off. Then, more briskly, "The eggs? They're good?"

Duvakin nodded, chewing slowly, bovine as he thought. What was Galya's angle? He watched her out of the corner of his eye, wondering whether she might be involved, might be one of the faceless menaces who were trying to do him in.

Don't be absurd, he thought sternly. If that were the case, it would have been easy to kill him the other night, or today, while he was unconscious. What then? Man-hunger, marriage fever? Duvakin remembered growing up, when there had been so many girls, so few boys. Bliss for the others, the lucky ones who seemed to have an endless stream of women. Somehow, though, even in a world that war had left with three women for every two men, even then Duvakin had usually been the one with no woman, while the other guy had all three.

Even more so in Magadan now, where it was the other way about; women were in short supply here, not men. Or Russian women, anyway.

What was her reason for sheltering him?

"So, little soul, you like them?" Galya asked, pleased. "Pity it's margarine I had to cook them in, and not butter! My mother, she'd cry her eyes out that she'd lived to see her daughter do that. You want a little vodka with them, maybe?"

Duvakin looked up, startled. "Little soul?" Even his mother hadn't called him that. Another reason for Galya's behavior, least explicable or believable of all, suddenly coalesced in his mind. That she really did like him. He thought of the clinic, but did not mention it, then looked around the kitchen. It was warm here, safe. And outside? Cafeterias, bologna breakfasts in his room. And someone who wanted to kill him.

"Some vodka would be very nice." He smiled weakly, not quite meeting Galya's eye; she could not have noticed, so quickly did she bolt from the kitchen. Duvakin watched the door, trying to fathom this frenzy of domestic bliss, without success. He felt somehow at fault, insufficiently enthusiastic.

He knew, though, he would certainly have to come back tonight. So he smiled more warmly when Galya emerged with her "little vodka," a faceted glass decanter filled with a vodka blushing the faintest rose. "Cherry pits? Galya, where ever? . . ."

She smiled broadly, basking in domestic triumph. "You probably have cherry vodka all the time, but I do like it with eggs."

"You shouldn't have," Duvakin murmured, but he felt his mouth water greedily as she filled his little glass, faceted like the decanter. Galya poured herself a businesslike dollop too and raised her glass.

"Your health!" he said mechanically, touching her glass.

"The future!" she answered brightly.

Duvakin coughed, choking on the slightly cyanic taste of the flavored vodka.

Somehow it continued all morning—the world of office, clinic, Dusya, and killer pushed farther and farther away. Galya was like a new bride, proud of her apartment, her skill in providing, her womanliness. She fed and watered Duvakin, pulling delicacy after delicacy from the secret places of her kitchen: apples, turnips, home-dried mushrooms, tinned fish. Slowly, Duvakin felt himself transformed into a drowsy column of food stretching from the little handmade cushion on his chair to the very back of his tongue. He felt stupefied, a shoat being fattened for some holiday. It was pleasant to talk, to be fussed over, to forget for a time the horror of the past few days—and yet, it was confusing, too. Each touch of Galya's hand, each cheerful look, each new dish seemed in some way another loop in a tangled skein.

At last, when his bursting head and stomach could take no more, he pushed back his chair, and said decisively, enunciating precisely, "Enough . . . I'd best go." He looked first at his hands, then at her; her face looked suddenly bare, attentive. She was not young; she was not pretty. Duvakin noticed how wide her eyes had grown, then looked at his own hands again. And you're so young? he thought, examining his hairy knuckles and scaling calluses. When he looked up again, her chin was trembling ever so faintly, almost invisibly, like the heart of some tiny bird. "To get my things," he added quickly. Then, after a pause, "That is, if I may? Come back, I mean to say," he mumbled.

The only answer was a quick, glassy film of tears that flowed smoothly over the doctor's eyes, to pool, tremble, and drop, a tear from each, onto her powdered cheeks. She lowered her head, nodded jerkily.

Confused, Duvakin stood up heavily. "My coat is in the hall?"

She nodded again, then asked, "What"—she cleared her throat—"what time?"

Duvakin was in the hall, shrugging on the coat. "What time what?" he asked, leaning back into the room.

"Will you be home? I mean here, what time?" She looked up, beaming again.

The question recalled the world outside, the things he had not yet done, the care he would have to take. He felt deflated, the dull throb of a headache just beginning.

"A couple of hours, I imagine . . . depending on the buses and what not." And whether or not I get killed, he thought with bitter humor. "There's not much to bring," he added, gratuitously, but feeling sorry for himself.

"I'll go back to the clinic then . . . smooth things over. I'll leave you the key, down in the post box?" She smiled wide, a trace formally.

"All right," Duvakin said, pulled on his coat, buttoned it, pulled on his hat and gloves. Then he stood for a second, uncertain. Galya studied her knee. Oh hell, Duvakin thought, might as well be hung for a goose as a gander. He walked stiffly over and planted an awkward kiss on the bristly hairs of her neck.

"Good-bye . . . see you later."

He walked out and shut the door quickly, not wishing to decide whether the sounds he heard were indeed sobbing.

The wind had picked up, Duvakin realized muzzily when he reached the street, really howling now from the northwest. The sky was dark with heavy clouds, and the air tasted of snow. So much for an early spring melt, Duvakin thought, and pulled his collar tighter. He ought to have been grateful, for the wind, the sense of weather drawing in, disguised him as well as any night. The few people about scurried through the streets with their heads down, their eyes grimly on their shoes.

He could not help recalling his first departure from Galya and the sharp bite of spring in the air then. Then it had seemed he was alive again, unfolding from the tight confines of some self-made shell, not only ready but even anxious to take on Magadan and anybody else.

Now he shuffled home like a dog with broken ribs, nervously watching over his shoulder for a danger he wouldn't recognize in a crowd of two.

Oh hell, Duvakin thought, hunching his shoulders. It was like some stupid game. He looked at the sparse lights f the city flickering on as the sky grew dark too early. A militia man standing idle by a wall newspaper was rhythmically flicking his black and white truncheon. Duvakin wondered whether the man would help him or push him f another attack came. He released his breath slowly, to conceal a sigh; it may be a game, he thought, but the stakes are real enough. There was nothing to be done. He would have to brave it through and just pray that his liaison with Galya was as secret as it seemed.

Traffic was light. About the only things on the road were lumbering buses and trolleys, sagging now beneath their sullen, sweaty load of workers on the way home. Duvakin paused at a crosswalk, well back from the road, then darted nervously across. He felt the wind push back at him; there must be a real storm coming, he thought absently.

The first flakes, he then realized, were already tumbling heavily down; he looked again at the crush of the trolleys, felt the heaviness of his belly, aching now from within and without, and decided to walk. Perhaps it would clear his head, help him watch for danger. He set out, glancing anxiously about himself. With the rhythm of walking, his belly gradually felt less painful.

The nearer to the water he got, the more crowded the streets got; the harbor was Magadan's heart, and even with a storm, begun now in earnest, the area was busy. Duvakin was nervous, but there was no alternative to his route. Fortunately, the men about him were as indifferent to his existence as they were to their own, so Duvakin was able to slip among them, head down and silent, cautiously eying each intersection. The anonymity was even seductive; Duvakin began to feel safe. Once past the gates to the wharf, though, things grew more sparse again, until by the Boulevard of Labor he was almost alone, a black dot plastered white on his windward side, struggling alone in the eddies and blasts of the wind. A few pensioners were out with their clumsy wooden shovels, trying to clear their appointed stretches of sidewalk, but the effort was vain. Once on Treefellers Prospekt, Duvakin had to chop his way through snow and muck almost knee-deep; quickly, he was winded and sweaty. The vodka gave him a pounding head, while all that damn food sat like a toad in his belly, making it even harder to flounder ahead. Here the road was impassable, totally empty of traffic. It looked as if Magadan, her spirit broken after winter had betrayed spring's early promise, had surrendered.

By the time he reached his building, Duvakin's head felt like it was a hard-boiled egg being peeled by the thick fingers of a clumsy drunk. He heaved himself into the clear space by the mud grates and mopped his brow. He looked back anxiously, but saw nothing behind him save a shifting curtain of wet snow. He caught his breath, dug a cigarette out of his moist and steamy coat; the cigarette was damp and pliable, would not stay lit.

Here, on home ground, the attractions of Galya's flat seemed even greater. Wondering, he studied the scarred and knobby stumps of lime trees that struggled dumbly before the apartment building. The problem was that so little made sense; how can you decide where to turn when you have no idea of what lies ahead? It was like one of those fairy tales, "this path leads to danger, this to trouble, and that to certain death."

He sucked hard on his cigarette, so hard he felt dizzy. The same questions chased themselves around in his head, leading him nowhere. The only fixed coordinates in this whole mess were a shit sack full of furs, two dead Rzhevskys, and a bruise on his stomach the size and shape of the Ukraine.

Fed up, he flicked his cigarette out into the snow and turned into the building. Say what you will, it gets your attention, he thought grimly, acutely conscious of his own powerlessness. What could he do, to help Dusya, Galya, even himself? His mind seemed to him as insubstantial and swirling as the snow outside.

He trudged heavily up the three flights to his room. The building was quiet, almost hushed. The snow outside probably, dampening sound and spirits. The usual noise and smells seemed absent somehow. Maybe no one was home from work yet, Duvakin thought, aware that the hairs on the back of his neck were rising. This is silly, he thought as he walked lightly down the dark hall to his room; there wouldn't be anyone waiting for me here.

Nevertheless, he realized he was tiptoeing.

He tried the knob of his door, softly turning the cold metal to make as little noise as he could. Holding his breath and biting his lip, he edged the handle slowly round, then pushed, gently.

The door held.

He pushed harder. It still held.

Duvakin slumped, surprised to hear his heart hammer with relief. He grinned at his own fears, dug out his key, and unlocked the door.

He looked quickly about through the door, saw that things seemed as he had left them, the room as empty. Detail was impossible in the murk of the storm, so Duvakin crossed stumbling to his bedside, where he fumbled around, found the cord, then followed it to the lamp.

The lamp lit.

He heard the door close, and he turned, his heart thumping.

Like a fragment of the blackest nightmare, he saw everything at once, the familiar room, the cozy light of the little lamp, and the lupine smile of the huge man who blocked the door.

And, like in nightmares, the craziest of crazy details made sense. He knew the man.

"You! Colonel—"

"Please, Vanya," the man held up a hand the size, it seemed, of a dinner plate, "General now ... General Polkovnikov. And tell me please, who's been walking on your face?"

* NINE *

Perhaps that is the function of nightmares, to make the senseless possible.

In so many dreams Duvakin had stood just thus, watching Polkovnikov, who always stood thus, tall as the door, broad, powerful, dangerous.

"General?" he said weakly.

Polkovnikov grinned wider, pleased with himself. "They called me worthy of it. Lieutenant General, to be absolutely precise, but . . ."

Duvakin's mind had emptied. He knew this was real, not a hallucination; Polkovnikov looked fleshier, his cheeks pulled downward, and his hair had gone grayish. He was well dressed, some sort of foreign-looking overcoat, dark, with a dark fur collar.

You've done all right, you son of a bitch, Duvakin thought vaguely, feeling suddenly that he must sit. He sank onto the daybed, keeping his eyes on Polkovnikov; from the bed the general seemed even more to loom above him.

The silence must have dragged on, for Polkovnikov's smile became forced, then disappeared, replaced by a look of irritation.

"So?" he finally demanded. "Four years you don't see an old friend, and 'you' is all you say? You're a *little* surprised, maybe?" The tone was, as Duvakin recalled it, half-bantering, with an undertone of seriousness.

Wide-eyed and vague, Duvakin considered the question, and realized that somehow, no, he wasn't surprised.

True, Polkovnikov and Moscow and that week of playing cheap spy four years ago, all that seemed connected, irretrievable, and immutable, so that it made as little sense to him to see Polkovnikov here as it would had, say, his mother (dead, what? thirty-some years) walked into the room.

But that week of playing at spy had taught him one thing—that life is stitched like a factory-made sweater; an accidental tug or a stray thread and suddenly, with no warning, you can end up with nothing more than a pile of dirty yarn. Four years ago that sort of thing had taken him from sleepy hotel security man to special KGB operative to state criminal and permanent exile. In a week.

And now, after four years of quiet, it looked like the sweater had come apart again—furs, Rzhevsky, the airplane, his apartment. The last time it had been Polkovnikov about whom everything centered; fine, he was here again.

"You're going to finish me off?" Duvakin asked feebly, his arms weak, as if he had grippe.

"What finish you off?" Polkovnikov looked genuinely puzzled. "Looks like this room would finish you off." He looked around with disdain.

The tone was real; Duvakin looked up, puzzled.

"Where've you been, Vanya? I've been waiting in this tip of a room . . ." Polkovnikov's nose wrinkled. "No decent place to sit, even." He looked back, and Duvakin remembered.

It was the eyes, those cold blue irises striated white that had always kept Duvakin powerless, unthinking.

As they had done just now. He felt anger returning, and with it strength. "Where've I been? You should know . ." he began, rising to his feet. You put me here, he thought bitterly.

In the nightmares it began like this. He would see the hated colonel, rise, and fling himself, flailing, at his tormentor. And discover that his limbs moved like he was on a peak-hour bus, slowly, against great weight. And each time, laughing, the Polkovnikov dream colonel sent him flying.

So now Duvakin just stood, tensing his muscles and measuring them against the colonel. General, he reminded himself.

Polkovnikov smiled, wagged a warning finger, as if to a child. "Come on, Vanya!" he said. "This isn't like you! A comrade from Moscow! May I sit, anyway?"

Duvakin mechanically indicated his armchair, the stuffing falling out. Springs and filthy wadding looked back pathetically.

Polkovnikov laughed. "I'm up all night, Vanya, it'll have to do. It's what, four in the morning?" He looked jokingly at his watch, a flash of gold.

Inexplicably, even more vividly than Rzhevskaya's flight, the fact that Polkovnikov's watch still ticked off Moscow hours, not Magadan ones, made Moscow palpable, real. Unbidden, Duvakin remembered Pushechnaya Street, the shops bright with colored paper and the shoppers in their leather coats; Gorky Street and its snarling streams of autos; above the city, looming, gilt, the university; and over there, off to the right beyond Kiev Station, Matveevo, where Tanya lived. Or used to, anyway.

For a second, Duvákin felt the full burden of the days past, as if the universe had without warning been translated into some foreign language, where even the gestures are different, making him want not even death, but never to have been.

And in that vertiginous moment, he felt something, a sly opposition, stir within him. Polkovnikov, a general now, and all the way here, from Moscow? Something big was afoot then. A second later it dawned that if Polkovnikov were not after Duvakin, then by heaven, the best friend Duvakin could have at the moment was Polkovnikov.

"Sorry . . ." he said, shaking his head, then stepping forward. "It's a shock . . . so much time . . ." He ineffectually held out his hand, which the general took in his massive glove.

"That's better, you son of a bitch," Polkovnikov beamed, almost as though he had quite forgotten how little reason Duvakin had to be glad of him. He was the traveler, to be greeted by people who knew him.

"You seem happy to be here," Duvakin said neutrally, not certain of how to proceed.

"Do I? The travel, I expect." The huge man deftly moved cups and a tin from a small footstool. "Or maybe it's just the being out again. In the field, so to speak. You know how long it's been?" Polkovnikov cocked his head. "Anyway, look," he said more solemnly, sitting carefully on the stool. "We have to talk."

"About what? Old times?" Duvakin tried to sound neutral, but there must have been an edge in his voice. It was like sometimes in summer when high thin clouds pass before the sun, not occluding it visibly, but making the light seem suddenly remote, chill, and inhospitable; something very like that dimmed Polkovnikov's eyes for a second. Then he laughed.

"I'd forgotten . . . Vanya the wolf whelp."

Duvakin knew that little was served in angering Polkovnikov, for not only could the man squash him like a puffball in the forest, but Duvakin even needed his protection. But, God, how tempting after so long to strike back, even if feebly. To cover his confusion, Duvakin sat back down on the bed, taking comfort from the smooth solid feeling of the wall at his back.

"Vanya," Polkovnikov said, extending a slim cigarette case covered in some sort of black scaly leather, "we can do this two ways. You can concentrate on the petty unpleasantries of the past—"

"Petty unpleasantries!" Duvakin looked up sharply. "My God, man!"

"Please . . ." Polkovnikov held up a hand. His voice was stern. "You are going to tell me Magadan, exile, reindeer, and so on. Correct? And I would ask you, you're cold? You sleep maybe on the street? And hungry? You've wasted away?" Polkovnikov emphasized by patting his own stomach, which seemed fuller than Duvakin remembered. Duvakin stared still at the general, then shrugged. He felt no desire to argue. Polkovnikov took the gesture as agreement. "All right, then, it's still life, right? You've even done well, the Party, an apartment . . . though you might keep it cleaner, Vanya." Polkovnikov's tone grew lighter.

"And the second way?" Duvakin asked dryly, to spare himself more jokes about his room.

Polkovnikov smiled, extended the case again. "That's the spirit, Vanya! The truth of the matter is that we need your help, and I'm asking for it."

"We?"

"I'm with the same people," Polkovnikov said neutrally, at the same time glancing meaningfully at the walls. Duvakin stared too, struck for the first time that in four years of living there, it had never once occurred to him that the room might be bugged. He had not even cared; what more could they do, he had thought. He was learning the answer to that question, so he simply nodded.

"Anyway," Polkovnikov continued, "seems a sorry thing to greet an old friend dry. You look like you weren't expecting me." Polkovnikov guffawed, pleased by his own joke. "Come on, it's almost dinner, there must be a restaurant somewhere in this town. I'll even buy!"

Duvakin stood, feeling numb. The thought of more food was appalling, and his body ached, pounded with the hurt of the morning, his general sleeplessness.

He clung grimly to one thought, the knowledge that the only way out of this crazy mess, if a way out there was, lay in Polkovnikov and the power he represented. Polkovnikov he owed nothing, not even civility. But a general now, in the KGB, and all the way out here? The crazy events of the week seemed, not focused, but nearer it, part of something big and serious. Big enough, maybe, Duvakin groped dimly, to get me out of it, and Galya.

"It's snowing, though . . ." Duvakin remembered. "It was snowing hard."

Polkovnikov waved an indifferent hand. "The restaurants will be open." He took Duvakin's arm imperiously. "Come on, you lead the way." The touch recalled other times this man had touched him, and Duvakin flinched, covering it by shrugging. "All right."

He glanced around, remembering his original mission, to gather the necessities of moving in with Galya. Of that no mention, he decided suddenly. No point in letting Polkovnikov know there was a Galya.

Besides, a part of him thought darkly, who's to say you'll ever reach her house again?

They walked downstairs, out into the snow. The snow still fell, the wind still howled, but somehow Polkovnikov's imperious progress through the drifts suggested convincingly that the snow was for others, not them.

"Where are we going?" Duvakin asked finally, slanting into the wind.

"Up ahead . . . I've got a car," somehow Duvakin heard in the wind.

On the boulevard a cab stood against the curb, snow thick on the roof and hood. Duvakin watched wide-eyed as Polkovnikov strode over, began brushing off the top with his arm. "Lend a hand, Vanya, don't just stand gaping!" he said. Startled, Duvakin leaped forward.

A few seconds' work got them into the empty taxi. Polkovnikov drove. Duvakin's questions sat pebblelike on his tongue while the general started the car, put it in gear, and, rocking the car back and forth, managed to batter and slither his way out onto the road.

"Sorry," the general smiled at length. "Not used to driving; been a while. In Moscow they drive you everywhere. Wouldn't do to be seen driving yourself, people would talk. They'd think you were on your way down." Polkovnikov concentrated, peering through the windshield. Duvakin studied him from the corner of his eye, struck anew by the man's size; folding two meters of general into the front seat of a broken-down Volga was almost a circus act. Listen to you, he thought abstractly, listen to you, you self-serving son of a bitch. "They drive us around in Moscow"—and a general too! Every one of Polkovnikov's two hundred centimeters oozed success, position, power. And most of it nicked from my hide, Duvakin thought acidly. And now I'm supposed to cluck over it, ask him about success, let him puff himself up like some louse-ridden pigeon. Well, piss on your mother's grave, generalissimo.

They drove silently for a moment, then Duvakin restricted himself to asking neutrally, "You know Magadan?"

"Not really . . . but you never know, they might know me . . . and I'm not here yet."

"How's that?" Duvakin forced his tone to remain flat; he did not want to be used as a dupe.

"Inspection, don't you know, just like Gogol . . . coming out to the provinces to inspect the troops. I'll tell you at the restaurant. Damn!" He swerved sharply to avoid a trolley bus that swung out to pass a stalled bus. They missed by millimeters; the engine lugged, almost stalled, then Polkovnikov remembered to downshift. "Wouldn't do to have an accident. This car is *already* in the garage."

"It's not really a taxi?" Duvakin asked quietly, struck by the thought that in a provincial city a taxi made an excellent disguise.

"Of course it's a taxi. I got it from the dispatcher."

"You know him then? You *must* have been here before."

"Never saw him before. He recognized Uncle Lenin's picture well enough, though, when I showed him a couple of shiners."

Duvakin concentrated on the rutted road ahead, trying to betray no reaction to this Polkovnikov, breezy with love of his own cleverness. Deliberately, Duvakin took the part of the bribed mechanic; what poor devil wouldn't be bribed by a handful of purple pictures of Lenin, fifties? What, half a month's wages?

Polkovnikov claimed never to have been in Magadan before, but he drove, if not with familiarity, at least with knowledge. He seemed alert, watching for streets, counting corners. As Duvakin thought about it, he realized there was something else too, a vibration of excitement.

"There it is," Polkovnikov said half-aloud, then he began cautiously to negotiate the slushy, frozen ruts that led more or less toward some building barely visible in the shifting gray and white of the flakes. Duvakin too leaned forward, peering through the foggy windscreen; outside was as vague and wooly as he felt within.

"The Fairy Tale, Vanya, you know it? The best in

Magadan, they say," Polkovnikov said as he moved the taxi into a snow bank, then gunned the engine, to let the car lug, stall, and die. Then he switched off the key. "Must be near the curb, I guess."

"The Fairy Tale?" Duvakin asked, aware that there was such a restaurant; he had never been there. "Aren't you worried about being overheard?"

"You've got a better place?"

Duvakin shrugged, not looking at the general.

"Anyway," Polkovnikov continued, "they won't know who we are. And besides, I'm hungry. There's nothing to eat at your place—I looked!" He laughed again, then heaved himself out into the storm.

Even in the driving storm a knot of would-be diners huddled miserably at the door, tapping now and again on the glass. Polkovnikov pushed indifferently through, grabbed the door handle, and pulled.

An ancient doorman half rose, apparently as erect as a curved back would allow, and in a tremulous voice informed them there were no places. Wordlessly, Polkovnikov gave the man a twenty-ruble bill, and he detumesced, creaking into his seat, there to stare involuntarily at his own cracked shoes. They pushed in.

The restaurant was not large, twenty tables perhaps, set around a concrete island that once must have held plants. A man in a red coat appeared and barked angrily, "There are no places, comrades!"

In the back a party warbled drunkenly, at one or two tables. Nearer the front a man slept, head on the table, one arm in a plate, the other hung dead toward the floor. There were no other patrons, but plenty of plates. Mounds of dirty dishes slid into empty bottles, which toppled into heaped-full ashtrays, the whole even flowing onto the floor in some places.

"Clean one of these, then," Polkovnikov observed mildly, then chose a table, where he sat, back to the wall.

After a second he stood, removed his overcoat, laid it over a nearby chair, and sat again, at ease. Hesitating a moment, Duvakin did the same.

"Cultured people check their coats at the door," the waiter sniffed, gesturing vaguely at the empty cubicle by the door. Then, looking about, he finally spotted the pair of shoes extending, prone, from behind the counter. Apparently accepting the inevitable, the waiter sniffed again, said, "They will clear your table in a second," and shuffled into the kitchen.

"No uniform?" Duvakin couldn't stop himself from asking.

"Uniform?" Polkovnikov looked blank for a second, then smiled. "No, not any more . . . wouldn't do in my line." Polkovnikov smiled mysteriously. "Impressive, eh?" he indicated with a wave of his hand. Their table, like all the rest, had not been cleared maybe since the Flood. Duvakin picked at some fish on a plate before him; it was stuck fast, partly buried in cigarette ashes and butts.

"Ah, well . . . the storm, I expect," Polkovnikov said in a worldly way. "Be a good fellow, Duvakin . . . clear away these things, will you?"

Duvakin sat a minute, indecisive, then slowly stood and did as asked. It was always this way with Polkovnikov; there was no good reason not to cooperate, until suddenly you find yourself up to your ears in trouble. There was a clearing station and a half-full cart across the room, but independence reasserted itself. He chucked the plates onto another table, piling them haphazardly.

The clatter brought the waiter out again, a glower pinching his dark eyebrows and recessed forehead. "No fights, comrades, this isn't the baths, you know," he snarled, then returned to the kitchen.

"Well, Vanya, at least we can be reasonably certain the help won't be spying on us!" Polkovnikov laughed. "I apologize for the mystery, but this is a matter of utmost gravity." His face now was suddenly sober, serious. His voice changed timbre too, indicating that now it was business. Duvakin's neck hairs bristled.

"All right, Vanya, long time, no see and all that, but I haven't dragged myself to the edge of civilization for jokes. I can't tell you exactly who I work for, it's a secret, but you can guess; you're not stupid. That last business worked out well, gave me a specialty, you see? Internal security," here Polkovnikov whispered, glancing about the restaurant. "Big stuff, delicate . . ." He smiled to himself a bit, thoroughly pleased.

"Give me a cigarette," Duvakin said nastily, in spite of himself impressed by the man who could boast about having done his dinner partner dirt. "That last business" had sent Duvakin here.

Polkovnikov heard the tone, and for a second he scowled. Then, brightening, he held out his elegant case. "Here you go . . . anyway, normally they wouldn't send me out here." His voice made plain the insignificance of Magadan and all who toiled there. "But unusual circumstances . . ."

There was a pause, which Duvakin knew he was to fill in with a question. He refused, instead smoking and studying the dusty stained glass of the far windows. They seemed to depict some sort of peasant scene, but the light outside was so murky and the glass so greasy that he was uncertain. The restaurant was carpeted, but smelled musty. Duvakin decided he would not care to see the place in a stronger light.

"They're taking this seriously, Vanya," Polkovnikov finally said, leaning forward intently.

"Taking what seriously, damn it!? I've had it with all these hints and winks and . . ." Duvakin suddenly found himself yelling, making his stomach muscles blaze, but clearing his head wonderfully.

"You don't know?" Polkovnikov sat up, blinking in surprise. "Half of Magadan dies in a plane crash, and you don't know?"

Duvakin still watched, uncertain of how to respond; his eyes, though, must have betrayed him. Polkovnikov nodded.

"You know then."

"I thought you said you were internal security," Duvakin finally asked, rather than reveal how much he did know about the airplane.

Polkovnikov regarded the room with apparent uninterest, then leaned across the table. "Let's say we know it's not a task for the air safety people. But you're right, normally I wouldn't bother. But this was the second . . . well, let's say queer story I heard about Magadan, so . . ." he shrugged. "Here I am."

He waited, but still Duvakin was silent.

"Damn it, Duvakin, you must know something about all this! And it's not like you can't be cranked in too, on general principles!" The general's nostrils flared wide; his eyes were glittering ice. Duvakin nodded thoughtfully. Some dangers were more abstract than a cafe manager's Zhiguli, it seemed.

"You're asking about the airport manager, I take it?" he answered as calmly as he could. Polkovnikov nodded once, stiffly, as he controlled his irritation.

Duvakin shrugged. "I'm damned if I understand any of it," he said. "It's like I caught my sleeve in the machinery, really." Methodically, he ran backward through his tale, the airplane, Rzhevskaya, Rzhevsky, and the toilet woman; of the accident, Dusya, and Galya he said nothing. Polkovnikov sat impassive and intent; Duvakin tried to make his tale as neutral as Polkovnikov looked, but even so, he began to feel again a knot of confused anger.

"So anyway," he concluded, trying for a light tone, "I

spent today lying around watching out for God knows what . . . waiting for you, it turns out. And that is all I know."

He looked at Polkovnikov hopefully, as if the man would see some answer immediately. And all would be well. He realized suddenly how passionately he hoped.

Polkovnikov didn't move, but there was, after a moment, a perceptible relaxing, a lessening of his attention.

"That's it?" he finally asked. "Nothing else?"

"A blown up airplane and a dead man aren't enough? You want maybe the pilot's hat size too?" Duvakin's anger was part disappointment that Polkovnikov had not seen any pattern, had had no answer; partly too he felt that more was asked of him than was right. Conclusions were for Polkovnikov, damn it! Polkovnikov scowled, dug out a fancy leather and metal lighter, lit a cigarette, then blew a deliberate blue cone in the general direction of Duvakin.

"Enough of that, Vanya. No need to get testy," Polkovnikov said mildly. "This business smells, Vanya, I'll grant you that for sure . . ."

"You mean you *do* know what's going on?" Duvakin leaned forward, attentive again.

"It's everywhere now, this stuff. My God, Vanya, you wouldn't *believe* the stories. Remember that house your friend had, that whore house?"

"Ishakin?"

"Him . . . remember?"

Duvakin nodded once, remembering far too much of that week and Polkovnikov's role in it.

"Vanya, we get guys now build two, three houses like that, plus maybe a yacht, to keep near the house in the Crimea . . . Foreman of the metro construction crews in Moscow, they found him with a whole marble house, out near Serebrenny Bor, all 'lost' from building sites. Or the manager of one of the new tourist places in Moscow—you know what he was doing?"

Duvakin shook his head.

"Guy's feeding *dollar* tourists, remember," Polkovnikov stressed the word with his eyebrows in a way Duvakin realized he had long not seen here, thousands of kilometers from the nearest dollar. "He makes meat weight by wrapping lung in the portions, sells the difference out the back door, then buys wedding rings. He had a box like *this* of them when they caught him." Polkovnikov held up what looked like a small torte box.

"So? Don't I seem to recall you had a pretty high opinion of all that?" Duvakin slipped deliberately into the familiar, aggravating his offensiveness. And not just because it was the black market which had won, the last time. It was Polkovnikov's air of virtue now, shock at the sins of others. What in the devil was so much fun about all this?

Polkovnikov casually leaned forward, draped a casual hand over Duvakin's shoulder, and squeezed. A thumb the size of a bottle neck dup deep into Duvakin's left collarbone; a twinge of self-defense told him the bone would break. Like that. He held his breath.

"Vanya, don't be unpleasant. The government is beginning to get a little worried. This corruption business is getting expensive. Times aren't what they were, Vanya, you know that? And the people don't like it so much."

Duvakin barely listened, intent only on not moving, to spare his collarbone. Fortunately, Polkovnikov meant only a warning; he smiled without warmth, then asked, "Is the waiter going to come?"

They both turned to stare at the door, which remained impassively closed.

"Vanya, go and see what's the matter, would you? See if you can't get me some food . . . soup, at least," Polkovnikov said imperiously, then turned his attention to the table, carefully rounding up crumbs with a knife, spilling them from the tablecloth into his cupped hand.

Again Duvakin considered for a moment, angry at being ordered about. Then, sighing, he stood. There was no winning. He shoved back his chair and went through the swinging door.

The kitchen walls were flecked with black, and there was a strong smell of burning. The waiter was at the back door flailing his arms, apparently trying to drive the smoke outdoors. Several pots filled with charred matter stood black on the stove. Nearer, a man in a high, once-white hat, the chef it seemed, was weeping bitterly, deep wracking sobs shaking his huddled frame. Two stout florid kitchen helpers, also in soiled white hats, dirty aprons, and black flip-flop slippers, were stroking him desperately, calming him, cheering him, "Now, Antosha, don't, Antosha . . ."

"Excuse me?" Duvakin said hesitantly.

The waiter looked back sharply, his face also florid. "You shouldn't be here!" he rasped, scurrying over. "Out! Out!"

"But he's hungry!"

"I can't help that now can I?" the waiter asked reasonably. "Come on, out you go."

"Not even soup? *That is*—" here he winked and pointed at the door with his thumb—"an important person. A Moscow person."

The words took a few moments to percolate; then the waiter paled, looked alarmed. "Moscow people?"

"Hungry Moscow people," Duvakin repeated, willing to be pluralized. "A borscht, at least . . ."

"A borscht? I don't know." The waiter turned to the sobbing figure. "Antosha is lamenting his lost youth. Hey, Mavruska, is there any borscht?" he said more loudly.

"Borscht? Borscht?" The chef Antosha surfaced suddenly, tears running down his vein-hatched cheeks. His eyes were an eggy blue, fogged with sorrow and, Duvakin did not doubt, vodka. "To make borscht first slice the

[149]

beets very fine . . ." he began to recite mechanically, more or less illustrating with a rusty knife the length of Duvakin's forearm. The two women cringed respectfully, while the waiter, alarmed, said, "Go back, sit down . . . There'll be a borscht. Moscow people, eh?" Then he scurried over to the wildly flailing Antosha, ducked beneath the arms, and gently pointed him toward stove. "In a second, in a second, sit, sit. There'll be soup." He smiled vaguely.

Confused, Duvakin retreated, accompanied by a wild clatter from the kitchen. He returned to his seat.

"What news?" Polkovnikov asked jovially, once more the jolly guest.

Duvakin thought for a moment. "It's confused, but they'll bring a borscht, anyway . . . they said."

"Anything to drink?" Polkovnikov asked.

"I'd be surprised," Duvakin muttered under his breath, not certain whether he ought to report on the disarray in the kitchen. "Ask when they bring the soup," he said more loudly. Apparently content, Polkovnikov dropped his cigarette into the ashtray already overflowing with butts, toyed with it a second, then returned to his original theme.

"They're getting disturbed, Vanya, up at the top. No more Red millionaires, that's what they're saying. Stuff like this, it's like things are getting out of hand."

"So what? You've come to arrest everybody?" Duvakin asked, trying not to be too openly antagonistic.

Fortunately, Polkovnikov suspected no irony, although he did notice Duvakin's face. "What's the matter? You don't believe me?"

"Sure, sure. What did they do to that restaurant guy?" Duvakin looked up, tired and strained.

Polkovnikov stopped playing with the ashtray and thought. "Punished him . . . ?" he said, a question in his voice.

"What, transferred him to another hotel? Maybe even put him in charge of a factory, instead? I'm surprised they didn't get a UN commission on them, brutality like that . . ."

"Vanya, I'm disappointed," Polkovnikov said softly, with an edge of warning. "I had thought you were above this sort of petty liberalism."

"Get off it, Polkovnikov," Duvakin could not work up genuine anger. He felt like he sometimes did trying to deal with Tungus or Chukchi shop girls; they each made sounds, but none of them were words, not in his world. "You know these campaigns are so much tripe. The big guys get a pat on the butt and a fist full of rubles." And guys like me, he thought, get sent to Magadan.

"Vanya, listen to me," the unexpected note of appeal in Polkovnikov's voice made Duvakin look up sharply, watchful. "Two things . . . one, you're right. This is not marble missing from a metro station lobby. This is a blown-up airplane and dead people. We are looking here at resources, plus some very unpleasant people. And two, you're wrong. The old man *himself* (here Polkovnikov indicated with both thumb and raised eyebrows the importance of this old man) is tightening the screws. You want to know how serious this is? His own *daughter!*"

"He had his *daughter* arrested?" Duvakin was surprised, even if uncertain precisely who "he" was; it didn't matter. That *any* of the big cheeses would have a relative arrested was unthinkable.

Polkovnikov made a deprecating gesture. "No, of course not . . . but two of her boyfriends were, circus bigwigs, sold train tickets that were allotted for circuses, sold even trips abroad, for a good stiff chunk." Polkovnikov had a "take-that" look on his face. "Look," he continued after a pause, his voice now conspiratorial. "There's nothing new here, for you, Vanya. What the devil, you don't need figures to know that Gosplan has jumped the rails, that we're in a bad way. *Everybody* says that things are bad, and could get worse. What if we have to start buying more oil; what if there's another war or the Poles or God knows, there's a million worries . . ." Polkovnikov tapped his finger on the filthy ashtray, apparently weary and burdened. "Anyway," he continued after a glance at the kitchen door, "that's why Moscow is so interested in this. This business here, it's too much." Polkovnikov's voice was so convinced that it took Duvakin a second to realize that nothing here was new. Wasn't this the same as last time, what Polkovnikov had then applauded as "initiative in service to the state"?

"Why?" he asked mildly.

"The plane, all right, the furs, all right," Polkovnikov waved his hand dismissively. "Even the interrogation, who cares? But one thing here, dear Ivan Pavlovich . . . *discipline*. What does this do to discipline? So once, twice . . . and pretty soon it's not a Party, it's a *bazaar*, everybody haggling over rags. And the peasants stand around and watch and get hungrier and hungrier. What happens if the question 'why?' is to pop into one of their empty heads? Then, my friend," here with a huge swipe of his arm Polkovnikov swept the table bare of the last pieces Duvakin had left, sending the ashtray slamming across the room to shatter against the concrete island. "Then things get political," he ended softly.

"Coming, coming . . ." the waiter said, emerging from the kitchen backward, his face bent over a tray. "Mind the crockery, gents, this is an *establishment*. Here you go, just the thing, a nice fresh borscht." He shuffled over, barely balancing a tray with bowls, finally succeeding in placing it on the seat of a neighboring chair. He ceremoniously placed a bowl before Polkovnikov, slopping a good half over the edge.

"Borscht?" Polkovnikov said, sliding back to avoid

the seeping ring of greasy, yellowish soup. "It looks more like broth and barley."

"Ah, well, perhaps it is, perhaps it is." The man nodded agreeably, placing a second bowl more or less before Duvakin. He stood for a second, rubbing his hands and watching eagerly, then remembered. "Spoons, spoons, of course . . . and bread!" He scurried over to their singing neighbors and gruffly took two spoons. He polished them with a thumb, then snagged a plate of stale bread from the snoring man across from them. He flung the three pieces clattering to their table.

"Eat, enjoy . . ." he said, backing away obsequiously, bobbing slightly, as if bowing.

Polkovnikov looked nonplussed. He grimaced at the bowl, then stopped the waiter's retreat with a raised finger. The man froze, a look of wild terror in his eyes.

"There is vodka?"

"Vodka? Vodka, of course there's vodka," the waiter smiled, nodded. "All the vodka you might want, only right now there's none. That is, usually . . . as a rule, vodka's what you can count on, but no . . . not right away." The man returned to backing up, as if he could feel the kitchen and safety behind him.

Polkovnikov held up the digit again. "Wine then?"

"Wine, wine, of course there's wine," the waiter almost squeaked with relief, scurrying forward with a soiled, faded menu. "Here's our wine."

The waiter stood rocking on his heels while Polkovnikov tried to make out the faded, blurred carbon copy; then, as if inspired by sudden thought, the waiter squeaked, "Serbian."

"How's that?" Polkovnikov looked up.

"Serbian . . . order the Serbian."

"What Serbian?" He looked back down at the menu.

"The Serbian . . . I recommend it highly, there was a

party here yesterday. *They* brought it." He waved vaguely at the singers. "*Imported* Serbian . . . very dry," the man whispered, for no reason Duvakin could discern. The effect, though, was conspiratorial. The waiter's eyes glittered eagerly. "Say Serbian . . . you'll thank me."

Polkovnikov looked inquiringly at Duvakin, who shrugged, then he laughed once, like a dog's bark. "All right, the Serbian." He handed the waiter the menu, then wiped his fingers on the edge of the tablecloth.

"You'll thank me, believe me . . ." the man repeated as he darted through the swinging door.

Polkovnikov stuck a cautious thumb into the soup, sucked at it, then spat. "Blessing it's cold," he observed mildly. "Hot, it would taste much nastier."

Duvakin fingered a slice of bread and listened to his stomach rumble. Thank God for Galya and her kitchen!

There was a silence as Polkovnikov picked at a button on his sleeve and Duvakin looked off into space, drumming his fingers; Duvakin could hear a faint clatter, then a muffled argument, followed by shrieks, and then silence. Outside there seemed to be no light at all now, as if the world were again engulfed in ice and night. Duvakin ached, and longed to get home, Galya's, *somewhere* . . . anywhere that he might lie down. There was more clatter from the kitchen, but Polkovnikov continued in silence. Duvakin would, he knew, have to push the matter ahead.

"So what's it all got to do with *me?*" he finally asked. "There's nothing I can do about it, is there? I mean, Lord, airplanes, beatings, dead people, and I don't even know what the devil is going on." He sat with his arms crossed over his chest, trying to comfort his thumping heart.

"Duvakin, I had hoped you wouldn't feel that way, but I guess I can understand it." Polkovnikov looked mournful, so clearly so that Duvakin suspected sarcasm. "So I'm even sorrier to have to tell you you're going to help. There's no choice."

"What else can you do to me?" Duvakin asked as casually as his dry throat would allow. "What's left?"

Polkovnikov spooned through his greasy soup, examining minutely the flecks which floated to the top. "One of the interesting capacities of human beings, we find," he said softly, almost like a teacher, "is that they can get used to anything, no matter how dreadful it may seem . . . and then when you take *that* away, no matter how little, then things seem worse. Things can *always* get worse . . ." He smiled, a thin-lipped, cheerless slash. Duvakin knew deep within that Polkovnikov was right, but he kept his face a stubborn blank.

"But," Polkovnikov continued after a short silence, "there is another question you might have asked me. You like it out here? You settled in?"

"You mean, maybe . . . ?" Duvakin asked, with excitement he could not keep out of his voice.

"I mean definitely. You've been a good boy. I imagine a successful collaboration and a good report from me would work absolute miracles with the Moscow registry people." Polkovnikov beamed, apparently disarmed by his own generosity.

Duvakin had guessed that Moscow might be within Polkovnikov's power, but he had not dwelt on it, concerned instead that he stay well clear of the general and his schemes. Now that the issue was raised, though, Duvakin felt a quickening of his breath. To wrangle a way back to Moscow . . .

He kept his tone as neutral as he could.

"Well . . ."

Polkovnikov laughed, his head back. "Anyway, you *like* this stuff, Vanya. You're lucky!"

Some luck, thought Duvakin and scrutinized the tablecloth. In fact, Polkovnikov had pretty much stated the choices. Enjoy it, don't enjoy it, but that was about it. He could help and maybe get back to Moscow. Or he could refuse and get himself the devil maybe wouldn't even know where. Dead, probably. For a moment he thought of how much he would enjoy nailing Polkovnikov's scrotum to a chair.

"Why me, Polkovnikov?" Duvakin finally asked. "Damn it, I don't know anything about Magadan, beyond what I told you. What do you want, for me to go around trying to buy up Magadan, like the last time?"

Polkovnikov laughed a bit too hard, rhetorically. "That's the spirit!"

The laugh goaded Duvakin.

"You *have* to have me, don't you Polkovnikov? That's why you're asking, you don't know who else to trust? How do you know me, come to that?" He eyed the man, challenging.

"I guess I know you, Vanya. You're honest. You couldn't scheme; you believe too easily. Four years and not so much as once did you try to go against your promise. Anyone else would have lied . . . easy enough to get a message through to Moscow."

Shame engulfed Duvakin like hot wax. He *had* believed them, he realized. He had not even thought of trying. He hung his head, appalled by his own credulity.

"Oh, come on, Vanya, don't feel so down. After all, I did say I *know* you didn't try, didn't I?" He winked meaningfully.

Just then the waiter reappeared, tripping as he crossed the door sill. He had two bottles, one in either hand. He recovered, reeling over to the table. He was noticeably drunk now. "Serbian . . . see? You'll love it." He placed the two bottles bang on the table, then fished in his jacket pocket for something. Perplexed, he paused, then brightened. With ceremony from his other pocket he dug a mayonnaise jar, which he placed before Polkovnikov. With a look of intense concern he studied Duvakin. An idea crossed his face; he said, "Just a second . . ." then scuttled over to the next table, where he got a water glass. Throwing a dead fly and the remaining liquid on the floor, he polished the glass with the edge of his jacket, then put it down on Duvakin's hand. "There! Your health, gents! Ooo! Cigarettes! May I, comrade?" The waiter snatched up Polkovnikov's case, fumbled it open. "Foreign? My lucky day! I'll take three, all right? God loves a trinity, like they say . . ." Sticking one cigarette behind each ear and one in his mouth, the waiter gave them a cheerful, bleary grin, and reeled back into the kitchen.

Polkovnikov burst out laughing, slapping his knee. "One of God's chosen," he said to Duvakin, who was still burning with anger at himself. "The dolt forgot to open the bottles!" Polkovnikov pointed, laughing harder. Then he leaned forward, gathering one into his enormous hand. "No, it's all right. One is already open . . . for quite some time, it looks like." Then he looked searchingly at Duvakin, those steely blue eyes seeking once again to transfix. "But, you see, that's why we've got to get to the bottom of this mess. Things are in a very bad way."

"He's just drunk, if you mean the waiter," Duvakin said wonderingly. "It's not like you've never seen one before . . . don't take it personally. The devil, Moscow's full of them, too, last time I knew about it."

"Only a drunk! Look at this place! Do you know how much money they waste in a place like this? And how many places like this there are?" Polkovnikov spoke quietly, but his words dropped like stones. "The whole cursed place is falling apart, and nobody is doing anything to stop it. Discipline, where the devil is discipline!?" Then, gravely serious, Polkovnikov said, "See, it's not the money that worries Moscow, it's that people get used to doing their own wiggling, once they start having to." Without thinking Polkovnikov slowly bent his butter knife double. "I mean Vanya, how long can this go on? Everybody's got his mouth wide open and stuffed full, and they're still stuffing, both hands and both feet. By God, Vanya, it gets worse every day. In Moscow already it's like wolves and an old moose, maybe not quite nipping at the old man's heels yet, but already they're quarreling about who gets to eat what . . . and everything else just goes to the devil's mother. Sell gold, that's the answer for everything . . . and so they dump so much gold the world price goes down, and we have to sell more still, just to come out even." Polkovnikov's voice sounded genuinely angry; Duvakin studied him, unable to decide how much of this was true. It was unsettling, to hear someone talk this way. Sure, things were never easy, or good, but you always assumed there was a reason for it being like that. The reason might be ideology or bad luck or even the greed of those in power . . . but it was a reason.

Polkovnikov seemed to hint that no one was in charge, that there *was* no reason, and that perhaps only chaos was at the helm; this was radically disturbing, like being told suddenly, in adulthood, that you were adopted. Duvakin tried to comfort himself that Polkovnikov was manufacturing this to persuade him, but a cold suspicion coated the bottom of his stomach.

Polkovnikov inhaled deeply, filling his lungs to capacity, then exhaled, like some old drawing of the four winds. Then he smiled. "Anyway, if it keeps up, either the whole works breaks down, and we have chaos, or else the peasants go up, like so much atom bomb . . ." Here Polkovnikov's large hands sketched a mushroom. "Or else we stop this *now*. Follow this up, *wherever* it goes. And punish them, damn it. The country's got to learn, we're a nation of laws, not a gang." Polkovnikov tapped a heavy forefinger in emphasis.

"And that's why I want you, Vanya. We can stop it, you and me. No silly spy games, no foreign currency. Just the old donkey method, me the carrot and you the stick.

Or the lever, if you want . . . but the point is, a boat's going on the rocks, and you've got to start pulling on the oars, am I right?"

"Concretely then! Enough with the fine speeches, what do you want?" Duvakin finally flared, sick of this day, this world. Tell me what I have to do so I can never see your face again.

Polkovnikov hesitated, studying Duvakin. Then, coolly, deliberately, he poured from the open bottle into each of their containers. Still silent, his eyes on Duvakin, he sipped from his mayonnaise jar.

And spat violently, then repeated.

"Christ in heaven! Benzine would taste better! Waiter!" he yelled, then spat again.

The drunk stumbled in again, wringing his hands and bobbing. "What cigarettes, comrade, a-i-i! What cigarettes! My whole life I'll remember your generosity, with my entire soul . . ." He reeled into the table and stopped, teetering on unsteady feet.

"Open this bottle." Polkovnikov pointed calmly at the remaining bottle.

"That bottle?" The man looked puzzled, then, illuminated, said, "Oh, yes, the Serbian! Lovely, isn't it? God's own sweet breath . . ." He took the bottle in both hands, shook it firmly, then began tapping it with authority against a folded napkin on the table. Polkovnikov and Duvakin watched in motionless fascination while the cork slid slowly up. One last whack and the cork popped out, propelled by a small fountain of wine.

Horrified, the waiter grasped the bottle with both hands, shrieking in short spasms like a wounded hare. Waving the bottle about, he drenched Duvakin, then spattered Polkovnikov, who shoved backward in his chair and stood up. "You'll rot for this, you swine!" he bellowed at the waiter, shaking an enraged finger. "Rot! Do you hear me?" Then he stalked out of the room. Duvakin also stood, grabbed his coat, and made to follow but felt his arm caught by the waiter.

"You don't want to try the Serbian? Pity . . . it's wonderfully good . . . imported Serbian." He winked, then sank slowly to the floor, cross-legged; one hand clutched the bottle lovingly, the other still held tight to Duvakin's arm.

Duvakin gently freed his arm and turned to catch up with the general.

"Be a good fellow, will you?" the waiter asked in entreaty from his place on the floor. "Cover me with the table cloth . . ."

"How's that?" Duvakin asked.

"Oh, never mind," the man said, pulling the cloth from the table they had vacated, then slowly winding it about his head, like a marriage between a tent and one of those Arab things. He tipped the bottle to his lips, drank deeply, then sighed with melancholy pleasure.

Duvakin shook his head and raced to catch the general. The man stood in the entrance way, smoking furiously at the storm. Duvakin stopped just behind him, thoughtfully put on his coat. His options? None, really. Don't play along, and next time you'll get run over properly, if Polkovnikov doesn't do you in himself. Play along, and hope like the devil for the best. For a second, Duvakin too studied the storm, then thought, and why not? Maybe there is something to be done. Maybe this time will be different. Besides, he added bitterly, he was like the sable in the ring trap again, able only to push forward. So be it, he thought. So be it.

He smiled slightly. It might even be pleasant, after so many years, to strike back, even if only a little. He looked at Polkovnikov's stiff, angry back, and swore a hopeful vow. This time, dear generalissimo Polkovnikov, if anyone is going to walk into an open manhole, it will not be Ivan Pavlovich Duvakin.

"All right, Polkovnikov, you've found yourself a partner. What do we do?"

"Splendid, splendid!" Polkovnikov turned with startling enthusiasm, as if he truly had been uncertain of the outcome. Numbly, Duvakin pumped the outstretched hand.

✳ TEN ✳

"These are place; you be sure?" the driver narrowed his slit eyes further, studying Duvakin. "Place here not clean. Bad people, not clean."

Duvakin clenched his fist, wishing he could tell this stammering Chukchi to press on, that he was mistaken. Instead he asked, "Is Leninka?" After a second he wondered how it was he had begun to speak mangled Russian too.

"Leninka, Leninka . . ." the leathery little driver acknowledged, then looked away blankly and braked the ancient truck. Duvakin shuddered as he heard objects slam against the bulkhead behind him, then opened the door, to climb down.

"Well, thanks, comrade," Duvakin said, reluctant to climb out into the cold that already gnawed at his legs.

The driver said nothing; instead he contemplated the burning lump of shag he pinned between thumb and pinky. It's your funeral, his huddled shoulders and nearly shut eyes said eloquently. Indeed, shrugged Duvakin and jumped down into the feathery roadside snow. Even before he had slammed the door, the truck was pulling away, to leave Duvakin in a deserted road, between an empty field writhing with susurating coils of windblown snow and a stunted forest of dark blue spruce. A pale sun was laboring its way clear of the sea clouds on the horizon, and Duvakin swallowed hard, to force back the sudden conviction that he was the last man in the universe. Not even a raven coughed, nor a sparrow twittered.

"So announce the arrival of Duvakin, most secret investigator, direct from Moscow headquarters," he said not quite aloud; even a murmur in that silence seemed a shout, the words battering through the pines in icy tinkling waves. The puffs of air from his mouth and the clasp of cold along his thighs reminded him that he'd best get moving; it was damned cold.

And damned early, he thought as he trudged across the road on the squeaking snow, looking for the entrance to Darmoved's residence.

That's how it was with Polkovnikov. The real question is why in the name of my mother's soul do I, poor mortal Duvakin, have to go see Darmoved, head of the local KGB; Darmoved, who specifically warned off even the head of the Magadan militia; Darmoved, who killed Rzhevsky? But the general somehow put things so that what Duvakin ended up arguing about was where to see him, at home or in the office.

Not that argument availed much there, either.

"In the house, Vanya, it's secret, you can see that?" Polkovnikov had repeated patiently in the freezing taxi. "You're supposed to be a secret inspector, investigating for the center. No real inspector would waltz in to announce that during reception hours, now would he? So you have to go to his house . . ."

"And do what?" Duvakin had asked sulkily, not willing to imagine the full dimension of what he was arguing about. "Why can't you do it?"

"What are you so worried about, Vanya?" the general had chuckled in frosty puffs. "You're not investigating him, just courtesy, let him know what's up . . . standard procedure."

Of course, Duvakin railed at his own fatigued credulity of the night before as he stomped heavily through the spruce. Of course, it's standard procedure—to drop in on the local KGB head at breakfast; to tell him that for four years you've *really* been a secret investigator for internal security, spying on the whole blighted province, and you're coming out now just to say that things look bad. Courtesy, to warn him that Moscow is about to yank the rug out, where he, Darmoved, was meant to have been in charge.

That must be jolly enough when it's true, let alone when the whole thing is like a bad dream of Polkovnikov's.

That was half of what had kept Duvakin awake all night, the lunacy of Polkovnikov's scheme and of his having agreed to it. The other half of it was wondering what other choice he'd had. Or more exactly, exploring fully in how many ways he had had no other choice.

And not just in a negative way, he had grown increasingly to realize as he tossed about in his stale sheets. Polkovnikov was the only rope Duvakin saw anywhere about him, with his ties to Moscow. As he stared at the black of his room, Duvakin had been unable to rid himself of feeling not free, of being unable to act for himself alone.

For one there was Galya, though God knows what his responsibility there was. When he had phoned, for caution using the public automatic opposite the bottle return station, where drunks had kicked out all the windowpanes, he recognized in her bantering urgency to have him back at her flat for the night that matters with her were getting deep. Duvakin felt confused; it had been only a few days. He could not understand the speed of her affection, nor did he feel comfortable returning it.

But then he *had* felt he had to phone her, and he quite carefully had concealed her existence from Polkovnikov. So there must be something.

Dusya too, though that was even crazier. Duvakin didn't know her, had not even been able to contact her again, and had no idea what—if anything—he might do for the Rzhevskys' orphaned daughter. A voice in the back of his mind, echoing with her own voice on that one call, nevertheless insisted that something must be done.

So, even though he had hardly slept and his stomach throbbed, Duvakin had been able to get up with a certain determination, and even hope, permitting him to get dressed, get down to the dispatcher's office, and flag a ride out toward where Polkovnikov told him Darmoved's residence lay.

What faint traces of determination had accompanied him along the narrow asphalt lane through the dwarf spruce abandoned him when Duvakin rounded the last curve and saw Darmoved's house. The house was bigger than most, and in good repair, with neatly painted trim and even a garage to one side, big enough for a couple of cars, maybe even a Chaika limousine. What really stopped Duvakin, though, was the front door. And the sudden realization that he, Duvakin, was going up to knock on it.

He couldn't do it. He stood still for a moment, trying to find reasons, explanations, to buttress that knowledge. His breath caught at his throat and his heart began to hammer. He couldn't do it. He turned around, relief at his retreat mingling with a certain self-loathing; because he was trying so hard to convince himself that he was right to retreat, it took a moment to see the guards.

Two soldiers in winter issue, white on white, relieved

only by the blue stud in the middle of each hat of white rabbit. KGB blue. With a start Duvakin realized that even their dogs were white. Save their red, slavering and horrible maws.

They were running right at him and not, he knew, for explanations.

"Hold it!" he shouted. "I'm expected!" Frantically, he dug through his clothing toward his inner pocket and his Party card. "*Stand*, damn it!" he shouted, as they kept on.

Either because he stood, when a true intruder would have run, or because he had ordered, where an outsider would have begged, the soldiers quickly reconsidered; their attack pulled short so close that Duvakin could feel the breath of the nearer dog hot against his knee.

Duvakin closed his eyes, to halt the trembling in his legs.

"Your business?" the senior of the pair asked, his voice rocking hesitantly between respect and contempt. Duvakin opened his eyes, glanced quickly at the pair before him. One was Russian, the speaker; the other was dark, Tartar maybe, Asian anyway. Both looked nastily competent.

And confused. Duvakin decided to stick with what had worked.

"Is my business," he tried to say brusquely, though he was betrayed by a squeak. "Is my business," he repeated. "The colonel expects me," he added when the first answer seemed to make the pair more edgy.

"Your name?" the senior one asked in the same neutral tone; he was reassured enough though to indicate to his dog with a flick of the chain that it should sit. The Asian, after a pause, followed.

"Look," Duvakin desperately shoved home the only edge he had, "you march up there," he indicated the house with a flick of his finger, "and tell Colonel Darmoved that it's Comrade Duvakin you're making stand here in the cold and then just see . . ." See what, he wondered, praying frantically that Polkovnikov had done as he had promised, telephoning the colonel.

"Duvakin?" the Russian asked, in surprise. "We expected . . ." he began, then stopped, as discipline reasserted itself. No discipline, though, could overcome the man's curiosity. After a pause he asked, "On foot?"

Duvakin blushed, feeling a fool, but also angry with Polkovnikov. Fine that he had to drag himself all the way to Leninka, and the general never even thought to ask how he would do it. Probably expected him to have a car; everyone in Moscow would. Or to bribe a taxi mechanic himself.

When he didn't have bus fare in his pocket.

"Yes, well . . . it . . . broke," he finally said. "And this is urgent." Instinctively, he returned to the angry, impatient tones he heard so often around headquarters. He was on the point again of pulling out his Party card, to persuade the still reluctant guard, but fortunately recalled that power lay in demonstration of power. How else had Polkovnikov managed so easily to get him out here? "Come on, hop to it, I'm freezing," he said gruffly, and turned back toward the house.

Duvakin had no idea how he forced his legs to walk up that frosty driveway, but it must have looked convincing. After a pause he heard a jingle of chain and the shuffle of boots receding down the driveway. His shoulders dropped a notch, in relief.

Relief, hell, Duvakin thought. He was at Darmoved's door. He took a deep breath, and knocked.

The door opened so quickly that the man must have watched the whole business with the guards; Duvakin almost fell forward, with the inertia of a knock.

"Duvakin?" he asked. "Where's your driver?"

"He . . . it broke . . . my car . . ." Duvakin stuttered.

What was all this concern about his car? Did no one ever walk to Darmoved's?

The man who opened the door studied him for a moment with almost an otter's face, bright quick eyes and a quick mouth, but without the air of chumminess an otter has. More like a weasel's face, Duvakin decided. Finally, the man shrugged. "If it's that important then . . ." He indicated that Duvakin should come in, then shut the door and helped him out of his overcoat. "This way . . ."

The last time Duvakin had penetrated into inner circles, back in Moscow, he had found life luxuriously furnished, and he must have expected the same here. The head of the Magadan KGB is not, after all, a night watchman. The hall, though, and what little Duvakin could glimpse of the rooms they passed, was curiously ordinary, even utilitarian. Rzhevsky's place was nicer.

Duvakin found the commonness of the wooden hallway reassuring, though he still clenched his jaw so hard his back teeth ached. His guide stopped at a door and knocked hesitantly.

"Ivan Ivanych?" He listened at the door, then smiled at Duvakin, looking remarkably like a weasel just finished with an egg. Duvakin scowled, reminding himself that he was important. The man opened the door, and Duvakin walked in, holding his breath.

The room was not large, but seemed spacious because of the large windows, almost doors, which opened out on a charming clump of birches. The room too was light colored, with none of the dark furniture usually found in offices. A cheerful room, Duvakin decided in surprise.

"Well?" a man said behind him; Duvakin flinched, but forced himself to turn slowly.

In a corner against a window leaned a youngish man in a bathrobe of some heavy, smooth material. It seemed he had been drinking something hot.

"Darmoved?" Duvakin asked, surprised. The man was too young and too slender.

He pursed his lips slightly, then put down the cup. "Usually, I'm addressed by my title. Colonel Darmoved." He squared his shoulders, facing Duvakin martially erect. He studied Duvakin with glittery brownish eyes, framed in large, foreign-looking glasses. "Well?" he repeated coldly.

Well, indeed, Duvakin thought. "It's important . . ." he glanced hesitantly at the weasel-man, who still stood by the door.

"I had assumed that Moscow wouldn't roust me out of my bed for trivial matters," the colonel said acidly, ignoring Duvakin's hint.

"Moscow?" Duvakin was startled. How did Moscow know about this?

"Your . . . chief, the general. They always forget the time difference when they call," Darmoved smiled, as if with mild annoyance. "Come on, man, speak up. I'm a busy man, and you are in my way. What is this confidential matter I'm to be informed of? You are Duvakin?"

Duvakin nodded, feeling sick to hear his own name, here. He glanced again at the man behind him.

Darmoved waved his arms in irritation. "Oh very well, Moscow shall have its secrets. Vaska, go see about the car." Darmoved watched his underling leave, then moved over to a large wooden desk, where he sat, gathering the robe carefully about him.

Duvakin stood, feeling like a schoolboy at examination. A schoolboy who has just forgotten everything in his head.

"They told you then"—he cleared his throat—"who I am?"

"Perhaps I know who you are." Darmoved smiled unpleasantly.

Duvakin felt his palms and forehead go wet. "I think

not," he said in a voice he did not recognize. "Who I really am . . ." he added, forcing himself to believe he really was what Polkovnikov had invented last night.

"An agent of internal security?" Darmoved asked, with a tart echo in his voice, not quite mockery. But not believing either.

Duvakin remembered his lines. "Assigned here four years ago, to observe the function of the Party—"

"And the execution of vital business. Word for word what they told me last night," Darmoved interrupted, now openly mocking. "And I am expected to believe that?"

Duvakin's stomach ran so cold he, for a moment, feared incontinence. Unable to speak, he shrugged.

"I did not become the youngest regional commander in modern times because of my credulity," Darmoved continued levelly, looking at Duvakin over the top of his glasses. "There is nothing in Magadan I don't know about, comrade Duvakin, Ivan Palych, assistant lecturer in scientific atheism, resident at twenty-eight Treefellers Prospekt, Apartment fifteen . . . need I continue? Nothing escapes me."

Unwanted, there popped into Duvakin's brain a confirming note; Rzhevsky had been picked up no more than fifteen hours after the old woman's theft had been logged in. That surely hadn't escaped him. Neither had Rzhevsky.

Duvakin trembled slightly. Polkovnikov had given him a story, one which last night had seemed convincing, that he had been investigating the Party for corruption, he'd begun to act (the old toilet woman's arrest), and now he had to inform the officer in charge that the trail led upward and that he, Duvakin, was acting on Moscow orders.

Which implied that Darmoved was either criminally incompetent, for not having noticed this, or complicit.

Duvakin didn't like the story so much anymore.

"So, unless you've something more to say . . ." Darmoved smiled and reached for the telephone on his desk.

"You know about the furs?" Duvakin squeaked, panicked to halt the hand before it picked up the receiver.

"That is state business that may not be discussed," Darmoved smiled like a tomcat with tailfeathers sticking to his lips.

"And the airplane? The one that blew up?" Duvakin couldn't remember whether he was supposed to know that or not, but he didn't care. Visions of a Rzhevsky, battered to death, were beginning to haunt his imagination.

Darmoved paused, studying Duvakin again, chewing on the inside of his cheek. After what seemed ages he ran a contemplative thumb along the edge of his jaw.

Duvakin felt a little clear space, and forged desperately ahead. "Ilushin sixty-two, Moscow bound, two, three days ago . . ." How many? He was getting confused.

"Also state business," Darmoved said less smugly, a little more puzzled.

Duvakin rummaged his memory for another card to throw down. Rzhevsky? He shook his head; something told him that was a secret best kept, yet.

Sounding as confident as he could, he said, "And me . . . state business too . . ." Remembering the confident rudeness of the section chiefs who plagued their office downtown, Duvakin sat, even dug out a cigarette.

Darmoved watched him, as if from a great distance. Finally, a little abstractly, he said, "Don't smoke, please . . ."

"What?"

"Don't smoke . . . it's bad for the equipment."

Equipment? Duvakin looked around, feeling foolish with the cigarette in his hand. Now that they could not have it, his lungs ached for the smoke. He rolled the cigarette in his fingers, feeling the tobacco dribble out of the tube. He had no idea of where he stood with Darmoved.

After what felt like silent ages, Darmoved said quietly, more to his blotter than Duvakin, "I am in control of this region. There is no reason for Moscow to question my . . ."

With a bump, Duvakin realized he was back on the map. Polkovnikov's map. "They question nothing, comrade Colonel!" Duvakin almost shouted. ("He'll be touchy," Polkovnikov had said offhandedly—this of a man with life-and-death power in the region!—"so assure him, it's just family, friendly.") "It's more . . . it's in the nature of a family matter." Duvakin smiled, trying to melt Darmoved a little. "The man who phoned, his comrades . . . there's a party worried maybe a comrade is involved, in maybe an unhappy way," Duvakin mumbled. What man, what party, what way? If Darmoved asked, Duvakin was sunk.

Darmoved slapped the desk hard and stood angrily, shooting his chair hard against the wall. "Family matter!" Duvakin tried not to cower. "Family matter? *Criminal* matter, that's what it is!" he shouted at Duvakin, then turned to face the window.

God in heaven, what are we talking about? Duvakin felt abruptly off the map again.

Darmoved addressed the window. "Very well, comrade . . . I am ordered to obey." He was acid with irony. He turned. "Provided . . ." He smiled. "*Provided* you produce adequate documentation."

Duvakin felt limp with relief. Home free. This is where Polkovnikov had drilled him.

"You're on the EVM? Central bank?" Duvakin asked offhandedly, praying he had recalled Polkovnikov's nonsense words correctly. He'll be impressed by that, Polkovnikov had promised. Correctly, it seemed.

"You're in that?" Darmoved asked, pointing at something with his chin.

In what? Duvakin twisted around, in the direction the chin indicated; he saw a glass-fronted bookcase, some portraits, and what looked like a desk with a television built into it. Wires as thick as a man's wrist disappeared into the wall.

A computer, Duvakin guessed hopefully. Polkovnikov had assured him there would be one; the plan depended on it.

"A computer?" he asked quietly.

"Data interface remote linkage, satellite transmitted, experimental model," Darmoved glowed with pride, as though the desk had sprung from his own loins. "I'm testing it for the Riga electron kombinat . . ."

Half the words were gibberish to Duvakin; he nodded sagely, watching Darmoved walk toward the object, then couldn't prevent himself asking, "It's ours? I thought all that stuff was foreign."

Darmoved turned as though stung. "Soviet science and technology leads the world!"

Duvakin remembered posting banners that said more or less the same on bulletin boards across Magadan in honor of Scientific Workers' Day, so he merely repeated his "naturally, naturally" nod.

Apparently mollified, Darmoved pulled a chair to the desk with the pomp of a pianist, then sat, squared his shoulders, inhaled, exhaled, and carefully touched a button.

Some sort of engine came alive with a kerchug, and Duvakin heard what sounded like rapid typewriting; over Darmoved's shoulder he watched the television glow into life.

Darmoved muttered to himself, "User code . . ." then carefully tapped out something on his keyboard. "Access

Khimki . . ." tap-tap-tap, "Priority . . ." tap-tap-tap, "Clearance . . ." tap-tap-tap.

Duvakin watched, half-turned in his seat, feeling both bemused and frightened. He hoped nervously that Polkovnikov had not betrayed him, that the magic phrases he had drilled him on last night would work; even knowing though that "Khimki" must be the new KGB operations center in Moscow, it was difficult to see this ritual of Darmoved's as something real.

"All right, comrade," Darmoved said ironically, over his shoulder. "Your confirmation?"

Nervousness brushed feathery wings on the inside of Duvakin's stomach; the schoolboy at exams again.

"Access program"—Duvakin cleared his throat, began again—"access program 'for three percent' . . ." he recited quickly.

Darmoved interrupted him. "Numbers?"

Duvakin opened his eyes, confused and worried. "Numbers?"

"In numbers or spelled out?" Darmoved snapped impatiently.

Polkovnikov hadn't said; Duvakin thought better of asking whether it mattered. He almost panicked, but then flung himself into an answer. You'll be right or wrong, he hoped. "Spelled out," he said, trying not to make it a question.

Darmoved addressed his machine again. He typed slowly, saying each letter, then "Enter . . ."

He looked up at the screen expectantly; Duvakin could not do otherwise. He saw his code word then, after a pause, letters began rapidly to appear on the screen, "A-u-t-h-o-r-i-t . . ." Just then a brilliant white dot grew in the center of the screen, seemed to explode over the screen, turning the whole face grayish-white, but only for a second. The screen turned black again, save for a flash-

ing band in the center, which blipped rapidly, then also
died.

Darmoved swore so coarsely Duvakin blinked.

"It's all right?" he asked, fearing his words might
have provoked the machine's behavior.

Darmoved waved a hand in disgust and mumbled,
"It's the gun, again . . ."

"The gun?" Duvakin looked up alarmed.

"The sending unit, the tube . . ." Darmoved wasn't
listening to his own words, instead fiddling around with
the keyboard before him. "We'll have to start again, with
the printer module . . . and use the telephone."

Duvakin nodded baffled agreement.

Darmoved punched away at the keys, now not saying
the letters aloud, nor, it seemed to Duvakin, being as
solicitous of the keys as he had been.

"All right," he said finally, "'for three percent'?"

Duvakin licked his upper lip. "That's right, then the
authority code . . ."

"Hold it, we're on wires now . . . slower . . ."

They stood silently, watching the motionless, silent
machine. Duvakin was just beginning to feel stiff and silly
when the machine kerchugged, typed, and spat a length
of paper.

"Code of authority?"

"Mikhail Fedorovich, then . . ." Duvakin again
wanted to recite his whole piece at once; again, Darmoved
halted him with a hand.

Tap-tap-tap, reverent, lengthy wait, kerchug, spit.

"Detail operational instructions of?" Darmoved
asked, turning about in his seat.

"Dark planet," Duvakin finished, hoping that he had
retained the rote phrases in the correct order.

Last night, Duvakin had tried to get some explanation
from Polkovnikov of what this careful learning of lines

meant, but the general wasn't particularly concerned that Duvakin understand.

"Just remember it all, that's the important job. The first one lets you into the program, but it's blocked . . . it's one of the most sensitive internal security areas we've undertaken. So the name will give you access; without it, the machine tells you nothing." Polkovnikov had smiled then, tapping Duvakin on the chest with a thick finger. "And if it doesn't let you in, then it doesn't confirm that Vanya Duvakin is who he says, and then . . ." The general had spat flatulently. Duvakin had shuddered, and remembered.

He stood at Darmoved's shoulder, in spite of himself breathing shallowly. The wait seemed interminable; Duvakin could feel his nerves edging toward panic.

At last the machine chugged into life and began typing furiously. Darmoved leaned forward attentively, reading the paper the machine was spewing. Duvakin tried too, but then remembered he was supposed to know all about whatever the machine was pounding out. He forced himself to stroll over to a window, where he tried to concentrate on the way the pale sun slid in and out of the flat milky clouds.

Darmoved whistled softly, almost simple breathing out, but Duvakin started.

"I'm—it's—all right?"

Darmoved stood, ripped the paper from the machine and turned, to study Duvakin. He glanced back at the paper in his hand.

"But why the Central Committee?" Darmoved asked, with what Duvakin prayed was respect.

"What why?" he stammered stupidly, acutely aware that he had no idea what was on that paper. He cursed himself for letting Polkovnikov put him there.

"If it's organ work, then it should be Andropov, not

Central Committee authority," Darmoved looked up, somehow respectful in his question. "Shouldn't it?"

Duvakin was baffled. "It's—ummm—Party, a Party matter . . . because . . ."

Darmoved nodded his head. "Of course, of course . . ." Then, totally unexpectedly, he smiled. "Family matters, like you said, eh?" He walked across the room and extended a hand to Duvakin. Numbly, Duvakin did the same, to get Darmoved's soft, dry fingers a limp second in his hand. "Very well then, keep in contact and so on." Darmoved still watched Duvakin closely, compounding the confusion and clumsiness he already felt.

"Of course, of course . . ." he mumbled, anxious to be away.

"Seriously, though," Darmoved asked, his voice now somber, "how long do you think you can keep it up?"

Duvakin stared at him.

"Oh, Party unity and all that. I know, preservation of authority, giving the masses positive examples . . . after all, I'm Party myself, I *have* to be . . ." Darmoved spoke calmly, as if man-to-man. "But law is something too, and discipline . . ."

"Certainly," Duvakin touched ground where he could. "There is that."

"Well, then," Darmoved flicked him on the shoulder with his hand. "And what do you suppose *this* does for law and discipline?"

"This?" Duvakin fumbled for illumination.

"Protecting these people, covering over their crimes?"

What in the world was on that paper? Duvakin wondered desperately. Crimes? "Well, you know . . ." he said vaguely, trying to edge toward the door. "It's not up to me."

"That's where you're wrong," Darmoved said crisply. Then, looking pleased with himself, he added, "Of course, that's why you're you and I am me."

Duvakin resolved to himself to walk right out of this entire business at the first opportunity; no more of this absurd floundering. And God grant that opportunity come. He eyed the door. "Comrade Colonel, I've got . . ." He waved vaguely at the door, then his watch.

"Listen," Darmoved smiled archly, "a word of advice . . . from one who knows. Burying dung doesn't make it into gold. It still stinks, and," he winked, "it can still stick to your hands if you aren't careful. That was my predecessor's mistake."

"Your predecessor?" Duvakin asked mechanically, still stepping slowly toward the door. Then, wondering what he was being told, he repeated, "Your predecessor?"

Darmoved smiled, immensely proud of himself. "Not important. Just remember, I tell you this, the youngest regional organ head in modern times!"

Duvakin remembered this was the second mention of what must be Darmoved's pride. "A great honor . . . very lucky . . ."

Darmoved sniffed disdainfully. "Lucky? That's why you're an errand boy. It isn't luck takes you from a Kolyma children's home to . . ." Darmoved spread his hands.

The suspicion, which had been growing in Duvakin, that Darmoved was a bit touched, withered like a freak spring flower. His neighbor Pavlovna had told him something of those prison camp children's homes. For the offspring, mostly, of the criminals and whores, who got a month off for pregnancy, and the occasional child of political prisoners who chanced to survive transport across to Kolyma. What scours and whooping cough didn't take, cold, bad food, and indifferent nurses did, while doing the devil knows what to the few who survived.

Darmoved had survived and prospered. Alone. Duvakin felt all his fear return. Coming face front with a shark might feel something like that.

Fortunately, Darmoved seemed to take no notice of

the horror Duvakin was certain had drained his face;
instead, he walked to his desk, pulled his robe tighter
about him, and reached for his phone. "So, fine, you have
my permission to intervene for a comrade . . . on *a limited basis.*" He stressed delicately but unquestionably that
he was retaining control. "And remember what I say—
duty, and keep your own hands out of the shit. You'll
thank me. Vaska? Get the comrade's coat."

It took almost all Duvakin's self-control to wait while
the weasel brought the coat, then showed him to the door;
his mind kept spewing bits of Darmoved grinning,
Rzhevsky beaten into grotesque poses, Darmoved, Duvakin blundering clumsily ahead.

And something else, too, he recognized as they went
back down the hall. There was something wrong about
this whole morning.

Not complaining, mind, Duvakin thought as Vaska
helped him into the overcoat. He had survived; Polkovnikov's plan had worked its wonder. If it was KGB who
had pushed him in front of the Zhiguli, then he was off
the hook, for a time anyway.

But still . . . Duvakin couldn't help recalling his own
lectures, the empty indifferent faces of his listeners, at-
tending on orders. It was the form to follow the set lecture
with questions from the audience, passed forward on
little bits of paper. Only there never were any. So Duvakin
always went prepared with his own stack of questions,
which he then answered, spontaneously.

And which his listeners found convincing. Just like
Darmoved seemed to have found this. Duvakin shivered,
shook himself, nodded at Vaska.

"Pity about your car," Vaska said, smiling in return.

Duvakin also smiled, stepped outside, said "Well
. . ." and shrugged.

"Odd the soldiers didn't find it," Vaska's eyes glittered. "They went back to look . . ."

Last night Duvakin had almost convinced himself that this mess was positive. All right, he had no choice. Someone was trying to kill him; Polkovnikov was threatening, and he had maybe not so much to lose. But in the black of night he had also grown hopeful, nearly confident.

That now, maybe, Duvakin could work things his way, for a change. Get himself out of trouble here, get himself back to Moscow . . . who knows?

The chill threat of Vaska's words, the bleak spruce forest, his knowledge that Darmoved now knew of his existence, all set heavily on his head and shoulders, like so many scruffy disease-ridden crows.

Wordlessly, Duvakin turned and started down the driveway toward the highway. Mother of God, he thought trudging drearily through the cold, I was going to help Dusya? This whole cursed world is an orphanage; just some of us find it out earlier. The wind lapped eagerly beneath his coat, and his feet rang hard on the steely tarmac.

* ELEVEN *

"Vanenka, come sit, darling. The blini are ready."
Galya brought in a dish piled what looked half a
meter high with blini, covered with a hand-embroidered
towel.

Duvakin turned away from the window where he had
been studying the dusk and froze; Galya looked almost
like the picture on some crazy tourist calendar, broad
smile, the platter . . . Russian Hospitality.

"Good heavens, Galya, all this for me?"

Galya blushed, beamed, and sat, then patted the chair
next to her. "Come, sit. It's good to have someone to cook
for."

Duvakin looked at the window again, glanced at the
apartment, and felt his spirits slip even lower. He walked
slowly over to the table, forced a smile onto his face, and
sat down. "Blini, eh? They look delicious."

"I started the dough last night. I thought you might
come back . . ." She smiled happily.

That smile was like another spoonful of ash on his

[183]

tongue. Duvakin buried his head, putting in blini as fast as he could force them. This was about the only thanks he could give the poor woman, he thought darkly, although his mind also registered distantly that the blini were delicious, and he was starved.

"You didn't eat lunch?" Galya asked as she piled another three or four blini on the plate.

"No! No more sour cream!" Duvakin managed to blurt as she poured the milky thick glop onto the plate.

"You don't like sour cream? Some jam then? Lingonberry, I picked them myself . . ." She was already ladling the thick purple stuff onto the sour cream. "You shouldn't skip lunch, no matter how busy you get at work. I'm a doctor, I know." She patted his head affectionately.

"I wasn't at work," Duvakin spoke absently, contemplating the gluey mass on his plate; it took him a second to realize that the atmosphere had grown distinctly chillier. Damn, what had he said? He looked at Galya.

The woman had only pulled back bare centimeters, but managed to look as far away as Moscow; her round eyes would have looked slaty and cold, had they not also been filmed with what must be tears. Duvakin stopped chewing. Galya's chin trembled faintly.

"Taking a bottle holiday then, eh?" she finally asked with very strained brightness. "Well, as you wish, but I had believed you for better . . ." She stood resolutely and stalked into the kitchen.

Duvakin slumped back against his chair. *Damn* it. And damn it again. Not enough to begin today with Darmoved, then spend all bloody afternoon freezing, out looking for Dusya, then crawl back to Galya's feeling like the lowest form of reptile, and her all open arms and kisses . . .

Last night he had thought he might help perhaps

everyone in the world. Now he felt powerless, or worse. Maybe even a danger for Galya.

Certainly a danger if she had to know any of this.

But how else to get her out of the kitchen, where he could hear her sobbing?

He stood heavily, trudged toward the kitchen. She stood at the sink, pretending to wash dishes.

"Galya," he said softly. "It wasn't like that. It's, it's something that it's better . . . you shouldn't know about it." Duvakin felt tongue-tied.

Galya nodded once, sharply, then straightened her back. "Well, you've the right, of course. But you might have been decent enough at least to tell me . . . there's another . . ."

"Quiet!" Duvakin snapped, surprising them both. "Will you listen one moment? And *don't* cry, *please!* Galya, please," Duvakin pleaded, cursing himself, his impotence, and the evil world in general. Reluctantly, he reached for her warm soft hand. "Galya, Galenka, listen, I can't tell you everything, but, well, yesterday I ran into a Moscow . . . colleague."

"Here?" Galya asked, incredulous and suspicious.

"In my flat," Duvakin said miserably. "He came for me. There's a matter he . . ." Duvakin paused, wondering what effect his words would have, dreading it. "Well, he wanted my help . . ." he finished lamely.

"On what?" she sniffed, inclined to believe but not yet permitting herself to.

On what can I tell you on what? Duvakin let her hand drop. That he's a KGB general in internal security, and I've been out to the regional KGB head, pretending to be KGB too, and now I'm up to my chin in God knows what? Duvakin knew he had no money, no power, not even hopes. But there *was* one thing he could give Galya.

Complete ignorance of this mess.

He shrugged. "I can't tell you . . ."

Her eyes stayed hard, more gray than green; though her chin still trembled, she held it sternly high.

The silence continued unbearably, until Duvakin muttered, "Because . . . it's a Party matter . . . and delicate."

"Say no more!" Galya said nobly, after a moment of searching his face. "From Moscow? Party matters? Say no more." She pressed his hand warmly and turned back to the sink. After a moment she began humming, something about brown eyes and bloody saddles.

Duvakin studied the plump back before him and sighed. Terrific. Galya has him figured now for maybe head of the Far Eastern Young Communist League at least, Polkovnikov wants God knows what of him, and somewhere out there is a man who pushed him in front of a Zhiguli. Not to mention a bloody sot of an Armenian who will be wanting him to come count red bunting. Of Darmoved he preferred not even to think.

Then he remembered Dusya and had an idea.

"Galya?"

She turned around and smiled, adjusting her hair with the backs of her wet hands. Her eyes looked uneasy, but she wanted to believe him, anyway.

"Galya, look, there is one thing. Maybe you could help me, professionally, so to speak . . ."

In some indefinable way, Galya became less a woman and more a doctor, cautious, filtering her answer through official considerations. "Yes?"

Duvakin thought disjointedly how best to put it. "Well, it's—how's the best way to locate a girl?"

Galya inhaled and grew hard, like sea ice. "*That* service is not my profession."

Duvakin blushed. "No, I didn't . . . I mean . . ." He took a deep breath and tried again. "A *young* girl, an orphan . . ." He felt he was in a taxi sliding on ice; all efforts merely pushed him deeper into trouble. Finally, he blurted out the tale of Dusya, her phone call, and his useless, freezing afternoon of wallowing about in Thirteenth Olympiad microregion; the reasons why Dusya was an orphan he managed to keep vague. "Anyway," he ended feebly, "with you being in children's ward and all, I thought perhaps . . ."

Galya sat slowly in a kitchen chair, keeping her eyes on Duvakin. Were the eyes warmer? It seemed so, but maybe he was wishing it?

"Why?" she finally asked.

"Why what?"

"Why do you want to help this Dusya?" Galya watched him narrowly.

"I explained. And not help, anyway. Make sure she's all right, you know, taken care of . . ." Duvakin felt wooden, as if perhaps fatigue was keeping his words from making sense. "Galya, she's a little girl . . ."

"Whose?"

Comprehension bathed Duvakin. "Good lord, Galya. I swear . . . it's as I told you, not mine, heavens, I only even saw her the once, she's just the daughter of a . . ." Duvakin couldn't think of a way to stumble around the description of Rzhevsky. "Of a Party comrade. She phoned me, damn it." Finally, disgusted, he sat heavily in a chair beside Galya. "Because she needs some help, that's why . . ." He toyed with a spoon, bending the head back and forth.

Galya reached over to take the spoon, but let her hand linger on his a second. "She got your phone number, and you still think she needs help?"

Duvakin felt nonplussed. "Maybe I told it to her mother . . ." he said, certain that he had not.

Galya held his hand for a second longer, then patted it, barked a short laugh, and said, "All right, I'll poke around, for you. I'll see what I can find out."

Duvakin was surprised how relieved he felt and realized that he must have been fretting about Dusya all afternoon. He remembered the blini; his appetite revived; he glanced at his watch.

"Galya, is it really after nine?" he asked, shocked.

"After nine, Vanenka . . . almost your bedtime, little soul." She smiled a broad, dimpled smile. The "little soul" caught in Duvakin's throat, making him cough. Then her answer sank in.

"After nine! I've got to get going!" He pushed the chair back, to find her hand on its back, preventing him.

"And where, at such an hour?" Her voice was cold again. All the work he'd just done, pffft.

"Out—oh, Galya, not for that, not for . . . it's the colleague I spoke of." Duvakin floundered. "But I'll be—" he began automatically, then realized he had no idea when he would be back; there was even the chance it might be never, he thought gloomily. "Well, it could be late," he said lamely, not quite meeting her eye. "But I will be back. Tonight."

He rose, shrugged on his coat, tucked in his neck scarf, wished he had some high boots, for the snow. When the drifts were deep like this, he usually got his socks soaked.

"No matter, Vanenka," Galya said huskily, after a pause. "Here . . ."

Duvakin felt something cold pressed into his right hand; he looked.

"A key?"

"I hate leaving it in the post box . . . dangerous, you know?" Galya said in a tremulous, joking voice while she tucked his scarf tighter into his coat, straightening his lapels. "You have your gloves? And where's your hat?"

"Right here." Duvakin held up his left hand vaguely, like a bird flapping. Then he stood, uncertain of himself. Galya watched him closely; he felt his neck flush.

"Bye," he finally said, bending stiffly to caress her

cheek, fragrant with old perfume and woman smell; small bits of powder stuck to his lips. In return, Galya gave him a hug so hard it made his eyes bulge, so swift he was on the landing with the door shut behind him before he realized what had happened.

Ah well, he squared his hat, ah, well . . . Galya behind and Polkovnikov ahead. Duvakin lit a deliberate cigarette, hoped fervently that he would see this landing again, and set off.

Outside, Magadan was returning more or less to normal, night crews scooping the mounds of cheesy wet snow into piles at the curb, where coal trucks with scoop chains laboriously backed up, slowly loading the snow. All over the town you heard the tinny tinkle of the backup warning bells as the crews toiled in the street.

Duvakin slithered and jumped, threading a careful way back to the Far East Hotel, his mind too much on keeping his socks reasonably dry to worry about Polkovnikov. Magadan is small, the central part no more than a few blocks, and as the newest of the city's few hotels, the Far East had the place of honor, overlooking the asphalt expanse of Lenin Square. In a few days Duvakin's crews would be draping a five-story Brezhnev down its front, beneath the promise "We Shall Make Each Day a Virgin Land!!!"

Duvakin finally made his way to the doors, a triple glass tunnel that contained only a decrepit doorman drowsing on a chair.

Duvakin tugged at the door. It was locked. He studied the doorman, who made no move at all. For a moment Duvakin thought perhaps the man might have frozen there; then he began a determined assault, rattling the handle and rapping at the glass with a coin.

After agonizing minutes, during which Duvakin began seriously to wonder whether he would have to stand on the street and shriek for Polkovnikov, at long last the doorman stood. Not so old after all, it seemed to Duvakin. The portly man came gloomily to the outside door, where he pointed a thick dirty finger at a sign hanging lopsided from a thread. "No Entrance Without Guest Card," it said.

"I'm not a guest; I haven't got one," Duvakin said, and pulled at the door.

The doorman shrugged, pointed first at his ear, then at the sign again. Then he turned as if to sit down once more.

Duvakin pondered a second, his hand still on the door; if he showed the doorman his Party card, he would surely get in, but at what risk, since none of this was happening officially? Secret, Polkovnikov had said. He might just push past, but the man looked bored, as if he might relish a good scandal on a slow evening. Inspiration struck.

He waved frantically, tapping again on the glass, indicating that the man should open the door. He must have looked convincing for at last the doorman fumbled with the bolt, opening the door.

"So?" he said cautiously, indifferently. Duvakin pushed on the glass.

"Young man!" the doorman said sharply, placing a strategic foot to jam the door. He drew himself up sternly, tugging at his tatty brown uniform smock. "You must have a hotel card to come in!" He straightened his uniform cap, which read, without explanation, "Red Dawn."

"How do new guests get in?" Duvakin asked slyly.

"What do you mean?" the man was suspicious.

"It's a new rule, right?"

"Yes, it is . . ." the doorman answered warily, a little mystified.

"So how can I get a card if I don't go inside? And if I can't go inside without one, then I can't get one, follow me? So let's say I've gone in to get one." Duvakin stepped smartly past the man's confusion and into the lobby.

He had never been in the Far East before, so he trusted to luck with the elevators. The low-ceilinged lobby of gray and black granite held nothing save an empty registration desk, an empty news kiosk, and an empty porter's station. Duvakin strode purposefully forward, praying the elevators were in the next hall; it was unlikely the doorman would pursue him that far. His responsibility was, after all, only for the doors.

The elevators were there, two slots slightly larger than phone booth doors. Duvakin pushed the buttons on both; one was, as he expected, turned off. The working elevator responded with phlegmatic squeakings and whir-rings. Duvakin looked around. The hotel was not large, but was built as if it were, with a warren of halls, restau-rants, and private rooms on the ground floor, even though only five stories perched on top. The lobby was vast, but utterly deserted. The dust on the sills behind him sug-gested perhaps that the hotel was abandoned. Duvakin shook himself, trying to lose the feeling of someone al-ways at his back. Across from the elevators was a huge dining hall set as if the Red Army chorus was coming for dinner, but without a soul in sight. Perhaps the cause was the cardboard sign on the door—"No Seats."

The elevator arrived and clanked open, leaving Du-vakin a step up of about half a meter. Duvakin heaved himself in, wondering how a guest with suitcases might fit in so small a space; although his head did not quite touch the roof, it was close enough to make him slouch. How in the world did Polkovnikov ride these? Taking a deep breath and with some effort not spitting over his left shoulder for luck, Duvakin pressed the top button. The doors began to close, then opened, closed, opened, as if in a frenzy of hiccups. Duvakin gave the doors a kick, they shut, and he creaked upwards.

Hotels like these, Duvakin knew, blossomed in the fertility of a paradox. Each city must have a luxury hotel for visiting powers and well-placed locals, but what kind of pull could a man claim if he were stuck here, in Magadan? Any real power would be nearer Moscow. And so these poorly made hotels *luxe* stood idle and dusty except for occasional groups of bureaucrats sent, presumably, for punishment.

Top floor, Polkovnikov had said last night, and toward it Duvakin clanked, his heart beating time with the ragged noises of the shaft. To calm his excitement, Duvakin read and reread the elaborate, barely comprehensible instructions for elevator riding.

The doors finally opened, hiccuping again, until Duvakin kicked them. He released his breath slowly, then felt dizzy. He realized he had barely breathed the entire slow way up. The floors of the hotel were stacked glass squares; from the small landing where he stood, there would have been a view of Magadan, except that all the panes were badly steamed, save a cracked one, which had been patched with two large sheets of plywood. The hall was painted black; surprisingly, there was no duty woman at the key desk.

Duvakin stood nervously, hearing nothing save his own shoes.

"Polkovnikov?" he whispered, wondering which of the twelve doors he could see held the general. Then, louder, he repeated the name. The same silence also repeated. He stepped gingerly down the hall, wondering whether perhaps he had misunderstood.

It was eerie to wander in what seemed an entirely deserted hotel, looking for someone invisible. The wind moaned at the edge of the plywood; radiators pinged and gurgled. Duvakin walked the length of the hall and back, both dreading and hoping for the appearance of *someone*.

It took a second trip to notice the door set flush in the black wall; it wasn't exactly hidden, but in a hall made of black panels, it was not designed to be noticed, either. Gingerly, Duvakin pushed; nothing. He pushed at the other side; it gave a bit, then popped open, revealing a set of carpeted stairs. Duvakin gaped at them.

"Polkovnikov?" Duvakin called faintly. No answer. He went up a cautious couple of stairs, repeated, without result. Duvakin shrugged his shoulders, then said half-aloud, as if there were someone listening to whom he must explain, "Top floor he said ..." That too met silence, and Duvakin shrugged again, then went up, his heart pumping hard.

This secret floor was carpeted in red, not black, and the windows looked out through a grill work of patterned cement blocks, but otherwise everything was like the floor below. Except, Duvakin noticed, that there were almost no doors. "Polkovnikov?" Duvakin asked again, seeing no one. Silence.

The silence deepened, until Duvakin could hear his own belt creak with his breathing. As in childhood, when on dark village lanes his body had been electrified with the sudden certainty that *something* was directly behind him, Duvakin whirled.

And found nothing. "Polkovnikov!" he whispered hoarsely, his voice giving out midword.

Duvakin thought of Rzhevsky, vividly dead now, huge powerful head split open, bleeding, jaw dangling broken. Who could kill Polkovnikov? he reminded himself sternly, recalling the tall power of the man. And who would push you in front of an auto? the empty hall answered back.

"Polkovnikov!" Duvakin bellowed, poised for flight at the top of the stairs, his heart rattling like an air compressor.

"In here!" he heard a muffled voice.

"Polkovnikov! Thank heaven ... Where are you?"

* Anthony Olcott *

Duvakin followed down the hall; there could not have been more than three rooms on the floor, all on the harbor side. He chose the middle door. "Polkovnikov?"

His fear subsided, Duvakin was left with the bitter awareness that a part of him had panicked badly when haunted by the fear of Polkovnikov's death. Which meant Duvakin, the fool, had come to rely upon the man who once before had kicked him down the ladder to here. Duvakin grabbed the handle, determined to be as distant, as self-serving as he could.

"Come in, damn it, Vanya, you're late," he heard Polkovnikov shout irritably.

"Late?" Duvakin dug his watch out of the layers of gloves and coat; although the crystal was almost totally opaque with moisture, it looked no more than ten past. Suspicious, he held the watch to his ear, where he heard the familiar "tick-bong." "You just said 'evening' . . ."

"Never mind what I said; haul your butt in here; the driver will be here any minute!"

Duvakin was scuttling obediently toward the invisible angry voice before he thought driver?

"Bloody weather . . ." he heard from somewhere deep in the suite and followed it. The rooms were grander than Duvakin had seen in ages—large chairs covered in orange and red cloth, sideboards of heavily varnished wood, faceted glass bowls, the one in the middle room filled with a large fruit, yellow, the size of a man's fist. Even in his awe, though, Duvakin recognized domestic goods. The lack of imported wares cheered him again; last time he had relied on Polkovnikov, it had been in a world where even the chairs were foreign. That the furniture was Russian made him hope that maybe the problems were too, and a simple Russian man could cope with them.

He found Polkovnikov in the last room, standing by a zippered canvas bag. The general looked more haggard

[194]

than yesterday, snappish. "Come on, damn it. I haven't much time. Khromoi's man will be here any minute. Give me a hand with this." He pointed to some blue artificial fabric that was sticking out of the bag.

"Khromoi?" Duvakin asked, tugging ineptly on the fabric. He recalled the name from somewhere, but could not place it.

"There's supposed to be some tubes in there, aluminum . . . yes, my host, your boss, regional Party secretary, he got me these rooms. Lovely, eh?" Polkovnikov waved a hand blindly at the air. "You've got the tubes?"

Duvakin handed them over, mystified. "Khromoi? The regional secretary's name is Omiyakhon, he's Chukchi . . . What's this thing?"

"I said the guy in charge, not first. Second secretary. You think they'd let some blubber-sucker run anything bigger than a reindeer race?" Polkovnikov paused, scanned the canvas bag, then swore. "Bloody hell, there's supposed to be clips of some sort."

"These things?" Duvakin handed the general a bunch of red channel-like plastic devices. "Why are you going to Khromoi's then?" he asked, wanting to add, especially if you're not here yet?

"That's the devil . . ." Polkovnikov took them, put them on the bed, then assembled the tubes into a shape rather like an inverted bowl. Duvakin was totally mystified. "Hand me the tent part, would you?" Polkovnikov said, straightening his back.

"Tent?" Duvakin looked about in confusion.

"Tent! Tent!" Polkovnikov snapped, waving one of his enormous fingers at the blue fabric.

It was heavier than Duvakin would have guessed, but there was no question it was a tent, not after Polkovnikov laid it out and, with a certain clumsy efficiency, clipped it onto the frame. "There!" he said, admiring his work.

Duvakin stared dumbly at the blue bowl, trying to understand the need for this enormous mushroom cap of a tent in the middle of a luxury hotel bedroom.

"In," Polkovnikov said, holding open a flap.

"Me?"

"Who do you think—Pushkin? Get a move on, damn it, there's not much time."

Baffled, Duvakin bent over, then tried to duckwalk in. The tent was too low; he was forced onto hands and knees.

"Move over, you fool." Polkovnikov said sharply, already on his knees. Duvakin slithered around the inside, finally curling up around the wall, to make room for the huge Polkovnikov. They bumped heads, got their feet tangled. By the time Polkovnikov succeeded in zipping the flap shut, they were so close Duvakin could smell the sourness of Polkovnikov's breath, as if he stood at the portals of the man's stomach.

"What is this for?" he asked in a stage whisper.

"Just a second . . ." Polkovnikov, already sweating, twisted around with a grunt to switch on something contained in a cloth pouch at the apex of the tent. Duvakin heard or saw nothing different, but Polkovnikov smiled and said, "There."

"There what? What's all this about?"

"Antisurveillance tent. That box up there sends out a jamming signal, and there's wires woven into the fabric to prevent detection, and special padding. They work, believe me. They're German; Nixon brought one the last time he came, and we couldn't get a thing out of his room. Him and that fat Jew of his would crawl in and pfft!— like they'd gone home. Finally, we had to send a man in to cut a square out of it to see what the devil it was made of."

For a moment Duvakin pictured a world leader's rear end disappearing into a tent pitched in the middle of a fancy guest room, and chuckled. Then a more serious thought struck him.

"Nixon, all right, but why do we need one?"

Polkovnikov looked at Duvakin as if disappointed, perhaps exasperated, then said, "You don't mind everyone knowing I'm giving you this?"

Duvakin twisted his neck; Polkovnikov had laid a small automatic pistol between them, a service Tokarev. "Mother of God! What do I need that for?" Duvakin's voice cracked. He pushed himself tighter against the wall of the tent.

"You know how to use it?" Polkovnikov ignored Duvakin's question. In the tent the air was growing thick and moist; it smelled of Polkovnikov's stomach.

"We shot them in militia training, sure," Duvakin said, still pressing away from the pistol.

"Take it then, and listen; there isn't a lot of time."

Duvakin could not drag his eyes from the pistol. "I can't use that! What am I supposed to do?" he squeaked. "I can't shoot anybody."

"Shut up and listen!" Polkovnikov hissed in a garlicky blast. "You never paid attention in the service, or what? But that's not it. Look, how did things go with Darmoved?"

Caught off balance and still watching the pistol nervously, Duvakin said, "With Darmoved?" He tried to pull himself together. "Things went well. The business with the computer worked just like you said. I'm to keep in touch, but can go ahead . . ." He hoped Polkovnikov's reaction to this would give him some inkling of the purpose of his trip.

In vain. The general nodded thoughtfully, waited. "That's it? Nothing else?"

"What else?" Duvakin was puzzled. "It was just like you said, he put that stuff into his machine, patted me on the butt . . ."

"No suspicions, welcomed you like a lost war comrade? Ouch! Damn it, a wire. Move your foot." Polkovnikov shifted heavily, forcing Duvakin further back into the wall of the tent. He sensed a cramp very near in his left thigh, tried to ignore it.

"Well yes, sure. I didn't think that was ... important." Who wouldn't have, he didn't quite dare say.

"*Everything* is important! Everything! You are my eyes!" Polkovnikov hissed, spraying Duvakin's face. Then, surprised, he said, "And where are you wriggling to?"

"Open the tent," Duvakin said grimly, squirming to try to reach the zipper. "Open that damn flap!" he repeated more stridently.

"Vanya ..." Polkovnikov's voice was placating, but the grip he clamped on Duvakin's elbow was not. "Vanya, don't take that attitude. You want to go to Moscow or not?"

That slowed Duvakin but did not stop him. "Lot of good Moscow will do me, when it's in a box they send me there, eh? Dead?"

"Dead? Who said anything about dead?" Polkovnikov whispered hoarsely; his surprise was genuine enough to make Duvakin feel a little better, even though still determined to get out of the tent.

"So what's the pistol for? Swatting flies?"

Polkovnikov waved his hand dismissively. "You've got too much imagination, Vanya."

"I have? You're the one's yelling and spitting ... besides, I'm nobody's eyes ...'"

To Duvakin's utter astonishment Polkovnikov hung his head, then looked up, a half-smile on his face. "I'm sorry Vanya. This is ... things are complicated, and there isn't much time. Let's start again, eh?"

Duvakin took a deep sour breath, to collect his wits, then began mechanically to recite his morning, from the

[198]

Chukchi on. As he talked, he mulled over Polkovnikov and grew ever more depressed. For the arrogant son of a bitch to apologize must mean things were in a very bad way.

On the other hand though, maybe Duvakin held more cards than he thought.

"Burying shit doesn't make it gold, eh? I like that," Polkovnikov repeated, shaking his head appreciatively. "And he knew about the airplane and the furs?" The general looked thoughtful.

Duvakin waited, feeling his breath slide almost syrupy down his throat. The silence stretched, until Duvakin could hear his own watch.

At last, Polkovnikov cleared his throat, coughed. "Well . . . things could be worse than I thought. Come on then. You'd best come with me."

"What!? Come where?" Duvakin looked at his watch. He was on the point of saying Galya would be waiting, but didn't.

"To Khromoi's," Polkovnikov answered matter-of-factly, twisting about to reach the zipper.

"Tonight? You said you were going; why do I have to go?"

"You told Darmoved you were."

"I did *what*?" Duvakin wiped sweat from his forehead.

"Khromoi's the comrade you claimed you were checking up on," Polkovnikov explained heavily, as if Duvakin were slow-witted.

"We already know?" Duvakin's surprise was growing. "Why do we have to go out there then?"

"Because Darmoved knows you're going . . ."

"But I never mentioned the man's name, I swear it!" Duvakin interrupted frantically.

Polkovnikov shrugged. "If Darmoved's any good, he

knows where you're going. And then, like I was saying, we don't know how long it would be until Khromoi knows you're coming . . ."

"I'm going to arrest him?" Duvakin squeaked, once more seeing the pistol, in horror.

"Do be quiet." Polkovnikov shifted uncomfortably, then said, "You *couldn't* arrest him, he's a Party secretary."

"So what do you need me for then?" Duvakin squeaked, now in exasperation. "It's not like I can do anything."

"It's not us who's got to do, it's *him*," Polkovnikov said hoarsely. "You're a secret investigator, remember? And what we want is names, bodies, numbers. If we hit Khromoi between the eyes with you, he'll maybe be happy to cooperate, and then we can tell Moscow what we've got out here . . ." While Polkovnikov talked he fished out a cigarette. Duvakin lay on his elbow, wondering whether a cigarette would even ignite in the tent now. Or was the heavy mustiness only in his head? It was like in nightmares, crossing a burning bridge, maybe, with horrible monsters ahead. And after each forward step they took away the boards behind. Were he to leave now, there was still the Zhiguli pusher out there. And Darmoved, who knew his name. And who had warned Pivovarov to keep everyone clear of the Rzhevsky business. And then too Polkovnikov wasn't the sort to let a simple refusal come between him and what he wanted.

Beyond all this hovered Galya, and God only knows what Duvakin could make of that. Terrific. Choices are easy to make—when there aren't any. Besides, a part of him hoped insistently, maybe sooner begun, sooner done. Or done for, he amended darkly.

"All right," he finally mumbled. "I'm a secret super spy, that's all I do?"

"That's my Vanya!" Polkovnikov brightened. "I can't

lie, Vanya, it won't be summer camp. Keep your eyes open and follow my lead. Remember, these are deep waters . . ."

Duvakin could sense Polkovnikov's excitement building beneath the cautioning words, but he could not share it. When you are a little fish, the waters are always deep. He cursed his luck again, then sighed. Reluctantly, he picked up the pistol. The plastic handle felt hot.

"Put that thing away, and let's go," Polkovnikov said, then unzipped the flap. The fresh air was like a roll in the snow after half an hour in the bathhouse. Duvakin let Polkovnikov unfold himself, then scrambled out after him. The general motioned silence, mimed putting the gun away. Still feeling as if the hand with the gun was that of a stranger, Duvakin hastily stored it in his suit pocket, then even more hastily dug it back out. Mercifully, the safety catch was on. He returned the gun to his pocket.

"Stow the gear, Duvakin . . ." Polkovnikov said, lighting his cigarette.

Dazed by the tent, the gun, and his fatigue, Duvakin clumsily followed orders, wadding the blue material more or less back into the carrying case.

"Let's go down, the car should be here soon. You want a grapefruit?" Polkovnikov waved at a glass bowl on the television, where there were more of those same fist-sized yellow fruits.

"Grapefruit?" Duvakin repeated mechanically. The word meant nothing to him, except the "fruit" part. Fruit in April he would not refuse.

"Grapefruit, grapefruit . . . like an orange or a lemon, but bitter. Some of our brownass socialist brothers ship us those things, and we send them rocket launchers," Polkovnikov spoke tensely, his irony heavy.

Duvakin took one of the fist-sized fruits, then realized he was squeezing it, kneading it—as if it might squirt not juice, but some omen of what the evening would bring. Oh well, he forced himself to think, Galya won't like a battered fruit . . . *when* I get home. He pocketed the grapefruit, took a deep breath, and followed after Polkovnikov. The pistol bulged in a clammy, familiar way against his thigh.

★ TWELVE ★

"Now, *that* doesn't hurt your eyes any, does it?" Polkovnikov said loudly to Duvakin.

Duvakin jerked his eyes open and thought, indeed. Khromoi's house looked like someplace a composer might once have lived, or Tolstoy maybe; a white house of wood, not huge, it was set on a knoll overlooking a small lake dotted with round boulders, each wearing a cap of snow. The setting was serene, white, glistening beneath the ragged moon and scudding clouds. Silver shadows danced across the gingerbread fretting and down the porch railing, carved with men and bears and roosters. The birch were crisp white against the brooding black of the pines; Duvakin felt a tightening in his chest. It was beautiful, and he was terrified.

It wasn't just that he felt desperately stupid about what he was to do and why he was there, although that clenched his stomach too; he had lived with *that* sense of nervousness before.

It was also Polkovnikov. Duvakin had felt him twist

and fidget the entire way from the hotel to here, constantly shifting position. They could not talk, of course, save for pleasantries. Khromoi's driver would have ears, as well as eyes for the road. Even so, Polkovnikov muttered to himself, never quite audible, but not inaudible either. His right fist clenched and loosened, clenched and loosened, the shiny black leather changing sheen as it stretched and relaxed.

Duvakin could guess only that Polkovnikov was scared. The thought in no way calmed him.

He tried to remember what he knew of Khromoi, but came up only with crumbs. Second secretary, he signed a few things, maybe even came to the office, though Duvakin could not have said when. Certainly Duvakin would have seen his photo, hanging on Red Honor Boards here and there, or on the rostrum at some parade or other—but who ever looks at the faces in those photos?

Their limousine pulled up to an old-fashioned wooden carriage entrance, as if this were a set for some Turgenev film, and just as in those movies, their host stood on the porch, waiting for the car to come to a stop. They did; the driver opened Polkovnikov's door, then his, and stood stiffly to one side.

"Welcome, dear comrade General, to our birthplace of the dawn!"

"Thank you, comrade Secretary!" Polkovnikov boomed in reply as he climbed from the car to greet his host. Duvakin scrambled out behind, forced to battle his way around the car through a snowdrift; the driver had parked too near the edge on his side. Then he had to trot to keep up with the two men, who disappeared into the house.

The house was as comfortably old-fashioned within as it was without; double doors led to a wide hall, where a plank floor went past several high doors, farther than Duvakin could have thrown his hat, to end in a staircase ascending to large windows that must look out onto the tarn. The oddity of the hall took a moment to emerge from his discomfort as he jogged after Polkovnikov.

There were no furnishings. No tables, chests, not even pictures or rugs. Their steps sounded hollowly off the highly polished floor. The driver had remained outside; Duvakin hastily followed Polkovnikov and Khromoi's quick steps to a door beyond the grand stairs.

"The house?" he heard what he assumed was Khromoi's voice say. "I find it large, for myself, but then there are . . . *social* responsibilities." He made the word sound distasteful.

"I can well imagine," Polkovnikov said affably, as Duvakin finally caught up with them. The room in which they had stopped was furnished sparely, with a desk, some chairs, a divan; more compelling was the view, full glass doors looking down onto the moon-lit frozen lake.

In so handsome a setting Khromoi seemed oddly out of place; he looked like everybody's pensioner uncle, a stout man who came barely above Duvakin's shoulder, saved from total baldness only by the wens and moles that dotted his head like currants in a sticky bun. His gabardine trousers were as full as a circus Cossack's and were tugged by old-fashioned suspenders right up to his breast bone. Below the waistband his belly sagged solidly, making him look respectable, a little stupid perhaps, and almost pregnant. Harmless.

What Duvakin could see of his eyes through the deep folds of flesh enclosing them suggested perhaps this impression was cultivated.

The suspicion deepened when Khromoi, after seating both of them on the hard divan and taking himself a seat opposite in an old-fashioned, heavy armchair, smiled and said, "All right, General, why have they sent you?" The manner was avuncular, but the question was not. Duvakin felt Polkovnikov stiffen.

"Maybe who sent me is the better question," Polkovnikov said, with what sounded to Duvakin's gloomy ear like nervousness.

"Who, why, it's the same question, eh?" Khromoi waved a puffy, liver-spotted hand. "Magadan isn't Paris; Moscow doesn't run cultural exchanges with us." He smiled again, seated formally on the edge of his chair. "They don't generally pay us much mind out here, as long as we do our job . . . and so far as I know," (he smiled, to show he knew very well how far that was) "we have been doing well. So there must be a problem. So . . . spare an old man the formalities, eh?" He put his hand on his heart. "I pray you . . . Anyway," he added, without the bantering tone, "on the telephone you said you were from Grigorii Vladimirovich's office."

Polkovnikov bobbed his head. "That's right, a friendly visit, friends of yours in the center, they've . . . there's been some concern . . ."

Khromoi, a wily old fish, would not rise to *that* worm. He sat, soft, pale hands clasped comfortably above his paunch. So? his deep porcine eyes asked.

"About the income," Polkovnikov went on reluctantly. "Why the income is down to—to crumbs." The last was spoken almost as a challenge.

Khromoi, though, was not rattled. He smiled, formed a plump little arch with his fingers.

"Crumbs? It might seem so to one from the capital . . . but among us here in Magadan, three milliard and kopeks still can be called a loaf." Your move, his air seemed to say.

"Do you know what the figures used to be?" Polkovnikov now was almost stern.

"For what?"

"The Magadan region, of course. Do you know the income used to be twice what it is today?"

"Nothing is what it once was, dear General—not you,

not I, not the region. For one thing, it used to be the territory was bigger, before they carved it all up . . ." Khromoi still looked imperturbed.

"I grant you, but the figures are adjusted for that." Polkovnikov leaned forward, urgent. "Comrade, the questions are beginning to get nasty."

Here Khromoi's smile faded slightly, but held. "And no one thinks fit to mention that when I first came out here gold nuggets lay in the riverbed like radishes on a plate? That now we must dig and blast to get out even so much as *this*? He measured off the tiniest portion of his little finger with his thumbnail, squinted at it with a tiny glittering eye. "That the trees used to grow right down to the water, just almost asking to be carted off? Or that" — here Khromoi beamed again, took out a Russian cigarette, slowly crumpled the cardboard into a spiral, at last lighting the tiny dab of tobacco on its end—"or that back then we had much less of a problem with our labor supply . . ."

Slave labor, Duvakin added mentally, staring in spite of himself at the jolly, chubby old gentleman who had been a slave master. Probably his fatigue made him more sensitive, imagining things, but he could not halt a tremor in his knees. He had known one or two of the guards from those days, just simple convoy guards, and they had never seemed right in the head again. Not crazy, different. Like they looked at the world with eyes that had seen too many men die. Die stupidly. They could be nice enough, those former guards, but always it was like the world for them was still us armed few and you ragged, dying many, all crowbait in different stages of decay.

And Khromoi here had been a guard of the guards. Duvakin had to look away.

Even Polkovnikov looked a little pale, Duvakin thought. He hoped it was not sweat he saw beading along Polkovnikov's upper lip.

"They know, of course, comrade Secretary, they

know. But these are not generous times," Polkovnikov said wearily, as though this were an old and far too familiar conversation. "Things are bad, comrade. In a word, the center needs cash. They're rationing in Kazan two years, *potatoes* I mean, to say nothing already of meat. Even in Moscow last summer it was July before the first tomatoes hit the market, and then there was no cabbage. There's no milk or milk products anywhere . . . and the birds eat more of the wheat than we can manage to get in from the field. Even *if* Gosplan projections are correct—and can you remember a time when they were?—things will be tight." Polkovnikov shook his head sadly, then lit a cigarette. "Already there's whispers begun . . . that there's hunger coming."

Duvakin was shocked, as if he had stumbled into the wrong room. His whole life, adult life anyway, he heard words like these on the bus, in the street. But to hear the general repeat them, and now to a regional Party secretary . . . All Duvakin's life the Party had assured him and every one else that things were perfect and still improving; so what if every empty store, empty sack, and worn-out shoe suggested the contrary? You could always figure maybe they meant elsewhere, and besides, the confidence of the state at least made it seem that life was under control.

Polkovnikov's quiet litany gave Duvakin a sudden stab of vertigo; and what if it *wasn't* under control?

"This is Magadan, General," Khromoi replied dryly. "The only tomatoes we get here are homegrown . . . and usually pickled green, to beat the frosts. And ask your friend here how much dairy we get."

"Would you like the projections on fishing? Fuel costs? Cod bank depletion? Competition with the Japanese?" Polkovnikov said dully. "Because it's bad already doesn't mean it can't get worse."

Duvakin expected, even hoped, that Khromoi would counter Polkovnikov, challenge him, maybe even accuse him of slander. Surprisingly, he merely pursed his lips, nodded, and said gravely, "It's a bleak picture, General . . . but I'll grant not entirely at odds with things we hear even out here. However, forgive a dim-witted old man for asking this, but what has this to do with us? We have met all our quotas . . . or most of them."

The general smiled slightly. "That is as may be, but that isn't what concerns the center so much right now. It's *results* the center notices now. Income! Income! Income! Moscow is watching these things, you may believe me."

"No doubt," Khromoi said, shifting forward heavily, to lean ponderously on his knees. "And Moscow has suggestions as to where this money bush grows? Eh?" He spat derisively. "The devil can take you smart center types! More income, the comrade says, and me with a port frozen shut seven months out of twelve, the nearest railhead thirteen hundred kilometers away, and to do the work in this paradise? Drunks, thieves, and some kind of museum exhibits who found out about the wheel last week!" Khromoi's eyes glinted with anger now, burning deep in their folds of flesh. His hands clopped forcefully on his knees. "You can tell your Grigorii Vladimirovich he's getting no more from me . . . and the two of you can just clear off!"

Duvakin watched in horror as the old man rose, wobbly and quivering like a bear in spring; not so lean, but as dangerous. It was no comfort that Polkovnikov also leaped up in alarm.

"Comrade, calm yourself, please! It's not what you think! It isn't for . . . it's not personal. It's the *state* that needs your help."

The combination of Polkovnikov's greater height, which returned him authority, and the word "state" stopped Khromoi, but did not make him sit.

After a space he said flatly, "What are you suggesting?"

Polkovnikov smiled with relief, then asked, "You want everyone to know?"

Khromoi looked down at his hands, then up to Polkovnikov again, evaluating, like a card player just before he bets. Then, still silent, he searched inside his pants pocket, took out an object about the size of Polkovnikov's cigarette case, only thicker, and demonstratively moved a wheel in its side.

"You have about a minute," he said simply.

"It'll have to do," Polkovnikov said quickly, turning to Duvakin.

I'm to speak now? Duvakin wondered in panic. Follow my lead, Polkovnikov had said; so where was the lead? He coughed.

"I ought perhaps to introduce you," Polkovnikov said smoothly. "Duvakin, Ivan Pavlovich, a Magadaner four years now . . ."

"The name is familiar," Khromoi said in a neutral voice, with one eye on the door. Duvakin felt prickles shooting through the underside of his scalp; he gave a calming scratch to his balding head.

"One of your workers, in fact, agitprop. He assists your Sutrapian with that end of things. Gets about a good bit, lectures, speaks to people, sees things, hears things . . . and sometimes helps us too."

"A Judas," Khromoi said matter-of-factly, examining Duvakin as if he had just found him in his soup.

Just then a heavy-set blondish man in tight jeans burst into the room. A fast look about slowed his near trot. "All is well, Vladilen Alexandrovich?" he asked diffidently, his big hands clenched at his sides. Duvakin leaped around wildly.

Khromoi scrutinized the two visitors for an agonizing moment, before finally saying, "Yes, quite well Lyonya, inform the others." Khromoi spoke offhandedly, but there was no question of his authority.

"Pardon me, Vladilen Alexandrovich, but . . ." The big man blushed uncomfortably; against his pale skin the result was spectacular. "But your, there's a problem with your . . ."

"I turned it off, Lyonya," Khromoi said patiently, returning to studying Polkovnikov and Duvakin, as if the guard had ceased to exist. Sensing the dismissal, the big man turned clumsily and left, with a parting, "Pardon me."

Polkovnikov laughed brittlely, nervous. "I am most impressed, comrade Khromoi." Duvakin watched Polkovnikov move deliberately, stiffly, to sit back down. Duvakin also relaxed, surprised to find he had one hand wrapped tightly about the pistol. He shuddered, looked at the door, imagining it burst open, burly guards with Kalashnikovs and felt boots lumbering in. And me with my toy pistol, he thought darkly. He crossed his arms, to get well away from the butt of the thing. Damn Polkovnikov, he thought darkly. Why was he making such a mess of things?

Khromoi acknowledged Polkovnikov's compliment with a bob of the head and turned to Duvakin. "And just what do you claim to have found during your snoops?"

There it was, the edge of the cliff, and Polkovnikov had only said, try to fly. Not how, not where. Just fly. Duvakin looked quickly at Polkovnikov, who was examining his shoe-tips. Unexpectedly, Duvakin's fright turned into anger. God damn Polkovnikov anyway! Throw me in and watch me drown.

"There's been some misdirection of commodities," Duvakin said as calmly as possible, trying to picture Rzhevsky's flat.

"What?" Khromoi leaned forward.

"Theft, Vladilen Alexandrovich." Duvakin concentrated on the older man's eye. "Valuable state property . . . furs, gold, diamonds . . ." he guessed.

"Timber, too!" Polkovnikov inserted loudly. Duvakin

looked in astonishment at the general. Who would steal timber? And how?

Khromoi, though, seemed nonplussed.

"This is what your sneaking about tells you?" he asked, studying Duvakin unpleasantly. Duvakin felt his fingers creep unbidden into his pocket, not to grip, but at least to touch the comforting plastic butt of the Tokarev. Then he remembered something of what the general had said back in the tent. Before abandoning him here.

"Theft from you, Vladilen Alexandrovich!" he said hurriedly. "No one has so much as *hinted* . . ." Duvakin groped for a direction. "But I've seen some things with your . . . well, not everyone is so honest . . . as you," he ended lamely.

"You have come to make a formal accusation?" Khromoi asked remotely, as if he stood away on a mountain.

Duvakin's heart caught at his throat. Have I?

Fortunately, Polkovnikov seemed to be back in working order.

"Yes!" he barked again. "But not against you, Vladilen Alexandrovich, good Lord, no . . ."

"Meaning?" Khromoi's question was as soft as before, but his eyes were fully open, glinting bearlike and crafty.

"Meaning, we'll grant that dear old Magadan is being squeezed of every kopek—I too am convinced of it— Where does it go, though? Eh? You remember why they always used to make the serf girls sing while they picked berries? So they knew all the berries got into the baskets . . ." Polkovnikov trailed off.

Duvakin was startled to hear himself add weightily, "Not all of Magadan's berries are going into your basket now."

Even more surprising, the old man agreed. "It's true," he murmured after a pause, his face now human, weary. "I am, and have been for a long time, an old man, General, a

simple man. And I find now I do not always understand
. . ." He shook his head heavily.

"Not so old, surely?" Polkovnikov said charmingly.
"There are many older, who at your age still had bright
horizons before them. Of course, they managed to catch
their affairs in time. Who are they, Vladilen Alexandrovich? Tell us their names, and we'll deal with them!"

Khromoi smiled slyly at the general. "I thought your
man here already had the names?"

Duvakin stared openmouthed at Polkovnikov; he had
never seen the man so inept. It was like watching some
famous footballer discover his shoelaces were tied together.

"He means who can we take?" Duvakin guessed, staring still at the general. "The situation . . ."

Polkovnikov gamely scrambled on. "*Something* must
be done, comrade Secretary, that's what worries the center. That's why they had me warn you. Corruption is being
looked at very sternly now. We can't afford to have every
swine in the country snout down in the trough, choking
down the swill as fast as he can wiggle his tongue. They
shoot people now." Polkovnikov's eyes were slate, crackling and excited. "What the comrade here has found re-
quires explanation . . . and *somebody* will have to answer
. . ." Polkovnikov left the inference hanging heavily in the
air.

"I CONTROL MY MEN!" Khromoi smashed the
threat back to the general.

Sometimes Duvakin stumbled on Chukchi dogpits,
illegal of course, but who could stop an enterprising soul
from snaring two of the half-wild, starving mongrels (descended from the brutes abandoned when Khrushchev
closed the Magadan camps) and chucking them in the
ring together? In those battles, just before the blood and
slaver, the air crackled like this.

Without thinking, Duvakin said calmly, "My experience is that you are mistaken." Then he stopped, wishing in horror he could bite off his tongue. Even Polkovnikov stared at him, blinking in surprise.

However, instead of replying, Khromoi levered himself out of the chair, paced heavily to the window, where he paused, studying the moon. When at last he spoke, it was to the window.

"Surely this is no concern for Grigorii Vladimirovich," he said softly, wearily. "You are correct. I can't deny that there have been a few . . . overly self-interested men, shall I call them? I deal with them as I can, and in a way that will make things clear to the others . . . but sometimes it seems like replacing the rotten logs in an old hut. Times are not what they were, you don't find the men anymore who come out here because the people need it, because the Party demands. Careerists, the whole lot of them! And I don't exclude Moscow," he turned to glare at Polkovnikov. Then, apparently indifferent, he shrugged. "But times change, people change . . . while the tasks remain. The people are still out there, their needs are still out there."

Duvakin watched the heavy old man, suspicious that this was some sort of set speech. The words were too common to be real. This was Duvakin's stock in trade, every agitprop man's—fine words about "the people" and their needs. To Duvakin a lifetime of reading slogans capped by four years of pushing them made the words rattle as meaninglessly as dried peas on a tin plate. The people, indeed.

And yet Khromoi spoke with a warmth that somehow made the impossibly trite abstraction sound real, alive. Duvakin recalled the bare entry, the idealistic name Khromoi's father had given him (Vladimir Lenin, the Kingdom of Heaven be his), and suddenly wondered, could it be that this wily old boar is what he claims to be? A Soviet man?

As if reading Duvakin's mind, Khromoi flared angrily, "Look at how I live! Is *this* the home of a Red millionaire? The Party gives me what I need, and I take no more! I have given my whole *life* to the Party, to the people . . . a claim not everyone can make." He studied Polkovnikov's expensive foreign suit with distaste. "But I am not a man blinded to reality either."

"Meaning?" Duvakin asked in surprise; the secretary had jumped in an unexpected direction.

"Meaning?" Khromoi shrugged, plump arms spread wide. "Meaning that I don't stop to change the whole world before getting done what I want done. Meaning, if it takes a little extra something to get Moscow's attention, well . . ." He made a shrewd face, like a clever peasant. "Look, you be square with me, I'll be square with you. Why is Grigorii Vladimirovich sticking his nose into this?"

Duvakin looked uncomfortably to Polkovnikov, who looked even more uncomfortable. "I can't tell you," the general finally whispered.

Khromoi shrugged, showed open palms of total hopelessness and infinite regret. "Ah, well, then . . ." He walked back from the window, smiling with regret. "And after four years of work . . ."

"*He's* under pressure," Polkovnikov muttered in disgust, self-consciously studying his cuffs.

"Beg pardon?" Khromoi paused in his slow advance.

"I said *they're* squeezing *him*!" Polkovnikov blurted, standing up again, apparently to replace his lost inquisitional edge with a physical one. "Squeezing him, you understand! And he wants me to check . . ." Polkovnikov trailed off, then said almost whiningly, "Think it out for yourself, can't you? Funds are short; demand is pressing. Prices rise daily. Money, that's the main thing, money!" Polkovnikov rubbed thumb against two fat fingers.

"Tphoo, you talk like a capitalist, General . . ." Khromoi spoke softly, studying Polkovnikov.

"Comrade, you are not listening to me! This is, I am telling you, an opportunity not to miss!" Polkovnikov spoke under such stress he seemed almost to gargle.

"For whom an opportunity?" Khromoi replied dryly, his smile thin, his eyes deep in their protective fat.

"My chief is . . . ambitious. He has dreams," Polkovnikov muttered, then savagely tore a cigarette from his case. "And he needs that money your men have been pissing against the walls!" His eyes were large, angry.

"Dreams?" Khromoi nodded appreciatively, chewing on one fat cheek. "Dreams, who doesn't have dreams?" He put his hands behind his back, rocked a bit on his heels. "I too have dreams . . ."

This would be the counter-offer, Duvakin guessed. Polkovnikov looked at his knee. "Dreams can be hard to realize," the general muttered vaguely.

"Money can help." Khromoi fairly twinkled.

"Power doesn't hurt either," Polkovnikov said neutrally.

A moment of watchful silence was evaporated by a radiant Khromoi smile. "How silly of me! Of course!" Khromoi demonstratively slapped his forehead. "The fur auctions are held in Leningrad; comrade Romanov would have a natural interest . . ." He trailed off, eying Polkovnikov speculatively.

"Well, we understand each other then, eh?" Polkovnikov said warmly, putting an arm on Khromoi's; to manage it he had to bend his knees.

"Perhaps, perhaps . . . depends on the dream, doesn't it?" Khromoi sounded odd.

"Surely, I need not articulate Grigorii Vladimirovich's?!" Polkovnikov sounded horrified.

Even Khromoi looked startled. "Good god, no! Yours! I meant yours!"

For a moment Duvakin felt disoriented, as if suddenly discovering the map he was using was for Minsk, and he was really in Pinsk. This business of Grigorii Vladimirovich and comrade Romanov and dreams . . . as he thought, though, he was less sure he understood nothing. Something about the oily beads of sweat that now oozed onto Khromoi's scalp seemed familiar. He felt his own palms go moist.

"Mine?" Polkovnikov said stoutly, "Nothing! Or shall I say that success will generate its own rewards?" He smiled slyly.

"Quite, quite . . ." Khromoi looked about, hesitating.

Duvakin, as much to confirm his own suspicions as to fill the air, asked, "And your dream, Vladilen Alexandrovich?"

Polkovnikov leaned forward, suddenly predatory. "As you say, it all depends on the dream, doesn't it, comrade?" His voice was more masterful, insinuating, than it had been all evening.

"You weren't briefed?" Khromoi looked surprised.

Duvakin's heart wobbled, but Polkovnikov seemed back in stride. "There were some surmises, but . . ." He shrugged invitingly.

Khromoi thought hard, his eyes going glazed with the effort. His breath came short. Incongruously, Duvakin recalled the first time he had tried to kiss a girl; moments before that clumsy wet lip bash he probably had looked a lot like the comrade there, deciding.

Khromoi grew redder with the effort, the dull glow of old coals, and the sweat thickened. "A metro . . ." he finally choked out, just as Duvakin began to fear for the man's heart.

"A what?" Polkovnikov leaned down courteously.

"A metro, a metro!" Khromoi was spewing now, like a steam pipe burst. "Eleven years they've promised, eleven years they've pocketed the cash, thanked me for the furs,

sent their daughters to me for diamonds . . . Eleven
years!" He clutched Polkovnikov's arm. "Try here, try
there, make him your friend, and don't forget comrade
this-and-that . . . and the metro? My metro? Always it's
complicated, Vladilen Alexandrovich, or not right now,
Vladilen Alexandrovich, the time isn't quite right, or let's
wait until after the census, Vladilen Alexandrovich . . ."

. Duvakin was astonished by Khromoi's passion; Polkovnikov seemed as surprised.

"A metro?" he managed to stammer, "Here?"

"No Soviet city of respectability lacks one," Khromoi
said haughtily. "Are we worse than Tashkent, eh? We're
Russian here, at least . . ."

Duvakin felt his jaw go slack. A metro? For a city of
90,000? On permafrost?

"Think of it!" Khromoi effused, obviously having
done as he urged often and with passion. "The Far Eastern
metropolitan, the Red Dawn express! An engineer's miracle! The northeastern-most subway in the world!"

Polkovnikov's mouth flapped silently, then finally
emitted, "A metro? Here?"

Khromoi drew himself up to full height, rocked back
on his heels, like an orator settling in to a four-hour
speech, and addressed the air beyond Polkovnikov's back.
"Anyone who can guarantee Magadan the construction of
a metropolitan underground rail system has my promise
of full support by the *entire* Magadan region . . . with all
resources."

This announcement was met by Polkovnikov's open
astonishment and Duvakin's firm conviction that
Khromoi was short a card or two of a full deck. Then
Polkovnikov beamed enormously and said, "*Done!* Shall
we wet the bargain?"

Duvakin was hit by a black, terrible question. And
what manner of man can *guarantee* a metro? His mouth
went very dry.

✶ THIRTEEN ✶

A gnawing of heat at his fingers made Duvakin more conscious; he slid the cigarette further along, took a puff, and noticed the first buildings of the city's edge.

The harsh yellow-violet light of the sparse streetlamps somehow made even the fresh coating of snow seem squalid. Log cabins, like something out of a museum about the evil tsars, tossed this way and that on this undulating sea of frozen mud and dwarf larch. The occasional apartment blocks were cracked, tilted, with black tar at the seams. There was no traffic, and Duvakin noticed no one on the streets.

It's a planet of dead men, Duvakin thought, shaking his head lightly, trying to ease his own sense of distress.

The car skidded rounding Twenty-fourth Party Congress, slamming into the granite curb. Unperturbed, the driver accelerated, lurched up the curb, then slammed back down. As he rolled over almost onto the driver, then smashed back into his own door, Duvakin recalled his other problem. He looked back; no luck, even that bouncing hadn't disturbed the general. And just how am I going to squeeze two meters of drunken general into a secret hotel room? Duvakin thought acidly. *This* close to the end, and the fool falls asleep.

Polkovnikov's sudden collapse was as surprising as anything else that had happened; one moment they all were madly toasting the Magadan metro—true, station by station, but still, they could not have had more than five or six—and the next, the general was snoring gently, like a baby steam hammer.

Khromoi had blinked twice in surprise, chuckled, and pressed some sort of hidden button. The blond Lyonya and a look-alike had appeared, hefted the general, and dumped him in the back of the car in which he and Duvakin had arrived. Duvakin had followed, glad to be going home, but exasperated with the general.

Now they stopped in front of the hotel, so close to a drift Duvakin had to shove to open his door. He looked again to Polkovnikov, hoping the blast of cold air had helped; it had not. He looked appealingly to the driver, who continued to chew absently at the tattered ends of a sparse mustache. I'm a driver, not a stevedore, his studied indifference said clearly.

Duvakin stared for a moment at his own hands, angry and impatient, then recalled his silly pistol. He pondered with pleasure pulling out the gun, forcing the corvine driver to carry the general inside, while he, Duvakin, imitated some steely foreign agent from a war movie. Sure, just take off your gloves, unbutton your overcoat, reach in your jacket pocket, and the element of surprise is yours, he thought bitterly.

Sighing, Duvakin stepped out into the drift and set like a weight lifter. Once he was firm, it was comparatively easy to reach back into the car, pull Polkovnikov forward, then half lift, half roll the general out of the deep backseat. About the same, say, as getting a dead horse out of a telephone booth. Duvakin staggered a step or two, but Polkovnikov was as long and clumsy as a rolled-up carpet. Duvakin floundered and sprawled into feathery, choking snow. He came up spluttering, gasping with the cold dusting that poured down his neck, plugged his nose.

The door slammed shut, and the car pulled away, its tail lights merry in the empty streets. Thanks for the ride, Duvakin thought, still sitting exhausted and incredulous in the snow. Anger with Polkovnikov swirled through irritation with his own inability to prevent the general from placing him in ridiculous roles; then Duvakin noticed the doorman of the Far East studying them sternly through the dirty glass door. As it had been after the accident, the idea that he was to be seen as a drunk as well was the last twig on the load; Duvakin stood, furious.

There was only one consolation, as he dusted his trouser legs; Khromoi was in their hands.

The avuncular old fool had blithely described, in detail, the whole fur-skimming operation; modestly he credited Rzhevsky with the invention, but retained for himself all credit as supervisor and inspiration. Duvakin had to admit that the scheme had the simplicity of genius; furs were simply removed from crates, the crates then officially sealed, and sent to random addresses as remote from Magadan as possible—a tractor repair station in Belorussia; a coal mine in Turkmenia; a mackerel-packing plant on the White Sea; anything, as long as the address was remote, small, and utterly unconnected with furs. What then happened, as Rzhevsky had predicted, was that some poor devil in his simple curiosity would open the crate, breaking the seals. Find the furs. And, obviously, panic. Either the man would then throw the crate away, if he was quick, or, more likely, summon the local officials, who as first order of business would compare the manifest with the contents of the crate. Finding about half of the furs missing, these then would concentrate solely on the poor fellow who had summoned them, because legal responsibility for the contents lies with whoever breaks the seal.

Meanwhile, Magadan gained a few more drops Khromoi could use to grease his metro into existence. Not that Rzhevsky hadn't found a use of his own for a pelt or two, Duvakin knew.

A nasty business, but, Duvakin thought almost happily, at least now no more clerks would face that same unpleasant surprise he had faced when first he stepped on that toilet sack.

Duvakin looked down the empty street, exhausted, but satisfied; perhaps the evening had at least been for something.

"Do you have my lighter, Vanya? I can't have left it out there, can I?"

Duvakin whirled at the noise. Polkovnikov was standing erect, graceful, not even very wet, wiping daintily at the snow on his sleeve.

"You're sober?" Duvakin asked stupidly.

"What else?" Polkovnikov replied offhandedly.

Duvakin was swinging his fists before he was even aware of it. "You son of a bitch, Polkovnikov!" he shrieked, hoping to concentrate all his rage into one titanic, lucky blow.

It was not even a near thing. Off-balance, falling, furious, Duvakin touched nothing firmer than snow before he felt himself plucked up and flung like an underfed alley cat into a drift, where he hit a buried flower box. He thought again of the pistol, but even before the stinging crack at his ribs and the choking noseful of ice crystals, he knew he was whipped.

"Don't you ever try that again," Polkovnikov said, his pale lips drawn tight.

Duvakin sat up, his eyes clogged with snow. He spat,

tried to speak, but could not. He scrambled to his feet, his anger throbbing even more inexpressibly as ice showered once more down his waist, ankles, neck. He gulped down huge gasps of cold air, trying to still his rage enough at least to breathe.

Polkovnikov, erect, majestic, stared down from his height as if he were on horseback. His nostrils flared slightly; the pink flush of his cheeks made even chillier the snap of his blue eyes. He studied Duvakin silently.

And what could Duvakin say? He stared back, his anger growing stale as he chose words with which to break the silence, then rejected them. Might as well rage at a Chukchi; Polkovnikov would no more reply to Duvakin's anger than would some moss-eating reindeer herder.

"Ah, the devil take it," Duvakin finally murmured, disgusted. There seemed nothing more to be said than that. "I'm leaving," he said softly, and turned away. "You can finish it."

"You know the penalty for unauthorized possession of a government weapon?" Polkovnikov's voice lanced into his back.

Duvakin turned around, enraged. "You've played *that* trick on me once before, Generalissimo." He dug clumsily into his overcoat, finally got his pistol out. He chucked it sidearm into a snowpile near the street, where it disappeared into the muck. "There—prove I had it. And you can't arrest me for illegal possession of a state fruit, either." Duvakin dug the grapefruit from his other pocket, with great pleasure squeezed it flat, and chucked it after the pistol; then, trembling, he glared at Polkovnikov, defying him to do something.

Polkovnikov glared back, then suddenly laughed. "Vanya, Vanya, Vanya . . . so maybe I underestimate you a little! You're right. That business at Khromoi's, I'm sorry." He shrugged, smiled.

Duvakin was surprised; threats, anger, yelling he was ready for, even force. But apologies, again? He thought for a moment, puzzled. Why apologize, unless there was more Duvakin was needed for? That must be it, Duvakin realized with a nauseating tickle in his stomach. There must be more yet. And Duvakin would be damned if he would do more. He looked at Polkovnikov, trying to concentrate on his face all the hate he had built up in four years of nightmares. As calmly as he could, he said, "It's too late, Polkovnikov. Do your own mucking out."

Duvakin turned and walked away. A few firm steps in silence, a few more. He fought the urge to stop, to turn, to say "Well?" For long moments there was only the sound of his footprints on snow and his own jagged breath; then a rustling swoop. Duvakin lunged away instinctively as Polkovnikov, panting lightly at his side, delicately took him by the elbow.

"Then tell me, dear Vanya," Polkovnikov said, "whether you know the penalty for unauthorized possession of classified information?"

Duvakin snatched his arm away. "What information?"

"That I'm here . . ."

"I couldn't very well not know that, could I?"

"True, but remember"—Polkovnikov's features were blandly polite, but made evil by those wicked eyes—"you are allowed to know only so long as you are involved. If you quit, it is no longer legal for you to know it."

Duvakin looked up into the murky sky, wondering if this is what drowning felt like. He had been dragging along, each day like the last, and suddenly, like stepping into a broken cesspit—Rzhevsky, Rzhevskaya, Galya, Polkovnikov . . .

"Why can't you just leave me in peace, Polkovnikov? Or shoot me and have done with it?" Duvakin addressed the sky, his voice flat and weary.

"You said you'd help, remember? . . . Besides, what

shoot? What's so dreadful about all this?" Polkovnikov gathered the world to him, with a broad sweep of both arms, then released it with an upward shrug. "Magadan, Moscow . . . it's *life*, Vanya. What's all this nihilism, this superfluous man stuff? You *like* being a lecturer in scientific atheism?"

"That wasn't my idea either, remember?"

"All right, so a militia man? You want just the park, some pigeons, and maybe a glass of bad beer when the line isn't too long? I had thought you for a man of *ambition* . . ."

"You thought me for a fool!" Duvakin snapped back. "Maybe I was, once—but you've given me a lot of time to study up, haven't you?" Duvakin was surprised at his own vehemence, but didn't care. "And it's a good thing too, or else Khromoi would be having us for late supper about now!"

"That was necessary, wasn't it?"

"You're claiming your muck-up back there was *planned*?" Duvakin sneered.

Polkovnikov studied him minutely, in silence, as if examining him for cracks. Duvakin felt his anger becoming self-conscious, as he remembered what this man had in his power to do to him. Still, anger it remained, as he recalled the feeling of abandonment at Khromoi's.

Polkovnikov, still silent, pulled out his cigarette case, and, unaccountably, extended it toward Duvakin. After a moment's hesitation, Duvakin took one.

"You really don't understand, then?" Polkovnikov finally asked, his voice melancholy.

"What?"

"What happened, what we're doing?" Polkovnikov dug in his breast pocket, tilting his head and releasing a small shower of snow from the top of his black fur hat. "Why we're doing it?"

"What's to understand?" Duvakin barked. "Khromoi

is a thief. You *claim* to be KGB. So, you arrest him; I go home, and . . ." And what? Duvakin had no idea and what; the unraveled life doesn't become a sweater again just because you stop tugging at the threads.

"You have matches?" Polkovnikov finally asked, having searched all his pockets. "My lighter's . . ." He waved vaguely.

Duvakin dug in his pockets, handed a crushed box of matches to the general, and waited, his cigarette on his lips.

To Duvakin's surprise, Polkovnikov lit the cigarette absently, cupping the match in his hand. "I don't know, maybe it's not even your fault. You know what it's like out in the West? Different prices all the time, new presidents, governments get changed like maybe you would your shorts . . ."

Sure I know, Polkovnikov, spend all my vacations in New York, Duvakin thought bitterly, wondering what all this had to do with Khromoi.

"We get spoiled here—the bus costs the same as it did back when you had hair; loaf of bread is still twenty-eight kopeks; the Party's in charge now since before we were born . . . and the whole time just three leaders . . ."

"Three?" Duvakin was surprised.

"Sure, three, plus Lenin, of course. The Americans have had, what, maybe twenty presidents in the same time; they fire them, they kill them . . . who could keep track?"

"So what?" Duvakin could not help asking, although deep down he was certain this information was only going to entangle him.

"So it makes us a little comfortable, that's what. We forget that even in a scientific, planned society like ours there's one thing going to happen anyway, that you can't stop."

Polkovnikov smiled; experienced angler, he thought his hook was well set.

"Death, Vanya . . ."

Duvakin waited; nothing more came. He drew a while on his cigarette. Finally, he said, "Seems clear enough. Through now? Because I don't see what in the devil that has to do with Khromoi or Rzhevsky, or me, come to that. 'Death' the man says!" Duvakin spat disgustedly. He turned angrily, took Polkovnikov's sleeve. "Look, why these fancy words? We're *through*. Khromoi's *admitted* it; he's been stealing, Lord I don't know, *millions*. Arrest him! Or is this a *family* matter?" He recalled Darmoved's insinuating inflection of the word, tried to imitate. He shook the general's sleeve. "Either way, *I* don't care! You understand? Just let me the devil alone!" Duvakin could hear his voice rising surprisingly near to hysteria, pushed by exhaustion and pain. He threw Polkovnikov's sleeve down, turned on his heel again, and was about to leave.

Then he noticed Polkovnikov's face, also exhausted. The man's head hung, his shoulders drooped. The general looked so beaten that Duvakin stopped and, after a pause, asked weakly, "Right?"

Polkovnikov snorted, raised his head.

"We were out there how long?"

"I don't know, three, four hours," Duvakin answered cautiously, wary.

"And Khromoi has seen neither one of us before?" Polkovnikov continued in the same monotone.

Duvakin nodded.

"And in under one hour he tells two total strangers that he is engineering a theft of state property so big he could buy a small republic. And you think Darmoved doesn't know?"

The question hit Duvakin like a thump in the head. Polkovnikov was right. Khromoi was demented, obsessed with his madman's subway. He had half of Magadan working full time to steal from the other half, so both halves could ride tubes through frozen gravel, and once the old man had begun to talk of it, he could not stop.

So how could Darmoved *help* but know about it?

But if he already knew, why then did he do nothing about it, but instead beat Rzhevsky to death? And why was Polkovnikov here, if not to investigate Khromoi? It was like trying to climb up a sandy river bank; each step upward seemed to slide him three steps back toward the water. But this was no brook sucking at his feet. The airplane, Rzhevsky, the mysterious man who was looking for him, who maybe had pushed him . . . He stood in the slushy snow, feeling utterly numb.

"Come on, Vanya, let's go talk about some facts of life," Polkovnikov murmured, taking Duvakin's arm firmly and heading him toward the hotel.

"Not back in that stinking tent you don't!"

"All right . . ." Polkovnikov faced about, now taking Duvakin's arm in his other hand as he studied the empty street. "But we walk and you listen. This is serious business, and we've got to keep moving."

Reluctant and stiff, but intrigued by the deep sense of worry in Polkovnikov's voice, Duvakin let himself be pulled up the block, toward the sparse shops on the west side of Lenin Square. At one in the morning Polkovnikov is worried about eavesdroppers? Nerves gnawed at Duvakin's stomach.

After a few score meters Polkovnikov took another careful look about, then said quietly, "Look, it's what I was saying before. We forget here what change *means*. It's *always* been the Soviet Union . . . Hell, there's not even been an event big enough yet to make us forget the Fatherland War. So, we've been almost twenty years now, same leaders, same prices, everything the same . . . and it's easy to forget how fortunate we are."

"What fortunate?" Duvakin sniped, looking at the shabby splendors of the square; mostly empty shops, a few struggling trees, the whole a spectrum of dirty white to dusty black, as deserted as the moon it resembled.

"Believe me, the people I'm chasing succeed, and you and everyone else will find out what fortunate. Tell me, Vanya, you look at our country and what do you see?"

Duvakin stopped, blinked. It wasn't a question he had ever put himself before. "I don't know . . . a place, buses . . . what do you mean?" You're born, you grow up . . . Duvakin couldn't imagine a country as something you thought about; it was there, period.

"That's what I mean, no one looks . . . *Think*, Vanya! Out here you've got what, Chukchis and Tungus and Russians, and in the south there's the blackbutts, then Caucasians and the Balts and we're all stuck together like soybeans in tomato sauce, our little round faces pressed tight against the glass. And it works, the whole damn mess works. You wait for a bus, it comes. You go to get something in a store—"

"You wait, it doesn't come," Duvakin interrupted with malicious pleasure.

Polkovnikov dug dryly at Duvakin's ribs. "You don't look so faint with hunger, Vanya . . . you see? And all of us little beans, each bean wants to be first in line and first on the bus and first with the big apartment. And what keeps this all from being just a god-awful slush of beans and sauce all over the tabletop? The container, that's what, the Party. And our leaders have kept that jar nice and safe for twenty years now, like I said. Problem is, though, the present beankeeper is getting on, and there's *lots* of interest in getting to be the next beankeeper . . . and if they should get to juggling around with the jar . . ." Polkovnikov's hands made a dropping smash, followed by silence. After a bit, the general added gently. "Then it doesn't work anymore."

"What's this got to do with me, for God's sake?" Duvakin was more puzzled than angry. "It's not like I can do anything."

Polkovnikov studied Duvakin with tight lips and tired eyes.

"I explained, Vanya, but I can again and again if I must. Moscow is coming up on a crisis. You remember Suslov?"

Duvakin thought for a moment, the name unfamiliar; then with a start, he did. The leader who'd died not long ago, the one they'd made so much fuss over. Even all the way out here they'd made everyone come in early for memorial meetings, and Sutrapian had decreed ten minutes of silence the day the man was buried.

Problem was, no one knew which of the leaders was which. It was like the time years ago, back when he was still in Moscow; one of them got himself chucked off the Politburo, just before May Day, Shelest maybe? The portraits of the leaders were already up all over town, and then, of course, the fallen one had to be removed. But other than Brezhnev, nobody knew which was which, so down they all came. Best to be on the safe side.

"Yeah, so?" he shrugged.

Polkovnikov answered patiently. "Suslov's the first of the big leaders to go, since Stalin, thirty years ago. Suslov is the first shoe . . . and it's got everybody waiting for the second." He spat over his left shoulder. "And when he goes, all hell could break loose, unless we take steps now."

"You talking about Brezhnev?" Duvakin asked.

"Brezhnev, Brezhnev . . . You see?"

Duvakin didn't. He stood, thinking, listening to the rustle of the few dead leaves still clinging to a lime tree.

It's true, he supposed, Brezhnev can't go on indefinitely; he looked perfectly healthy in the pictures, young even, but twenty years is twenty years, no matter what your Party card number is; he'd been in the Great War, too. Duvakin tried to remember what it was like when Khrushchev disappeared, but he could not; it was too long ago. Then Duvakin had still been in Krasnaya Sosna, so it had taken days for the news of a change to ripple out. Stalin's death he remembered, of course, tears pouring down his face like everybody else. He was brand new to the militia then, a rural recruit posted to his native mudhole. And those tears came *because* it seemed nothing could come after Stalin except the end of the world, the end of the universe. But something did, some names he recalled poorly, then Khrushchev.

Really, it was more like mushrooms than a change you could think of, by people. The leaders just appeared, like they'd always been there and maybe it was you who was only just noticing.

On the other hand, Duvakin realized, if you think of the nation as like his office, only bigger—this one licking Sutrapian like he was covered in sour cream, that one spreading rumors that Sutrapian was a Jew, this one reporting on everybody else to the KGB, to get a jump on the apartment lists. It was a madhouse, like going to the peasant market in raspberry season. All you want is your half-kilo of berries, and forty, fifty of the devils yell at you, flatter you, insult you, all trying to get you to buy *their* berries, or at least, not buy *his* berries. Imagine that sort of chaos spread out over the whole USSR. Duvakin shuddered. "But what's that got to do with Khromoi?" He suddenly realized he could not make the final connection. There was no answer. From the corner of his eye, Duvakin studied Polkovnikov, who stood there next to him, worriedly rolling a cigarette back and forth between two fingers. There, in the snow lit by the bruise-indigo light of a failing street lamp, Polkovnikov looked suddenly human.

"And what am I supposed to do?" Duvakin turned to face Polkovnikov directly, staring up into the man's slender, stern face. His tone was curious now, not hostile. A problem so large it worried even Polkovnikov was sobering.

The general shook his head, touched Duvakin's elbow, indicating they should move forward on their circuit of the square. Then he spoke, his voice very low.

"Second secretary, way the devil out here, it's a funny position. You've got a staff, you've got people below you . . . but above you, apart from some blubbersucker they keep in his igloo except when they bring round the Africans or Vietnamese, there's not much. Sure you report to people, to some names in Irkutsk, Khabarovsk, back in Moscow. But it's easy to begin to feel independent. After all, the sun checks in with you half a day before it gets around to warming Moscow . . ."

"Khromoi's a counterrevolutionary?" Duvakin asked, not following.

"I didn't say that, and if you do, you'd better be sure of who's nearby. I said it's a funny position, one that should make an experienced man suspicious . . ." He trailed off. Then he added softly, "At least, a fellow could make a good case with all that. As I suspect our friend Darmoved is trying to do."

Duvakin felt addled. "Wait a moment. What's all this got to do with Darmoved?"

Polkovnikov examined the deserted, snow-choked square minutely, then leaned down to whisper in Duvakin's ear. "Darmoved is trying to force Khromoi and his operation to work for him . . . we think, anyway."

"Operation?"

"Enterprise, whatever . . ." Polkovnikov still whispered. "I suspect that's what he was pressuring Rzhevsky for, on the excuse of the complaint you signed, so he could force Khromoi to cooperate with him." He straightened up, as if all were now explained.

It wasn't. "Cooperate on what?" Duvakin asked. "Why did he need me for an excuse? He's KGB. Anyway, what would Darmoved want with Khromoi's furs?"

"Not much, maybe . . . furs are furs. Sure, it's money; sure Moscow could use it. But hell, if it's all just so Darmoved can buy a dacha in Gagra and a Bulgarian fur coat and a set of Japanese tires, the devil can have him." Polkovnikov was silent, thoughtful. Then he said even softer, "However . . . what's the most valuable thing there is in this country?"

Diamonds? Duvakin wondered. A car?

"Going abroad?" he finally ventured cautiously.

Polkovnikov shook his head.

"Influence, Vanya, connections. You buy enough of that and you can do *anything*, go abroad, buy a house . . . maybe even, if things work out right, you time it right, maybe you can take over the country. A little connection buys more connection, until you get people with ideas. And right now is a bad time for people to be getting ideas." He took a deep breath, exhaling a frosty roiling column of steam, smoke, exhaustion up into the purple-gray night. "Look," he continued softly after another deliberate examination of the square, "Darmoved is young, he's ambitious, he's successful. To me, that spells good solid connections, at the top. And you know who's at the top?"

"Brezhnev?"

"No, fool . . . of the KGB. Andropov, that's who . . ."

Duvakin knew that, like almost all Soviet citizens. Of the big leaders, the ones in charge, the average man could name two, usually. The first secretary. And the head of the KGB.

"Andropov, now," Polkovnikov spoke as if to himself,

"Andropov is a sly one, your deep type. Not a rank-and-file organ man, for one thing; for another, first KGB chief to get himself on the Politburo with the big boys. There's talk he's even pushing for Suslov's job, now that the old man's dead."

This was heady, rarefied stuff for Duvakin, who like all but a handful of his fellow citizens assumed that new leaders grew, like tree fungus. As if for the first time examining what lay around him, Duvakin began to get some inkling that his world was *caused*, not simply a product of chance.

"And?" he prompted, to move Polkovnikov forward. The general was quiet, reflectively, anxiously toying with his cigarette.

"And? If I tell you, Vanya"—the general turned a very grave, sober face toward Duvakin—"then there's no going back. This is classified so high you can't tell even your dead mother." He waited.

Duvakin wanted desperately to turn and walk away. Brezhnev, Andropov, KGB, Polkovnikov . . . it was more than a mortal man could bear. Or should bear.

But there was the other question, which Polkovnikov had not answered; why had he been used as the excuse? Maybe there was no answer; the *fact* still remained. Because he had stuck his foot on that woman's sack, Rzhevsky had died. To Rzhevskaya he had denied responsibility, and she had died too. And Dusya was orphaned. Other strands unraveled too, Galya. Finally, even himself. Duvakin was responsible, somehow, for all this. He could not see how, but could see that he could not now simply walk away.

Perhaps that's what Magadan was still for—so you couldn't escape.

"Well?" he croaked, at last.

Polkovnikov laughed, clapping him on the shoulder. "That's the old Vanya! But remember, not a word!" He pulled Duvakin urgently close, whispering the hot sour words in his ear. "There's talk that a group of the old guard in the organs are trying to move their man up, maybe even force Brezhnev to retire. So's they can put Andropov solidly in the saddle, no questions. Failing that, to jockey him in soon's the old fellow pops off . . ."

"And what's that got to do with Darmoved?" Duvakin whispered back.

"Moving himself up while pushing the clique, most likely . . . at least, that's what I'm checking. We're checking . . ." He grinned.

Duvakin walked for a bit, contemplating the gray slush at his feet. This business of factions sounded tame, too small to warrant all the fuss. He decided in for the soup, might as well stay for the lunch. "And so what if Andropov does take over?"

Polkovnikov stopped, turned to face Duvakin. "You can't be serious, Vanya?"

Duvakin looked blank.

"You know how this town came about? The organs were in charge; they ran this place like their own personal game . . . and there were dead men up to here." He held his hand to the level of his nose. "You want a whole country like that? Back to the old days. No laws, no protection, just this?" Polkovnikov held up his fist; enclosed in the black leather glove, extended in the frozen air, the fist looked enormous. The general brought it smashing down into his other palm, where it thumped savagely in that silent city where millions had slaved and died. Duvakin shuddered.

Then suddenly, like having a curtain pulled back, he realized something was wrong. He snatched away the arm Polkovnikov held so solicitously.

"Hey, wait a minute! You're KGB too! How come you're not—"

"One of the conspirators?" Polkovnikov beamed at

Duvakin like a teacher at a prize pupil. "I swear, Vanya, the frost has cleared your brain out here. You're starting to think. I know we'll find a place for you when this is all over."

Duvakin made an impatient gesture with his hand, even though he felt a gratified warmth about his heart. Let's see the place before you get excited, he reminded himself sternly, nevertheless recalling vividly the Novoslobodskaya metro stop, where he used to get out for his Moscow room. "Answer me!" he said, rather more imperiously than usual.

"The organs aren't all crazy, Vanya. There's good ones, take their responsibilities seriously. And then there's bad ones, renegades, you might say." He smiled, making clear on which side of the angels he stood.

"Andropov?" Duvakin asked, not quite able, even alone in the center of an empty square half a globe away from Moscow, to inquire aloud whether Andropov, one of the most powerful people in the world, was a renegade. Better his tongue should choke him.

Polkovnikov, though, understood. He shrugged. "All I can tell you is a story . . . a true story. A Moscow widow I know, a general's widow," Polkovnikov stressed, "lives in a closed building, two doormen, fence around the whole compound. She goes on vacation, leaves a spare key with the neighbors, a prosecutor and friend of Andropov's, it turns out. Not even a Russian, a Jew of some sort. She comes back, finds a fur coat and two diamond rings are gone. She phones the militia. They come, ask a couple of questions, discover that the prosecutor has a young daughter, a known addict and thief. And they can go no further. The widow complains, takes it to the procurator's. Same thing . . . the door is closed, they tell her. Finally she demands and gets," Polkovnikov stressed, thumping his forefinger on Duvakin's chest, "an audience with Yurii Vasileevich himself . . ."

"With Andropov?" Duvakin asked, surprised that one could arrange to see such a person; somehow he had assumed one was only summoned.

"Andropov, Andropov. Anyway, the widow tells the story, tells her suspicions, that the daughter took them, asks his help, and you know what Andropov answers?" Polkovnikov's eyes were cold, glittery. "There are laws, he says to this poor woman, there are laws against slander . . . Go home and quit entertaining such *dangerous* fantasies about a valued worker of the Fatherland . . ." Polkovnikov's eyes, even in the poorly lit square, seemed almost crystalline with anger. "Does that sound like a nation of laws to you?" Then, apparently needing no answer, he took Duvakin's arm again, heading them toward the hotel. His tale, he seemed to feel, was self-explanatory, complete.

And so it was, Duvakin thought with gritty fatigue, though not like the general had intended. Generals' wives, fur coats, diamond rings—it was nothing Duvakin could care about. It was not his world.

What he did hear, though, was the passion of the general's voice, his fear of a future that made even him, a general, tremble. Until tonight Duvakin had thought nothing could frighten Polkovnikov. Now that something had, Duvakin felt an utterly unexpected emotion.

Exhilaration. Polkovnikov was telling him the truth. Whatever was going on was serious enough to scare a general.

Duvakin could not say he was glad to be where he was, in the thick of this mess; nor was he happy about all the deaths. But there was no going back; he could not now simply lift his foot from that toilet woman's sack, returning all to what it was.

Given that, Duvakin was in an enviable position. Unaccustomed, too. For the first time in long years he felt in control.

Not full control, certainly. He still did not know who had pushed him, or why, did not know who had killed Rzhevskaya, orphaned Dusya. But he did know that Polkovnikov had buckled beneath the weight of this intrigue.

And he, Duvakin, had not.

For the first time in long years, he felt a glimmer of confidence that events could somehow be bent around to his advantage. He did not see fully how, nor when; he did know, though, that for the first time he saw himself rising above the general. Exhausted as he was, the thought made him feel more alive than he could remember feeling, perhaps since early manhood.

"Sounds like a nasty business . . ." he finally said vaguely, realizing they had come to a halt before the doors of the hotel.

Polkovnikov laughed.

"So it is, Vanya, so it is. All right, so we'll see then, test matters a bit. In the morning, same time, elevenish." Then, a beefy handshake, one last squeeze of his arm, a toothy smile, and Polkovnikov headed for the hotel. The doorman, Duvakin noted idly, stood at attention. Suddenly, Polkovnikov halted, turned back. "One thing, though, Vanya . . . Find that pistol!" He smiled blandly, waved a hand toward the piled snow. Then, with a "Tomorrow!" he disappeared into the Far East.

Thoughtful, exhausted, Duvakin wandered slowly over to where he had fought with Polkovnikov. Galya would be waiting, he realized with a warm sense of pleasure; maybe that would work out too? He reached up, snapped off a short branch of the stunted shrub at the curb, to poke about with.

So, we're after the head of the Magadan KGB, he thought, trying through articulation of it to make the idea seem less crazy. He toyed with the branch he had snapped, noticing that the buds were swollen, the leaves anxious now to emerge. Duvakin thought idly of the stale confines of life within the bud, the exhilaration of release. He smiled, half at himself, half at the possibilities of the future. What will be, will be. Even with a pistol. He eyed the snowbank where the pistol had flown.

Suddenly filled with hope and a determination the content of which he could not articulate, Duvakin began poking furiously at the snowbank, searching for the gun.

* FOURTEEN *

Duvakin grunted, rolled onto his back, stared at the ceiling. Then, stretching, he wriggled his toes.

The time? he wondered idly, disinclined to move even his arm to see his wristwatch. The sun peeked in dusty shafts around the heavy curtains Galya had contrived from old rugs; late enough that he would call this a lie-in, and luxuriate; not so late he had to hurry. His stomach still ached a bit, and a tentative hand would tell him that his face was still scabbed, but by heaven, he felt all right, he thought.

In fact, he acknowledged with a small smile at the ceiling, things seemed not so bad at all. Last night Galya's greeting had been warm, saved from the maternal only by the rubbery tussle that followed her solicitous presentation of stuffed cabbage and homemade bread beer. He watched the dust motes jiggle and dance in the shifts of sunlight and considered the memory of Galya's back bucking silver with sweat before him, recalled her moist, salty kisses of thanks as he dropped into sleep. Damn it, it wasn't what you'd call a bad life.

He sighed, wishing for a cigarette, then realized that he wanted a cigarette because he smelled one, noticing that second the faint blue intestines of smoke curling torpidly in the sun at the corner of his vision.

Duvakin turned on his side with a grin, to greet Galya and the morning.

The smile froze stupidly, drained of content; Galya sat smoking in her chair, a hard look on her face.

And a pistol in her hand. Pointed, his mind noted absently, at him.

For a moment Duvakin suspected that he was still asleep, the sight of Galya with the gun was too much in the manner of dreams, all the crazy elements of his week jumbled together.

"So, awake?" she said calmly, if superfluously, then took a pull at the cigarette. For a space the red tip glowed as furiously as the dull glow of Galya's gray-green eyes.

No dream, Duvakin knew; anger, powerlessness, and above all a sense of tremendous fatigue, that life could so seriously grow demented in so short a time, rose up around him like spring melt. He yawned, tempted to go back to sleep. Then he sat up.

"That's my pistol."

Like Galya was a muddled clerk in a bathhouse coat check. Yes, that's my hat, that's my coat. And that's my pistol.

"Glad to hear it, since it was in your jacket that I found it." Galya's voice was cutting.

Duvakin studied her, trying to fathom the situation. Galya was one of them, whoever tried to push him in front of the car? Why not then push him off at night, or put ground glass in his meat pie? Why wait until now, and with his own pistol? But why else point the pistol at him?

On the off chance the pistol simply happened to be

aimed his way, Duvakin gathered himself and the bed-clothes into a heap at the foot of the bed; as he suspected it would, the small black circle of the barrel followed him. He wound the bedclothes tighter about him, knowing that a blanket or two would make scant difference to the minute lump of lead that Galya now pointed at his mid-riff. Curiously, however, he was not, he realized, afraid. He felt more the unlucky clown in some provincial circus, his act a rising crescendo of mishaps. And was this the climax?

To be shot by a doctor, his new ladyfriend?

He sighed again, then looked Galya imploringly in the face.

"Put that down, Galya, what say?"

For a space Galya considered the question, then re-affirmed her answer by raising the pistol even more de-cisively.

"Some questions first, Vanya . . . if that's your name . . ." she added nastily. Duvakin was quite taken aback by the bitter viciousness he heard now in her voice. The butter and cream voice of "little soul" was, it appeared, long gone.

"Of course that's my name," Duvakin was exasper-ated. "That's what I told you it was, didn't I?"

"Told me a lot of things, didn't you?" She took an-other puff of cigarette, then deliberately crushed it out in a saucer at her elbow. Looking up and smiling a nasty, gold-flecked slash, she added, "Suppose by sheer chance some of them had to be true."

"What?" Duvakin was confused, with anger very near. "What lies have I ever told you?"

Galya shrugged, this time her chin trembling ever so faintly, like well-made beef aspic. "Who knows? Your name, your job, your plans, your . . ." Her voice broke over a word that sounded like "feelings."

"Damn it," Duvakin said softly, "I don't know who's

been putting nonsense in your ears, but whoever it is deserves a splinter in his tongue. Every word I've ever told you was true as truth, the breath of God himself!"

"And this?" Galya readjusted herself primly in the chair, covering her rosy plump knees with one hand and showing him the pistol with the other. Duvakin felt addled; the gesture was somehow affecting, endearingly feminine, and yet he knew he ran a very real risk of being shot. Galya had not been slapped together from almond paste!

"What this? The pistol?"

"The pistol, the pistol . . ."

"So?"

"So, as I recall, it's not something the Party usually issues to agitprop workers. In fact, as I figure it, Vanya . . ." She paused, to clear her throat of a quaver that was slowly driving her pitch upward to a squeak. "In fact, I figure this pistol makes you one of two things, a spy or a criminal." The obstruction in her throat returned, but a quick massage with her plump left hand allowed her to say, "And I'd like to know which one I've let soil my sheets." The control she was exerting could not prevent a bright sparkle of tears from glazing her eyes.

Duvakin slumped back against the wall, feeling utterly eviscerated.

Not a word, Polkovnikov had said, not to anyone. And especially not to Galya, he thought, remembering the nauseating twisting the casual threats against Tanya had given his stomach, four years ago. Galya was no Tanya, but still, to do that to someone he . . . his mind balked at naming the emotion he felt for the plump, aging, dyed-blonde doctor who now pointed a faintly trembling pistol in the vicinity of his sternum; instead, it offered up a complex memory of soft dumplings, the smell of real coffee, and the unnameable pleasures of deep night.

Call it whatever, he couldn't let himself drag her into this mess any further.

So what could he tell her, that she wouldn't shoot him?

To Duvakin's surprise, what flooded swiftly over him there was not fear, not despair, not even disgust.

It was loneliness.

Duvakin suddenly felt, with the force of a boot to his belly, utterly alone. He had never been a social man, but he had felt at least he was one of the many, enduring daily life with the rest, begrudged existence by no one, taking what pleasures chance offered, and sharing what he would, as he could.

Now, here, huddled in a bed in Magadan, with Galya pointing his own—or more properly, Polkovnikov's—pistol at him, Duvakin felt at the center of rings and rings of hostility, hated, hunted.

And alone.

Unexpectedly, he wept.

The pain of the automobile accident, the gun, Galya, Polkovnikov, the ignominy of Magadan, and all the insults major and minor of decades of life as a man suddenly, like a garlic press, so squeezed his soul that he could not choke out his bitter, blinding tears fast enough.

Duvakin could not have said how long he sobbed mindlessly on the bed, but it could not have been terribly long, for soon shame began to burn dry his cheeks. As if the tears had been pus of some sort that had to be lanced before he could think, Duvakin found his mind clearing, awakening. He took a huge gulp of air and sat up.

Bumping, to his astonishment, into Galya, who now sat next to him, arm hovering irresolutely in the direction of an embrace. The pistol Duvakin glimpsed by the saucer, across the room.

"Don't cry, Vanya," Galya said hesitantly, still not

entirely trusting him. She patted his thigh roughly, while Duvakin ground the horny heels of his hands into his scabby cheeks, to stem the last trickle of tears. "Don't cry . . . you're in trouble?"

Duvakin nodded, then snorted, the word seemed so inadequate.

"A pistol, you . . . that's a government pistol." Galya was not precisely fishing; more like she held out handles for him to grab, if he wished. "A Moscow colleague . . ." She smiled more warmly, then hugged him. Her arm felt protective, strong. "Come on, you can tell the doctor."

Duvakin leaned his head against the wall, letting his blanket cocoon drop. And what choice was there? If he didn't tell her, he lost his last friend; if he *did* . . . who knows? So *tell* her, he thought, at the same time thinking tell her *what*? That people are killing each other because Brezhnev's an old man? And one of them wants *me* to help stop them? Mother of God, she'd take him for touched!

"That's just it, Galya. It's secret, government work," he finally said, staring at the ceiling. "They said I couldn't talk about it."

He felt her fingers stiffen, then almost fling away the arm they had held.

"Secret!" She spoke the word as if it were covered in spiders. "Secret! And haven't I heard *that* before!" Disgusted, she stood, straightened her skirt, and with dignity said, "Well, once learned, twice burned. You can pack up your secrets and go back to your hovel, or to the devil or . . ."

"Wait a minute," Duvakin demanded. "What do you mean, twice burned?"

"Just what I said." Her manner was frosty, professional. "Last time I smiled proudly each time he said 'secret work,' until it turned out our little beauty the secret was from Kiev and could get him residence permis-

sion there . . . as man and wife, only, you understand."
She spat at her foot. "That's once. And there won't be a
twice." She stalked out of the bedroom.

Duvakin had never been accused of infidelity before;
it was novel enough to have even one woman. He found
the accusation degrading, like being taken for drunk.
After a moment of surprise, he jumped up, wrapped the
blankets about himself, and followed Galya.

"Galya! Wait! It's not that way. You don't understand."

She stood in the kitchen, sobbing over the stove.

Duvakin was even more surprised by her misery. That
she needed him, he knew. That she clung to him, he knew.
And yet the torment of these tears suggested more. Love?
He recalled Rzhevskaya's wild sobs. Slowly, tentatively,
he crossed the kitchen, to stand behind her. He watched
her dimpled arms quiver. After a moment he put a clumsy
hand on her shoulder, which she jerked away.

"There's no one, Galya," he said lamely. "It's a dirty
business they've caught me up in, and I don't want you to
get tarred."

"And chasing round after your bastard brats isn't tar, I
suppose!?" she flared, even seeming to rise. Her eyes were
the green of a stray cat's.

"Brats?" Duvakin stammered.

"Brats!" she sprayed him with hot saliva, then turned
her back.

Understanding that she meant Dusya, Duvakin felt
torn. He wanted desperately to find out what the doctor
knew, whether the girl was all right.

But to pursue that now would only confirm what
Galya accused him of.

"Dusya isn't mine," he said in what he hoped was a
calm voice.

"That woman was too old, eh? Or you're not properly
loaded, maybe?" The viciousness of her jibe was softened

by the quaver in Galya's voice, muffled by being addressed into the sink.

"Galya, it wasn't like that," Duvakin protested gently, unable to think what more to say. "It just wasn't like that . . ."

Galya stopped sobbing, but did not turn around.

Duvakin stood wrapped in his blankets, surprised that he wanted so much to make Galya not cry. It wasn't that he wanted to make her happy, not in the way he had trembled like some month-old pup in his haste to please Tanya, back in Moscow. He did not love this woman, he reminded himself sternly. Probably, anyway. Sometimes he even felt pushed into her arms by those same hands which had pushed him before the Zhiguli, felt bound to her by chains of blintzes and omelettes and homemade jams. But still, he wished she would not cry.

"Whose dirty business then, Vanya?" Her back was still turned.

"To tell the truth, I don't know," Duvakin said, startled himself at how uncertain he was of Polkovnikov's employ. "But it's a man I know from Moscow, a general, and he's involved in internal security . . ."

"And just what in the devil do you know about internal security?" Galya turned around, her red-rimmed eyes derisive. "Look at you!"

Duvakin glanced from his blanket-wrapped bottom half, which he clutched with both hands, to his deathly pale arms, whose muscles slumped unpromisingly into a soft belly still purple and yellow with bruise. Involuntarily, he sucked his stomach in. "It's not wrestling they have me do," he said plaintively.

"And a good thing," Galya sniffed dryly. "I can't imagine what they want you for."

The tone reminded Duvakin uncomfortably of nasty children squabbling at a village pump, but his pride was stung. "They want me enough to send me back to Moscow, when this is all through," he said, with an unthinking "take that!" tilt of his nose.

Galya's eyes opened like large parasols of green and white; she stepped back, bumped the stove, where gas began to hiss, then she groped for a chair, her eyes still on Duvakin.

"Moscow?" she asked, when she was seated. Her upraised face was tear-stained, clogged with powder.

"Moscow," Duvakin affirmed, puzzled at her reaction.

"To live? Not just to visit?"

"To live . . ." Duvakin was growing alarmed, suspecting faintly where her thoughts ran.

"Vanya"—she smiled passionately—"Moscow!"

Duvakin had the words "They only offered me!" on his tongue before he realized how cruel they sounded; manfully shuffling for another way to say the same thing, he hit only upon "You've never been before?"

"Been? Of course I've been, who hasn't been to Moscow? But you know what it's like to get a residence permit? Besides," she shrugged, looking away from Duvakin, "there's the contract."

"Contract?"

She nodded her head vaguely, as if the word were an ancient enemy. "You think I stay because I like it here? I am perhaps a collector of blackflies and mud?"

"You have your passport, don't you?" Duvakin was alarmed. "You're a doctor really?" He too fumbled out a chair, sat heavily in his clumsy blankets. One hairy white knee slipped free, which he hastily covered.

"You need a reference to get out too, Vanya, and when we signed on, the contract was guaranteed service for ten years, in return for a list of considerations as long as your arm . . ."

"We?" Duvakin asked.

"Berezkin, my husband . . . my ex-husband. A village boy with big eyes," Galya's voice was flat, as if this story were not told easily or often. "Sweet-talked a stupid village doctor into marriage, then took the doctor to the Party, volunteering her services wherever there was a deficit, providing they promoted him too. They gave us Magadan, where you will note doctors do not precisely lie beneath each tree, and my oil-tongued devil convinced me that for this apartment, a Black Sea vacation every year, a car, special rations, ten years was nothing . . ." She shrugged. "Do you have a cigarette?"

Duvakin slapped automatically at his chest, then recalled he was in his undershirt. "They're in my jacket . . ." He pulled his blankets more modestly.

"Next to your pistol?" Galya smiled sweetly, making Duvakin blush.

"You want me to get them?"

"No, it's all right." Galya put an imperious hand on the table; her manner was growing more regal as the tale progressed. "So . . . for a time things were marvelous. We got supplemental food packets and good wages; he was rocketing up in headquarters . . . lots of 'secret work.'" She looked tauntingly at Duvakin, then continued. "Then one fine day he walks in, announces he is being transferred to Kiev. Marvelous say I, raspberries and bread and fresh milk. Sorry, he tells me, but his 'patroness'"— Galya's lips pursed—"a widow, had taken rather a shine to him, and would prefer he went alone . . ." She trailed off, studying her knuckles, then continued brightly, "So, it's like the old days. I've still got four years of my sentence in Magadan!"

The conditions of this sentence were infinitely better than those of any of the others sentenced to Magadan, but still, stuck is stuck. "I thought I was a lifer, until last week," Duvakin said lightly, trying to cheer her up.

"But now *Moscow*, perhaps!" Galya's voice swelled with hope.

"Your contract, though?" Duvakin pointed out, not feeling it necessary or polite to voice his first objection, that he had not yet thought beyond going alone. "You can't—"

"There's a paragraph . . ." She trailed off, blushing slightly and her voice drying out. "There's a bit about allowing exceptions to preserve the family unit."

"Family unit . . ." Duvakin's question collapsed, as suddenly a large number of pieces fell into place. Family unit, that meant marriage. And marriage meant a way out of Magadan, for a trapped and tricked Dr. Berezkina.

Which meant she needed a man. But not just any man. One who looked like maybe a ticket out of the mud. But who could be sure, so you have to try every likely number that wanders through the clinic.

Until finally you find a balding agitprop man with a badly scratched face. And an empty head, he thought with bitter anger at himself, his foolish hopes.

Wordlessly he rose and let the table, trailing his blankets behind him.

The sulfurous black pitch of his loneliness returned, but he was kept from self-pity by anger. He should have known; nobody falls like Galya had, not without a reason. At least, not for a beat-up tattered old exhibit like Duvakin.

He put on socks, trousers, buttoning his fly slowly. The pleasures of her warm apartment, her table, her bed now mocked him, brass he had taken for gold. A tool, that's all he was, something Galya had tried to bend to fit her ends.

And you? he thought as he slipped on his shirt, once again catching his little finger in the ripped cuff. And you have been coming here in the purity of your soul?

He sat on the edge of the bed, surprised by the force

of his own objection. It was true, he thought as he toyed
with one shoe, his hands were not exactly clean either
when he first came here.

But still . . .

He had thought the choices were his, not hers. He put
on one shoe.

And what choices were there now? He stroked the
other shoe as if it were a small animal.

His Magadan life of agitprop and Sutrapian and
bologna in his meager room was exploded, gone.

Grunting a bit as he bent, he put on the other shoe,
pulled the laces tight.

So, go back to the apartment and wait for Polkovnikov's wrath, provided the pusher didn't get him first.
Stay here, and be a ticket to Moscow. He sat up, head
ringing with blood. Attractive choices.

For a moment he let himself feel pinioned. Then he
decided, all right, everyone is in this for himself. Galya
wants to go to Moscow; Polkovnikov wants whatever he's
after, and Duvakin will keep an eye on Duvakin. He stood,
put on his jacket. His decision sat poorly on him, like a
new shirt, sensible perhaps, but stiffly uncomfortable.
His back unnaturally straight, he walked across the room
to pocket the pistol.

"Some breakfast before you go?" Galya called from
the kitchen, her voice artificial.

Duvakin took a deep breath, about to say no, then
thought why not, a man has to eat. Besides, he knew there
was one more body to account for. Dusya.

Make things up with Galya? He couldn't. Leave her?
He walked stiffly out of the bedroom, to the kitchen.

Silently, Galya produced kasha and fruit gelatin and
cheese and clotted milk, as if, Duvakin thought with deliberate bitterness, she could keep him if he got so fat he
could no longer fit through the door.

Yet he ate it all, and drank her coffee too, his body

grateful to receive what his mind balked at. Galya essayed a comment or two on the weather, the food, her day, each of which Duvakin answered politely, without pursuit.

At the same time he began to feel ridiculous. What was so wrong with all this? his stomach, the pragmatic side of him, asked.

Finally, as he sat smoking, studying the gray rings ascending dizzily in the sunlight, Galya stood and said with brittle jocularity, "Well, some of us have to work for our bread. They'll be wanting me down at the clinic. Just pile the dishes in the sink, will you?"

She bustled about for coat, hat, boots, purse. Then, dressed and composed, she stopped on the threshold of the kitchen, to say formally, "I apologize for my actions. I was worried . . ."

"About your ticket," Duvakin muttered into his cup, loud enough that she knew he had spoken, but not so loud that she heard. She chose to ignore it, and immediately Duvakin felt a prickle of shame.

"Your Dusya seems to be . . . well, nothing went normally," Galya struggled to report officially, without letting her questions color her voice. "No record of an accident like you mention. No record of her being taken to the child welfare people. No history of treatment at our clinic or any of the others I know about."

Duvakin still felt ugly. "You're saying I made her up?" he asked his plate.

Galya hesitated so long that Duvakin finally looked up, turning toward her. "Well?" he prodded her.

"Well, it seemed odd . . ." she murmured. "So finally I telephoned the city committee." She must have noticed the horror on Duvakin's face, for she rushed ahead. "Officially, Vanya! As a doctor! Said I had heard such-and-such, that I was concerned for the well-being and safety of the child and . . ." She stopped again, studying him.

"What did they say?" His hostility was now almost fully replaced by curiosity.

"That's what made me wonder . . . 'That matter is under official consideration. Inquiries must be addressed to the proper quarters' . . . like I was asking about a criminal or something. It *worried* me, Vanya, made me wonder. I've grown fond of you," she said hesitantly. "But *that*, then you with the pistol . . . that frightened me, I suppose. I lost my head, perhaps."

Duvakin could concentrate only on Dusya. Damn it, how could he track her down? It was like the earth had swallowed her. Would Polkovnikov be able to help? After mulling in silence, he finally said, "Ah, well . . ." not quite consolingly, not quite superiorly.

However, Galya took this as an olive branch. She smiled brightly, a shade artificially. "Silly of me, *really* it was. I see that now. You know what you're doing, I see that now. You know what you're doing, of course. I mean, what harm could come of an unloaded pistol anyway? See you this evening," she ended half-declaratively, half-interrogatively, and left.

Unloaded pistol?

This week had surprised Duvakin so often that he was almost accustomed to this chill sensation creeping along the floor of his stomach, driving out all other thoughts. Almost accustomed.

He dug the pistol from his coat pocket, fumbled with the latch that released the clip. The empty clip. Hastily, he pumped the chamber action; out popped absolutely nothing.

Unloaded pistol.

He turned the little Tokarev over and over in his hands, as if trying to massage from it some reason why Polkovnikov would so seriously present him with a totally useless lump of plastic and steel. It wasn't even heavy enough to use as a club.

Duvakin glanced at his watch, realized he ought to be moving. In a daze he stood, fumbled his way to the hall and his coat.

The logical thing, of course, was to ask Polkovnikov why, dear general, did you forget my shells.

Simple peasant caution told Duvakin very loudly that that was a bad idea. The general did not forget things.

So, what to do?

Since it's illegal to own a private handgun, there weren't many bullet stores. The Tokarev was standard militia issue, but that didn't mean he could ask to borrow a bullet or two from the first militia man he met. His exposure to the black markets made Duvakin not doubt that bullets *could* be found, given time, luck, and money.

He put on his hat; he had empty pockets and a bare half hour until he must meet Polkovnikov.

And such luck that he was up to his eyebrows in this mess, destined perhaps to leave Galya's hall and walk out into an oncoming truck.

He shrugged. And what was there to do? He could not go back, he could not run away.

Robotlike, he walked out the door, toward the shaky elevator.

Duvakin tried to think, but he was able to concentrate successfully only on not mumbling; the mass of whirling thoughts he was trying to sift down to hard facts left him muzzy and distracted. The deep snow of yesterday was settling like curds in cheesecloth, rivulets of whey draining off under a bright blue sky, making everything look wet and heavy and glistening. "It's almost May . . ." Duvakin muttered vaguely as he neared the hotel. At the entrance, he stopped, looked up at the grimy facade toward where Polkovnikov waited for him. The sky was blue; the people of Magadan bustled about their affairs like so many sow bugs . . . and I'm off to God knows what. Then, pulling his wits together like a man about to edge out onto thin ice, he squared his shoulders and went into the hotel.

The doorman, having seen him with Polkovnikov, acknowledged his status by looking straight through him. If you are a secret, then who am I to know? his blank face said. The hotel was still deserted, the restaurant still boasted no available seats in its echoing expanse. Duvakin clanked upward, the elevator and his heart making similar noises.

Suddenly, an idea struck him. What if Polkovnikov had a pistol? As the doors hiccuped and stuttered to open, Duvakin pondered; *of course,* he must have a pistol; it wouldn't make *sense* to trust matters solely to Duvakin.

Well, then, it would make no more sense for Polkovnikov's pistol also to be unloaded.

His brain half pictured scenes of stealing a clip from the unsuspecting general, and Duvakin knew, his mouth dry, that he must try. There was no choice.

He gave the doors their necessary boot and walked up to the secret floor, thinking heavily. He pushed open Polkovnikov's door.

"Polkovnikov?"

There was no answer, but he could hear water running somewhere, so he advanced, trembling with hope. If the general were in the shower, now . . .

"You read German?" Polkovnikov suddenly called from wherever he was, the bathroom.

"Me? No . . . why?" Duvakin was surprised and alarmed. German?

"I think that's what this is, but I can't figure out what I'm supposed to do with this . . ." Polkovnikov appeared in the room holding a brilliant foil packet printed with a photo of a delicious omelette.

Duvakin examined the incomprehensible packet, then asked, "What is it?"

Polkovnikov smiled, pleased to be the one who knew. He answered offhandedly, "Instant food." He used the foreign words. "Means just add water and cook. Comes out like that; cosmonauts, mountain climbers, those kind of types use it. They issue us these, so there's no trouble about food when we're in the field."

"Except if you forget to bring a Nazi with you," Duvakin said with dour pleasure, angry that his plan had so quickly failed. "You can't eat downstairs?"

"Tphoo! That swill?" Polkovnikov, still in his suspenders, made a face. "Big day today, Vanya, need some energy!" He made muscles like some Young Pioneer, then smiled. The general was as excited as a five-year-old on New Year's Eve. Duvakin felt his chest squeeze, his breath get shorter. "You eaten?" the general added as an afterthought.

Duvakin nodded, but Polkovnikov handed him a tin of something anyway. "Here, try this. I've got coffee on . . ." he explained disappearing into the bathroom again.

For a moment Duvakin studied the tin; a creature like a spider or louse was painted in lurid red on the label. "What is that?" he asked nervously.

"Crab. Try it. There's no bread, but try some of those rusk things by the bed. They're sweet, sort of," he bellowed from beyond the closed door.

"Just the rusk, thanks . . ." Duvakin shouted, suddenly aware that his chance perhaps had come. How much time did he have? Could he have?

To cover any untoward noise, he bellowed, "What big day?" as he made for the closet by the bed.

"Lots to do, not much time!" Polkovnikov answered. "I've got to be wrapping this up, for the holidays."

Duvakin fumbled breathlessly with the catch, then began quickly to pat the pockets of Polkovnikov's other suit, hung with care in the closet. "In Moscow?" he asked stupidly.

"Of course in Moscow. The holiday's a good time for these sort of matters." Polkovnikov's voice sounded nearer; Duvakin's brain seemed frozen, but his fingers, thank heaven, continued to scamper. "So where do we go?"

"Darmoved's . . ." Polkovnikov answered, then after a pause, grabbed the door handle. "*Damn* it . . ."

Duvakin thought his heart had stopped. He distantly felt his fingers tell him there was no pistol in any of the general's pockets before he snatched back his arm. "You—" He cleared his throat, tried again. "You lost something?"

"Is there a glove or something out there?" Polkovnikov stuck his head through the door. "Fucking pot got so hot I burned my fingers."

Duvakin looked about helplessly, certain his distress must be shrieking all over his face. Fortunately, Polkovnikov seemed more concerned with his fingers, on which he blew with lusty enthusiasm. "Get me a sock or something at least! The damn pot is boiling all over the place now!"

"A sock?" Duvakin parroted stupidly.

"Second drawer, hurry, damn it!" He disappeared.

A wild cunning suddenly focused Duvakin. Acting on chance and instinct he rushed to the bureau, pulled out the top two drawers simultaneously. His left hand fumbled in the second drawer for socks.

And the right, inspired, flitted about in the top, for guns.

"*Second* drawer, I said," Polkovnikov boomed over Duvakin's shoulder; Duvakin withdrew both hands as if they too were scalded. "It's all right though, Vanya." The general chuckled. "Shows you how cool I am! I wasn't thinking . . . used a towel. You want some coffee?" He held up the pot.

Duvakin was trembling so badly that he could only shake his head. That Polkovnikov appeared to have noticed nothing was a blessing, but Duvakin still did not have the bullets. The nearer he was to this huge, powerful, dangerous general, the more he was certain he must.

"You all right, Vanya?" the general asked, concerned. "You look pale."

"I . . . it's nothing . . . just . . ." he waved vaguely at the bathroom, suddenly aware how much fear made Galya's breakfast want to come out. "May I?"

"Use the other one, by the door. It's a mess in there." Polkovnikov chuckled, then poured himself a cup of murky coffee. "The maid is going to hate me . . ."

Duvakin dashed into the other room, searching for the proper door; apparently this suite could be divided as needed, so there were a couple of necessaries. He tried one door. A closet, with Polkovnikov's overcoat. He closed it, opened the other door, to the bathroom.

The coat! He reversed the doors again, heart pounding. Faster than he knew they could move, his hands patted down the bulky woolen coat.

"The *left*-hand door, Vanya!" Polkovnikov called through the opened connecting door, while Duvakin, sphincter taut and tongue stiff with paralyzed, unthinking fear, pulled out the general's pistol from his outer pocket.

A Tokarev.

Pushed beyond thought by need and apprehension, Duvakin in one swift move pocketed the general's pistol, replaced it with his own.

"The left? I got it . . ." he squeaked as he waddled, buttocks clenched, inside.

When he emerged he was, if not composed, at least

not frenzied. A quick check had informed him he now had bullets. For what, for whom he had no idea, beyond fearful suspicions. But, come what might, Duvakin could at least go down kicking.

Polkovnikov was finishing his coffee. "All right?" he asked with more interest than he usually showed in Duvakin's health.

"Too much yogurt for breakfast," Duvakin muttered dismissively. "It's nothing."

Polkovnikov seemed relieved. "I hope so," he said as he rose to put on his suit jacket. "We've got to be on our toes this morning; it's bear we're after." He winked.

"Bear? What do I do?"

"What you're told," Polkovnikov said offhandedly, his power more complete now that he was dressed. "Come on, you can start by getting the tent, we're running late."

The tent? Duvakin turned to the nylon bag in the corner. "We need it?" He could accept that this room was bugged, that Khromoi might be bugged. But they were going to Darmoved's . . .

"Just get it and come on, will you?" Polkovnikov snapped irritably. "This isn't for next year's plan, you know."

Trying to digest the idea that even the head of Magadan's KGB might be bugged, Duvakin stepped to the bag, hefted it, and turned to follow.

★ FIFTEEN ★

"**S**mell that air, it's soft as the hair on your mother's arm!" Polkovnikov said jauntily, striding through the sloppy muck of the sidewalks. "I *told* you it was just a spring storm, Vanya!"

Breathless, struggling with the satchel, and unable to match Polkovnikov's long stride, Duvakin scurried behind, walking three steps, jogging two. To his astonishment, they had simply exited the hotel and cut right, around Lenin Square. Busy with keeping pace, still shaky from his search for the pistol, Duvakin had failed first to understand. When he did, he stopped dead.

"No!"

Polkovnikov stopped too, turned.

"What no? We're going to see Darmoved, remember?"

Polkovnikov doubled back, took Duvakin's arm in a grip that permitted no dispute.

"But in his *office*?" Duvakin's fear kept his heels firmly rooted.

"It's where the man works, isn't it?" Polkovnikov was

still jolly, excited about whatever he thought would be the pleasure to come. "Come on, Vanya; don't be a goose."

Reluctantly, Duvakin let himself be urged step by step toward the oldest building on the square, a sinister yellow and white wedding cake of plaster statues and curlicue trim and towers made to look much taller than they really were.

KGB headquarters, Magadan.

In the days when Magadan was a kind of amusement park for the NKVD, the personal fiefdom of the state police, this building had been the de facto government center, where tubby little men decided the lives and, more often, the deaths of their millions of rag-clad prisoners.

Demoted by Khrushchev, the building, if anything, became more remote, more intimidating. The entrance parade doors had light voile curtains; the only auto entrance was barred by a high gate of black steel, and no sign of life ever showed in its windows. Not so much as a geranium. The roof bristled with antennae and mysterious metal shapes, and the building was so girded round by rumor, dread, and reputation that usually people crossed over the street or cut across the square, rather than touch the sidewalk before it. Some people, Duvakin knew, even insisted the sparrows did not light there, and it was a fact that the original plan, to have the new twelve-meter Lenin put against that building, had been dropped, when it became clear no one would be willing to work so close to the building's walls.

And me? Duvakin thought bitterly. I'm waltzing in to see the colonel in charge. With a pistol.

Polkovnikov more or less frog-marched Duvakin up to the corner, then down the block, to a small door set deep into the granite foundation of the building. Duvakin would have sworn he had never noticed the door before; a corroded brass plaque the size of a postal card read simply "Reception." Duvakin hefted his satchel, the handles biting into his shoulder, set his jaw, and with conscious effort followed the general in.

Polkovnikov stopped so suddenly Duvakin rammed into him.

"Steady!" Polkovnikov said, turning back nastily. "The comrade here wants to see our papers."

Duvakin readjusted his skewed hat and noticed the desk Polkovnikov's bulk had hidden. It was set virtually athwart the doorway, allowing entrance only by sidling through a narrow gap. Assuming that one passed the inspection of the dour young man seated at the desk, Duvakin was astonished to note that the guard was not Russian, an Asiatic of some sort. The man's hair was bristle cut; his eyes mere slits above cheekbones like steel traps, and his expression was totally blank.

Not so Polkovnikov.

"They've taught you to read as well, eh, roast beef?" The general smiled as he produced a small cardboard folder from inside his breast pocket, then held it forward.

The guard's color turned slightly more olive, but he remained impassive as he reached for Polkovnikov's pass; just as he touched it, the general let it drop with a plop to the desk.

"And here I thought you people were clever with your hands," Polkovnikov remarked casually, making Duvakin glance with alarm at the guard's pistol. He had been lucky once and did not relish the prospect of Polkovnikov queering things again. Luck dislikes working back-to-back shifts.

There was no need for worry. The color of horseflesh, the guard shot to his feet, saluted crisply, and said in perfect Russian, "My apologies, sir!" His black eyes burned a smoldering hole in the air beyond the general's shoulder. "On what business, sir?"

Polkovnikov lazily picked up the folder, replacing it in his inside pocket. The guard, who proved almost as tall

[263]

as Polkovnikov, still trembled at stiff attention, his hand at his brow. The general studied him minutely, then shook his head. "Just a visit, little friend. We'll find our way . . ."

Polkovnikov stepped past the desk, making for the stairs; Duvakin squeezed awkwardly through the small space, snagging his bundle on the wall and almost dropping it, before he caught up. Halfway up the dark stairs, Polkovnikov said, as if to himself but perfectly audibly in the well, "So we're even shipping camelfuckers out here now. Next thing, they'll be making a Turkoman Patriarch."

Before they left the stairwell to go down a long blank corridor, Duvakin glanced down at the guard, who stared stonily ahead, his ears two crimson strips.

"What was that about?" he whispered hoarsely.

Polkovnikov half turned, his face dark. "Ah, they make me mad, breeding like god-damned rabbits, expecting to be treated like white men . . ." He waved a dismissive hand. "Come on, Vanya, you can introduce me to your friend Darmoved." The general's excitement had turned grimmer, less controlled. Duvakin tried to gather his wits; gloomily he suspected he would need them.

The building was something out of a nightmare—long, high-ceilinged corridors in murky half-light, a narrow liver carpet muffling their steps. Most doors were high, padded with frayed leather, the color of old blood; some were frosted glass. At intervals there still stood the coffinlike boxes where guards used to stick prisoners in transit, so one prisoner might not see another. Occasionally, there was the tentative tapping of a typewriter, a muffled voice or two. Duvakin grew rapidly disoriented as he followed Polkovnikov around corners, up another short flight, even down a flight of stairs. The building, which on the outside had seemed four simple floors of office, proved inside to be chopped up into some sort of maze. The deeper they penetrated the more trapped Duvakin felt; when an inquisitive eye peered from an anonymous door, Duvakin was unable to resist the temptation to slap his pistol once more.

"Here we are," Polkovnikov whispered, stopping at an innocuous door. "You ready?" he mouthed.

Duvakin would never be ready, he knew, not for anything in this building. He swallowed, then suddenly wondered how Polkovnikov had known his way through that maze; *was* this his first trip to Magadan? Duvakin felt a shadow of suspicion cross his heart. What if he were being led into a trap?

Just as that possibility hit him, Polkovnikov turned the door handle, pushed, and entered. "Tell the colonel we're here, that's good lads," Polkovnikov boomed jovially to the two men who sat, openmouthed, in the narrow antechamber. Duvakin recognized the man called Vaska, then, more slowly, that this must be some sort of observation room. His mouth still open, the other guard stood slowly up, trailing his earphone cord, reaching slowly inside his coat.

Polkovnikov shook a finger like a stern uncle. "No, no, don't you dare, little friend . . . think how upset *he'd* be," Polkovnikov poked a thumb at the wall. Then, grinning, he pushed open the next door and stepped through.

Numbly, Duvakin followed, inanely nodding to Vaska as he passed. As inanely, the startled man nodded back.

Duvakin, in Polkovnikov's wake, saw a large office, hung with the standard portraits, Lenin, Brezhnev, some younger man in glasses. Small behind his enormous desk stood Darmoved, his eyes huge, his mouth open. When he noticed Duvakin, his eyes narrowed.

"What is the meaning of this?" he asked in a chill, unpleasant voice, apparently to Duvakin, but with his eyes firmly on Polkovnikov.

The general in his turn stared insolently at Darmoved, a half smile on his lips. "Tell the man, Vanya . . ."

Duvakin was growing used to Polkovnikov's tricks; he didn't even care much any more. Perhaps the security grew from seeing the miracle Polkovnikov's cardboard folder had wrought at the entrance. Duvakin shrugged, then said, "The comrade here wants to talk," indicating Polkovnikov with his thumb.

"Normally my guests"—Darmoved flicked a thin hand at the formal entrance doors that stood studded and leather-bound across from his desk—"are announced . . ."

Immensely pleased with himself, Polkovnikov sat in the leather armchair opposite Darmoved, removed his overcoat, leaving it draped from his shoulders, like an actor. He smiled. "To all three of you?"

Darmoved flushed the color of summer borscht and walked stiffly to the door they had come through, where he said something harsh and low, then shut the door. Which then, Duvakin noted, became invisible in the paneled wall. He thought again of Rzhevsky, beginning to understand how a side of beef like that might get beaten to death by a newt like Darmoved. A newt with reinforcements beyond the wall. In spite of himself, Duvakin noted that the carpet was dark red. Like in the old days, so blood stains wouldn't show.

"You must be Polkovnikov then." Darmoved smiled. "I had heard you were in the city." For effect he let the implication hang a bit, then he added, with a tip of his head at the now-invisible door, "Clever of you, that . . ."

Polkovnikov smiled his feline best, then purred, "At your service, and nothing to it, really. We in the center know the little tricks of you provincials. Besides, the architects' plans for the place are easy enough to dig up when you've got my access." Polkovnikov studied his nails casually while Darmoved and Duvakin digested this; Duvakin had no idea what effect it had upon the

colonel, but he found it distinctly unnerving. That Polkovnikov would have dug out maps not only of Magadan,
but even of buildings, and the Lord knows what else as
well, suggested plans far deeper than they had seemed so
far. Duvakin swallowed, to clear his ears.

Darmoved may have been having similar thoughts,
for he sat slowly at his desk, examining Polkovnikov
grimly. In his turn the general kept a mocking eye on the
colonel, radiating palpable superiority. There was an uncomfortable silence; then, not moving his eyes, Polkovnikov said, "Open the tent, Vanya . . ." He waved vaguely
at the center of the room.

Looking as serious as he might, Duvakin did as he
was told, trying to make a convincing professional job of
it. Even though he had done it once before, the task took
ages, and Duvakin had, inexplicably, several red clips and
a couple of tubes left over.

The entire while Darmoved sat in expressionless silence, as if every morning at this time a man came to erect
a blue nylon mushroom in the center of his reception
area. Polkovnikov simply smoked and whistled, ir-
ritatingly, through his teeth.

At last, sweaty and disarrayed, Duvakin stepped back
to admire his handiwork; the tent was straight, even crisp,
and as inconspicuous as galoshes on a pig.

"Please . . ." Polkovnikov ordered Darmoved in politely, as if it were the living room he pointed his finger at.
"A little chat . . ."

Darmoved permitted himself no more inquiry than
raised eyebrows, but did not budge.

"Our Temple of Solitude," Polkovnikov said
jocularly, but standing to emphasize his insistence. "To
keep us from stray eyes and ears."

"For legitimate business there are no such here," Darmoved answered with strained casualness; the colonel's
knuckles were white on the desk.

Polkovnikov leaned forward, putting his plate-sized hands on the desk, to speak directly into Darmoved's face. "As your superior, I insist . . ."

After a second's hesitation, Darmoved rose stiffly and marched over to the tent. He hesitated again, then, as if surrendering entirely, he got on all fours and crawled into the tent. At the sight of the colonel's khaki posterior, Polkovnikov winked gaily at Duvakin, then whispered, "He's ours now . . . your turn, Vanya, now you . . ."

Ours? For what? Duvakin wondered, on the verge of protesting. With two in the tent last time he thought he'd die, and now three? Then Duvakin remembered Vaska and the others beyond the wall, and agreed that the more private things were, the better.

Inside, the air was already foul and did not improve as he and Darmoved slithered about to make room for the general. With tremendous grunting and groaning they finally all fit; sweat gleaming from his hawklike nose, Polkovnikov switched on the device at the top of their little dome. "There . . ."

"This is all necessary?" Darmoved asked breathlessly.

"Party business of an embarrassing nature," the general replied flatly. "As you would know, if you'd been doing your job."

At that moment Duvakin was glad the tent allowed virtually no movement; with his shoulder jammed against the colonel's thigh, he felt the jibe pass through Darmoved like an electric jolt.

"I do my job!" he strangled out.

Polkovnikov shrugged in the dark-blue light. "Even better, means we've bagged a co-conspirator, Vanya. Quite a haul you've made, chum."

"What are you insinuating?" the colonel demanded, twisting his face awkwardly to Duvakin.

Duvakin shrugged, as much as space allowed. He

opened his mouth to begin accusations of Khromoi, but before a sound emerged, Polkovnikov interrupted.

"Vanya and me, we just yesterday had the most interesting chat with a colleague of yours," Polkovnikov stressed "colleague" oddly.

"Khromoi . . ." Darmoved said flatly. "Your 'family friend'?" he asked Duvakin.

"You see, Vanya? It's just like I said, you're never alone when you go out visiting," Polkovnikov joked, then grew more stern. "So you admit the connection, then?"

"What connection?" Darmoved asked, exasperated.

"That you have been conspiring with the second secretary to steal from the Fatherland?" Polkovnikov demanded in icy procuratorial tones. Duvakin felt a shiver of confusion. He was having trouble recalling their true quarry, Khromoi or Darmoved. Khromoi had been stealing, but here it was Darmoved whom Polkovnikov was hectoring. And why had there been no word of Rzhevsky?

Darmoved grew frosty and distant. "Your accusation is unfounded. The matters you speak of are under official investigation." Then, as an afterthought, Darmoved added a sarcastic, "Sir."

"Pretty poor job of it then," Polkovnikov said nastily, his breath sour and fuggy. "Or maybe one of your eyes goes blind when you investigate, maybe that's it, huh? *That* Moscow would find interesting . . ."

Smiling confidently, Darmoved wheezed, "Both my eyes work fine."

Polkovnikov turned to Duvakin. "Some eyes, eh Vanya? Your toilet woman spots a fur-stealing business worth Lord knows how much, while gimlet-eye here . . ." Polkovnikov shrugged, made a flatulent noise, then snapped back at Darmoved, "What were you doing, counting thumbtacks?"

Darmoved relaxed so sensibly that Duvakin felt it through his shoulder and so turned to look more carefully at the colonel's face. Sweaty, ashen, and breathless, Darmoved still managed to seem sardonically confident. "You're worried only about Khromoi and his furs?"

"*Only?*" Polkovnikov boomed; in the tent, the question was deafening. "You know how much they've been stealing?"

"I make it seven, maybe eight million last year alone," Darmoved said with aplomb. Duvakin felt his mouth drop open; who could imagine such numbers? "Of course, that's just the furs . . . look, it's damned uncomfortable in here. Can't we get a breath now?" His face was slick with sweat.

Duvakin knew suddenly he agreed, and must shift position. There was nowhere to go, though, and Polkovnikov squeezed his calf painfully.

"Stop kicking, Vanya!" the general barked, then spoke more neutrally to Darmoved. "Why was Moscow not informed?"

After an unpleasant pause, Darmoved conceded, "I didn't know everything yet. I was still looking . . . am still . . ."

"You need to know more than that the state is losing eight million rubles a year?" Polkovnikov asked sternly.

Darmoved loosened his tie, gulped air. "Look, this is senseless! Talk you want, we'll talk, but let me out of here!"

Polkovnikov was unmoved. "Why was Moscow not informed?"

Darmoved seemed not to hear; he was staring at the zipper opening beyond Polkovnikov's back and breathing heavily. Duvakin, too, found it difficult to think of more than the air, now so thick it caught at his nostrils like sour cream.

"Why was Moscow not informed?" Polkovnikov repeated insistently.

"Damn it!" Darmoved snapped, "the man's a second secretary! I can't just have him arrested!"

"Why was Moscow not informed?" Polkovnikov's words dropped like plump globules of molten lead onto Darmoved's shiny forehead. "Why was Moscow not informed?"

Inexplicably, Darmoved relaxed, to answer formally. "Because of the suspect's rank, I informed comrade Andropov's office directly, to place myself under his instructions."

With a gasp Duvakin glanced at Polkovnikov; so it was true? He was about to open his mouth when he felt the general's fingers close tight about his ankle, then squeeze. Hard.

The general looked at him, to make certain the message had been received, then lazily looked back to Darmoved. "Now that I'd call antisoviet, Colonel . . ." Polkovnikov drawled. "To claim that comrade Andropov's office would 'instruct' you to murder—"

"Murder!?" Darmoved screeched, startled.

"Rzhevsky, he means," Duvakin said helpfully, curious to see Darmoved's reaction.

"That—" Darmoved turned the color of old liver. "That was a mistake, I swear it. The guy wouldn't . . ."

Polkovnikov spoke again, still in that lazy, drawling way, like they were discussing sports, or girls. "That's what you'll tell them when they serve you your own kidneys for lunch? It was a mistake? Rzhevsky had some awfully powerful friends, did you know that?"

"They told me to find out where the money's going," Darmoved gasped, fanning himself weakly.

"Who told you?"

"Comrade Andropov's office. They said he had to

know where the money was going . . ." Darmoved's voice grew fainter; Duvakin wondered whether they might all be smothering. Cooking, maybe. His shirt clung to his spine like a membrane.

"Into his own pocket's not a good enough answer? Maybe because it also goes into yours?" Polkovnikov was the only one who seemed unaffected by their ludicrous tent.

Darmoved shook his head, unable to say more.

"So let's say I go back to Moscow, ask around in Andropov's office—where naturally no one will have ever *heard* of this nonsense—you know what *that's* going to look like? Like you were conspiring to aid and abet . . . Remember"—Polkovnikov smiled icily despite the sweat bucketing down his face—"we have the death penalty again."

Darmoved rallied himself. "It's not that. The money's going someplace, back to Moscow. Comrade Andropov's office suspects a plot . . ."

"The metro," Duvakin croaked, his voice congealed in the foul air. "You didn't know?"

"What?" Darmoved managed.

"The metro . . . Khromoi wants to build a metro, so he's bribing Moscow people," Duvakin repeated patiently, puzzled by Darmoved's incomprehension. Polkovnikov had said the colonel would certainly know.

Darmoved, though, simply waved a fatigued hand and looked disgusted. "Some inspector you are, if you believe that nonsense. Who would be stupid enough to build a metro here?"

"So?" Polkovnikov's voice was still scornful. "It's still theft; it's still illegal . . . and you're still helping. Or isn't *mil-li-ons* theft, to you?"

Darmoved glowered scant centimeters from Polkovnikov's face. "You believe it too? That bedtime story? That someone could seriously claim even the faintest glimmer of sense in building a metro here? I won't ask why anyone would think we need one, or why the center would give us one. Towns this size are thicker than fleas in a bathhouse! But permit me one little question. Who is *crazy* enough to dig tunnels in permafrost? Eh? You ever seen the stuff? It's harder than concrete; you'd be blasting every whisker of the way, and then you turn around and the stuff *flows*! There's nothing worse to build on, to say nothing of *in*! Christ! And what little isn't permafrost, *that's* granite . . ." Darmoved fell back against the tent, straining its seams.

"It's *your* worry that Khromoi is a fool!" Polkovnikov spat dismissively. "That money is still going somewhere. Arrest him."

"That's it, isn't it?"

"What?"

"The money *is* going somewhere, and you can bet not for metros!" Darmoved managed a sarcastic glance at Duvakin.

"For what, then?" Duvakin asked, puzzled. Last night he had thought Khromoi demented, but honest. Polkovnikov hadn't made out that Khromoi was a liar either. "If not for a metro . . ."

Darmoved looked almost comatose, sunk deep within himself. Duvakin thought it was the air, until Darmoved, eyes almost shut, whispered, "A lot of the money goes to Leningrad offices, before it disappears. Andropov . . ." Darmoved opened his eyes, raised himself up slightly. He studied Duvakin and Polkovnikov a moment in silence, then murmured, "If a breath of this gets out, Andropov will have your skin made into throw rugs."

Polkovnikov winked, patted the tent comfortingly. Just us old friends here, so to say. Duvakin shivered, in spite of the fug.

Darmoved hesitated a moment longer, then, as if collapsing, wheezed, "Andropov's men think they've spotted a young bull who's maybe trying to get a jump on the old boy, speed things along . . . especially now with Suslov gone."

Even in such syrupy air, Duvakin could recognize the argument Polkovnikov had given him the night before. Only then it was Andropov who was the young bull. Duvakin felt his neck hairs crackle against the tent.

"Who?" Polkovnikov barked, then, more slyly, "Who's so big they don't just squash him?"

Darmoved took a deep breath, then said, "Romanov . . ."

"Romanov? What Romanov? Not—?" Polkovnikov sounded shocked.

Darmoved nodded. "This money, or a lot of it, seems to head in the direction of Romanov, then sort of disappear. It's got the Moscow people pretty jumpy, I can tell you, and Romanov, he's a deep one."

Duvakin felt his eyes open wide, then dry. Romanov's name he knew too; it was an old joke.

The ghost of Nikolai II appears to Brezhnev on Nevsky Prospekt, in Leningrad. "Well, Leonid Illich, greetings! I see everything's different now! Revolutionary names, eh?" the tsar asks.

Brezhnev says kindly, "Nonsense, Your Highness! Look, Nevsky, the Winter Palace . . ."

"Oh?" the tsar says. "But the empire? That's gone, isn't it? No more colonies, subject peoples?"

"Well, to tell the truth," Brezhnev admits uncomfortably, "if anything we've a bit more in that line . . ."

"Hmmm . . ." the tsar says, frowning. "Censorship? Secret police? Hunger? Corruption? They're gone, at least?"

Brezhnev scowls, then glumly shakes his head.

"Now just a moment!" the tsar's ghost says angrily. "You people make a revolution and kill all the Romanovs and—"

"Oh-ho!" Brezhnev interrupts with relief. "Not so! Our man in charge here now is a Romanov, you see?"

In a rage the tsar claps his forehead in his hand. "So *nothing's* changed?!"

"Well," Brezhnev ponders anxiously, then brightens, "not so, Your Excellency! Vodka! The vodka is forty percent alcohol now, not thirty-seven percent, like in your day!"

"Lyonya, Lyonya, Lyonya," the tsar says in disgust, "all that fuss for three percent?"

That Romanov? Duvakin wondered. Like Andropov, a young comer on the Politburo, head of the Leningrad region. Famous as strictest of the bosses, purest of the pure.

Last night, when Polkovnikov had suggested there was one plot, Duvakin had accepted the fact without feeling it; now, when Darmoved suggested a twin plot, but in favor of Romanov, Duvakin knew it was true. Perhaps not these plots, or not these men. But men like Polkovnikov and Darmoved believed now there were such plots—and men who believe plots possible are but one step from making plots of their own.

Duvakin felt that same thrill of fear he had been skewered by the night before, when sensing suddenly the delicacy of his life's fabric against the ballooning push of chaos. He saw again the twinkling rain of airplane bits and knew that if intrigue had begun at the top, then suffering would come, and not only at the top.

Polkovnikov, though, seemed unperturbed, even amused. "Romanov? Making himself first secretary? Tphoo! After sixty-five years of us drumming into everybody's head what devils the Romanovs were, how could he *dream*?"

"Comrade Andropov's office is considerably alarmed . . ." Darmoved answered stiffly.

Beneath his fear something else nibbled at Duvakin,

but it was hard to concentrate in the sweatbox of the tent. A plot in favor of Romanov seemed not only possible, but somehow familiar.

Polkovnikov, though, pressed on. "Listen, little friend, your stories are very thrilling I'm sure, but my colleagues back in Moscow—your superiors—see it like this." Polkovnikov smiled the half-smile of superiority Duvakin remembered so clearly, from four years of nightmares. "We have theft, and we have a murder. Rzhevsky's friends want blood, and the state wants its furs. So we can give them a thief and call him a murderer—"

"I can't arrest Khromoi!" Darmoved interrupted in panic. "Not without clearance! He's a second secretary, for God's sake."

Polkovnikov continued as if he had heard nothing. "Or we can give them a murderer, and call him a thief . . ."

"I'm not a murderer," Darmoved muttered sulkily.

"And Rzhevsky's not dead?" Duvakin could not resist jabbing, catching the drift now of Polkovnikov's plan.

Darmoved glowered at him. "That was duty . . . an investigation."

"I recall something you said about laws," Duvakin goaded again; if Darmoved could be forced into arresting Khromoi, then the last of the pieces arrayed against them would be gone.

"I can't arrest a second secretary! I'm not big enough!" Darmoved hissed. "They'd crucify me!"

"Well, Vanya, looks like we'll leave it for Rzhevsky's friends to sort out . . ." Polkovnikov said jocularly to Duvakin, even clapping him on the shoulder.

"You arrest him!" Darmoved clutched at Polkovnikov's sleeve. "You're high enough, a general in the KGB, for Christ's sake! I'll testify, I swear I will!"

Duvakin was astounded; the man who yesterday had seemed so remote, controlled, was now begging? Then he recalled Polkovnikov's story, of the widow and Andropov. Could it really be that despite Khromoi's own admission of massive theft, Andropov would protect him, and punish Darmoved, solely for arresting a superior?

Polkovnikov shook his head, smiled nastily. "The honor is yours."

Duvakin felt almost sorry for the ashen-faced colonel. He thought of Khromoi, the bear masquerading as a harmless old fool, and knew why Darmoved looked so stricken.

Suddenly, he realized what had seemed so familiar about Romanov's name, and Duvakin's heart froze.

Last night, at Khromoi's . . . when Polkovnikov had claimed to be working for Romanov in approaching Khromoi.

And today Polkovnikov works for the KGB, and Andropov?

Duvakin turned in shock to Polkovnikov, who was smiling victoriously. He would have asked, but something else stopped his tongue, another memory.

The punch line of that stupid joke, "for three percent." Those had been the words Polkovnikov had given him to establish his identity with Darmoved.

"Can't I at least clear it in Moscow?" Darmoved whined miserably. "If I don't do that, Lord, his people will have him outside and me inside, two minutes flat—and then where will you be?"

"Your choice, swillbucket. You should have thought of this while you were dancing on Rzhevsky's head!"

"It was them! I never touched him!" Darmoved jabbed toward the wall where his men were hidden.

"Don't know as Rzhevsky's friends will see the difference." Polkovnikov was impatient, no longer interested. "Believe me, you could be sent so far away, you'll think Armenians are white men! How does political education officer for an Afghan infantry unit sound, eh?" Polkov-nikov winked, relentless. "Wouldn't be hard, lots of open-ings . . . and these are big friends."

Darmoved paled, sweating even worse. "God . . . all right, on what charge?" he capitulated miserably.

"We'll see . . . theft, for a start. Malfeasance. Currency manipulation, bribery, and who knows, maybe with a question or two we can think up something serious?" He slapped Darmoved chummily on the shoulder. "You could end up a hero! Come on, Vanya, we'll take the colonel's car . . ."

Polkovnikov unzipped the tent and crawled out; the air of the office rushed in cool and fresh as the first blizzard of September. Duvakin sat still, trying to rear-range some vague and sinister thoughts, but the colonel in a frenzy flung himself through the door, to lay gasping on the carpet, his legs still in the tent.

"Is everything all right, comrade Darmoved?" asked a puzzled and businesslike voice. Duvakin started; he had forgotten that there might be guards outside.

Mouth dry, Duvakin felt for his pistol. For a second he pictured emerging, pistol at the ready, forcing them all to raise their hands, to back slowly against the wall, while he . . .

What? Escaped through a KGB headquarters designed by a badger, to emerge in a town set at the edge of the world, separated from safety solely by millions of hec-tares of dwarf cedar, reindeer moss, and snow?

Simpler just to shoot himself, he thought, his heart hammering.

Darmoved also hesitated, laboring heavily for air, then crawled the rest of the way out.

Feeling a fool, Duvakin waited, then finally crawled out too, into a circle of beefy armed guards. He stood quickly, then staggered. Two quick lungfuls of air helped, but the room still wobbled and rocked.

Vaska studied Darmoved solicitously, clearly ready at the slightest gesture to have his crew of well-fed thugs fling the two strangers straight to the devil's grandmother.

Insouciant, Polkovnikov had lit a cigarette and was half sitting on the desk, enjoying the sight of Darmoved wheezing, ashen.

One thing was clear to Duvakin, even as his head spun. Polkovnikov had no fear of Darmoved. Not for the first time, Duvakin wondered who the devil Polkovnikov was, what he was about. And just how powerful he was.

With a glare at Polkovnikov, Darmoved straightened himself, mopping his forehead. "It's all right, Vaska," he muttered. "The general has . . . some business."

And like so much sugar in hot water, Vaska and his men disappeared, closing the concealed door after them. Darmoved's shoulders slumped again, and Polkovnikov laughed.

To still his head, Duvakin sat, wondering why Polkovnikov was so intent upon breaking Darmoved. To use him to arrest Khromoi seemed senseless if there were an equal chance Khromoi instead would arrest Darmoved.

"Well, shall we go then?" Polkovnikov asked jovially, as if it were to the movies they were headed, then indicated Darmoved should lead the way.

Duvakin looked up at the towering general, wondering which story was true, Polkovnikov worked for Romanov, Polkovnikov worked for Andropov? Both? Neither?

Then he felt Polkovnikov take his arm in that huge, strong hand, to half hoist him to his feet. "Let's go, Vanya; we've got the bastard, I think . . ." He chuckled, then leaned over to whisper. "But keep your pistol ready. We might need it, eh!" Then a jolly cuff on his shoulder sent Duvakin staggering toward the door.

The general was trembling with excitement; Duvakin's own tremors were from fear.

★ SIXTEEN ★

They went out another way, through more empty halls, past closed doors. Where the sun struck through the large panes, it was warm, but the unlit halls seemed cold. Anxious heads appeared from some rooms, but Darmoved calmly assured them all was well, or ordered them back in, to their work. Otherwise, nothing was said.

The garage was across a small courtyard in the center of the building, like a skywell; a drab hangar of concrete sprayed over steel held a Chaika, a Niva, several Volgas, a Zhiguli, crates, boxes, and mountains of materials, lost in the shadows. A chauffeur appeared, plump and greasy as a salami, but he too was dismissed. Darmoved would drive himself.

They got into the Zhiguli, Duvakin in the rear, and jerkily Darmoved backed them out of the hangar, killed the engine, started it again, hopped forward, and killed it.

"Can't drive, eh?" Polkovnikov laughed wolfishly.

The first officer of the KGB drew a deep, ragged breath, then clamped a pale jaw, to expel it through his nose. His eyes crackled, but he said only, "So you drive."

In the back Duvakin half listened to Polkovnikov's affable acceptance of the offer and the fuss while they changed seats. His mind was pounding, struggling to assemble into some coherent order all the fragments of this week; most urgent were Polkovnikov's last words.

"You wouldn't be *afraid* now, would you?" Polkovnikov mocked, as his eyes flickered back and forth from Darmoved's pale, strained face to the rusting iron gate that barred their way.

Stiffly Darmoved stared ahead and said, "Blow the horn."

The third bleat brought another Asian face to a small hole cut high in the left-hand wall. Darmoved rolled down his window, half crawled out to hold up a bright red cardboard pass, and yelled, "Colonel Darmoved!" Finally the gates creaked open, to let them out.

A ghost of memory crawled up Duvakin's spine. Once before he had sat like this, Polkovnikov at the wheel, their business done, the guilty party their passenger . . .

Fear for a second overwhelmed him, making his breath short too; too much was unknown, unknowable. Who had pushed him? Why? What did Polkovnikov want? The pistol? The airplane? Dusya? In panic he grabbed at the door handle, prepared to leap and run if only the door would open. The handle lifted, the lock unlatched, and a damp cold breeze hit his face.

"You all right, Vanya?" Polkovnikov asked in surprise, his eyes watching him in the mirror. Even Darmoved half turned, his face ashen and apathetic.

"Yes . . . it's not . . . wasn't closed," he mumbled, then sat back, relieved. The air, the change of position, Polkovnikov's apparent concern, and above all, that the door opened, all helped restore some calm; what had most sobered him, though, was the scene he had glimpsed on the square, where a ragtag squad of middle-aged women in black padded jackets was toiling to shovel the last of the snow and slush onto an old Auroch truck. Other trucks came down each of the four sides of Lenin Square, stopping at each lamppost, where tipsy workmen slowly propped ladders. Trudging upward, they painstakingly filled each tube of the lamp's precast holders with red flags, which then whipped gaily in the wind. Decorating had begun for May Day, 1982.

He glanced toward where the reviewing stand would be, curious about their major coup, the new Lenin. Memories of that project, the headaches of coordinating the three shops, the endless wrangles over design, the knowledge that he had helped plan all this gave Duvakin new confidence. This wasn't life, it was a lunatic week. Sure enough, he saw with satisfaction, the base was already in place for the reviewing stand, and the framework for the Lenin was already crawling up the side of the four-story building next to it. One of the enormous shins had even been brought, laying half the length of the building.

His Lenin. The one he had ordered. In his other, real life.

The realization cleared his head. This was not like the last time. He was not going to go quietly into the noose. He put his hand on the pistol and stared out the window, determined now that things must be puzzled through.

They drove in silence, Polkovnikov smiling faintly and Darmoved grim, his jaws knotting, through the town and out onto the Highway of Dawn, following the curve of the bay toward Siglan and Cape Alevin. Duvakin watched the rocky coast, a jumble of crags, birds, ice, and surf. In most places the road had been hacked from the cliffs by prisoners. How many of them had been chucked dead of exhaustion into the sea below, to wash about until rot, gulls, and seals had disposed of them?

Those men had died because of plots too, victims of

the ambitions and schemes of other men they had never seen or known. People said times had changed, but look—Rzhevsky dead, the plane to Moscow, orphan Dusya, the attempt on his life . . . and all for what?

Darmoved kills Rzhevsky to get information about this plot, this Romanov business, and so advance himself with Andropov. Khromoi's reasons for stealing furs were no better; he stole from the state to bribe the state into having the state build a metro on which a man of his rank wouldn't dream of riding. The airplane?

Like drawing a third ace, the answer fell into Duvakin's lap. The Rzhevskys! He remembered the wealth of their apartment, the pride of their industrious nest-feathering. Rzhevsky was no man for selfless mad dreams of civic betterment; he must have been stealing his share as well from what Khromoi was stealing for his metro. And if Rzhevsky were helping himself, then no doubt all of Khromoi's helpers had dipped in for their shares as well.

But why kill the wife? Not to mention a whole plane-load of passengers? Then Duvakin remembered Rzhevskaya's words. She had phoned to arrange a ticket the night before. Someone informs Khromoi of that call. He assumes that Rzhevsky is bolting, after the arrest of the toilet woman, protecting himself by informing on others. And so . . . poof goes one airplane.

Duvakin felt as lucid as if a fever had just broken, and as sick. He knew that if he were right, the 160 other people who had died to stop Rzhevsky had never entered Khromoi's unhinged old mind.

They pulled up before the house where Khromoi waited, standing uncertainly on the stoop. He was in simple trousers and shirt, as if on vacation, his braces tugging the pants to a seemly pensioner's height, at his ribs. Polkovnikov braked the car; Darmoved rolled down the window as the old man approached.

"Good afternoon, Colonel, General," he said jovially,

a question ghostly behind this hearty greeting. "An unexpected pleasure, so soon to see you again, General. Taking the air?" he asked, bending forward far enough to see into the car. Duvakin watched the porcine eyes, aglow with hidden intelligence, ruthless, mad intelligence.

"Good afternoon, Vladilen Alexandrovich," Darmoved replied mechanically. "Spring, a drive in the air . . . come with us for a moment," he ended more sharply.

"It's kind, I'm sure," Khromoi demurred uncertainly, "but the hour . . . I haven't dined . . . and I've work."

"No one is more tireless, Vladilen Alexandrovich," Darmoved replied, "but the Moscow comrade here brings news that falls near to your heart."

"My metro, you mean?" Khromoi inhaled sharply, as Polkovnikov's head shot around to glare at the colonel. "You managed to arrange a commitment so soon!?"

Polkovnikov bobbed a quick nod before the secretary looked anxiously over his shoulder, then whispered hoarsely, "Will it take long? My coat?"

"Leave your coat, you'll find it quite warm enough," Darmoved answered. "Come, just a moment of your time . . ."

And that easily the trap was sprung. Even before Darmoved finished speaking, the secretary opened the door, motioned Duvakin over, and sat heavily in the rear seat.

Duvakin noticed in astonishment that the old man's eyes were shut. Khromoi wiped his cheeks, then snuffled softly. "Forgive me," he muttered to no one in particular. "I am a foolish old man." Then, more loudly, "Can it be after so many years that my dream is finally to come true?" He leaned forward again, to seek reassurance from Polkovnikov; the general muttered something inaudible while, wasting no time, he put the car in gear.

They rattled out of the yard, bouncing heavily on the small potholes; four men in a Zhiguli is no joke, particularly when two of them are well over a hundred kilos. As they heaved past Khromoi's guardhouse, Duvakin noticed the startled faces of a couple of men, but the secretary seemed oblivious.

Excited, he sat forward, bumping Duvakin's knee. "What did Grigorii Vladimirovich say?" Khromoi asked anxiously. "How certain is it? I couldn't announce the plans, could I? For May Day?"

Polkovnikov looked ashen, suddenly, and Duvakin felt another click of understanding. The general was in a dangerous position now, caught between his two stories. Duvakin felt his confidence rise a notch, to see the general discomfited.

"You drunken old fool! A metro? Here?" Darmoved spat derisively. "Pigs'll lay eggs before they build a metro here!"

"I don't understand, General." Khromoi's voice was more formal now, a bit worried. "I think perhaps you ought to take me back . . ."

"I think perhaps we ought to have a talk, instead," Darmoved turned half about, imitating the old man sarcastically. "In a more formal setting . . ."

"Talk? About?"

"About," Darmoved shrilled, "theft of state property, currency violations, conspiracy, bribery—that's what comes to mind first."

"You milk-wet whelp, Darmoved." Incongruously, the old man laughed. "You stupid son of a bitch, I feel sorry for you. You've really put your pecker on the chopping block this time, you know."

"Have I now?" Darmoved smiled more confidently, studying the secretary unkindly. "Have I now? And what would you say to a full confession?"

"Confession? Of what?" Khromoi seemed startled, perhaps alarmed; he turned to Polkovnikov. "General!

What is this about? I demand that you stop this car!"

Polkovnikov pretended deafness, concentrating on the road, so Khromoi pulled himself forward, using Duvakin's arm as a grip. Darmoved turned almost completely around to press his advantage.

"A confession of who ordered furs stolen, of how they were stolen, of the money . . ."

"Fascinating, and who might be the author of this story?" Khromoi was more confident.

"Local author, fellow name of Rzhevsky." Darmoved's answer dripped with acid; the air seemed to crackle.

"Rzhevsky?" Khromoi crossed his plump arms and stared out the window. "For the first time I hear this name. And I might warn you that the procurator—who is an old Party comrade—doesn't enjoy such fictions."

"Perhaps not . . . particularly when he hears them while sitting next to you on the prisoner's bench."

The secretary shifted his weight, shaking the tiny Zhiguli. Polkovnikov, as silent and attentive as if he were at the theater, lit a cigarette.

"And just why would he be sitting next to me?" Khromoi asked pleasantly.

"Because of the criminal incompetence with which he handled enquiries about misshipped furs. Or shall we call that aiding and abetting? This is among other matters, of course." Darmoved smiled, going for the throat.

"Rzhevsky told you that?" Khromoi asked, forgetting that he had never heard the name. For a second he battled anger, then relaxed. "Ah, well, after that toilet woman, I suppose. Still, the Party will understand. It's all for the metro, you know that?" Khromoi suddenly addressed Polkovnikov. "This isn't building some dacha for myself or buying foreign cars; this is a metro, understand? For the working people of this city . . . the Party . . ."

"The Party is a bit fed up with thieves right now,

Vladilen Alexandrovich," Polkovnikov interrupted dryly. "Moscow rather prefers to decide about metros and such things by itself." He took a drag on his cigarette.

"Thieves? What thieves?" Khromoi maintained his august manner. "No thief steals what has no owner."

"The state is the owner." Polkovnikov's answer was mild, but Duvakin could feel crackles of lightning behind it. The territory was growing familiar.

"And who is the state? The Moscow comrades who take the money aren't the state? The people who will ride the Magadan metro, *they* aren't the state? Don't give me that old nonsense, comrade ..." Duvakin heard Khromoi's breath go more labored. "See here," he added after a moment's silence. "I thought you had promised to *help* with the metro." He looked accusingly at Polkovnikov. "You promised that Rom—"

"I rather fear," Polkovnikov interrupted hastily, "that there's nothing to help. The metro's impossible; nobody can build such a thing on permafrost." He took a drag on his cigarette; Duvakin was surprised to notice the general's hand tremble.

"Soviet science can do anything!" Khromoi declared stoutly.

"Not build a metro in frozen muck," Polkovnikov said gently, as if loath to break an old man's heart.

"It is money? You want more money?" Khromoi asked nastily. "Well, all right, if it must be, there's always money can be found. You're a greedy bunch of bastards back in Moscow, but all right, money's no hindrance. Furs, gold, diamonds even, though that's a bit trickier. Those mountains," he said, waving a proud plump hand at the Kolyma peaks, "have everything."

"Except a metro, you bloody fool," Darmoved sniped savagely.

"Let's hear your laugh when you're sent to guard salt flats on the Caspian, you filthy little reptile!" Khromoi whirled. Then, more calmly, "Besides, with your confessor dead . . ." He smiled eloquently, blew on bunched fingertips to show the matter had dispersed to nothingness, and winked at Polkovnikov.

Darmoved paled. "How did you know?"

The secretary was serene. "A tragedy . . . such heavy fog, and a whole airplane . . ." He shook his head lugubriously, until unnerved by Darmoved's snort of laughter in the front seat. "So *that* for your Rzhevsky!" He made a fig at Darmoved.

"There was no fog," Duvakin blurted. "It blew up."

All three men turned to him, startled; the car jerked as the slush on the verge caught the wheel, and Polkovnikov had to turn back, to attend to the Zhiguli.

"Don't interrupt the gentlemen when they're chatting, Vanya," Polkovnikov said softly, as if Duvakin were an ill-mannered child. Then, in a more normal voice, to Khromoi, "But the comrade's right, you know. It was the *wife* you blew up. Not to mention a bank supervisor, first assistant at the truck parts factory, two accountants . . ."

"But when the man telephoned me about the ticket . . ." Khromoi objected, then slammed his mouth shut. A bit late; he had just confessed to murder.

Which made Darmoved's job a lot easier, Duvakin recognized. Murder was no family matter.

But then, to his astonishment, Polkovnikov continued.

"But you do have a point, Vladilen Alexandrovich. Rzhevsky *is* dead. The colonel here got a little overly enthusiastic . . ."

Since Darmoved's office, Duvakin had assumed the point of Polkovnikov's game was to use Darmoved to destroy Khromoi; why then reduce Darmoved's authority? It was almost like Polkovnikov was playing, pitting the two men at one another. As the thought formed, Duvakin recalled another time, when *he* had been the puppet.

Suddenly, he had a horrible suspicion of what the general was really up to.

"Now, comrades," Duvakin distantly heard Khromoi say, voice mellifluous, resonant, convincing. "Let us be reasonable. It appears that none of us has entirely clean hands. In my zeal to serve the people and my Party, I perhaps did exceed the bounds of the necessary . . . and you, Darmoved, perhaps in your sincere desire to scour the union clean of such blemishes as Rzhevsky . . . even you, General, in your desire to advance the fortunes of comrade Romanov and, naturally, our Party, our nation—perhaps all of us committed the error of excessive enthusiasm. But is this a sin? Our hearts are pure, even if our hands are a bit clumsy. Wouldn't the wisest thing be—in view of our experience, our motivations, our past services—wouldn't it be best to accept each other's quite justified criticism and then return to our labors as wiser and better men?"

"Keep it in the family, eh?" Darmoved asked ambiguously.

"Family," Duvakin knew, meant high Party, inner circle, that interlocking web of connections, associations, and obligations into which were not woven simple lecturers in scientific atheism. Such as, say, himself.

His heart began to pound; he had no idea what he could do, but he would do something, rather than be used as a scapegoat. Again. He dug into his coat pocket, for the pistol.

"So Darmoved can go back to killing prisoners, and Khromoi can go back to stealing and blowing up airplanes?" Duvakin shrilled, struggling to keep his voice under control, hoping to shame Polkovnikov out of the silence he was maintaining.

The general, however, would not be shamed. "Prisoners resist, Vanya," the general observed mildly, like a teacher. "And I'm sure Mikhail Fedorovich doesn't regard Vladilen Alexandrovich as a thief . . ."

"How do you know about Mikhail Fedorovich?" Khromoi asked, surprised. "He's never even let me meet him, just talked on the phone, when he needs money—"

Several things happened at once.

Khromoi slammed his mouth shut again.

Darmoved turned to Polkovnikov with surprised, shrewd eyes.

Polkovnikov blushed, sweat coming shiny to his head.

And Duvakin remembered two things. "Mikhail Fedorovich" was another of the code words Polkovnikov had given him. "Mikhail Fedorovich" had *also* been the name of the first Romanov tsar.

"My God," Duvakin said in sudden illumination, "this was all because of my toilet woman, wasn't it?"

The two passengers turned to him, while Polkovnikov's neck flushed redder, convincing Duvakin he was correct.

And thus in great danger.

"You're this Mikhail Fedorovich! You're conspiring—"

"Shut up! You're hysterical!" Polkovnikov snapped, his jaw mottled white and red. "Comrades, this is dangerous antisocialist slander, the man's . . ."

Duvakin noticed disjointedly that the other two were listening carefully and realized that his only hope lay in continuing to pour fuel on these sparks. "You're a traitor. You didn't come to investigate any scandal; you came to stop one! You were afraid for Romanov's plot after that report I had to sign."

In rising fury, Polkovnikov turned savagely to slash at Duvakin, but with feeble result for Duvakin shrank into his corner.

"So, General, you are a traitor," Darmoved hissed with obvious pleasure, much more the figure Duvakin had first met.

Polkovnikov turned back, struggling mightily to master himself. "Strong words, toad, usually used for people who conspire against government officials"—he jerked a thumb at Khromoi—"to advance themselves with criminal factions of state renegades and who beat useful citizens to death. The word fits you better, wouldn't you say?"

Khromoi too had an iron to warm. "You lied! There never was to have been a metro, was there?!" He hauled himself forward to lean over the seat.

"Metro?" Duvakin barked. "He was bleeding you white! He was—"

Like a bear in a pit, Polkovnikov turned back to swing again at Duvakin, and at the same moment Darmoved launched himself at the general. Off-balance and confused, the general turned again, fighting wildly to throw off the little colonel. Unable to cope with all this, the Zhiguli slithered, then stood hesitantly on its two left wheels. Duvakin clutched wildly at the door handle and watched, horrifed, as Khromoi loomed above him. It was Khromoi who decided matters. Pitching forward, whether to join the fray or because inertia gave no choice, the man's weight toppled the Zhiguli onto its side; spewing majestic sparks, the car rolled onto its back, to slide dreamlike along the Kolyma Chaussee toward Magadan, upside down and stately, until it smashed with astounding force into a stakebed truck from which were leaping frenzied Chukchi women.

Dazed, Duvakin stumbled out, disentangling himself from the heaving mass of Khromoi, only to run hard against a small metallic object. He stepped back to see, first, a pistol aimed at him, then high above, the general's lips, thin white slashes, like razor scars. Trembling, they said, "I should have killed you the first time, you worm. This time you die!"

Bleeding, dizzy, Duvakin still knew what he had been told. "It was my signature! You knew I would know you, so you came for me first!"

The vicious grimace on Polkovnikov's face as he pulled the trigger and the hollow click that followed told Duvakin the last and most bitter truth.

Polkovnikov had not tried to kill him after his first attempt because he had decided to use Duvakin instead. Duvakin was clever; he was intended to figure all this out.

As slowly as in one of his nightmares, Duvakin dug into his pocket; with a trembling hand, he pulled out the pistol.

"I've got the one with the bullets, Polkovnikov . . ." He saw without comprehension that their car was burning now, flicking the encircling Chukchis a dancing orange; somewhere he heard sirens. "I was supposed to figure out you were framing me, wasn't I? And when I tried to shoot you, you could shoot me." He held the pistol awkwardly, almost as if he were lecturing. Then the last act of the role Polkovnikov had designed for him struck. "My God . . . and then you were going to kill them, too, and blame it on me." He pointed at the other two men, who were standing dazed and wide-eyed in indecision.

Duvakin was stunned. To have died, a state criminal . . . He let his arms drop, unable to do more than gape at the man who so cleverly had maneuvered him toward that death.

Oddly it was Polkovnikov who saved him.

The smart thing for the general would have been to appeal to his equals, to make it a family matter. Instead, in panic, Polkovnikov tried one more shot at Duvakin, then turned and fired at the other two, in a fury of fruitless clicks. Then, horrified, the general turned to run.

Darmoved caught him at the knees, sending him into

the slush. Slower and long unused to physical exertion, Khromoi took somewhat more time to reach the general's head, which he began kicking savagely, while landing a blow or two on Darmoved as well.

Duvakin, meanwhile, stood trembling violently in the center of the fire-flecked circle, pointing a pistol at a murderer, a murderer, and a frustrated murderer.

Absurdly, one thought alone echoed through his useless brain.

And what of Moscow, now?

· SEVENTEEN ·

What saved Duvakin that afternoon was paradox.
The Khromois, Darmoveds, and Polkovsnikovs of
the union are not arrestable. Their actions become crimes
and are punished as crimes only by decision of the Party.
Sods of the microscopic significance of Duvakin rarely get
close enough to such eminences even to tip a hat, let
alone swear formal citizen's complaints of murder,
murder, and attempted murder. One *word* to the militia
men arriving on the scene by *any* of the three, to say
nothing of a united front, and Duvakin would have been
on his way to the devil's mother-in-law.

On the other hand, the Khromois, Darmoveds, and
Polkovnikovs of the union usually do not roll about
brawling in the muddy slush like drunken truck drivers,
cursing and bloody. Normally, the class found by militia
men in that condition show their papers first and give
their explanations afterward. And so the militia man in
charge of the arriving squad could be understood for
having assumed the affair should be handled in the nor-

mal way, with three hefty swings of the truncheon, and all
bodies in the back of the Black Maria. As for Duvakin, a
well-dressed man standing calmly with a militia pistol
must be official, and so it could be understood too that
Duvakin was seated cordially in front, while the whole
mess was whisked off to the militia station.

Understood. Not forgiven.

Even in his most disjointed state, Duvakin knew that
he was like some figure from the cartoons, who has just
stepped blithely from a cliff, but who, because he has not
yet realized it, will hang for a small space in midair.

The width of the abyss that now separated him from
other mortals and safety grew more evident as he sat in
the militia station, hearing the normal noises subside
slowly into an awed silence, broken only by flurries of
frightened clerks and the distant rings of telephones,
hastily answered. Occasionally, faces appeared, to peek in
wonder, perhaps in pity, at the dazed, battered man who
slumped apathetically on the splintery bench in the waiting room. It was some minutes before one of the braver
sorts thought to tiptoe forward and pry the pistol from
Duvakin's fingers. Duvakin watched indifferently, as if the
fingers were not his own.

The magnitude of his folly grew still clearer when
Pivovarov emerged, his face the color of a sailor's bed
linen.

"A word with you, Ivan Pavlovich?" he half whispered, shocked into formality.

Duvakin stood, on feet that felt frozen, to clump into
the captain's office where the files lay as chaotically as he
remembered. He sat, Pivovarov stood.

"You are aware . . . the identities of the men I have
. . . you had me lock up in there?" he asked softly, holding
up three sets of documents, as if their touch alone could
wither his hand.

Numbly, Duvakin nodded.

Pivovarov shook his head slowly. "You poor, stupid son of a bitch . . ." he said, as caressingly as a mother. "You know that I'm going to have to put all this on your head?" The captain held up a new file, let it drop with a flump on the desk. "I'm sorry, but my man had no idea. I can't just let him . . . because you're crazy. Can I?"

Duvakin, still numb, shook his head, then croaked, "You're releasing them, then?"

"I *can't!*" he exploded in exasperation. "You've sworn out the complaint, and we logged it, before—" He broke off in awe. "Anyway, I phoned Khabarovsk, and they're so confused they're sending a commission on the first plane. Christ in heaven, Duvakin"—Pivovarov seemed almost respectful of folly so grand as this—"you kicked over the bucket this time!"

Duvakin nodded again, then sat in silence. Finally he asked, "I can go home?"

Pivovarov thought, then decided. "They didn't *say* anything about you, actually . . . sure, what the devil! We know where to look for you. Go on home, say good-bye, get your things together."

These last words fell on Duvakin's forehead like taps of a hammer. He knew without comprehending that he was a dead man. He stood heavily, turned, and walked out the door. As he passed the door to the corridor of cells, he heard distant voices shrieking in argument. It appeared the three sharks he had pulled into his rowboat were awake again, and thrashing savagely.

Mechanically, he stumbled outside, hailed a taxi, and rode in exhausted silence back to Galya's. It was not until he fumbled in an empty pocket to pay the driver that he realized what he had done; then he shrugged. Galya's apartment must be home now. Where he would wait to be crushed. Indifferently, he bore the cabdriver's abuse until Galya appeared, to pay and lead him gently away.

* * *

The first evening and night were a blur of dread; Galya at first was excited and importunate, then silent, watching Duvakin stare wide-eyed at the doorknob, waiting for it to turn. The next day was no better. Duvakin sat in the armchair and smoked, wriggling his toes when the sun made them too hot. He was surprised; they were still his.

On the third day he accepted that he was still alive. He could not account for it. Alive and free, for today at least. No one would arrest him on the first of May.

He was still trying fruitlessly to puzzle things out when Galya burst in, pink with laughing, and demanded that he come to the May Day festivities at Lenin Square. Numb, too stiff with fear to protest, Duvakin let himself be dragged, stumbling like a drunk, out to gape with the rest of the town at the twelve-meter Lenin that strode purposefully above the square named in his honor. Fully assembled, the Lenin towered above the crowd, stern, cloth-capped head staring firmly at the future, which lay somewhere beyond his outstretched right arm.

Which had been built in another shop and clutched, therefore, another cap.

Even in his distraction Duvakin recognized the day was more like the first of April than the first of May. A mistake of the magnitude of the two-hatted Lenin ought to have disappeared in seconds; instead, the order to dismantle emerged from Party headquarters a scant hour before the spontaneous people's demonstration was scheduled to begin. By then most of the workers were scattered about the city; those they were able to locate were already drunk, so it was all that the Party could do to remove the conflicting head and arm before the workers of Magadan staggered past, waving willow branches and banners.

Apart from the ten-meter headless amputee, the sole witness to Magadan's May Day proved to be Omiyakhon, the first secretary, who stood on the deserted dias blinking in dazed confusion, grimly waving his arm. Unaccountably, the other notables failed to appear. At first the people of Magadan reacted to these aberrations with merriment, like schoolboys when the teacher steps out into the hall; there was more drunkenness than usual, more raucous shouting, more stumbling and falling, until the parade began to tangle and clot. The iron-faced militia men who ordinarily would have beaten the drunken marchers into strawberry compote watched one another nervously, waiting for orders. None came. Finally the militia elevated its gaze, determined to ignore what it had not been ordered to correct.

Duvakin was too preoccupied to absorb this chaos, but others more alert, like Galya and the women around them, passed quickly from boisterous excitement to nervous alarm, as the number of things wrong with the orderly celebration of May Day grew beyond bungling into something more sinister. The headless Lenin, the empty dias, the rising drunken hum as the parade degenerated into a crowd, were to respectable Magadaners what earthquakes, eclipses, and two-headed calves had been to their ancestors, omens of deep and mysterious perturbations of the known universe.

Finally Galya grew so alarmed she plucked at Duvakin's sleeve, to insist she was cold and wished to return home to the warm feast she had prepared. Duvakin stumped clumsily after her, marveling at the first small bubbles of hope percolating through the tar pit his brain had become. Perhaps something else was going on?

In the depths of another sleepless night, though, Duvakin realized that hope was foolish. He could not escape the consequences of his act. He returned to watching the doorknob, waiting for it to open and swallow him down to hell.

The next morning, however, brought more sun, a humming Galya, and *still* no reaction to what he had done. Galya had asked nothing of him since he returned, apparently content that he was there. With a start, Duvakin recognized what a danger he was to her and resolved to leave immediately. At that moment she brought in hot water and towel, and with a deftness borne, she later explained, of training in maternity, she shaved him, then gave him a round moist kiss on the forehead.

He sat up, feeling more alive. "Maybe I should move back home, then?" he said, trying to seem callous, persuading himself it would be a good thing to get clear of her before the rock poised above his head descended. "Go back to how it was?"

Galya began to weep, almost silent save for a chuffing noise, like a leaky valve. She did not, as he might have expected, curse him, beat him, rage at him. Instead she sat, costly Hungarian mascara zebra-striping her cheeks, hair straw in both color and texture falling in stringy strands around a lined, desolate face. It seemed to Duvakin that her eyes stared wet and hurt straight ahead, facing life and the death eventually to come, alone.

Unable to explain why, Duvakin moved next to her on the bed, put an awkward arm about her, and patted her sturdy shoulder. Tears came then in torrents, great quivering sobs, while Duvakin could only pat her and say gruffly, "There, there, Galochka . . . don't cry, all will be well . . ."

He almost believed it himself, then.

* * *

Later, he got up and returned to work. There was a
fuss from the secretaries, a jibe or two from the fellow
clerks. Sutrapian emerged drunk as a priest, to growl a
threat or two about the Lenin, complain about the length
of his absence, then, astonishingly, to clasp Duvakin in a
hairy embrace reeking of pear brandy. He sobbed a few
disjointed phrases about how unjust life is, kissed Duvakin on both cheeks, and gave him his first assignment.
Blinking and wiping his cheeks, Duvakin returned to his
old desk and chair and sat; it was that easy to return to
work.

Physically, at least. Mentally, Duvakin was like a man
who cannot fully wake up. His body made the motions,
but it was as if his eyes never focused, or all his limbs
were numb. All his actions had a dreamy, ineffectual
quality, almost as if he no longer believed in his own
existence.

Magadan seemed as stunned as Duvakin; the chaos of
May Day continued. Life grew more erratic. One day no
buses ran, then suddenly there was no bread. A few days
later bread returned, but then cheese disappeared. Suddenly there were frozen Japanese chickens everywhere,
even the vegetable stands and news kiosks; without re-
frigeration they soon rotted. People mumbled that the
official side of things had taken a turn for the worse, but
having no alternative, the Magadaners went about their
business.

Duvakin saw quickly enough that these ripples of
chaos were deep, powerful vortices inside Party headquarters. Small announcements became a daily thing; so-
and-so of the city committee or the trade union or the
harbor had been replaced, at his own request, for reasons
of health. Name of replacement as follows. "Purge!" the
people who followed these things began nervously to
whisper, but Duvakin paid little attention. Preoccupied,
he continued with his routine, trudging around with bul-

letins, enduring Sutrapian, and puzzling out the disappearance of Dusya.

The new jumble of Magadan's civil structure made it hard to know whether the stone walls he constantly encountered were official or accidental. Unwilling to tease fate by tugging at whatever held him still suspended, unpunished, at first he limited himself to tedious "interviews" with pompous orphanage directors, cautious, furtive trips out to Thirteenth Olympiad microregion, and attentive listening. All of which confirmed only what he knew; Dusya had fallen from the face of the earth.

He grew bolder after one morning when the sparrows rowed in the fuzzy yellow catkins and the sun glistened on hills striped mud and pale green. As Duvakin trudged to work, a bony hand touched his elbow and hissed, "You need a new shirt, jeans maybe?"

Duvakin had turned and almost stumbled with surprise. It was the toilet woman. "Phoo . . . if I'd known it was you . . ." She turned away in disgust.

Duvakin grabbed her arm, astounded to see her. "You ought to be in prison!"

"Well, you ought never to have been born, you slimy half-breed!" the woman shot back. "Trying to get an honest old woman into trouble . . ."

Heads were beginning to turn, but Duvakin was obsessed. "No, no, I didn't mean . . . How is it you're out? I mean—"

The toilet woman drew herself up haughtily. "Released officially," she smirked. "So *that* for you!" She turned and made a ritual flip of her skirts, high enough to bare a blue and white kneeback pale above filthy men's socks.

"But why?" Duvakin pressed on, feeling suddenly that this was vital to himself, his own well-being. "They never release anybody, you know that."

This was so true even the angry toilet woman had to

acknowledge it. She shrugged. "I didn't ask questions the day they swung the bars open. Maybe they were busy with other things."

The crowd flowed around them, until with another shrug and an impudent fig at Duvakin's nose, the old woman joined it, and disappeared.

Duvakin's first reaction was superstitious dread of unexplained phenomena. As he thought, however, he grew bolder, allowing himself to hope.

If the toilet woman's crime had been dismissed and he had not yet been touched . . .

He was still hopeful when he returned that evening to Galya's, but far from bouyant. A diligent day had turned up nothing on Dusya.

"I'm sure she's well taken care of, Vanya," Galya assured him at dinner. "The family was well-connected, you said, and there was the grandmother."

In some obscure way, though, the child had become a talisman of Duvakin's fate. He had to convince himself all was well with her before he could begin to accept that he too had been spared the consequences his actions should logically have brought.

Relations with Galya were not easy. It seemed enough for her that he returned at night, sat at her table. She must have sensed the shadow that sat over Duvakin, but said nothing. For this Duvakin was grateful. Although in his heart he began slowly to accept the unthinkable, that there would be no consequences of his folly, what he could not accept were the consequences if he were wrong, if retribution were still to come. Galya surely would not be spared.

But still nothing happened. Duvakin still hung in midair, kicking his legs dreamily.

Just before the end of May, Sutrapian assigned him an especially honored task, to explain to a gathering of Party activists at the Magadan glassworks the significance of the decisions just taken at the recently concluded Central Committee meetings. Confidently, Duvakin pocketed the paper, confidently strode out onto the podium before his torpid, thick-skulled audience, and expertly reeled off decisions and their decreed significance. Among these items was an extraordinary fact, which stopped him cold.

Andropov had been promoted, to take Suslov's old job. Further, he no longer was head of the KGB, replaced by someone unknown. A Ukrainian, and a proper Black Hundred, by the smell of the capsule biography included.

Duvakin stood silent so long, turning the paper over and over in his desperation to elicit more information, that two or three of his more alert listeners assumed he was through and so began to applaud. Duvakin stumbled from the stage, his dread now returned tenfold.

As ill luck would have it, that same night Galya first timidly raised the question of Moscow. Duvakin shuddered so visibly and grew so morose that she assumed their joint transfer to Moscow was still forbidden for conversation. She let the subject drop, to concentrate on domestic bliss.

His fear back, Duvakin began to gorge, darkly aware that no one gets such food in labor camp. Baked fish, oatmeal, blini, beef aspic—what didn't Galya make for him! And always coffee, often enough brewed with real milk, and even Moscow cigarettes, which she procured somewhere. Afterward, Duvakin would burp and smoke somnolently in the big armchair, listening faintly to Galya's chatter and watching the doorknob.

In the summer, Magadan was not so bad; they went for rides in Galya's auto, berry picking in the glades along the coast, mushrooming west of town, or out to one of the many tarns which dotted the foothills. All was luminous in the northern summer light, and Duvakin even found himself enjoying the staid matrimonial scenes they played—Galya's careful lap robe when they ate on the ground, her matronly distance when they walked in public, and the delicacies with which she stuffed him.

More fully, though, he knew that his feet still hung above nothing, and he feared the future. Galya soon learned that talk of marriage or the civil registry or Moscow made him draw in his head like a box turtle, and so she confined her campaign to elaborate illustrations of her wealth, competence, and obvious advantages as a wife. In midsummer she became convinced that Dusya had something to do with Duvakin's collapse and the consequent stalling of her campaign for Moscow. Duvakin remained stubbornly silent about what had occurred that April night, believing absurdly that to spare Galya that knowledge might mitigate for her whatever disaster befell him. About Dusya he talked readily enough, and Galya threw herself into the search with the zeal she normally gave to shopping.

Even Galya found headway impossible to make, despite her skills. The offices of city government, the Party, and the ministries, were all in fantastic disarray, officials missing, gone, out of town without explanation, or suffering from unknown illnesses. More ominous, the few people she turned up who ought without fail to have known the Rzhevskys paled and denied ever having heard the name before. "Something queer is going on," she finally conceded to Duvakin, "and I can't seem to do much about it."

Duvakin grew gloomier and gloomier, convinced now that Dusya's disappearance must presage his own. He fretted sleeplessly in the silver-purple of summer nights and gorged on Galya's food, in dread of the turning doorknob. For the first time in his life he even began to grow stout, rising gasping from meals with a clogged belly and thighs tugging at his pants. His suit grew taut, but here too Galya showed her skills. Watching her move buttons and let out seams, Duvakin thought glumly how very little he had to give her, save trouble. The circle about him seemed to draw still tighter in late August, when Sutrapian failed, without explanation, to return from a summer holiday. Duvakin trudged to work each mosquito-cursed morning blackly certain he would not return home again that night; when he did he was as certain he would never see work the following morning. In the agitprop office affairs were anarchic, but Duvakin and his fellows carried on as though there never had been such a person as Sutrapian.

Autumn began to draw on, the days shortening noticeably. The sun began to set before ten, then before nine.

And then one morning at his desk Duvakin read a short notice of a trial just concluded in Khabarovsk, and suddenly the noose about him seemed to slip and grow slack. Certain Party workers, functionaries, bureaucrats and other trusted officials of the State, 317 of them in all, were convicted of abusing their positions by conspiring to steal furs and other valuables from the State. Staggered, Duvakin sat, and reread the notice. The information was the same; virtually the entire Magadan Party structure, from the level almost of staff typists right up second secretary, was to be jailed, while the second secretary himself, V. A. Khromoi, was to be shot. Duvakin looked up, dazed and unbelieving. All about him in the office he could hear a shocked hush melting into nervous titters of relief. It must be true then, he thought. The purge was over. And he was unscathed.

In the days which followed Duvakin began tentatively to let himself believe that the impossible had happened, that he would escape, that in destroying one another the three men had forgotten to destroy him. The coviction grew when five shiny new Ilushin 68s arrived from Moscow, importing an entire replacement Party infrastructure to Magadan. Duvakin's new superior, a Balt named Apshusiems, plonked a black bottle of resinous balsam liqueur on the desk, toasted Duvakin's health, and assigned him a lecture to read.

Paradoxically, as the conviction grew that he *had* been forgotten, Duvakin's elation began to curdle into disappointment. If he was forgotten, then so was Moscow. This, he realized bleakly, meant he was stuck in Magadan forever. Worse, with Moscow gone, he had nothing to offer Galya. He began to drink more of her flavored vodkas, growing even stouter. He was distracted with her, grateful for her attentions but then angry he had nothing to give. He felt in her debt, then he felt trapped and powerless. He grew testy and moody, staring for long periods at his shoes, smoking sulkily.

One day in late September, when the fog rolled off the Sea of Okhotsk as thick and cold as brine slush, Duvakin could bear his drone's life in Galya's apartment no more and stormed doughtily out into the chill gloom, where he collapsed almost sobbing on the broken bench in their courtyard.

This was worse than the last time, when he had been played for a fool. The last time had been horrible, like stepping through a trapdoor to plummet whistling down a shaft. But then at least you *knew* you were falling.

Now? He might still hang in the air or might be on solid ground. Moscow might be gone forever, as forbidden him as it had been on his last night there. Or maybe Polkovnikov no longer guarded the city, and Duvakin could freely go there?

There on the bench he raised his puffy face and acknowledged what he knew; no one in Moscow would want him, even if he could go there. He had helped no one, not even himself. With a heart like a frozen pebble, he also knew that soon Galya would recognize his impotence as well, and then he would have only Magadan. The fog rolled in as salty as the tears that oozed down his face, but much colder.

The next morning, still a little drunk, Duvakin heard the doorbell ring. He was sitting in his undershirt, unshaven, contemplating the taut band of his largest trousers. Soon he would have to search for new pants, he thought blackly, then waved a hand. The devil, let Galya look . . .

"There's a letter for you, Vanenka," Galya returned from the hallway, puzzled by the envelope she carried formally before her. "Registered. It looks official . . ." she whispered, her face ashen, her voice trembling.

Duvakin looked up, wide-eyed, his heart hammering.

"For me?" He ran a hand over his bristly chin, ashamed of the stubble. He reached for the gray square, noticed his hand trembled. "Registered?"

Galya sank onto a stool opposite, her knees like bread loaves; she studied him with silent alarm. Duvakin pondered the envelope, receiving no clues; it was squarish, the gray of a militia uniform, with the address typed. The registration number and sticker were glued on with a blob of yellow paste. Trembling violently, he forced a thumb beneath the flap.

"It's official . . ." he murmured, withdrawing a typed sheet folded foursquare. It took two readings to realize that his downward plunge had at last begun. The letter read:

COMRADE DUVAKIN, IP, IS URGENTLY REQUIRED TO PRESENT HIMSELF BEFORE AN EXTRAORDINARY PARTY COMMISSION AT 28 KOLYMA CHAUSSEE, IN CONNECTION WITH VERIFICATION OF QUALIFICATIONS IN THE EXCHANGE OF PARTY DOCUMENTS, 11:00 HOURS, 28 IX 82.

Below was scrawled an illegible signature, overstamped in purple ink.

"My God," he whispered, his face pale. He unthinkingly handed the paper to Galya. "It's a purge . . . today . . ."

Galya also blanched, then decided to meet matters head on. "You've got nothing to fear, Vanya. It must be simple routine. Come on, we haven't much time, mustn't be late." She hauled him resolutely to his feet then hustled him through preparations.

Duvakin himself was like a rag. As he shaved he kept stopping, trying to peer through the mists to see what this remarkable letter might mean. The purge was over, wasn't it? And there had been no questions for him, had there?

This couldn't really be it, could it? His turn?

His hand trembled so badly that he gave up shaving his neck. They would shave him in prison anyway, he thought gloomily. Galya fell short of actually beating him to get dressed, but it was a near thing; dread would shoot through him with a spasm, and he would simply stop, sock dangling, to stare hollow-eyed ahead.

At last, though, they were out—walking because Galya was out of gasoline coupons.

The day did nothing to lift Duvakin's fears; it was drizzling, and the air was as damp, chill, and importunate as a homeless mutt. From heaven knows where, Galya had obtained a large, sturdy unbrella, beneath which they scurried to the appointment. Duvakin thought repeatedly that he heard footsteps close behind and so could barely walk, whirling about at every step or two. Each time, apart from sullen soggy pigeons and an old woman or two trudging past with bags full of empty bottles, the streets were deserted.

"It's our footsteps, echoing, silly," Galya finally said tersely. Unconvinced, Duvakin nevertheless quit turning, so that during the entire dreary trudge to 28 Kolyma Chaussee, he felt steely fingers poised millimeters from his neck.

The building proved to be the reception office for the Magadan Regional Executive Committee, in the shadow of the KGB building.

"What do they want?" Galya half whispered, her eyes round and gray; the green, Duvakin knew by now, disappeared when she was worried. He shrugged, for he had never had occasion to come to the building before, and any speculations he might have were too bleak to confess. His heart hammered at his neck so hard he could barely hear.

The waiting room was tiny, with just barely enough room for a long wooden bench with broken slats, tattered copies of a newspaper in Chukchi, and a sign on the wall next to a closed hatch, announcing that the workers of this office were engaged in a socialist competition for efficient service.

Duvakin sat heavily on the bench in an open half-space, forcing a decaying native woman and an equally decrepit old Russian man to move further apart. The woman looked ahead impassively, but the man began an incoherent tirade about veterans and the respect they deserved but did not get. Periodically, he jangled the medals he wore scattered across a plump expanse of greasy topcoat.

Galya was more self-possessed. Crossing the room confidently, she rapped sharply on the hatch, then after a short silence, rapped again, shouting "Girl! I say girl!"

A third rap finally opened the hatch, and a plump woman with purple-red hair and thick glasses that greatly magnified her stupid expression leaned out.

"What?"

"We're summoned—" Galya began importantly, holding up the paper, but the woman was even faster.

"You'll be called," she said in a bored voice, sliding the hatch shut again.

Galya though, was no child; she had stuck the umbrella tip in the slot. The hennaed woman realized it, slammed hard a couple of times, then exploded.

"Citizeness! This is an office! Stop this hooliganism this minute, or I'll—"

"You forgot to ask our name, didn't you?" Galya smiled pleasantly.

"That's my business? Your name is your name, what do I care what your name is?" she shrieked, realizing that it was true. "Well, we're very busy; what can you do?" She grew defensive. "I mean, look, is it fair, there's all of you, and just one of me!"

"Duvakin, I.P.," Galya said sternly, her back stiff. "*Party member . . .*" she added weightily, but without needing to. The woman had disappeared, to reappear instantly at the open door.

"*Please . . .* I hadn't realized. Why didn't you *say* something? They told me, straight away, just as soon as he gets here . . ." She was flustered and a little frightened, so plump she quivered.

His heart accelerated; the other people on the bench eyed him and edged away nervously. A *somebody*.

Galya crossed the room in three quick strides and, in the guise of giving him an encouraging squeeze, yanked him to his feet.

"Go!" she whispered. "This is important, Vanya."

And step by heavy step, he did.

Banishment. *That* wouldn't be so bad, maybe. Further north, say, or out to one of the Arctic Islands? Novaya Zemlya?

Prison. For what? Criminal possession of the gun, say; that might be bearable. Couple of months, a year? Political would be worse, though. Antisoviet activity, loss of civil rights . . .

Labor camp. He wouldn't come back from that, not at his age.

The hall was dark, but small too, a sort of box. The

woman squeezed herself against the wall to open the door while Duvakin tried to figure out how they could cast what he had done as a capital offense.

The door opened slowly, to reveal the commission, a troika. The first man, in a uniform Duvakin did not recognize, was young, early forties, and had a sunburned nose. He tried to look sternly out from behind plump pink cheeks and a peeling bald head, but instead, he looked comical. That was bad; if he knew he appeared silly, he would be doubly vicious, to prove he wasn't.

The second man, the head examiner, was older, but vain. His hair was dyed black, and he cultivated a thin moustache, the precise width of his tuberous nose.

"Ah, comrade Duvakin! Come in, come in!" he said extending a puff-pastry hand not quite to shake, not quite to receive the documents Duvakin held in his hand. "Comrade Kruglopuzov," he pointed to his right, "I am Blokhodavkin," he thumbed his chest, "and this . . ."

Duvakin took one manful step into the brightly lit room, to feel suddenly as if the floor had given way, his whistling plummet to doom shrill in his ears.

"This is comrade Darmoved."

The inclined gray head at the chairman's left looked up, and like a wolf greeting lunch, Darmoved opened his mouth. He was, Duvakin registered faintly, not in uniform.

"Your documents! Comrade!" Duvakin realized that the chairman was repeating, puzzled and impatient; eyes riveted to Darmoved's, Duvakin held out his Party card, passport, and other documents, to place them blindly in Blokhodavkin's hand. Then the chairman read a long and complex statement, which Duvakin heard only as shards of phrases.

Duvakin noticed distractedly that the room seemed to be retreating backward up a long dark tunnel, while only

Darmoved's eyes grew bigger, yellow, smoldering with malevolence. Duvakin heard ". . . antisocial activity . . ." and ". . . dangers of an unparalleled . . ." and ". . . extraordinary vigilance," but he understood nothing. Like a bird the snake, he watched only Darmoved.

There was a silence.

"Well?" Blokhodavkin asked impatiently.

"Well what? Sir? Comrade?" Duvakin asked weakly, realizing from his far end of the tunnel that the question was to him.

"The Party rewards you with a course of study at the Institute of Scientific Atheism, and you say well what??" Blokhodavkin rumbled ominously, like thunderheads on a stifling summer evening.

"A course of study?"

"In Moscow! Understand?!" The chairman raised his voice, exasperated.

"Moscow?" Duvakin could not tear his eyes from Darmoved, who though absolutely still, seemed to seethe with hate. "Moscow? Sir . . . comrade sir?"

"Moscow! You see?" he turned to the man at his right. "I told you he'd be speechless, the lucky devil. When it's Moscow they're always speechless, and don't we know why!" He laughed a bit jealously, then thrust a sheaf of papers in Duvakin's unresponding hands. A quick glance told Duvakin they were something official, with stamps.

Still he could not tear his eyes from Darmoved; he saw from the corner of his vision how the other two men turned expectantly to Darmoved.

Slowly, deliberately, the man stood. Duvakin stepped back, until the doorknob jabbed him in the pelvis. He sucked on his teeth so hard that salty blood popped from his gums onto his tongue.

"The institute is a great honor . . . even at your age, Duvakın." Darmoved's irony was heavy. "Your comrade will envy you." Then, like a marksman aiming a pistol, Darmoved slowly raised and held out a small folder of red cardboard. Duvakin stood as if nailed to the door.

"Well? Take it!" Blokhodavkin snapped, and reflexively, Duvakin did so. Darmoved's hand was dry and rustled like old papers.

Duvakin stood dumbly with the folder in his hand. Comrade?

The chairman stood, shook Duvakin's hand gustily; Kruglopuzov handed back the passport; Darmoved curled a lupine lip, and the fat receptionist appeared, virtually to carry Duvakin back out to the waiting area.

Galya leaped up.

"What is it? What was it? Vanya!" She held him as she had long ago, walking down the clinic corridors after the accident, propelled him to the seat on the bench, which the others, deferential, had kept open.

"Vanya! *Speak!* What is it? What did they . . . ?" Galya squeezed his arms so tight his mouth dropped open, but no sound emerged. Instead, he held up the papers, which she snatched, rifling through them while she let Duvakin sink stunned onto the bench.

At first his brain raced, but the clutch was not engaged. Only slowly did the ideas move, jerking and bouncing through his head. Darmoved, on a credentials commission? In civilian clothes? And he had done nothing to Duvakin? Except glower?

There could be only one explanation, which Duvakin's brain kept jumping back from. But there it was

Darmoved had been demoted.

Broken to the ranks, even. Junior member of a petty regional commission, way the devil out here? It was a bare step above stevedore.

"Vanya!" Galya shrieked, hugging him, squashing his nose against her creaking, jiggling chest; then, remembering propriety, she stood straight, smoothing her dress. "It's an insult, really, a course like *this*, for a man of your age and experience." Then she squealed again, unable to contain her glee. "But *Moscow*!" She even hugged the papers to her as she bounced rapidly up and down, before stopping, pink-faced, to beam.

Duvakin still slumped, astounded. Darmoved demoted, Khromoi shot . . . And me not only untouched, but *rewarded*? He turned his new Party card over in his hands, wondering what all this could mean.

Galya was growing businesslike, with gusto tackling the tasks she saw ahead. "They'll handle the registration, it says, but I wonder about the apartments. It couldn't be that they won't give us a flat. Shura says her uncle says that the apartment situation in Moscow is absolutely appalling. You're Party too, of course . . ." She was dressing him as she spoke, anxious to have him away from the other gaping citizens and at work on the new life to come.

Duvakin felt something slip from the Party card as he went to put it in his pocket, a little square of newspaper that fluttered to the floor. He bent, picked it up. There was no date, no indication of where it was from. The clipping, a scant few lines, said only:

> The Ministry of Foreign Affairs announced that its new cultural affairs attaché to the Soviet Embassy in the brotherly People's Republic of Benin, Major V. S. Polkovnikov, was warmly received today in Porto Novo.

"Where's Benin?" Duvakin interrupted Galya's torrents of plans to ask.

Surprised at these first words since he emerged, she stopped, then asked suspiciously, "Is it a city, or what?"

"A country, I think . . ." Duvakin crumpled the paper in his hand, beginning to understand.

"One of ours? Africa then, it must be in Africa, the rest I can keep track of," she said firmly, then waited for an explanation. When none came, she shrugged, and took up where she had been. "The car we can sell, or maybe it would be better to ship it; I don't know how long it would take us to get one there. I'll have to have Shura ask her uncle. Most of the furniture is trash, but still, well, I'll see . . . and then . . ." She paused just outside the door, to ask in an entirely different voice, "The wedding . . . We are getting married?"

"Of course!" Duvakin said, staring off into space and wondering why Galya was hugging him so tightly and crying. Of course! Africa. He pictured Polkovnikov, huge, sweating, nostrils quivering high above a crowd of pitch-black brother peoples, a diplomatic smile bolted to his lips . . . and in his heart the writhing, gnawing knowledge that Duvakin was not only alive, not only unpunished, but even back in Moscow.

He had not been rewarded.

He had been made another man's punishment.

Even so . . . Moscow! he thought, feeling like an enormous rock had been lifted from his chest and the sowbugs and millipedes that had fouled his soul for so long had scurried away from this sudden light.

"When? Vanya darling, when?" Galya asked anxiously, Duvakin assumed about the move.

Moscow! He recalled the streets, the shops, the crowds . . . "As soon as possible! Next week, this week, as soon as possible!"

To his surprise, Galya hugged him again, pinning his arms to his sides.

Then the rock dropped back down, and all the bugs returned.

Darmoved was demoted. Khromoi was shot. Polkovnikov was broiling in Africa, basted with the nettles that Duvakin was strolling free in his beloved Moscow.

That meant at least one more pair of hands in this. More maybe if those conspiracies had been more than threats they used to club each other with.

Hands Duvakin did not know. Hands who even now were using him as a tool, to torment Polkovnikov. And what if only the plotters were gone, and the plots still lived?

As vividly as the day it occurred, he saw Rzhevskaya's plane puff, expand, and rain to earth in a glittering shower of aluminum shards and human flesh.

Who knows? But why make things easy if they changed their minds?

"Only one thing," Duvakin said sternly, now grabbing Galya's elbow firmly. "No airplanes! Understand?"

"No airplanes?" she stammered, confused.

"I insist! Train, boat, we go to Moscow on land!"

Somewhere between confused and angry, Galya said loudly, "But that's such a hard way to get to Moscow!"

"There're worse," Duvakin said grimly, taking her arm.

ABOUT THE AUTHOR

ANTHONY OLCOTT was born in Red Lodge, Montana, a town better known as the birthplace of Ernest Hemingway's fictional character Robert Jordan. After winning a scholarship to Phillips Exeter Academy, Olcott went to Stanford University. He first visited the U.S.S.R. in 1969, at which time he decided to become a Russian specialist. Seven years later he had a Ph.D. in Russian, a job at the University of Virginia and the uncertain suspicion he liked being a student better than being a teacher.

Although between trips to the U.S.S.R. he worked at a variety of jobs (translator, bartender, book buyer), Olcott turned periodically to teaching. He has taught post-graduates through junior-high students, from Stanford to Moscow (where he taught English at the Moscow State University). During his Russian travels he not only spent time in the major cities, but also in smaller cities such as Voronezh, Lomonsov, and Sumgait.

His first novel, *Murder at the Red October*, in addition to becoming a sales success was a nominee for the Mystery Writers Association Best First Novel Award in 1981. Married to a prominent teacher, Olcott now devotes full time to writing and coping with his two children.

THE HASTINGS CONSPIRACY

ALFRED COPPEL

The time is a year or two from now. Relations between
Britain and America have cooled as Britain's socialist
government leans steadily to the left. But as long as
Britain remains a member of NATO, the Soviet Union
will be unable to achieve its ambition – the annexation of
Western Europe . . .

Then Soviet leaders realise that they can break the uneasy
alliance – by persuading the British government that the
United States plan to invade and occupy Britain . . .

"Astonishingly original and frightening . . . this is Mr
Coppel's best book yet"

Colin Forbes

0 552 11982 2   £1.75

CORGI BOOKS

ALFRED COPPEL

THE APOCALYPSE BRIGADE

A world on the brink of disaster . . .
A private army willing to fight to the death . . .

The Apocalypse Brigade describes the world as it may be
a decade from now, where superpowers are held in thrall
by both terrorists and OPEC. It is a world on the edge of
apocalypse, where private citizens are prepared to act
when their weakened governments are not . . .

"Mr Coppel is a wily writer. He knows how to keep things
churning . . . and he knows when and how to spill a little
blood and when and how to turn back the bedclothes . . .
That he has a certain and unswerving understanding of
the true nature of the world today is clear almost from the
very first page"

The New Yorker

0 552 12079 0   £1.95

CORGI BOOKS

GIRI

義理

MARC OLDEN

"Ludlum, look out, Marc Olden is here"
Walter Wager, author of *Telefon*

GIRI
*to the Japanese, a term meaning duty or loyalty, the most
binding obligation of the samurai warriors. But to an
American, it means something else – revenge!*

Combining international intrigue, Oriental philosophy,
deadly violence and burning passion, *Giri* is a gripping,
fast-paced thriller in which East clashes with West, and
the ageless code of the hunter versus the hunted is put to
the ultimate test.

"Anybody who loved *Shibumi* and *The Ninja* shouldn't
miss it"
James Patterson

0 552 12357 9   £1.95

CORGI BOOKS

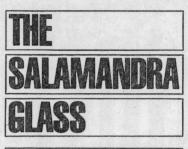

THE
SALAMANDRA
GLASS
A.W. MYKEL

The heart-stopping novel of international suspense and intrigue by the author of *The Windchime Legacy*.

Michael Gladieux thought he'd finished with The Group, a highly specialised unit he'd served with in Vietnam . . . until his father is murdered, his body found with a note accusing him of Nazi collaboration during the war and a glass pendant anchored to his heart with a shiny steel spike.

Who was Michael's father? Why are Washington and The Group so interested? Michael's search for answers leads him on a terrifying quest – to find his father's killer. What he uncovers is far more deadly, as he becomes the one man capable of stopping the twisted legacy of THE SALAMANDRA GLASS.

Rivals Ludlum at his best!

0 552 12417 6   £2.50

CORGI BOOKS

FREDERICK FORSYTH

THE MASTER STORYTELLER

The Day of the Jackal

One of the most celebrated thrillers ever written, THE DAY OF THE JACKAL is the electrifying story of an anonymous Englishman who, in the spring of 1963, was hired by Colonel Marc Rodin, Operations Chief of the O.A.S., to assassinate General de Gaulle.

"Mr. Forsyth is clever, very clever and immensely entertaining" *Daily Telegraph*

"In a class by itself. Unputdownable" *Sunday Times*

More than 7,500,000 copies of Frederick Forsyth's novels sold in Corgi.

0 552 09121 9   £2.50

CORGI BOOKS

RED DRAGON

DRAGON

THOMAS HARRIS

RED DRAGON
". . . is an engine designed for one purpose – to make the
pulses pound, the heart palpitate, the fear glands secrete"
New York Times Book Review

RED DRAGON
". . . is an extraordinary book. A thriller in its own right, with
pace, tension, and a capacity to prickle the skin with excitement, but more than this, a superb study of character, seen and
understood and created in depth . . . Enthralling, frightening,
totally professional. It is quite simply the best of its kind that I
have read in twenty years"
Lord Ted Willis

RED DRAGON
". . . simply comes at you and comes at you, finally leaving you
shaken and sober and afraid . . . the best popular novel published since THE GODFATHER"
Stephen King

0 552 12160 6   £1.95

CORGI BOOKS

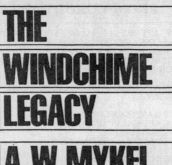

THE
WINDCHIME
LEGACY
A. W. MYKEL

RIVALS LUDLUM AT HIS BEST!

Sentinel is the most advanced computer ever built, possessing a capacity many millions of times greater than the human mind. But Sentinel's supreme control over the US defence network is threatened . . . one of its creators plans to sell the blueprint for another Sentinel to the Russians.

When the KGB send their top spy to bring back the information, Sentinel's two most highly-skilled agents are assigned to intercept him. But one of them soon discovers that they are up against more than just the KGB . . . for a secret plot to bring about Hitler's last dream – the Fourth Reich – has already begun . . .

"A page-turner that I could hardly wait to finish"
Washington Star

0 552 11850 8 £2.50

CORGI BOOKS

OTHER THRILLERS AVAILABLE FROM CORGI/BANTAM

☐	11982 2	THE HASTINGS CONSPIRACY	*Alfred Coppel*	£1.95
☐	12079 0	THE APOCALYPSE BRIGADE	*Alfred Coppel*	£1.95
☐	12140 1	NO COMEBACKS	*Frederick Forsyth*	£1.95
☐	11500 2	THE DEVIL'S ALTERNATIVE	*Frederick Forsyth*	£2.75
☐	10244 X	THE SHEPHERD	*Frederick Forsyth*	£1.95
☐	10050 1	THE DOGS OF WAR	*Frederick Forsyth*	£2.50
☐	09436 6	THE ODESSA FILE	*Frederick Forsyth*	£1.95
☐	09121 9	THE DAY OF THE JACKAL	*Frederick Forsyth*	£2.50
☐	12393 5	BALEFIRE	*Kenneth Goddard*	£1.95
☐	12160 6	RED DRAGON	*Thomas Harris*	£1.95
☐	12433 8	A COLD MIND	*David Lindsey*	£1.95
☐	12417 6	THE SALAMANDRA GLASS	*A. W. Mykel*	£2.50
☐	11850 8	THE WINDCHIME LEGACY	*A. W. Mykel*	£2.50
☐	12510 5	WOLF TRAP	*Frederick Nolan*	£2.50
☐	12357 9	GIRI	*Marc Olden*	£1.95
☐	17160 7	THE CIRCLE	*Steve Shagan*	£1.95
☐	12369 2	MOTHER LOVE	*Domini Taylor*	£1.95
☐	12307 2	RED SQUARE	*Edward Topol & Fridrikh Neznansky*	£2.50
☐	12583 0	SUBMARINE U-137	*Edward Topol*	£2.50
☐	12271 8	THE ASSASSIN	*David Wiltse*	£1.95
☐	12490 7	THE SERPENT	*David Wiltse*	£1.95